CLARA
REEVE

CLARA
REEVE

Leonie Hargrave

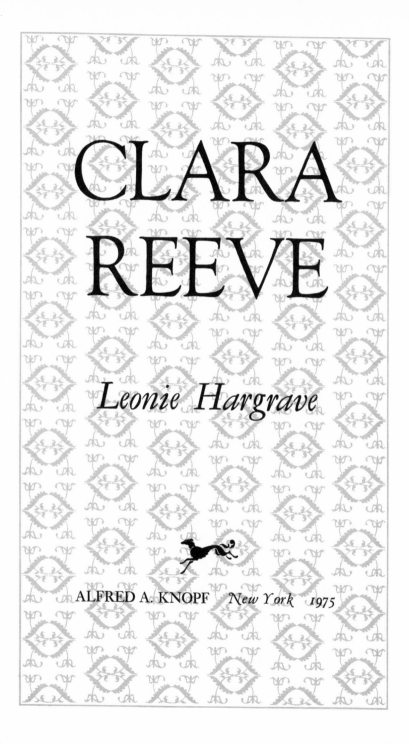

ALFRED A. KNOPF   *New York*   1975

This Is a Borzoi Book
Published by Alfred A. Knopf, Inc.

Copyright © 1975 by Leonie Hargrave

Library of Congress Cataloging in Publication Data
Hargrave, Leonie.   Clara Reeve.
  I. Title.
PZ4.H2765Cl   [PS3558.A62416]   813'.5'4
ISBN 0-394-48490-8   74-25267

Manufactured in the United States of America

First Edition

For Jeff and Charlotte
Happy Anniversary

Contents

BOOK ONE

BOOK TWO

BOOK THREE

Contents

MY FAMILY

For my readers' greater ease in apprehending and remembering the sometimes tangled matter of this chapter, I have included here a little genealogical table, which, though leaving out a great many Reeves, Trowbridges, and Jerninghams, should give a fair notion of the relations among the principal figures of my story, so far as these were known to me in the year 1850.

Richard, Viscount Rhodes
(1642-1703)
CREATED 1ST LORD RHODES, 1688

Charles, 2nd Lord Rhodes
(1691-1749)

Clarence, 3rd Lord Rhodes
(1735-1774)

William, 4th Lord Rhodes
(1760-1834)

Howard
(1796-1834)
M.
Eliza Trowbridge
(1804-1840)

Douglas, 5th Lord Rhodes
(1798-)

Rev. Augustus Reeve
(1779-)

Zaide
(1805-)
M.
Conte Visconti
(1796-1835)

Dora Rhodes M. **Robert Reeve** **Lydia**
(1824-1850) **(1818-1850)** **(1810-)**

Niles Visconti
(1835-)

M.

Clara Reeve
(1844-)

Josiah Jerningham
(1786-)

BOOK I

Écoutons la légende, écoutons!
—LAKMÉ

CHAPTER ONE

My Cousin Niles

ON A COLD AND OVERCAST THURSDAY in March of 1850 my mother was laid to rest in Highgate Cemetery, and on that same day I met my cousin Niles. Niles was fourteen then, and I still some weeks shy of six; yet I remember our first meeting with a distinctness that seems almost unnatural now when so much that was dearer to me, so much it would be a solace to recall, has quite faded away. Could I but bring to mind with this same vividness a single hour of those days so little time before, when both my parents were alive and I secure and happy within the charmed circle of their love. How I have longed to possess not the uncertain, phantom-like images of them that were my sole inheritance at their deaths, but full-length studies alive with the circumstantiality and minute observation of some great modern portraitist, a Frith or an Alfred Hughes.

Vain longings! Many a night, in childhood and long after, I have lain awake rehearsing that slim stock of memories. Often and often have I tried to wrest from them a richer color or a deeper significance, but the attempt has always been beyond my powers. At least I have been able to preserve these few dim fragments intact. I have been told, by those who make it their business to understand such matters, that from some lingering patches of paint on a crumbling wall or from bits of broken stone delved from the earth the entire dimensions and intent of a work of art may be surmised. May be it is the same with our lives; and so, rough and discontinuous as I know they are, I should like to open this history by reviewing once again those infant memories.

Of my mother, I recall principally her smile, a smile in which her eyes shared equally with her lips—sparkling blue eyes and lips rather fuller than would accord with an ideal notion of beauty. In both these particulars—and, as I have been told, in many others —I bear but faint resemblance to her, for my own eyes are of a brown that approaches nearly to black, and my lips vary from the ideal by their thinness, as does, indeed, my figure. Oddly enough, I've also been told by those who remember her that our chief point of resemblance is precisely . . . our smile. What more can be said of this smile but that it was the unfailing fountain of my early happiness? In the worst distresses and loneliest hours of my orphaned childhood, I needed only to close my eyes and think of how she had smiled to me for an answering smile to come to my lips—and tears, some times, to my eyes.

I remember a gay, striped silk frock, all warm reds and silvery grays. To my child's eyes it seemed a magnificent creation, its tiers of flounces, even those about the wrists, sprigged with innumerable silk rosettes, the bodice pointed à la Sévigné, the skirts quite full, though nothing like the fullness one may achieve today, as this was before France and the general progress of history had introduced crinolines. Strange to say, though my aunt Jerningham has confirmed that this indeed was one of my mother's gowns, I do not remember my mother *wearing* it. It exists in my memory as an inert and lifeless shape, a simulacrum such as one might see upon a dressmaker's form in the window of a shop. But for all that, it belonged to my mother, and I treasure its memory accordingly.

I remember—but how dimly!—a walk we took to the rectory of St. John's Church in Clerkenwell, where my grandfather, the Reverend Augustus Reeve, was curate in his later years. Here were my parents married, here I was baptized, and here, on the momentous day of this walk, I was permitted my very first taste of tea. Amazing that an adult human being can come actually to savor that bitterness!

I remember a narrow, gloomy garden walled with sooty brick where my mother's spaniel, Fad, made a great uproar retrieving the sticks she tossed to him. My aunt Jerningham has asserted that this scene must be a product of my fancy and that my mother never possessed any more imposing pet than a canary-bird, who, however, answered to this same name of Fad, or Fadladeen, after the chamberlain in a romance of Thomas Moore. Can memory have transformed a canary-bird into a spaniel? Rather, I suspect my aunt may have invented this tale from a sense of delicacy and a desire not to involve my feelings with Fad's fate after his mistress had passed on. In any case, whether bird or beast, after my mother's death I was never again to see him.

Lastly, I remember that dear, calm face framed by a bonnet trimmed with a bow of blackest crepe. Beads of Whitby jet glittered on her high collar. By these tokens I know that this must be my last memory of her, that she was dressed in mourning for my father, whose ship, the *Cranleigh*, went down in a storm off Saint Govan's Head on January 12, 1850. A scant two months later she, too, died in giving birth to a son who, unable to face this darker world alone, quickly followed his parents to that brighter one which, I hope and trust, they now inhabit.

Of my father, alas, I can recall no more than a bit of gold braid depending from his uniform, which I would play with as though it hung from his shoulder on purpose just to be my toy. His face and figure, his carriage and address, or how he dealt with me, whether with sternness or indulgence—of all essentials such as these I have no recollection.

Yet I am certain that I was, perhaps more than most children, happy and well-content, else in the years that followed I should not have felt so unhappy, so discontent. Mine is not a rebellious temper, but I suffered inwardly with a consciousness that my fortunes had suffered a most terrible reverse with my parents' deaths. Of my uncle and aunt Jerningham I shall have more to relate hereafter, but I may say at once that in retrospect I cannot accuse them of any exceptional lack of charity. My uncle was motivated by a strict conception of justice and duty, which his actions never violated. My aunt's character, though less consistent, was warmer and kindlier. To both of them I owe a debt of gratitude larger than I can ever repay, or express.

Such, so pleasant yet so obscure, are my earliest recollections. May be that queer unaccountable creature, Memory, slumbers such times as we are happiest, as a dog will doze before a glowing hearth, and can only be awakened by some calamitous event.

Or may be, like Janus, Memory is double-visaged and can discern future as well as past, can single out, amid the cloud-wrack of the shifting world, just that scene or face that will one day come to figure most prominently in the long sweep of our days. Love at first sight may occur more frequently in literature than in life, but surely we have all known instances of it. The bonds that were to unite my destiny to that of Niles Visconti were more complex than love, though love of a kind would one day add a strand to that mazy knot. I dare say the word does not exist that could fairly represent the sum of our conjoint experience, but if it did, it would needs be as strong a word as Love or Honor or (this, too, was a strand in that knot) Enmity—one that could bear the soul's full weight.

To return to that original, too vivid moment when we first met. My aunt Jerningham had dressed me in my best frock and led me down to the parlor, where my mother lay in state. It was a small room, and very few people sufficed to fill its chairs and the one ottoman. My aunt directed me to sit on a stool placed near the foot of the casket and then left me that she might circulate among the mourners still arriving and to receive, as after myself the nearest of kin, their commiserations. I soon came to feel uncomfortably conspicuous. The mourners would look at the casket and then at me and shake their heads and sigh. My aunt Jerningham possessed an instinct, not to say a relish, for the pathetic, and no doubt she'd placed me so much to the fore in order to heighten the "effect" of the spectacle.

I am ashamed that I cannot claim to have felt any more profound sensation on this occasion than embarrassment. My heart could not grasp the fact of death's finality, its absolute, inflexible decree. Much less could I conceive that the wooden box beside me contained all that remained on earth of the mother I would never see again except in dreams and reveries. I studied the fringe of the worn Turkey carpet, the cruciform pattern of brass nails on the dark-gleaming casket, the roses molting on the mantelpiece, with the same dazed and unmoving calm with which I had been taught to observe the Sabbath.

I was awakened from these benumbed contemplations by a stir at the back of the room. My uncle Jerningham rose to grasp the hand of a young man some decades his junior. He insisted that this youth take his own seat directly in front of the casket. (This chair was a relic of the reign of Queen Anne; it had been my mother's pride and privileged seat, which no one had thought to trespass on until this hour.) Such deference by age towards youth was odd enough, but there was something even more odd in this stranger's person and manner, a singularity that irresistibly drew my attention.

With the advantage of hindsight, my fascination is perhaps less to be wondered at. My uncle Jerningham and the other mourners gathered in that room were upper tradesmen, and as such their comportment and style of dress declared them, while Niles Visconti was emphatically a gentleman—nay, an aristocrat. Pride of birth and breeding fairly shone from him. Further, though from the vantage of my six years he seemed fully mature, I must even then have recognized the disparity—a matter of nearly two feet— between him and the other men in the room. When fully grown, Niles attained to something less than average height, and he was then fourteen. His stature, compounded with the fairness of a porcelain complexion and a pronounced delicacy of feature, made him seem a kind of miniature adult, such as children were often represented in portraits of earlier centuries.

I remember how, before the undertaker's men came to remove the casket to the hearse, Niles sat on that frail Queen Anne chair, still as a statue, his thin hands not joined in prayer, as my aunt Jerningham had insisted mine must be, but resting side by side on the black stuff of his trousers, as though for him prayer could offer no easement nor reward. I remember the fixed stare of those dark eyes, the lips compressed and pale. He seemed to be smiling at some bitter jest unknown to all but himself. Oh, the very faintest smile, to be sure—but I had seen it. I fear I must have studied him most shamefully to have formed so clear and ineffaceable a record of him as I still possess, and yet it may have been no more than a glance. A disease, as we have learned, may be initiated by creatures invisible to the naked eye, and a tragedy may be set in motion by no more than a slip of the tongue.

CHAPTER TWO

At Highgate Cemetery

OF THE FUNERAL AND THE SLOW JOURNEY to Highgate, I preserve only shadowy memories, their outlines melting into a Lethean mist. I recall that my aunt wept a great deal and that my uncle appeared angry. I know my cousin rode with us to the cemetery, but I had ceased to take such close notice of him. Instead, my attention was directed to the window of the coach. There, against a background of louring cloud, long fluttering pennons of the deepest black would intermittently appear and disappear. I puzzled over what they could be, knowing that a display of banners, however somberly dyed, was not a customary feature of funeral processions. Plumes, yes—the horses and carriages would be abundantly decked out with these. But flags?

As I write these memoirs, half a century later, a solution to that mystery has occurred to me. These "banners" must have been the crepe bands fixed to the hats of the hired mutes who walked alongside our carriage. As I was small and the window was placed well above my level of vision, I would not have seen even the tops of their hats, but as the wind rose and fell, it would lift the trailing bands of crepe and let them collapse, some times by turns, some times all together. A slight enough mystery, to be sure, but suggestive by its very triviality of the still benumbed state of my feelings, my shocked reluctance to touch the wound of deep-hidden grief.

Yet something—I believe it was the sight of the open grave—touched that wound and wrenched it wide. Despite the pain of that wrench, despite an anguish that amounted nearly to horror, some quirk of childish pride made me try still to keep that grief secret. I slipped away from the mourners gathered round the grave and ran I knew not where—nor cared, so long as it was away. Un-

consciously, I sought the safety of insensibility, but my new awareness pursued me inexorably through that labyrinth of solemn
angels and marble crosses, markers and monuments, an awareness
that my mother was no more, that she would never smile at me
again, that she was lifeless as the turned-up clods of earth beside
her grave. Dead! And the whole world an emptiness.

The deeper I penetrated into this stony wilderness the greater
was my agitation. At last, half in exhaustion and half overcome by
my terror of being lost, I threw myself upon the steps of a
miniature chapel composed in the Gothic style, all of spines and
spires and spikes, and there let burst all my accumulated bitterness
and despair. Spirit and body both were convulsed by a sorrow that
every aspect of the scene about me seemed to encourage and confirm—the cheerless season, the leaden sky, the endless recession of
sepulchral images. My grief would abate a moment from its utmost
fierceness, and then the sight of that stark landscape populated
solely by absences, by Death, would renew my tears and my
terror.

My readers must not suppose this terror was inspired by any
supernatural dread. I had thus far in my life escaped being
frighted by tales of ghostly visitations. Indeed, at that moment,
such a possibility would have been consoling, for the sharpest pang
of bereavement consists in our knowledge that we shall never,
never see whom we mourn again. *Never*—that word was a knife,
and I twisted it in my heart.

It was in this extremity of sorrow that my cousin Niles discovered me. Without a word, he sat upon the chill white step of
the monument and took me in his arms and there let me cry. My
tears fell to the sleeve of his coat and were absorbed—and what
different tears they were now! They seemed to reveal a warmth
at the very core of my grief. A tenuous warmth, may be, but
vital for all that. Niles, by his simple act of charity, had let me
know that my loneliness, though awful and immutable, was not
absolute.

"Clara?"

Though I was somewhat recovered, speech still failed me. In
answer I could only look up to his face.

Tenderly he smoothed my hair back from my forehead. Gently

he dried my cheeks with a black-bordered handkerchief. "Clara, we must return to the carriage soon. Your aunt and uncle are quite worried. Do you feel you can stand up?"

I nodded dumbly. He helped me to my feet and, as well as might be, brushed off the bits of leaves and grass that clung to my rumpled pelisse.

"Better? Very good, then. If you wish, I can carry you—for some part of the way at least."

He made this last suggestion so doubtfully that despite myself I had to smile. Niles seized on this change of mood and insisted vigorously on my mounting to his back. He would be my dapple-gray and I his rider. An astonishing suggestion! Properly, I know, this is a sport for boys, but I was intrigued and, with no sense of my impropriety, agreed to ride pick-a-back. Niles, after all, was a grown-up, and the wishes of grown-ups were to be deferred to. We set off at a canter back the way I'd come—but in how altered a mood it would be impossible to say. Niles quite simply amazed me from my misery.

How quickly he had taken the measure of my character, how deftly learned to "sound me from my lowest note to the top of my compass." Often, in later times, he would again be apt at charming away my darker moods with such moral sleight-of-hand. These sudden shifts from the forlorn to the frivolous were the very hallmark of his character, by which I was at once captivated and thrown into confusion.

After a brisk trot along the gravelled path, my dapple-gray grew noticeably slower, then came to a halt beside a great granite sarcophagus, where I was obliged to dismount. While Niles rested on this bulky tomb to recover his breath, I recognized, not far ahead of us, the site of my mother's grave. The mourners had quitted the spot, and now two gravediggers were filling in the earth over the casket. I approached respectfully, my sorrow moderated for the moment by a kind of awed curiosity, and stopped before the marker, a thin white slab propped on its side against another headstone.

Niles had come up behind me unobserved. He asked if I could read the inscription on the stone.

"Somewhat," I answered. "This word is 'Dora' and this below

it is my father's name, and this is the year, and then how old she is. But here where it says—*The dead shall be . . . raised?*"

"Yes, that's right."

"I can't make out the next word at all."

"*Incorruptible,*" Niles assisted.

I repeated the word, and continued: "*And we shall be . . . changed.*"

"You read it very well. Do you understand it, too?"

I confessed that I did not.

"Well, St. Paul, who wrote those words in a letter to the people of Corinth, said that it was a mystery, which means that it's hard even for grown-ups to understand." Niles' lips tightened into the same bitterish smile I'd remarked earlier that day.

"My aunt Jerningham says that mother has gone to heaven to be with the angels and with my father. She says they will be very happy there, and some day my brother and I will go there, too."

"Then you shouldn't cry now, should you, if your mother is happy."

"Aunt Jerningham says I ought not to, but heaven seems so . . . I don't know."

"Far away?"

"Yes, terribly far."

"You'll find as you grow older that things that once looked terribly far away come to seem nearer. Once I thought Italy was the farthest point on the globe. Now I've been back and forth five or six times."

"Is it nice? Italy, I mean."

Niles laughed. "Oh, very."

"Some day I'd like to go to Italy. Mother always said the finest music in the world was in Italy."

"Do you like music?"

"Very much."

"Then some day I will take you to Italy, and we'll see the operas and hear the choir at St. Mark's and all the rest of it. And when we've finished with Italy, I'll take you to Germany. They have fine music there, too. Finer, some say, than in Italy."

"What is 'incorruptible'?"

"Ah! When we die, you see, we'll have a new kind of body.

Our souls are immortal, but our bodies aren't, and so they die. In heaven, though, our bodies shall be immortal, too. St. Paul said, in that same letter, *For this corruptible must put on incorruption, and this mortal must put on immortality.* Which has always sounded to me rather like changing into a better suit of clothes. At least that's a way to try and understand it. St. Paul is often hard to understand."

"Are you a minister?" I asked, taking his hand as we set off on the path towards the gate where the carriage waited.

"No. I'm much too young to be anything at all."

"But you mean to be a minister when you're old enough?"

"No." There seemed more of sadness than of bitterness in the smile that accompanied this denial. "No, I think not. A minister must be a very good person, and I'm not always very good."

Some precocious sympathy for feelings far beyond the ken of my six years moved me to return that smile. "Neither am I," I confided to him.

He squeezed my hand.

CHAPTER THREE

Which Treats of Antecedents

As my deceased parents' lodgings on Amwell Street were too small to accommodate the great tribe of Jerninghams who had attended the funeral, the dinner was to be held in my uncle's residence in the far-off suburb—as it was then considered—of Bayswater, and thence, to Worcester Terrace, our coach proceeded. My cousin made some attempts at conversation during this journey, but my uncle defeated each attempt by a word or a glance. It cannot be that he felt my mother's loss too keenly to reply (though such was my aunt's case), for on other occasions, when a death has touched him even more closely, I have known my uncle to dwell for hours, with a kind of solemn enthusiasm, on the themes of Mortal Corruption and Divine Justice. Rather, I suspect, he was embarrassed by the presence of this boy who so naturally assumed the manners of a man, whose clothes and accent were markedly superior to his own, and who possessed, though he neglected to employ, the title of Count (albeit an Italian title). Too often we refuse to credit persons of a very pronounced character with feelings of delicacy or tenderness. As society is ordered, shyness must afflict even the strongest man at times, though it may be dissembled by many masks. My uncle adopted an air of taciturnity, and later, when circumstances allowed, of open hostility, but his initial motive was not much different from that which prompts some unseasoned miss to blush and turn her face aside from the dashing young dragoon who has asked her to dance.

Before I may advance this narrative even a few weeks further, to the moment Niles was formally repulsed from my uncle's house, I must first begin to untangle the complex skein of my antecedents. Already, I have introduced relatives with the surnames of Visconti, Jerningham, and Reeve. Yet another name must be added to this list before these various branches will compose a tree—that of my great-grandfather, William, fourth Lord Rhodes, who was the friend and, very briefly, the successor of the Tory Chancellor Lord Eldon. As such, he was one of the most notable men of his age, but I fear we now live in another age, in which neither Lord Rhodes nor Lord Eldon is much remembered.

I thought to interpolate here some account of my great-grandfather's career, so far at least as it touches on my own story, but instead I shall refer the interested reader to De Quincey's essay in an 1839 issue of *Tait's Magazine*, "Recollections of Blackthorne." In that essay, De Quincey speaks of his long-time patron and host as "of all Tories the most uncompromising, of all parents the fondest." Imagine, then, such a parent's distress when his eldest and dearest son—Howard, who was my grandfather—eloped to Gretna Green with the only daughter of that notorious Radical pamphleteer James Trowbridge. The fond parent waged sore battle against the uncompromising Tory and even obtained a kind of victory, for while refusing from that time forth to admit Howard within the gates of Blackthorne, he did fix on him a comfortable

income of some ten thousand per annum; nor was there any talk
as yet of disinheritance. No doubt Lord Rhodes expected that the
simple passage of Time, which has made Tories of more than one
Whig, would one day lead his prodigal to views more in keeping
with his station in life. But when Howard, in May of 1832, took
an active and public role in the agitations for the Reform Bill, the
Tory could compromise no longer. So bent was Lord Rhodes on
preventing Howard from succeeding to his title and estates that he
did not scruple to compromise his own wife's good name; but of
that, hereafter. It suffices here only to note that, with the assistance
of Lord Eldon, then Chancellor, the fourth Lord Rhodes arranged
that the fifth of that title would be his second son, Douglas, who
would inherit, as well, Blackthorne and all other moneys and properties pertaining to the Rhodes estate. It must have been a painful
decision, for the man had doted on his elder son, while the younger
had been a source of endless aggravation and expense, a light-
minded, callow youth (by De Quincey's report) wholly given up
to the pleasures of table and stable.

There was a third child born to Lord Rhodes, a daughter by his
second marriage, Zaide. De Quincey is reticent concerning this
daughter, saying only that she too "co-operated in breaking her
father's heart." At a later point, my own story will compel me to
expose the scandal that De Quincey quite properly veils. For the
present, it is enough to say that Zaide was married off to a relatively obscure nobleman of the Kingdom of the Two Sicilies, by
whom she was to bear an only son, Niles. This Conte Visconti (the
Visconti of Ischia were a junior branch of the powerful and ancient Milan family) died less than a week before his son was born,
and so Niles received the title of Count with his first breath of air.

A few more words will suffice to make clear the relation that
existed between Niles and myself. In 1824, a daughter had been
born to the prodigal Howard and his wife, Eliza, and that daughter,
Dora Elizabeth Rhodes, was wed some nineteen years later to a
newly commissioned lieutenant in Her Majesty's Navy, Robert
Reeve. It was through my mother, then, and through Howard
Rhodes, that I came to occupy my own slim perch on the Rhodes
family tree. I cannot therefore claim full cousinship with Niles, but
rather a bond of the second degree, a bond that had been further

attenuated by a years-long lack of correspondence and intercourse between the separate branches of Lord Rhodes' family. Douglas, upon becoming fifth Lord Rhodes, displayed no inclination to establish a connection with either his brother's offspring (Howard having predeceased his father) or his sister; that is to say, with either my mother or Zaide. The furthest extent of his charity towards the former was the wreath he dispatched to her funeral and the letter he sent the Jerninghams expressing his grief and begging them to excuse his own absence on that occasion. Towards his sister, especially after Niles' birth, he showed a less consistent disregard, but the history of that relationship is too complex to be summarized in this initial outline. Indeed, the vagaries of Douglas's conduct towards the surviving members of his family will constitute a fair portion of the narrative that follows.

As for Zaide—or I should rather say, the Contessa Visconti— her long residence on the Continent had made her, if not forgotten, little mentioned by her own family. This, I fear, was the *purpose* of her being established abroad.

The appearance of Niles Visconti at my mother's funeral had come, therefore, as a considerable surprise to my aunt and uncle. They were but dimly aware of his existence; his presence in London was totally unknown to them. Niles had learned of my mother's death in the newspaper and had presented himself at Amwell Street quite on his own initiative.

My relation to the Jerninghams is much more simply accounted for. My aunt Lydia was the youngest daughter, as my father had been the youngest son, of the Reverend Augustus Reeve. Mr. Jerningham was the friend, and very nearly the contemporary, of that gentleman. Earlier in life, because of his reforming tendencies, Augustus Reeve had suffered disappointments in his career. A living he had been led to expect was denied him, and he was obliged to bring up his numerous family on the little income he derived from the curacy of St. John's Clerkenwell. Lydia, as a result of her father's allegiance to the wrong banner, had had no expectations whatever, and when Mr. Jerningham, who was a prosperous tradesman of the strictest principles, proposed for her hand, there was no question but that she must accept. She did; they were married; my own childhood destiny was fixed.

It was not a matter of course (as Lydia was later to explain) that the Jerninghams would take the place of the parents I had lost. At first, Mr. Jerningham had strenuously opposed the suggestion. He held that the responsibility for my upbringing ought best to be assumed by a Reeve, either my grandfather himself or one of his sons. I do not think that it was any lack of liberality on my uncle Jerningham's part that made him wary of assuming this responsibility, but rather a sober sense of his unfitness for the demands of parenthood. His own marriage had been childless, and he had reached, at the time I came to live with him, his sixty-fourth year. Few characters are so resilient at this stage of life as to be capable of forming new habits and affections. My uncle Jerningham's character was of the most unbending kind, and he recognized that the best and wisest course would be to establish me with a household in which the presence of a six-year-old would not be quite so revolutionary an event as in his own.

Children are all of them savages in a way, and parents must be their missionaries, introducing them to the usages of civilization and instructing them in the principles of religion and morality. However, this is best accomplished bit by bit, and the most successful missionaries learn to overlook the less mischievous barbarities of their flocks. I do not mean to suggest that children should be left ungoverned and that nurseries be allowed to revert to the jungle, but the contrary extreme, of expecting a child to possess the deportment of a matron and the discretion of a diplomat, is surely just as inadvisable. In short, tolerance is an essential virtue if parenthood, or childhood, is to be other than an ordeal, and tolerance, alas, was the virtue which my uncle Jerningham principally lacked.

Lydia, with less of philosophy in her composition, argued for my adoption, and while not a passionate advocate, she was persistent. She pointed out that her father's health had already rendered him incapable of most of his pastoral duties. Mrs. Reeve being dead, the responsibility for my well-being would fall mainly on the shoulders of his elderly housekeeper, a woman of whom my uncle disapproved for the hint of gin he had some times caught upon her breath. Then my various other uncles were shown to be incapable or unqualified. Two had remained bachelors. A third, in the service of the East India Company, had removed himself and his family to the other side of the globe. There remained as a real possibility only Gilbert, the Reverend Reeve's second son, who had also taken orders and was then vicar of a workingman's parish in Birmingham, where he was attempting to support a family of six children and his wife's two maiden sisters on an income of £240. To this Gilbert my uncle Jerningham had written immediately after my mother's death, suggesting that he might without disservice to his own family increase the sum of his dependents from nine to ten. Gilbert refused point-blank. My uncle Jerningham professed to be shocked at such a lack of charity in a man of the cloth. He was never to know that a letter from Lydia had preceded his own, in which she had advised her brother to reject her husband's proposal.

Lydia persistently urged my adoption without ever directly alluding to what she knew was her strongest argument—her own childless condition. Through me she might yet enjoy the fulfillment of motherhood. Being then forty, she was bent on not letting this last opportunity slip through her fingers. Yet, for all her efforts and stratagems, she might not have succeeded had it not been for the timely, and inadvertent, aid of my cousin Niles.

As I was not present at the event, I reproduce here my aunt's report of it. Some three weeks after the funeral, Niles called at Worcester Terrace, to Mr. Jerningham's renewed consternation and his wife's delight. My aunt could remember little of their initial conversation, except that it was "gentlemanlike and *very* amiable." Her attention seems to have been more engrossed by his costume than by his talk. Niles' own tailor could not have given a more particular account of what he wore on that visit and how he wore it: his morning coat buff, single-breasted, and of the nicest cloth; his waistcoat tawny and cut in the clerical style that fastens up one shoulder (what is called an M.B.), the buttons fashioned from bloodstones; his cravat, a black Joinville, was tied loosely and "drooped to perfection"; his inexpressibles (so long as she lived, only once did my aunt ever stoop to saying "trousers") were the deepest shade of burgundy; his boots (I can see my aunt throwing back her head as she said this) "nothing short of sublime." Rather than mar this *tout ensemble* with crepe, Niles expressed his mourning with a ring. In short, the very beau ideal of dandyism, and the

first representative of that creed, surely, to have been admitted to
the Jerningham drawing room. My aunt's wonderment is not really
to be wondered at, especially if one bears in mind the diminutive
scale on which all this elegance was exhibited.

After sufficient gentlemanlike and amiable conversation, Niles
inquired after myself. Was I well? As well as might be expected
this soon after my loss. And living, of course, with the Jerninghams? Of course. And would continue to? Mr. Jerningham made
an equivocal reply. In fact, after a second refusal from Gilbert
Reeve, my uncle was then thinking of sending me to Gloag Hall,
a charity school in Lancashire, established specially for the orphaned
and indigent daughters of naval officers. Niles pursued the subject
until he had wormed some hint of Gloag Hall from my uncle,
and then, with a definite air of coming to my rescue, he presented
Mr. Jerningham with a letter from his mother. Contessa Visconti
proposed that, should my more immediate relations find themselves
unable or unwilling to support the trouble and expense of my
bringing-up, she would be quite happy to assume that responsibility
herself. Niles' holidays were approaching, and he might escort
me on the journey, by rail and coach, to Venice. My uncle was as
much dumbfounded by the extent as by the apparent want of
motive for the Contessa's generosity.

"An extraordinary communication," Mr. Jerningham said, returning the letter to Niles.

"Thank you. May I tell my mother that you will consider her
offer?"

"You may express my appreciation of her offer, but as to accepting it, that would be quite impossible."

"Not at *all*! I assure you, Sir, my mother is quite sincere. I know
Clara a little, and my mother very well. They would dote upon
each other."

"No doubt. No doubt."

"If it is a question of the too informal tone of my mother's
note, she has empowered me to approach her solicitor here in
London, Mr. Hosmer. I am sure he can draw up terms to meet
your satisfaction."

"I question neither Contessa Visconti's sincerity nor her generosity. But"—he furrowed his brow—"well, after all . . . Italy."

"Italy? Why, it's the cheerfulest place there is. Nothing could suit my cousin more. Removed from the painful reminders of her parents' deaths, refreshed by the novelty of the scene—and Venice is, of all cities, the novelest—invigorated by a more healthful air and friendlier climate, Miss Reeve would bloom, she would flourish, she would *thrive*."

Niles had little conception of my uncle's character if he thought that he would in any way advance his cause by such arguments. Had Italy been universally approved as the cheerfulest, healthiest, happiest country in the world, there would still have remained an insuperable objection to any good Englishman going there: it was Catholic. My uncle entertained a pious horror of anything that smacked of Rome, Popery, or Dr. Pusey. He would not enter a church where he suspected candles had been burnt or confessions heard within the last few hundred years. The very sight of that boot-shaped silhouette on the globe was painful to him, and here was this wisp of a boy proposing to him that he should send his own niece to the reeking bedchamber of the Whore of Babylon— to *Italy*!

"Impossible," he repeated.

My aunt, who appreciated the cause and strength of Mr. Jerningham's distress, interposed before Niles could make matters, if possible, worse. "We wouldn't want, you know, to send Clara to a Catholic country."

"But, Madam, if the only alternative is sending her to Gloag Hall, surely you would not wish to deny her the advantages of—"

"Advantages of damnation!" my uncle roared at him. He rose, trembling with rage, and advanced on the young pagan. "Advantages of idolatry! Advantages of Hell!"

Niles fled the house in terror, leaving behind his gloves of lavender kid and a brand-new Wide-awake. It was only with the greatest difficulty that my aunt was allowed to have the cook's boy deliver these to his hotel. My uncle was all for throwing them onto the ash-heap.

So my fate was decided. In the interests of my salvation, Mr. Jerningham was prepared to sacrifice his own comfort and peace of mind. Niles' mention of his mother's solicitor dispelled any notion of Gloag Hall, for if the Contessa were really determined to

have me, it would be more feasible to secure my removal from a
charity school than to tear me from the arms of near kindred.

I was not to learn of this incident until some twelve years had
passed. When I did, I was for several months consumed by a secret
self-pity and vain regrets. Italy inspired in my breast no thrill of
reverent horror, but rather a vision of sunlight over vine-clad
hills, of musicians strolling through picturesque ruins, of fountains
plashing, of gondolas and gondoliers, of golden temples and blue,
blue, blue skies. No doubt this girlish conception was as wrong-
headed and mistaken as my uncle's. Italy, as I have since learned
very well, is neither Arcadia nor the Infernal Pit. But how many
tears I wasted over this dreamland of my own imagining, and
how bitterly did I blame my guardian for having denied me the
chance to live there!

To do Mr. Jerningham justice, I must say that he acted with
greater wisdom and a finer sense of his niece's best interests than
anyone could then have known. I dread to think what a different
life-story would be mine to relate if he had been persuaded to
accept Contessa Visconti's offer and I had been sent, all guileless
and guideless, to live at the Palazzo Albrizzi.

CHAPTER FOUR
My Uncle Jerningham

THE HOUSE IN WHICH ANY PERSON spends his childhood becomes
for him the prototype of all houses whatever. Let that person
begin to read a book and let there be mention of a parlor, a scullery, a staircase, and the image that rises before his mind is of the
parlor in which he passed his Sunday afternoons, the scullery where
he hid from his playfellows behind a wooden tub, the staircase
which he climbed each night to reach his tester-bed. It is to this
house he will most often return in his dreams, and which, however education may later revise it, is the template on which his
entire notion of Taste is cut to form.

In my own case, alas, that revision has been drastic, and when I do return in dreams to Worcester Terrace, it is more often with a shiver of dread than with a smile of pleasant reminiscence. I was not happy there.

Its exterior was identical to all the other houses in the row. Together they formed a uniform black mass of brick protected by a palisade of sharp iron pikes. At intervals, this double line of defense was broken by narrow doorways and wide bay windows. The possibly subversive effect of the latter was combatted in two ways: they were never opened, and they were hung with heavy draperies.

Such was the general character of the neighborhood. Within, the same theme was carried on with the full resources of contemporary decorative art. Each piece of furniture, whatever homely purpose it might be meant to serve, was dressed up as a miniature fort. The armchairs bristled with miters and turrets; the parlor table was supported by a whole battery of flying buttresses; the pier-glass was almost engulfed by the crocketed canopy that framed it, while the mantel and fireplace beneath it would have been a fit tomb for any gentleman of the Middle Ages, albeit snug. Everything, down to the thistle-shaped bell with which my aunt would call for tea, was in the most severe and prickly Gothic style that Industry could contrive.

Often nowadays people will complain to me about the superior comfort of those times and how our new style of furnishing sacrifices ease to elegance. I can only suppose that these people grew up in another era. In Worcester Terrace that sacrifice had been accomplished long since. No single item of its furnishings pandered to a false sense of comfort, and not a few, the dining room suite especially, actively mortified any poor pilgrim unlucky enough to sojourn with us.

The reader may suppose from this account that my uncle was a passionate collector. In fact, he came by these furnishings through no deliberate act of discrimination, but in the ordinary course of his business. He managed the London office and was a junior partner in the firm of his brother, Nicholas Jerningham. Worcester Terrace had been furnished by a process the opposite of Natural Selection, for all the oddities and freaks of taste that the British public had been unanimous in refusing became, in mass, the fabric of *our* daily lives.

I begin to detect a too acerbic note in this description, and I fear that I have exercised a sarcasm against Mr. Jerningham's furnishings that I would secretly like to employ against the man himself. There is no help for it. I did not love him with that full and open love which his position as my uncle and guardian warranted. I would like to say I *could* not, that duty alone cannot command the affections, but I will leave it for my readers to judge whether, and how much, I am to be blamed. Let me endeavor, at least, for the remainder of this chapter and the next, to deal with Mr. Jerningham in a spirit of more justice, if not of actual charity.

He was a man of notable physical presence: tall without angularity, heavy without stoutness, dignified in repose, and vigorous in movement. He had the long, lean, thoughtful face so common among the natives of Yorkshire, in which county the Jerningham family had its origins. The very type, I have often thought, of the Yeoman, but varying from that type by marks acquired through a lifetime of rigid self-constraint. The frame that Nature had intended for strenuous effort the demands of Commerce had chained to a desk; the strength that might have wrested treasure from the earth or contested with violent seas was wasted upon the phantom hordes of debits and credits, accounts current and accounts rendered, profit and, ultimately, loss. His real strength smoldered deep within him, like the latent fires of a volcano.

The practice of religion provided him with his only release for these trammelled energies. In all but formal allegiance he was Evangelical, but a fear of being imputed an enthusiast prevented him from following his principles to the logical conclusion of professed Non-Conformism.

Religion may have afforded Mr. Jerningham a certain relaxation of his habitual tensions, but it offered no more immediate *comfort* than did his furniture. His lips might repeat Paul's words, that in Christ "we live, and move, and have our being," but his eyes were ever fixed on the awful issues of Death, Judgment, and Eternal Misery—and to these issues, under his tuition, my own gaze was turned. I was made to understand how my soul lay under a dreadful weight of sin, for which I would one day surely suffer endless torments of everlasting flame. Some mention must have been made of Heaven, but that was not a subject that provoked Mr. Jerningham to eloquence.

Such an approach to Christian doctrine is better suited, perhaps, for the conversion of a reprobate and hardened sinner than to incline the heart of a six-year-old girl to the love of God. Well, wiser minds than mine have debated these matters for centuries, and probably the debate will continue as many centuries more. There will always be those who strive towards God, and those who yield to Him; those who hold themselves erect before His judgment and those who would melt in the warmth of His love. I know my own nature to be more of the yielding and melting variety, for the first article of my faith is that—

> . . . *all must love the human form,*
> *In heathen, turk, or jew;*
> *Where Mercy, Love, & Pity dwell*
> *There God is dwelling too.*

Mr. Jerningham, could he read these lines, would surely condemn such a lenient doctrine, and as doctrine it probably errs on the side of the sanguine. If so, I must thank Providence for having favored me with a teacher so well able to correct that fault as Mr. Jerningham.

Such were my uncle's principles; his practice was in keeping with them. Every aspect of our daily lives was adjusted to the end that we would not stray from the paths of righteousness. The Sabbath, of course, was scrupulously observed, but, in addition, each weekday evening repeated Sunday on a reduced scale. In the hours between our rising from dinner and my retiring to bed, Mr. Jerningham would read aloud from Scripture, usually a passage from Paul or the Prophets, followed by the appropriate chapter of Dr. Casbolt's *Commentaries*, of which we possessed all twelve volumes.

As he read, my aunt and I would ply our needles. My own task, once I had learned the rudiments of embroidery, was usually to copy out, stitch by stitch, a verse from Revelation. To this day, whenever I hear one of the pithier maxims from that book—such as "Fear none of those things which thou shalt suffer" or "As many as I love, I rebuke and chasten"—I can *see* the words as they appeared on one of my samplers. I know the shape and size and color of each letter; my fingers feel the incessant small motions of needle and thimble, the tension of the cloth in the hoop; I am seated, once again, beside my aunt, and my uncle's even monotone becomes a single sound with the crackling of the logs. And I must smile. For strange to say, those long, dull, eventless evenings, oppressive as I often thought them then, have become, by the alchemy of time, a golden memory. I will not try to explain my paradox. Those of my readers who have known such evenings of quiet and motiveless labor, week by week and year by year, will understand me; the rest must accept it as a mystery.

CHAPTER FIVE
Rage and Its Issue

IF THE ONLY REPROACH that could be made against my uncle were his partiality to pious exercises at the expense of other pastime, my childhood would indeed have been exemplary, in a quiet way. Sometimes, however, and more frequently as I grew older, Mr. Jerningham would lose mastery of those fierce energies pent within his heart, and they would erupt into furious, ungovernable rage. There would be little warning beforehand. His bony hand might tighten round the lion's head that glared from the carved arm of his chair; his cheeks, normally sallow, would be suffused with blood, and one might observe the vein that ran slantwise across his high, white forehead darken and begin to throb. But a knowledge of these signs was of no use in avoiding his wrath. Denied a pretext in the present, he would rage against something my aunt or I had done to annoy him an hour, a day, a week past, and because there was no telling when his anger might flare up, I lived for months on end, may be for years, in a perpetual state of dread.

Among the myriad instances of such outbursts, two stand out

in my memory with particular clarity. The first occurred shortly after I'd come to live with the Jerninghams, and so it is likely to have been my first acquaintance with this darker side of my uncle's character.

It was on a Sunday evening early in June. The air had been cooled by showers through the afternoon, and high above us, as we walked down Worcester Terrace towards St. Mary's Church, a fleet of coral-pink clouds sailed eastwards across a sky that grew steadily a deeper and deeper blue. The balmy air, the ever-changing spectacle above, the breeze that sighed through newly-budded leaves—such evenings are a kind of tender against the life we hope to live hereafter. Even a child may feel their benign influence, but for an adult sensible of the weight of the years, and of the pain, the waste, the disappointment these years may bring to all alike, such moments can be inexpressibly precious. One inhabits for a little while the calm, harmonious halls of Eternity, and the whole creation echoes with the Redeemer's promise: "Come unto me, all ye that labor and are heavy-burdened, and I shall give you rest." Such, I know, is my response, and such, I believe, was my aunt's on that evening long ago. Her eyes would lift to watch the coursing clouds, then slowly trace them to their source in the radiant West.

Then, as though this had been no more than a painted screen which burst all at once into flame, the beauty and stillness were shattered. My uncle, trembling in every limb, his face transfigured by his passion into a mask of wild, staring anger, had grabbed hold my aunt's arms and was shaking her roughly about, raving all the while in a voice I could not recognize as his, so shrill it was, so terrible, so void of *meaning*. I clung to my aunt's skirts in terror of this roaring stranger who had been my uncle. I felt her body hurled this way and that. I was certain he meant to kill her right there on Worcester Terrace on our way to church. There was a pause in the struggle: I waited for the final blow to fall.

My aunt hissed at her husband between clenched teeth: "Josiah, release me at once!"

He did. She took two steps back from him, dragging me stumbling after her.

My uncle, whom I never knew to laugh otherwise than when these fits were upon him, began to do so now. Under ordinary circumstances it would have seemed a hearty, healthy kind of laughter, but following such violence it was uncanny, as though one were to encounter (as I once did) a foaming glass of wine resting on the lip of an ancient tomb.

My aunt, more accustomed to the progress of her husband's rages, addressed him again in an ordinary tone of voice. "Pray, Josiah, compose yourself."

"And you!" he replied, in a manner at least half-coherent. "What of you? Don't think I'm blind! Staring and goggling! Jack-in-the-box!"

"There are *neighbors*. We are standing in the public way."

"Ah, yes, neighbors! And so we preen our feathers, do we? A wonder you're not dancing, I suppose. You want music? And a monkey, eh? *Eh?*"

"Josiah!" Her tone matched his for subdued ferocity. "Silence yourself at once. Clara, give me my bonnet."

I retrieved the bonnet from where it had fallen to the pavement. As I handed it to my aunt, Mr. Jerningham cast on me a look of unqualified contempt. Of hatred, even? Perhaps.

"So, Lydia, I see you *have* a monkey now."

From that moment I became, along with my aunt, the destined object of his future rages. Indeed, I soon supplanted her as his preferred victim, since I could not contest against him.

Before I advance to the second instance, I ought to explain what lay behind my uncle's behavior on this earlier occasion. For, though his actions were extreme, they were never unmotivated or, in his own estimation, unjustified. In this case, he had thought that his wife, by the attention she had devoted to the beauties of the evening sky, had violated the laws of propriety. To a degree, he was correct; most authorities do maintain that a lady ought not to divert her gaze from the direction in which she is walking. However, circumstances alter cases, and a rule devised for the exigencies of Regent Street should not possess the same force on a deserted avenue in the suburbs. Some of my readers may disagree, but even taking the strictest view of the matter, it must be admitted that my uncle's reprimand was out of proportion to the offense. A word—at most a frown—would have sufficed.

In the next four years, I was to witness many more displays of Mr. Jerningham's temper, but none so intimately painful, none that was to impress so indelible a mark on my spirit, as the two recounted here. In the interval between them, I even learned, instructed by my aunt's example, to discount these periodic explosions, as the natives of West Indian islands learn to discount the hurricanes that annually devastate their fields and houses. They would retreat to their cellars; I, within myself. There, at last, my uncle sought me out.

It was a weekday afternoon late in the summer of 1854. I had been having tea with my dolls in the tidy walled-in garden behind our house, while my aunt watched my play from the window of the back parlor. The dolls were seated in a row on the white cast-iron bench: Alexandra, as eldest and handsomest, occupied the bench's one cushion (a damp, lumpish thing, but never a murmur left *her* lips); beside her sat the raven-haired, rosy-cheeked Mademoiselle Latouche (a noisy, naughty creature, Mademoiselle Latouche, though cleverer than her sister); finally, slumped in a corner by herself, was the sport of the family, their impoverished cousin, Chloe. My aunt herself had made Chloe from odd scraps of cotton and duck. A sillier, more comical rag-doll than Chloe never was seen, with her floppy yellow bonnet, her orange yarn hair, and bright mother-of-pearl eyes popping out of a round, grinning face. There they sat, sipping their tea and chatting with each other and with me, who alternately acted the parts of their mother, their hostess, and the maid who attended them. In this last capacity, I had left them to fetch an imaginary plate of biscuits from the steps of the house. When I turned round, plate in hand, I discovered that a jay had perched himself, bold as brass, on Chloe's lap and was endeavoring patiently to peck out her eyes. Now if this had befallen either Alexandra or Mademoiselle Latouche, it would have been a tragic event, but as it was only Chloe whom the jay attacked, poor foolish Chloe, it was a comedy—or less than that, a farce. Chloe sat unprotesting as the jay struggled to remove her bright button eyes, and her two cousins regarded her plight with imperturbable calm. I was beside myself. I called to my aunt to look, but she had left her seat beside the window. Chloe and the jay together tumbled off the bench. The jay gave out a great *screech* of indignation. It was too much for me. Limp with laughter, I collapsed to the steps.

The next moment I felt myself hauled up by my pinafore and

swept, as by a gale, through the ground floor hallway of the house and up the stairs and into my uncle's study. Once I had been set back roughly on my own feet, I found myself facing Mr. Jerningham, who was seated at his desk. He was in one of his rages, but this was not his usual rage. His hands trembled, his eyes burned, the vein in his forehead throbbed—but he was silent.

When he did speak, it was in a tone of icy, cruel deliberation more frightening than his former headlong incoherency: "What demon has possessed you, child?"

How could I answer such a question? I hung my head and waited for his abuse to begin, knowing that it could only last so long and that then I would be sent to the safety of the nursery.

"Pardon me, Sir."

"Well? Is that all you have to say?"

"I'm very sorry, Sir."

"*Why* are you sorry? Speak up! Look at me."

"Because . . . I was laughing," I hazarded. I knew, of course, that laughter was sinful on the Sabbath. Like every child, I had been taught the little song that goes—

> *We must not play on Sunday,*
> *But we may play on Monday,*
> *On Tuesday, and on Wednesday,*
> *On Thursday, Friday, Saturday,*
> *Till Sunday comes again.*

The second stanza prohibits laughter as well. But this was not a Sunday, else I should not have been allowed into the garden at all, else my dolls would have been locked away, else my aunt would not have been sitting idly at an open window.

"Indeed!" my uncle said with a jeering smile. "I would have known that in the City. Can you tell me what caused such laughter?"

"The jay, Sir . . . he was. . . ." His examination had reduced me to such a state of quivering terror that I could not go on. I really believed that if I finished the sentence, if I said that the jay had been pecking at my doll's eyes, that Mr. Jerningham would gouge out mine.

"Yes? Go on."

Terrified into silence, I could only stare and weep.

"Obstinate, too? Well, I have a cure for that." He opened the top drawer of his desk and took out a small box of inlaid ivory and teak. I recognized it as having belonged to my mother. Mr. Jerningham handed me this box and bade me open it. I obeyed, though now it was my hands that trembled, while his had grown quite steady.

"Set the box down here on my desk. Now, unwrap the tissues. Hold up the article you find there, hold it higher, and tell me what it is."

I held up a slim limp length of a kind of rope. It was about ten inches long and fashioned from what seemed innumerable strands of light brown silk. To either end small gold eyelets were fixed.

"Well?"

I shook my head and whimpered.

"When your mother died, Clara, your aunt thoughtfully removed a lock of her hair. From it, this watch-chain was made. It was to be given you on your twelfth birthday. Clara, do not look at your feet when I am addressing you."

I raised my eyes.

"If your sainted mother had witnessed what I did today, if she had seen you, as I did, rolling on the ground and screaming—shrieking, I should say—with laughter, she would have been very ashamed of you. I have no doubt that she *did* see you and that she *is* very ashamed—and very angry, too. I have no doubt she would have punished you. Do you, Clara?"

"No, Sir."

"But as she is not here, I must act in her place. Hand me the watch-chain, Clara. Lift your chin."

I did as he commanded, and with no other warning than a sudden grimace, he lashed at my neck. The eyelet's sting was sharp as the bite of a hornet. I screamed, as much from sheer horror as from the pain. Five more times I was compelled to stand still while he whipped my neck. Then I was ordered from the room.

There—it is written! And now that it is, and the ink is dry, I wonder at myself for having quailed before the task. How long my hand hesitated before I could begin this chapter. Now that it is almost done, I feel a giddy relief—as though I had confessed some long-buried guilt of my own.

Perhaps the larger guilt *is* mine. I have stored up these memories too long. My imagination has made an ogre of Mr. Jerningham, and though I profess a Christian forgiveness of him, my heart, I fear, is sealed against him. Now the wound is once again exposed, I hope it may heal.

I hope, as well, that my motive in rehearsing these painful scenes is not solely a desire for self-vindication, though that must have its share in any composition of this sort. My conscious object, though, has been to trace certain tricks and turns of my character to their childhood source. Many of the events of my larger story, if they are not to seem altogether incredible, must be viewed in the light of much earlier experiences, for the Woman's actions often spring from the fears and misapprehensions of the Child.

To take a small but telling example: as a direct consequence of that first whipping, I have never been able to laugh in an easy, natural manner. Rather than call down on myself again so terrible a punishment, I learned to control my breath in such a way that no alteration in my face or voice would betray my secret mirth. Like the use of whalebone, what began as a determined effort of the will became, through long use, inherent. My character, thus, became the mirror image of Mr. Jerningham's: anger stifled in his breast, and laughter in mine.

In more decisive ways, as well, my nature was shaped by his. Like any other subject of a despotism, I developed the twin habits of acquiescence and distrust. The acquiescence may have been superficial, but the distrust was profound. I have always feared that beneath the even tenor of my daily existence there exists an abysm of terror into which my next footstep might hurtle me. I form friendships slowly, and love, of that impulsive, swift-blossoming type celebrated in so many modern romances, is altogether outside the range of my sensibilities. For me, love must be the product of years of mutual sympathy and active association; a tree rather than a flower.

Because I am distrustful, I am also incurious. Believing that danger lurks everywhere, I have usually been content to remain fixed, statue-like, in some safe niche to which no novelty may intrude. This, of course, is not an absolute principle, or else I would have no life-story to relate beyond the synopsis of my meals and a catalogue of my needlework. But it is true to this extent: that in a choice between what is familiar and what is unfamiliar, my preference has ever inclined to the former. I am *afraid of knowledge.* It is as simple as that.

I have one fault, however, which I can by no means blame on the influence of Mr. Jerningham, and that is a passion for my own Psychology. Give me my head, and I will trot on for pages of blissful self-absorption. But whoa back, enough! My actions will reveal what stuff I'm made of more surely than a mile of galloping analysis.

A final word before I leave the subject of this chapter: on the matter of corporal punishment. It is judged proper that a girl, because of her presumed greater delicacy, be birched only about those portions of her anatomy which are customarily bare; that is, on her hands or neck. I can only suppose that the adults who follow this rule were never themselves punished upon their necks as children. In fact, it is inexpressibly painful. Pray, reader, if you have daughters, do not discipline them *more* cruelly than you would your sons!

CHAPTER SIX
Lydia

FROM THE HOUR OF MY MOTHER'S DEATH until the tragic moment of her own, Lydia Jerningham was my constant companion and dearest friend. She epitomized in her sole self the contradictions and diversity of a room full of quarrelling relations—mothers, daughters, sisters, in-laws, and all degrees of cousins and aunts. My feelings towards her were as diverse and contradictory: I loved her, I laughed at her, I rebelled from her, I wept for her. I was her confidante and her victim, her pupil and her nurse. She could amaze me endlessly and bore me to tears. She was as various as the seasons, as changeable as the weather, and as unpredictable as her own timepiece.

Lydia was thirty when she married, her husband fifty-four. It was not a love-match, but few women entering their fourth decade of filial dependency are likely to reject a willing and respectable suitor on that account, nor is that suitor's age, so long as he is still robust, apt to be a great deterrent. By thirty, one has learned to forgive others for being forty, or even fifty-four.

Whether some kind of love eventuated from their union it would be difficult to say. Mr. Jerningham, in the intervals between his eruptions, was not one to display his feelings before me, but the heart's deepest impulses are often, for that very reason, those best secured from public view. Lydia, on the other hand, was liberal with her testimonies, but they were, on this subject as on most others, inconsistent. "Mr. Jerningham," she once told me, "has been the pea in the slipper of my existence. I'd have been happier married to a Red Indian, or a pauper, or a marrow from the garden." Other times she could wax quite sentimental, calling him her popinjay, her hearthstone, her "other Albert" (a reference to the Prince-Consort, and the highest possible encomium); but all these more fanciful endearments she reserved for when he was absent. To his face, she never ventured upon anything warmer than "my dear husband," or some times, in an inveigling tone, "Josiah." Yet if my own experience has taught me anything, it is that the public and the private aspects of marriage may be quite distinct. Misery may cloak itself in a show of high spirits; the converse is just as possible.

In her person, my aunt realized that ideal of cheerful heaviness and smiling substantiality so often associated with those mid-century years. Her crinolines were responsible for some part of this impression; her manner, at once portly and delicate, for another part; but even without such assistance the impression would have been strong, thanks to Nature, a generous appetite, and Mrs. Minchin, the Jerninghams' inspired cook. Lydia's cheer never glowed brighter, nor was her smile so broad, as when she sat down before one of that worthy woman's apple tarts or a plate of her scones. Indeed, those joints and gravies, those puddings and pasties made epicures equally of husband, wife, and ward.

In one other important respect wife and husband were in complete agreement—the respect of Propriety. Lydia lived for Propriety. It was her morning and her evening star, her alpha and omega, the axis round which the whole great globe of her being revolved. The Propriety at whose altar she worshipped was not the same Propriety, exactly, as that adored by Mr. Jerningham. His was a rather more unified conception, verging on monotheism, while Lydia's tended to shift in the winds of fashion. It was not God's but Mrs. Grundy's watchful eye she lived in fear of.

Behind Mrs. Grundy, however, a more august presence made itself felt—the Queen's. Our house on Worcester Terrace came in time to be a kind of shrine to the Royal Family. In every room, almost on every wall, the faces of the Queen and the Prince-Consort, the Prince of Wales and the Princess Royal, looked down on us from a dozen chromos and a score of china plates and teapots acquired at the Great Exhibition. The Bible of this religion was the *Illustrated London News*, every number of which was certain to afford some glimpse behind the curtains of the Royal Residences. Not all that was done at the courts of Buckingham and Windsor could be emulated, even on a reduced scale, in a Bayswater villa. However earnestly my aunt might study the rules of precedence, she was given little opportunity to apply them at her own dinner table. All that was splendid, lustrous, and regal in the Pantheon of the Royal Household remained as inaccessible as a dome frescoed by Veronese to the wondering throngs below it; but this was, after all, only the outward aspect of their majesty. Its intangible core could inspire even the humblest cottagers to model their domestic life on the same principles of diligence, dignity, and sobriety. If there was a ludicrous side to my aunt's identification with her Sovereign, there was, inseparable from that, a side that was sublime. In her own unassuming way, Lydia Jerningham was as much a visionary as Teresa in her convent cell, though my aunt's vision, may be, was of an humbler, more domestic kind; namely, that she should educate me into a Princess, the very pattern of all virtues and accomplishments.

On the face of it, this was an unlikely undertaking. Neither my expectations nor my aptitudes were out of the ordinary, but she took up her task as though the plain deal of my character were very Parian. Even if Mr. Jerningham had not insisted that the ex-

pense of a governess was beyond his means, I doubt that my aunt
would have been willing to surrender my education into any other
woman's hands. Through me, because I was a child with a child's
regardlessness of the strict divisions of adult society, she was able
to live the better part of each day in a Kensington Palace of her
own devising, where she was the Baroness Jerningham and I the
Princess of Bayswater.

I was delighted to co-operate in a fantasy in which I was assigned so flattering a role. Even the most arduous problems of
arithmetic seemed tolerable when the unfolding of them was pref-
aced with "As Your Highness must appreciate" or "As Your
Highness must now clearly see." Sad to say, once we had advanced
a little way into the *Elements* of Euclid (needless to say, in a translation; young ladies did not in those days attempt Latin or Greek),
neither Her Highness nor Her Ladyship appreciated or very clearly
saw the inalterable necessity for the base angles of an isosceles
triangle always being equal. We did not on that account abandon
geometry, for when Reason faltered we could rely on Faith. As
my aunt remarked, "*What* we learn, my dear, is not at all important, so long as we devote a specific amount of time to it each
and every day. Understanding will come in its own good time.
We shouldn't presume to *force* it."

Each and every day, therefore, I did devote a specific amount
of time to the study of History and the use of the globes; I read
the classics of English Literature (provided they were not *novels*)
in the improved editions of Thomas Bowdler and James Plumptre;
I practiced Drawing by copying the oaks and oceans represented
in *The Young Ladies' Artistic Miscellany*. After a time, I became
so adept at this form of plagiarism that I was able to re-assemble
landscapes of my own out of the various formulae in the *Miscellany*, with a special predilection for seas and mountains, preferably
side by side in the wildest kind of weather. This, though I had
never seen any body of water larger than the Thames, nor any
promontory higher than Primrose Hill.

In one subject our progress was more real and consequently
more satisfying. Lydia possessed a tolerably tuneful pianoforte (it
represented the better part of her marriage portion) and a fair
talent for performing on it. Music occupied a place in her life

analogous to that which religion occupied in my uncle's: it was the unifier of her scattered energies, the arena in which her soul's inchoate aspirations could become focussed and articulate. Her execution might some times be wanting, but her taste was knowledgeable, her expression full and true. Fullest and most true, I think, when she played Mendelssohn, whose graceful songs, at once lilting and complaisant, lively and silvery-sad, seemed to issue from her own inmost being. What student could help but take fire from such a teacher? I would willingly have surrendered every other occupation, and my aunt would almost have allowed me, for the chance to devote myself entirely to the keyboard, much as some luxurious bush, if left unpruned, will encroach upon the whole garden with its eager tendrils. Such singleness of purpose, while it may produce great artists, was not suitable for the education of a gentlewoman. The bush was trimmed for the garden's sake; my practice was limited to a sensible half-hour every afternoon.

There was another plant in that garden which, let the gardeners do what they would, was anything but luxurious. Alas for my pretensions to gentility, my study of the French language never ripened into a real and applicable skill. I mastered the grammar well enough to make my way, at a kind of unsteady canter, through prose of no more than average difficulty. I even cleared the hurdles of five or six of that language's best-approved classics, though this accomplishment was more in the nature of working out vastly elaborated riddles than of enjoying what better scholars have assured me to be masterpieces of literary art. Often, as I would sit staring at the conjugation of some painfully irregular verb, I would reflect that of all the unhappy consequences of our first parents' sin, the unhappiest was surely the collapse of Nimrod's great tower and the sundering of the peoples of the world into so many mutually incomprehensible nations.

Despite my native incapacity, I might eventually have won to a tolerable degree of competence by reciting the litanies of my grammar book, as have countless English boys and girls before me; I might have—if the venture had not been doomed from the start. My instructress in this, as in all else, was my aunt, and my textbook was the same volume of handwritten paradigms that she had

copied out as a young girl under the tuition of a certain Madame
Roland. This lady had claimed to be the widow of one of
Napoleon's officers, but, in the light of what I now know, I
very much doubt that she ever saw any more of France than may
be glimpsed from Dover on a day of clear weather. Madame
Roland's accent, which Lydia learned from her and I from Lydia,
was such as no Frenchman, however provincial and uncouth, has
ever spoken or heard. In fact, her accent obeyed all the rules of
correct English pronunciation, with now and then a trace of
Cockney in the vowels. Anyone overhearing us speak this pidgin
French to each other would have been overcome with hilarity, if,
that is, our mistaken purpose were suspected. Fortunately, we had
learned to speak our "French" so rapidly that it was for all intents
and purposes a language private to Lydia, myself, and, if that good
widow were still alive, Madame Roland.

The day would come when we would be grateful for possessing
a private language, but not before we had experienced the colossal
chagrin of discovering the error of our ways on a memorable
evening in May of 1863. The great French actress Rachel was then
in London performing in Racine's tragedy of *Bérénice*, a play I
had thought I knew by heart, as it had been one of the first texts
I had had to decipher. Never, so long as my uncle was alive, had
I been allowed to attend the theater, but after his death, my aunt
decided to relax that prohibition. The Queen, after all, was known
to be partial to a good play, and the Queen could not be in error
in matters of conduct. So, to celebrate my nineteenth birthday,
we went to see *Bérénice*. From the moment the curtain rose and
Antiochus addressed the audience, we realized that something was
amiss, and each sequent, unintelligible verse deepened our morti-
fication. We left at the interval. In the carriage returning home,
my aunt's embarrassment slowly gave way to such fits of laughter
as would have done any schoolgirl credit. Laughter did not come
as naturally to me. I sat beside her silently, while tears of hilarity
rolled down my cheeks. Altogether, I think it was one of the
delightfulest evenings of my life.

From the preceding sketch, my readers may have gathered that
Lydia Jerningham was a most mercurial and light-headed creature,
the veriest Titania of guardians, a Falstaff among aunts, and

truly, this is the light in which I like to remember her. She had a darker side to her character, however, which could be very dark indeed. Just as my uncle would some times erupt into towering rages, my aunt was capable of as sudden and as inexplicable declines. Her blithe spirits would plummet abruptly, to lodge for days and even weeks in a morass of melancholy and hypochondria. When I say this, I do not mean to disparage the very real pain she experienced during these "megrims," as she termed them; only to suggest that the source of that pain, and its remedy, lay outside the understanding of medicine. There was nothing she could do but take to her bed and endure what could not be cured.

It was my duty at these times to be at her bedside and answer to her needs, which could vary with wild celerity. The sash must be raised or lowered; the curtains drawn or parted; the counterpane was stifling her, yet once it was removed, instantly she took a chill. But these caprices were as nothing compared to the gusts of passion that accompanied them. She would weep, would groan and wring her hands; in anguished, rambling soliloquies she would reveal all the accumulated bitterness of her wedded life to my uncomprehending, rapt attention. Lear never raged against the heavens and humankind half so vehemently, for in the worst of his distresses he possessed the comfort of witnesses worthy of his grand ravings. My aunt had only me.

No; she had, as well, another ally, whom she trusted more, though the trust was falsely bestowed. When her megrims became too much to bear, she would have recourse to Macpherson's Sulphurous Compound, one of the numerous patent medicines of that time which, under the guise of relieving suffering, imposed sufferings much greater than any they might have relieved. Macpherson's Sulphurous Compound was nothing else than laudanum, an alcoholic tincture of opium, and by its use my aunt had become, unknown to herself, a confirmed addict of that noxious drug.

Though the laudanum relieved her megrims (which were no more, I suspect, than an anxious craving for that narcotic), it also was responsible for the prostrations and lamentations I was so often witness to. Any man alive, and any woman, holds within himself the potential of an equal wretchedness, a misery that may be quite independent of the facts of his existence. There is pain

enough in this world, and injustice, and ill-fortune, to drive all its
inhabitants to despair if they will but fix their gaze thereon steadfastly, as Capuchin monks, so that they may not forget their
mortality, sleep in the coffins in which they will one day be buried.
My aunt's use of opium had become inseparably associated with this
habit of exclusive concentration upon her own distresses. Self-pity
was, in the strictest sense of the word, her vice.

The more fantastic pleasures of the drug, the visions and
ecstasies that De Quincey and other addicts have testified to, were
also erratic visitants at my aunt's sickbed, but what "local habitation and name" these airy nothings may have taken remained
largely a mystery to me. At these moments, Lydia's manner grew
calmer but less connected. Three words recurred ever again, three
words she would pronounce with a kind of raptured imprecision.
They were: *teapot, trilobite,* and *Amanda.* The first and last need
no gloss; trilobites, I have discovered, were a form of crustacean life
that became extinct some millennia ago. I cannot guess where my
aunt would have heard of them, or what significance they possessed
for her. Their conjunction with the imaginary Amanda and teapots conjures up visions that put me distinctly in mind of my most
beloved author, Lewis Carroll. That one should suffer the horrors
of addiction for the sake of private adventures in Wonderland
strikes me as a very poor bargain indeed. Perhaps I am mistaken.
More often than not, reports of the Ineffable, except by the
greatest poets, have a tinny, not to say ridiculous, sound. The
fault may be in human speech rather than in the visionary's apprehension. Perhaps; I only know that I would never sell *my* soul
to Macpherson's Sulphurous Compound for the sake of a teapot, a
trilobite, and Amanda, whoever she may be.

Once I had seen my aunt through two or three bad spells, the
duty of listening to her complaints, especially when the opium
had taken the edge off her eloquence, was more conducive to impatience than active empathy. It is a sad but certain truth that
we become quickly inured to miseries that are too much advertised, and from indifference it is only a little way to active
resentment. Some times, I confess, I went that little way, but
usually I sat beside Lydia in a trance of boredom and staunch
insensibility.

Not so when she began to recover. Once she'd put her medicine aside, her nervous irritability was such that the slightest cross, the least deviation from velvet perfection, the sight of a mote of dust upon the mantel, or the sound of the wrong note on the piano could send her into transports of pique. Not rage; that was Mr. Jerningham's prerogative. She did not burst out all at once, but her tyrannies—against the maids and Mrs. Minchin and myself, would have done credit to an empress. When it was I who had offended her (may be the hem of my frock was wet from brushing up against a dewy shrub; may be I closed a door too audibly), her punishments were ingenious and cruel. She did not whip me; that, too, was *his* prerogative. Often, indeed, I wished she had.

The punishment I remember most clearly, and dreaded most, was to be made to stand on a particular step halfway up the stairs to the second floor. This hallway was hung with daguerreotypes of the tombstones of both the Jerningham and Reeve branches of the family, a form of decoration less fashionable of late, though by no means extinct. The tombstone that confronted me as I stood upon this particular step was my mother's, and my feelings as I studied that inscription, hour upon hour, were an excruciating complex of desolation and remorse. It almost seemed that the little infraction of which I had been guilty was somehow linked by a chain of secret, subtle causes to my mother's death. Reason told me this could not be so, but, in the twilight of that stairwell, Reason could not always rule my mind. There in ghostly grays and blacks was the tombstone, and every word graved in its granite was a reproach: "What! Are you here again? What have you done now, evil child!"

"Nothing!" I would plead. "I broke a cup—only that."

"You have broken your dear aunt's heart, Clara," the tombstone would reply. "And *mine*. And *mine*."

Soon or late my aunt would call for me. Her temper would be past, and the forgiveness that I begged was freely granted. There might even be a sweet-meat waiting for me, or, which I loved more, a fairy tale. She was inconsistent? Yes, God bless her, she was.

Yet in *one* thing she never varied. Through all the campaigns of the some time secret, some time open war she waged against her husband, she never once betrayed me to him. Often, may be, she could not come to my defense, but she would never, even when put out with me for reasons of her own, assist one of Mr. Jerningham's attacks. As my aunt she could be infinitely capricious, but as my ally she was unswervingly loyal.

CHAPTER SEVEN
An Invitation

THAT LOYALTY WAS NEVER more severely taxed than on the day, in June of 1862, when the post brought me an invitation to come with my aunt for a week's visit to Blackthorne, my great-uncle's residence in Sussex. Mr. Jerningham was firmly opposed to my accepting. To his astonishment, his wife was as firmly in favor. She argued with him, and what is stranger, won the argument. I was not to know that our visit had been an item of controversy until I was seated beside Lydia in the railway carriage that would take us to Lewes. If I had, I know my impulse would have been to side with my uncle. Blackthorne represented the Unknown: had the invitation possessed all the alluring sweetness of a siren-song, this alone would have been sufficient to deafen me to its enticements. In fact, Lord Rhodes had written in a tone as nearly approaching to hostility as was still consonant with his hospitable purpose. I marvelled at my aunt's temerity—she, the ever-compliant, the reed that bent before her husband's lightest whim, whose life for twenty years had been a series of strategic retreats! I marvelled even more that she had triumphed over him.

"But how?" I insisted. "What ever did you *say* to him?"

"I merely pointed out that this would be a priceless opportunity for you, and one that might not offer itself again. 'Blackthorne,' said I, 'is one of the chief jewels in England's crown.' That was very pretty, don't you think?" Smiling a smile of quiet self-approbation, she smoothed a wrinkle from her travelling rug. "See how neatly I can manage," that smile and smoothing seemed to say. "Who could defy my calm authority?"

"And that was all? He was persuaded?"

"No," she conceded. "Not by that alone. I pointed out, too, that in view of the nearness of your tie to Lord Rhodes, any refusal of his kind invitation would suggest something like a lack of family feeling."

"In order not to offend Lord Rhodes' *feelings*, my uncle consented?"

"It was a consideration, surely."

"But still not the deciding one."

"I wouldn't venture to say, my dear, what consideration was decisive. One way and another, he was persuaded. Let it rest there."

Her tone, the quick, sly look she darted at me, the pouting expression of her lips—in all these were commingled an annoyance at my persistence and an amused assurance of complicity. Lord Rhodes was rich; he was my great-uncle. These two facts together had almost the force of a syllogism. Yet, somehow, though the handwriting was clear and bold, I had managed till now not to glance at the wall from which it stared down at me. I was being shipped to Blackthorne like a load of goods to be inspected and approved, and I must co-operate in this venture, must present myself as a probable and pleasant candidate for inheriting some part of Blackthorne's wealth. This was Lydia's understanding; undoubtedly it would be Lord Rhodes', as well.

I rose from the seat, blushing. "After all, Aunt, I think I would rather not go."

"Nonsense, my dear. Sit down. You've already written to accept. Lord Rhodes' coach will be waiting at Lewes."

"You can send him a telegraphic dispatch. Say I am taken ill."

"Clara! For shame!"

"I would rather tell a small lie now, than to . . . to seem to be. . . ."

"You will seem to be nothing but what in fact you are. The grand-daughter of his brother. What guilt in that?"

"But a whole week! To have him studying me, to *know* I'm being studied. I would as soon spend that time seated outside a church with an alms-cup in my hand. Don't ask me to, Aunt, please."

"I ask you only to sit down and behave like a sensible, well-brought-up girl."

"I refuse to act a part!"

"For goodness sakes, child, no one has suggested that you should. Be your own sweet self. If your impulse is to retire into corners, then follow it. If you are asked questions, answer. As for the rest of it, I trust you know the difference between a knife and a fork. Nothing else is required. Remember, *he* invited you. His motive in doing so is not for us to debate, or speculate upon."

Her words might have persuaded me, but her smile again belied the disinterestedness which they professed. I felt perfectly on fire with shame. I reached for the handle of the carriage door, fully intending to leave the train even without my aunt's permission, but Fate was quicker. The noise of the engine, which had been mounting steadily throughout our little duet, drowning us out like the orchestra in a German opera, now reached a crescendo. The carriage lurched, I fell back against the seat, the columns of the station platform began to recede at an ever-quicker tempo.

All the real fire of my indignation was lost in the spectacle of that journey. As well could I have disputed theology while being lifted up bodily to Heaven as now to continue any discussion with my aunt. Living so near Paddington Station, I had of course *seen* railway engines, both at rest and in motion, but nothing in my life had prepared me for the experience, at once exhilarating and terrible, of hurtling forwards in space at such prodigious speeds. With the expansion of the suburbs and the proliferation of railways, this form of travel has become so commonplace in our time that few of my younger readers will appreciate what an awesome thing it was, that first railway trip, for they will have been initiated to its mystery at an age when all things are awesome—and also, therefore, rather taken for granted. I was eighteen, and my notions of the Possible were firmly grounded in the bedrock of precedent. Now that bedrock heaved, my notions crumbled, and I was borne along, amazed, through the realm of the Impossible, a country of dreams, at a velocity of forty miles an hour!

The speed of our passage was not the only source of that amazement. The very face of the city, that London in which I had passed my entire eighteen years, was altered out of recognition. The moon, as I understand, has a dark side, which is always turned away from the earth; here was the dark side of London, the London of squalid courtyards and teeming tenements, of mile upon mile of soot-blackened tumbledown brick. Like some great fire-breathing bird, our train glided above the rooftops of Lambeth and Kennington, and from the windows of our carriage I viewed the dark face of an alien and ominous city, the London of poverty. The infernal regions, I think, would offer a first impression no more dismal than this.

Then, with the same magic swiftness, a new kind of landscape, as lovely as the last was grim, began to unfold. Green pastures and fields of corn, bright with the sunlight and the tenderness of June, rolled past like the waves of an endless and endlessly verdant ocean. No spirit long pent within a city could help but feel the expansive and vivifying effect of this swift plunge into God's own green and glowing world, and for me, pent up a lifetime of eighteen years, the pleasure was extreme. If South London were a Hell, this was, with even less exaggeration, Heaven.

Some times, far back from the path of the railway, one could catch a glimpse of some fine mansion, its leads gleaming pearly-gray in the noonday light. Less striking, though no less picturesque, were the clusters of lower roofs that wore droll bonnets of thatch (a novelty as striking as one's first sight of wild deer or wooden shoes or whatever else one never sees in cities). These cottages peeked out from covertures of oak and yew, box and beech. How I longed for my water-color box! I wanted a record of every hillside, every farmhouse, every tree. Here was the England I had seen so often celebrated in the pages of *The Young Ladies' Artistic Miscellany*, but transformed, resplendent, alive. Part of my pleasure may have sprung from the delight of recognition, as when one sees the original of some great cathedral made familiar by engravings, but the larger part was simply a heartfelt gratitude for the world so marvellously flying by me.

Among so much that was beautiful, my thoughts could not help but grow calmer. My alarm of only a few minutes before seemed excessive, if not baseless. I was not, after all, incurring any guilt in accepting this invitation. My uncle might well be as curious to meet me as I to meet him. If another motive lay behind this curiosity, it was no concern of mine. I would think no more about it.

Of course I did. It was impossible not to, and hypocritical to

deny it. What I thought, finally, was this: that as I was related to
Lord Rhodes, and as he was said to be quite rich, I *might* some day
inherit something from him. However, the degree of that relationship was not close, and the nature of our tie was not such as to
predispose him towards me (nor me to him). It was not likely, then,
to be a large inheritance. How much, *I* could not estimate. (The
Jerninghams, at the conclusion of their argument, had settled on
an annuity of two hundred pounds as being the upper limit of what
might be hoped for. The least I might come into was not liable to
be less than a lump sum of five hundred pounds, but even this might
be forfeited, so Lydia had argued, if I spurned my great-uncle's
invitation. Though the event would prove these calculations wrong,
the figures seemed probable.)

I determined to act towards my uncle with a normal cordiality,
but to do nothing with the *purpose* of pleasing him or making
myself an object of interest. In any case, my resources in those
respects could be but scant. I was a girl of the middle classes,
possessing only moderate charms and little cultivation. Many would
have judged me too young to dine in adult company. Whatever
Lord Rhodes' character might be, this could not be a recommenda-
tion. He would, I assured myself, think me dull, and I must be
willing to abide in that character for the duration of my visit. At
some trifling cost to my vanity, my conscience might be salved.

I did not reach that conclusion quite so directly, nor, once
reached, did it abolish my qualms once and for all; but when they
did return it was not with the panic force that had overpowered
me at Waterloo Station.

We reached Lewes in the mid-afternoon and found a landau
waiting for us. The coachman secured our boxes behind and asked
if we would like the top folded back in order better to take in the
view. Reckless of our complexions, we agreed. The roof came
down, we took our seats, a crack of the whip—and we were on
our way to Blackthorne, which lay some five miles south of the
town.

What a superior form of travel, after all, is a carriage by comparison to a steam engine! The thrill of extreme speeds, the convenience of swift arrival, the greater comfort of a railway coach,
even, as some claim, its superior safety—what are these against an
hour's ride with a spirited pair in good turnout? Yet I did not enjoy

that hour as I might have, for despite all that I had preached to myself on the virtues of dullness and disinterest, I was too keen to see the fabled Blackthorne to pay attention to the prefatory beauties. The road followed a while the bank of the Ouse. At every turn I expected Blackthorne to become visible. We crossed a bridge and rode through a tunnel of shade sloping downwards through a civil wilderness of broad-leaved elms. At every clearing in that forest I strained to see Blackthorne. We climbed a long hill from the crest of which my aunt insisted she could glimpse, far off, the shimmer of the open sea. My own vision was too poor either to confirm this, or deny; my *conviction* was that this was the sunlight glinting off the roofs of Blackthorne. Downwards again we drove, into a wide valley striped with the contrasting golds and greens of field and pasture and pied with stands of beech and elm. In the middle distance, the road forked. Set back from its left branch was a high iron gate, and behind the gate stood a tall, dignified freestone mansion.

The pace of the horses quickened. They sensed they were near their home. Delight conquered all my brave resolves. I must tell my admiration or burst!

"Aunt! There it is! Blackthorne! Oh, is it not lovely?"

The coachman turned round in his seat. "This is the lodge, Mum. We've a way to go before we reach your uncle's house."

CHAPTER EIGHT

A Kind of Magnificence

JUST AS IN GREEK MYTHOLOGY there is one muse responsible for each distinct category of the arts, so there prevails among the great families of England a tendency for each to produce some particular kind of genius. One might be distinguished for military prowess, another for statesmanship, still another for episcopality. The genius of the Rhodes family was a gift for making good marriages. Again and again through their history, the fortunes of the

Rhodeses have been rescued at the eleventh hour by some prodigy of matchmaking.

Of all these marriages, the most prodigious took place in 1759, when Clarence, third Lord Rhodes, secured to himself the hand and purse of Miss Marianne Spottswood, of the Virginia Spottswoods. Miss Spottswood's grandfather had amassed a considerable fortune in the slave trade; her father trebled that fortune while serving the Virginia colony as governor. And the issue of all these labors—of ships sailing, slaves toiling, peculations received, and heiresses wooed and won? It was this paragon, the noble pile and broad gardens of the greatest of the Georgian country houses, Blackthorne.

It is not Blackthorne's beauty, nor its nobility, nor yet its amplitude that constitutes the real force of the first impression it makes upon any visitor, but rather a sense of its ponderous inevitability. That vast classical frontage rises above its grounds like some great, gray limestone cliff. It seems no artifice of man at all, but a product of the earth's deep grindings and groanings over the centuries.

While still some distance from the entrance, our coachman brought the carriage to a halt. Tipping his hat back with the handle of his whip, he announced in a tone of possessive pride that *this* was Blackthorne. Had his accent been less rustic, I might almost have supposed that he was my great-uncle, who, in order to study us unawares, had been playing the part of his own servant, like the Prince in *Lalla Rookh*. Since those days, I have noticed that the servants of other great houses often adopt a similar attitude, as though the mansions in which they serve are no domestic form of architecture but temples where they minister, like Ganymede, directly to the gods.

"It's very pretty," I said, with a sense at once that words had failed me.

"Oh, it's more than pretty, Mum," the coachman said reproachfully.

"It's magnificent," my aunt supplied.

"Ah, that's more like! Magnificent top to bottom. And all carved stone, too—none of your brummagem stucco or your brick. How many windows would you say, Mum?"

"Oh, very many. I'm sure I couldn't imagine."

"Take a guess, Mum. Remember, there's two courtyards inside, and then all the windows on the west front we don't see from here. How many windows?"

"An hundred?"

"Oh, Mum! More than that!"

"Two hundred?"

"There's three hundred and forty-eight separate windows. Not panes of glass, mind. There'd be no numbering them at all."

"As many as that," I murmured.

As we resumed our progress towards the house, my aunt would rhapsodize over this or that aspect of the grounds or the architecture, more for the benefit of the coachman than for mine. His quizzing had reduced me to such a state of witless embarrassment that I could not remove my gaze from the handle of my parasol. I felt as though I were being studied by hostile eyes from all three hundred and forty-eight of Blackthorne's windows, a tribunal unanimous in its judgment that I was a small, shabby, ignorant girl whose trespass within the august precincts of Blackthorne would be soon and soundly punished. Such a conviction of one's own relative littleness is, more often than not, the *second* impression induced by great works of architecture. The might of stone columns and massy walls is not without an object; it is might *over* someone— over, in this case, me.

The carriage halted before the main entrance, where the grandeur of the building was brought to a focus of opulency by a broad stone staircase mounting to a portico, or porch, worthy by virtue both of size and execution to stand before a cathedral. Down this staircase descended a figure, a gentleman proportioned in the ordinary human scale and dressed in the ordinary London fashion. Very well dressed, may be, in peg-top trousers and a snuff-colored frock coat in the same expansive style—what was called "a very heavy swell." This in itself was reassuring. The manner in which he greeted us, the affability with which he handed us down from the carriage, his own matter-of-factness about the Aladdin's Cave into which he conducted us and where he was (he informed us) himself a guest, all these were calculated to give us ease, a commodity of which both my aunt and myself stood much in need. The actual sense of what he said escaped me in those first minutes;

but I knew that he was not, as had been evident at a glance, my great-uncle.

"Lord Rhodes is in good health, I hope?" my aunt inquired.

"Lord Rhodes is never in anything else. The only time he sees his physician is when he invites him to dine. For that matter, it may be the only time he'll see us. He's deuced fond of his horses. Rides like Mazeppa, you know."

"Mazeppa?" I asked, and won thereby a deadly look from my aunt.

"Lord Byron's Mazeppa," he explained, a little abashed. "A fellow who got into some kind of romantic entanglement and was tied to the back of his horse in consequence. 'Away, away, my steed and I,/We sped like meteors through the sky,' and so on for a great many lines, as far as the Ukraine, where he finally was untied."

"My niece has had no occasion to read Lord Byron," Lydia said, in a tone that announced her willingness to feed both of us at once to whatever lions of Worldliness and Impropriety stalked the halls of Blackthorne.

"I dare say it's no great loss for her. He's much overrated."

"She *does* esteem Lord Tennyson."

"Ah yes, Lord Tennyson is an excellent poet."

A heavy silence ensued. During this exchange, I had been able to observe our companion more closely, and all that I observed confirmed my first good impression. Living with the Jerninghams I had had as little occasion to meet young gentlemen of fashion as to read Lord Byron, but here, I was persuaded, was the very model of the type. He conveyed an air of manliness and quiet strength that all the calculated extravagances of "fashion"—Dundrearies drooping to the tips of his collar, a watch-chain stout enough to secure a small boat, the bold tartan of his waistcoat—could not diminish. These were but the ivy on the oak.

"I know not where Mrs. Lacey may be," our not-quite-host remarked. "I would undertake to show you to your rooms myself, if I could thread the labyrinth of the upper halls. But without at least a compass, I fear we might be wandering for days."

"Mrs. Lacey is Lord Rhodes' housekeeper?" I asked.

"A little more than housekeeper, and less than wife. His cousin, I've been given to understand, by some twelve or thirteen removes, as am I, through her, to an even remoter degree—for she's my aunt, you know." He stopped short, his ruddy cheeks grew ruddier. He must have thought I would construe his remarks as a reflection on the distance of my own relation to Lord Rhodes.

He was relieved from this difficulty by the appearance of the lady in question, a plump, pleasant matron of middle age, in a widow's cap and half mourning.

"Mr. Mainwaring exaggerates, as usual," she announced from the doorway. Then, to ourselves, with a slight but not a slighting curtsey: "Mrs. Jerningham. Miss Reeve. I'm delighted to discover that my tardiness has not left you to bake in the carriage. Please excuse me. And thank you, Godfrey, for presenting me in my true and ambiguous character."

"Mrs. Lacey, I stand abashed," he replied with complete composure, in a tone, indeed, almost affectionate. "With these ladies' permission I shall retire to the Temple of Pan to pursue my studies and lick my wounds."

Directly he'd left, Mrs. Lacey conducted us to our rooms. Every step of this brief journey—through the high-vaulted entrance hall, up the great staircase, and along another, dimmer hallway—revealed fresh causes for wonderment, but no mere inventory of Blackthorne's rooms and treasures would convey the sensations they produced in those first minutes. I felt as though I were once again plunging through the world at breakneck speed, racing over rooftops, seeing streets fleet by me soon as glimpsed. In truth, Blackthorne put me in mind more of a city than of any individual dwelling I'd ever entered. Its principal hallways were as broad as many London lanes, and its plan was almost as bewildering as the older quarters of the City, and for a like reason, that it had taken shape over several centuries, its final Georgian increment being a kind of casing for the original Jacobean structure.

A city, therefore, but a city how transfigured, whose coffered ceilings gleamed with gilt; whose walls coruscated with panellings of silk or glowed with the richness of damask! At regular intervals, vistas would open onto gardens that stretched, it seemed, for miles; but noble as they were, these views were surpassed by imaginary vistas into the ideal realms of the imagination. Both the third and fourth Lords Rhodes had been collectors of daring and discernment, and Blackthorne had become, throughout, a gallery of the finest English, French, and Italian art. The merit of this collection

I could not, with my little experience of the fine arts, appreciate, much less its rarity. The very names whose masterpieces these were—Greuze and Guardi, Titian and Turner, the divine Guido and the immortal Claude—were then as unfamiliar to me as the subjects they portrayed, the views of foreign cities and ideal landscapes, the pagan deities, and the courtiers and courtesans of ages long past and lands far distant.

As she whirled us past all this magnificence, Mrs. Lacey maintained a steady flow of information about the house and its present inhabitants, from which I gathered that Mr. Mainwaring was her younger brother's son, that he possessed the livings of Rodmell and Glynde, though he dwelt, usually, abroad, where he devoted himself to some kind of scholarship, of which folly Mrs. Lacey hoped this latest visit to his native England would cure him.

"He's fanciful to a fault, and as much given to expressing his *ideas* as any lad fresh down from the university. Apart from that, a finer gentleman was never born. On a horse, he's a match for anyone in the county, Lord Rhodes not excepted, though he *will* say, because he thinks it sounds original, that he'd prefer to read a page of Horace than to ride about on horses. He will pun all night on a single pint of claret. It distresses Lord Rhodes no end when he talks so. I've remonstrated with him. Lord Rhodes has been his benefactor almost since the boy could say "Thank you, Sir," and one ought in such cases not to offer contradictions unnecessarily. Generally, you will find Lord Rhodes the most temperate and unexcitable man in existence, but when he is crossed he *can* be quite fierce, and once he has been roused he is unrelenting. Dear me, yes!"

Had my attention been given more fully to what Mrs. Lacey said, I might have worked myself into a fine state of nerves over the ogreish character she imputed to my great-uncle, but deluged as I was by fresh impressions of all kinds, I had not the wit to sort out what mattered from what did not. It was all remarkable—Mr. Mainwaring's puns equally with my great-uncle's reputation for bearing grudges, the sweep of the staircase equally with the green hillside I could see from the window of my room. High above that hillside, a lark tumbled in the golden haze of a late summer afternoon. I raised the sash. The air swept in, carrying the strains of that giddy, heart-swelling song.

CHAPTER NINE
Another Kind of Magnificence

SEVEN O'CLOCK WAS THE DINNER HOUR at Blackthorne, which allowed me fully two hours to become acquainted with my apartment, to dress, and to fret. Lydia had announced that our journey had brought on a small megrim and she had taken a dose of Macpherson's Sulphurous Compound to soothe her nerves and compose her digestion. I was left to my thoughts, which were a volatile mix of anxiety and exhilaration, of soarings upwards and dizzying swoops down.

Let me at once confess that the principal source of my distress was a concern for my toilette. It was a needless distress, for my aunt had exercised taste and discretion in helping me select my new frock, a simple dress of white book-muslin worn with blue ceinture and a narrow neck-ribbon of the same sky-blue. In the dressmaker's mirror, three days before, I had thought myself a proper Cinderella in it, but now I worried whether it was sufficiently *en grande tenue* for dinner at Blackthorne. Against the rich silk coverlet of the bed, where it was laid, it seemed *too* simple; even poor. Further, I decided that its blue trimmings would call attention to what I then thought the chief flaw of my appearance—my brown eyes. What Cinderella ever lived whose eyes were not a sparkling blue? My hair, likewise, was dark, almost ebon. The more I studied my face in the mirror of the dressing table, the more I fretted. It seemed . . . foreign, a gypsy's face.

Well, I was eighteen, and this was to be, in a sense, my *début*. I doubt there is a girl in England who has not, in the same circumstances, wished to reconstitute herself in some equally drastic way. If I could find that mirror again, and if it could be compelled to show me the same features it presented then, I would not find much therein to regret. Even the defects of my person were such as the fashion of the day approved. I was small, and smallness was the vogue. I was slight, and so I might achieve an acceptable silhouette without lacing myself into a faint. My complexion was pale to the point of anemia, and anemic complexions were prized above the rosy cheeks of high good health.

Even at eighteen there are limits to a girl's self-fascination. Soon enough, the other appointments of my two rooms—yes, two! —drew me away from the toilet table. Here, alone, unhurried, and unashamed, I might forget my manners and goggle at the sheer mass and majesty of wealth that overwhelmed even this obscure corner of Blackthorne. The central marvel of my bedroom was a great four-poster japanned in scarlet, black, and gold, a specimen of the vogue, a century past, for chinoiserie. Gilt dragons peered out from the four corners of a pagoda-shaped tester, which rose, like an independent work of architecture trapped within the confines of the room, to brush the tall ceiling with a posy of fantastical flowers. The curtains of the bed were gathered about the posts. Wishing to study the quaint figures painted on the ancient silk, I unloosed the braid fastening one of these panels, and, as I did so, a silvery tremor of sound, like music played in another room, startled the air. I paused; the sound died away. I touched the silken curtain; the music was renewed. The mystery was soon solved. Each of the blossoms in the bouquet at the top of this pagoda was a bell fashioned of colored glass. The slightest motion of any part of the bed would set the lot of them delicately jangling. An admirable conceit for a Chinese temple, but rather unsettling when applied to a bed. However was one to sleep in it?

All the furnishings of the bedroom carried out this oriental theme in the same style of gilded whimsey. There was a screen before the toilet table which represented the whole geography of Asia. Willows drooped, rivers twisted, mountains reared, clouds hovered, and the waves of a pastel sea lapped at the foundation of pagodas much like the one in which I was to sleep. Through this landscape a crew of jolly Chinamen wandered in bucolic idleness. The same cheerful bonzes had strayed onto the wallpaper, where they led a life of equal ease, together with some herons and assorted birds of paradise. Other herons, of marquetry on a field of satinwood, flew across the bowed drawer-fronts of a commode. Another pair, blazoned on the sides of great china vases, were perched on the shelf of the mantel, from which vantage they regarded me with beady-eyed disapproval.

This aviary-bedroom opened into a private sitting room, or boudoir, decorated in a much calmer and less populated style. To this room I betook myself, with a sense somewhat of escaping the bustle and chatter of a party of strangers. Here all was brightness, grace, and quiet ease. One's attention was not assaulted at every glance by encrustations of the grotesque and curious. The settee, of striped silk, did not pretend to be anything but a settee. A number of chairs of differing design and tables suited to various purposes were disposed about the room, as though by hazard. Yet, despite this apparent heterogeneity, there seemed a unity of taste and a harmony of part to part in this room, which the bedroom, for all its consistency of style and theme, altogether lacked. One was encouraged to be comfortable here without being tempted to sloth. Some few objects of interest were unobtrusively displayed: a shelf of Meissen figurines, a vase of fresh peonies, and, hung to either side of a casement window, a pair of still-lifes so unremarkable as to seem, to my untutored eye, a reproach to their rich frames, as though porridge were to be served in golden bowls.

On closer study, these pictures seemed even homelier. A pear, a walnut, a peach, some grapes, a milk jug, and the top of a teapot were scattered about in a fog of brown oil paint: that was all. You could see the strokes of the painter's brush, like ripples on the surface of the canvas, and so thinly was the paint laid on that you could see the actual weave of the canvas itself. What slapdash, trumpery things, thought I, and yet I could not shrug them off. I would walk back and forth between them (the other was even cruder: a pot of cheese, a pile of plums, a loaf of bread, and what looked to be a grocer's reckoning, in French), puzzling over them, annoyed with them, and—tell it not in Gath!—increasingly charmed and satisfied.

As I was standing thus engrossed, I heard, behind me, the door to the hall being opened. I turned to see, framed in the doorway, a tall woman in a dusty travelling cloak and battered straw bonnet. Her hand rested on the knob; her back was towards me. She was addressing someone who must have been, to judge by the volume of this lady's voice, a good distance down the hall. A loud voice, and its tone was scolding, but even so its quality was musical, as though these words were a little recitative prefacing her formal aria. "Please, my good woman, do not put yourself to any further trouble on my behalf. You forget, perhaps, that I have lived at Blackthorne more years even than you. All its mysteries are known to me. I have catalogued every closet's skeleton and known the ghosts by their first names. Certainly you must allow me to find"— she turned towards me—"my own room."

Her face was veiled, and she stood in shadow. A mutual surprise had rendered each of us immobile as a statue. So convincingly had my visitor declared this room to be her own that I felt I owed her an apology, yet I hesitated to address her until she had lifted her veil. That little bit of black gauze separated her from me as effectively as a foot of solid masonry; while it covered her face she remained in another room.

She lifted her hands to the hem of the veil but did not raise it. "You are Clara?"

I nodded.

The veil lifted to expose wide, loose, rouged lips that formed an ironic, pouting smile. "Clara Reeve?"

I managed a more articulate assent to this, and my effort was rewarded by a display of the entire face. It had once, I could see, been handsome, perhaps as little time before as six or seven years, but now age had performed its melancholy miracle upon her flesh. Some faces wear the emblems of their mortality with a kind of philosophic nonchalance, as though their wrinkles and pouches and jowls were so many old clothes which the wearers actually prefer for their greater comfort and convenience. This was not such a face. It was not that the lady sought to *disguise* her decay. The color added to her lips and cheeks was not intended to deceive; rather, it was a little gesture of apology to anyone who might be distressed by the raw reminder of her face—that we will all of us one day be as cruelly ravaged. Yet, even without the folly of a deliberate effort, something of youth did cling to these wasted features. It was there in the vivacity of her expression, in the firm clench of the little jaw, in the liveliness of the gray eyes, in the sense she conveyed at almost every moment that, though the fortress of life were beleaguered, it had not been broached. Appetite and strength of will had not departed from her with her beauty, nor so long as her being still knew the hungers and the satisfactions of a worldly life would she ever attain to that higher beauty, which time cannot touch, the beauty that is the glow of the spirit's growth.

Was I so prescient as to gather all this at a single glance? No, I have abused the privilege of a much longer acquaintance to draw meanings from this lady's face and clothes which would only be revealed during the whole unhappy history of our relation. So, to retrench: I saw a rather remarkable old lady, whose smile made me feel a little uncertain of myself, a little more inclined to step back from her than to advance to meet her—an effect which she seemed to be aware of, to judge by the words she then addressed to me.

"But I must have frightened you out of your wits, my dear, bursting in on you like this, appropriating *your* room—which I see now that it is, though I can claim a kind of excuse, in that it was mine *once*. But my dear brother, whose grizzled seeming much belies the delicacy of his true nature (we ought never to trust appearances), must have wished to spare me the pain of too vivid a reminiscence. Dear Douglas, such a gentleman."

"Then you must be the Contessa Visconti," I ventured.

My guess was rewarded by a kiss upon each of my cheeks. Dust sifted through her veil as it brushed my face. She smelled overpoweringly of musk.

"I bear that unfortunate name, yes. But *you* are forbidden henceforth to address me by any other name than aunt, or, if you like, Zaide. And I shall call you Clara. It's shameful that we should begin our acquaintance so late in life—so late, at least, in mine. I did have some hope I might find you here. When I wrote to His Lordship—and we must all have a care, Clara, not to diminish *his* dignity by omitting these little marks of deference, for age has rather stiffened him, just as it has made me looser." She flexed her wide lips in a leering grin. "All *too* loose, my brother would say. When I wrote to him—a month ago?—I did suggest that our visit might be in the nature of a family reunion."

"Has Niles come, too, then?" I was conscious of my boldness in referring to my cousin thus familiarly, but it seemed to be the style his mother favored. In any case, she seemed not to notice the liberty, much less to balk at it.

"Niles, of course, and his fair bride, too. The whole tribe, in short."

"I had not known that he was married."

"Just this February. Yes, I am become the Dowager Countess. I fade away suddenly like the grass. In the morning it is green, and groweth up: but in the evening it is cut down, dried up, and withered. Very sad, very true. What is it from? Not Shakespeare?"

"I think *The Book of Common Prayer*."

"Ah, then I wish your worthy Mr. Jerningham had been here to hear me spouting from so irreproachable a text. I have always blamed Niles for managing all that so poorly, though of course it was no embassy for so young a lad. With a little more tact, some assurance that, though living in Gomorrah, we were nevertheless stout and righteous Protestants, he might have secured permission for you to come to Venice, if only to say hello."

"To Venice? I'm afraid I don't understand."

"Oh dear, have I stepped in it? Of course, you were only six then, you wouldn't have known. Well, since it's out, it's useless to pretend it's not." She proceeded to inform me of the letter she had sent, through her son, to the Jerninghams. This was my first knowledge of the Contessa's offer, and the shock of it did nothing to steady a mind already discomposed by so many novelties. The Contessa must have sensed my confusion, for she shortly excused herself to dress for dinner.

Indeed, the hour did not allow of delay. I went to my aunt's room and roused her from the murmuring slumber induced by her medicine. Dreamily she let me assist at her toilette. Somnolently, she attended mine. Together we set off to find the drawing room.

"Amanda," she whispered at the head of the stairs, taking my arm and bearing down quite heavily, "I must confess to you that I find this all *very* upsetting."

CHAPTER TEN

A Family Dinner at Blackthorne

THOUGH WE HAD FEARED TO BE LATE, we found the drawing room empty. A solitary moth, prematurely awakened, flitted among a dozen lighted tapers, as if undecided which would afford him the most glorious demise. Finally, he committed himself to the topmost candle in a stand of four that stood upon the mantel next a glass-belled clock. The flare of the moth's death drew my aunt's attention to this clock and roused her to wonder whether we had come to the right room. It was now some minutes past the hour appointed for dinner. Lord Rhodes himself might be unpunctual, but would all his other guests as well? Or had we misunderstood Mrs. Lacey and come down too soon? Useless to debate those questions between ourselves, but what alternative was there? We could not roam the hallways of Blackthorne seeking an answer.

More minutes passed. Outside, the shadows lengthened across the lawn; within, the darkness advanced more rapidly. Those candles, whose burning had at first assured us that this was the room intended for our reception, seemed now to mock at us in the thickening gloom, like the will-o'-the-wisps that lead late travellers astray.

Eventually we were discovered, though not before Mrs. Lacey, unable to find us in our rooms, had impressed half the household staff to search us out. That good lady herself, in a flutter of apologies, conveyed us to the *rose* drawing room, where the company had been awaiting us the long while we had waited for them in the *oval* drawing room. In her eagerness to assume the whole guilt for our tardiness, Mrs. Lacey forgot that we had not yet been presented to Lord Rhodes, who stood by scowling impatiently at her recital and pulling at his mustaches. Without an introduction,

my aunt and I were not in a position to offer any other apology
than our blushes.

"Very good, Mrs. Lacey. This is not an assize, you needn't
plead. They were lost and you have found them. Splendid. Now
we may dine." Pushing past Mrs. Lacey, he offered his right arm
to my aunt. "Mrs. Jerningham, will you do me the honor?"

Lydia quite literally flinched. Small as the company was, she
had been certain the other ladies would take precedence over her.
She glanced at the Contessas Visconti, but they seemed unconscious of Lord Rhodes' act of anarchism. And if her host did mean
to slight these ladies, what choice was there except to take the arm
he offered her?

"Clara?"

I took his left arm. There were flecks of mud on the rough
tweed of his coat. Evidently he had not seen fit to change from
the afternoon.

"We don't stand on ceremony here," he said to me. "Blackthorne is not London, and often there are not gentlemen enough
to go around."

"Oh, it's much nicer like this, *en famille*," Lydia observed
brightly, in her best French.

"Exactly," he agreed, with, it seemed to me, a rather grim
smile.

The doors were opened and we proceeded through the hall
down the stairs to the dining room. Lord Rhodes set a brisk pace,
but in this, as in his other rudenesses, I found a kind of relief. His
muddy sleeve, his shortness of speech, his rush to the table and haste
to seat himself before his other guests were seated: all these
solecisms tended to counterbalance our original fault and, in effect,
put me at my ease. My aunt, I could see, was outraged, but I,
with fewer preconceptions of how aristocrats habitually behave,
was only astonished, as by some prodigy exhibited at a fair, an
arithmetical pony or a waltzing bear. I was genuinely curious to
see to what use he would put the silver and the napery, but, if I
expected further marvels, he disappointed me. His deliberate affectation of bad manners could not withstand the sight of a table
setting. Once he was seated, he dined like any ordinary gentleman.

In the course of that meal, Lord Rhodes spoke to me three
times: once, to ask if I found my room comfortable; a second time,

urging me to taste the partridge he was himself so abundantly enjoying; finally, just before the desserts were brought in, to say I was welcome to Blackthorne. I assured him that my room was comfortable, the partridge delicious, and myself thankful to be his guest.

For the length of my visit, no greater intimacy than this was ever to be established between my great-uncle and myself. He never referred to the past, except once perfunctorily to regret my parents' deaths, nor did he show any curiosity about my present mode of life. As for opinions, the self-replenishing source of virtually all polite conversation, he seemed to think that I had none, except about the weather. He never failed to join with me in deploring the rain that kept us indoors and applauding the sunshine that allowed us out. Once, later in my stay, I went so far as to express, unprompted, my admiration of Blackthorne's gardens and of a variety of white rose peculiar to them. "Very pretty, so they are," he conceded with a scowl. That evening, vase upon vase of those same roses filled my room with their pallor and heavy perfume. A singular attention! Thereafter, I was more sparing of my praise, lest I again incur the rebuke of such largesse.

Lord Rhodes showed himself more companionable to my aunt. Discovering her veneration of the Queen, he plied her, through this and all our succeeding dinners, with tidbits of royal gossip more intoxicating than an equivalent number of glasses of claret, which beverage, I might add, was also very freely dispensed at his table. In telling of the Royal Family's visit to Blackthorne, he shouted down the length of the table to Mrs. Lacey, directing her on the morrow to show my aunt the state bedroom which Victoria and Albert had inhabited for three days in the spring of 1849. From that moment, Lydia ceased to note even the most glaring improprieties of our host. He had led her to the Holy of Holies and let her touch the veil that shrouded the Ark of the Covenant. When, in addition, it was known that Lord Rhodes had been present at the funeral, just six months before, of the Prince-Consort, that he had ridden in a carriage close behind the hearse, that he had witnessed at first hand the tears of the inconsolable widow, Lydia's heartstrings were stretched almost to snapping and her conversion was complete.

That first evening, Mr. Mainwaring sat to the right of my aunt, and to his right sat the Dowager Contessa Visconti, to both of whom my readers have been already introduced. They formed an odd contrast: he in evening clothes so superbly tailored, so exactly "right," that they seemed, like the chitons and togas of the ancients, garments of some timeless world where the currents of fashion are stilled; by contrast, the Contessa wore a frock twenty years out of style and looking as though it had done her service every evening of those twenty years. A stranger surveying our dinner party would have been quite misled as to our relative stations. Both my aunt and Mrs. Lacey—even, for all my earlier fretting, myself— were more richly and modishly attired than the Contessas Visconti, while Niles and his uncle were quite overshadowed by the elegance of the young clergyman.

Yes, Niles was present at that dinner. He had been placed on my left. The moment he had assisted his wife to sit down, before he was seated himself, he addressed me in a manner at once cordial and courtly.

"Ah, my dear Miss Reeve. I was so delighted when my mother told me that you were here. We have met before, you know, though I dare say you won't remember. It was quite twelve years ago, twelve very altering years."

"I assure you, Count Visconti"—I touched the hand he held out to me—"that I remember quite vividly. I was in a great distress, from which you rescued me."

"No!" He slipped into his seat without having to move it back from the table, in a single motion rather too sinuous to be really graceful. "Let's have *that* out at once. You shall not call me Count. Let it be cousin or, better, just Niles. And if our brusque language had not dispensed with intimate forms, I should insist on 'thou' as well. Now, let us begin again. Good evening, Clara. I dare say you don't remember me."

"No, I assure thee, cousin—" I shook my head, smiling ruefully.

"It won't do. I shall end by not being able to talk to you at all."

"Am I being a bear? I don't mean to. It's only that I've never escaped a sense of the absurdity of my ancient and honorable name. If it were English, you know, I would be addressed as Count Viscount, which you must admit has the ring of parody."

"And if," I suggested in a half-whisper, "my great-uncle's surname were Lord. . . ."

"Lord Lord!" Niles tittered appreciatively.

"What if you wore mufti—is that the right expression—and called yourself Mister?"

"No *Mister* Visconti suggests a dancing master or some revolutionary fanatic, or both, since these days they are not distinct categories."

Our conversation continued along this pleasant if not very purposeful course, neither saying much, but Niles saying it some times quite amusingly. Of the thousand conversations I may have had with Niles in the course of time, nine hundred have been little different—small talk, whimsies, tittle-tattle. If only, I have many times wished, those nine hundred had been all; if only (and it is an evil wish) life could be lived always at this level of lightness and nonsense! Wicked or no, that wish is never granted. However lightly they are touched, bubbles will burst. But they are lovely, aren't they, as they float downwards through the air?

The twelve years between our previous meeting and this had wrought no momentous changes in his person. He had gained some few inches and pounds; even so, one scarcely could believe this was the nephew of the robust and grizzled Lord Rhodes. The contrast was absolute. Niles' silken hair loosely curling down to his collar, his smooth face and glowing complexion, the chiselled, frail perfection of his features, the quick intelligence of those dark eyes; set against these Lord Rhodes' bare pate and bristling white mustachios, his thick, blunt nose and heavy jowls, the pock-marked flesh, his general air of sullen immobility, his pale eyes bleary with a lifetime's excesses. It was the difference between David and Goliath, Ariel and Caliban, blooming spring and hoary winter, though one could see at a glance that the mere increment of years could not transform *this* spring to *that* winter.

Once again, though, I anticipate myself. My attention during most of that first dinner was engaged mainly by the dishes and the niceties of the service, not by any minute observation of my cousin. Most of his attention was devoted, necessarily, to his young wife, Renata, who was under the disadvantage of speaking no English. For the duration of her stay at Blackthorne, she was able to converse only with her husband and mother-in-law. Mr. Mainwaring, who had some acquaintance with the classical Italian of Tuscany, made some attempt to communicate with her, but Renata knew only the dialect of Naples. After a few baffling exchanges, Mr. Mainwaring declared that the difference between the Neapolitan and Tuscan dialects was as large, at least, as the difference between Hebrew and Greek. Thenceforward, his attentions to the young Contessa were limited to the standard *Buon giorno*s of greeting, *Buona sera*s of leave-taking, and some shrugs and smiles of self-deprecating frustration.

Altogether, we made a very uncommunicative party. Accustomed as I was to long silences at the Jerninghams' table, I was not made greatly uncomfortable. Mrs. Lacey and her nephew seemed to suffer most, and they both struggled valiantly to rally our flagging discourse. Mrs. Lacey had the greater handicap in this, for at her right hand sat Renata, with whom she could not speak at all, and Zaide, on her left, did not show herself disposed to pursue any subject with her hostess. Mr. Mainwaring had the advantage of having made the Grand Tour and was able endlessly to solicit the Contessa's opinion on this or that city, or view, or church, opinions which at first were delivered with the utmost brevity. (Of Siena she said only: "Yes, it is quite charming. Everything is striped.") Then, either warming to the gentleman or tiring of his too mechanical questioning, she began gradually to offer more developed judgments, rounded out with curious and uncommon pieces of information. For a while it seemed that she might single-handedly rescue us all from the threat of silence, but then, during a remarkable account of her expedition to the top of Vesuvius, Lord Rhodes interrupted her.

"Still the same, eh, Zaide?"

"I beg your pardon, brother?"

"I said you are still the same."

"And I begged your pardon. How am I the same?"

"A bluestocking, you know. Of the deepest, darkest blue."

A deeper and darker red suffused her rouged and hollow cheeks. "Have I been where no lady ought to go? Are volcanoes then another male prerogative?"

"Volcanoes, is it? Sorry, but I hadn't been attending. I had just wanted, this last half hour or so, to get in a word to Godfrey."

"Have I been monopolizing your conversation, Mr. Mainwaring? I know I'm liable to do so. You must excuse me."

Lord Rhodes cleared his throat complacently. The Contessa fixed an angry gaze at the poached salmon on her plate and said no more. Mr. Mainwaring assured her that he had been fascinated by her story and begged her to continue.

"Really, there is no more to say. It was a volcano. It rumbled and smoked and belched, and one stared at it, as one does stare at anything that rumbles and smokes and belches."

Mr. Mainwaring made one other notable attempt to open a subject of common interest. He had been speaking in a subdued tone with my aunt, who, owing either to the laudanum she'd taken previously or the claret she was drinking now, had grown progressively less sequential in what she said. Mr. Mainwaring was under some strain to follow her from thought to thought. Then, when he seemed to be most confounded, he brightened.

"An interesting observation, Madam." Then, turning to include Lord Rhodes and myself, he said: "Mrs. Jerningham has mentioned trilobites. Though fossils are still some distance from my own investigations, I have lately had occasion to pick up Mr. Darwin's interesting book. A most remarkable production it is. Though you may think it strange in a man of the cloth, I find myself very much persuaded by his reasoning."

"Darwin?" asked Lord Rhodes, startled from his sullenness. "You don't mean the fellow who says we're all come down from monkeys?"

"I can't say, Lord Rhodes, that I can endorse his theories so far as that, but still—"

"Damn it, Sir, there are ladies at this table. Wait till the port comes, and I'll be happy to deliver you my opinion of Darwin or any blackleg scoundrel you may name."

That fairly ended Mr. Mainwaring's efforts for that evening. During the rest of the meal, little could be heard but the chink of silver on china and melodic murmurings of Italian between Niles, Renata, and Zaide. Once my aunt had the misfortune to spill half a glass of claret on the damask cloth. A little later, Lord Rhodes did the same, with, I suspect, the charitable motive of lessening Lydia's embarrassment. When Mrs. Lacey, at her master's cue, rose, I for one was quite happy to follow her from the room.

CHAPTER ELEVEN

A Stroll in the Moonlight

WE WERE SERVED OUR COFFEE in a drawing room that looked west-wards across the terraces of Blackthorne to a plantation of cypresses, their boles and branches forming a vast ornamental screen behind which the last embers of the day glimmered and grew gray. Zaide waited until Mrs. Lacey was seated and then found a chair for her-self at the opposite end of the room. In this conflict of loyalties, Renata favored Mrs. Lacey above her mother-in-law, perhaps be-cause the light, being stronger where Mrs. Lacey sat, was better suited to the hemming of the handkerchief she had taken from her sewing box. My aunt joined Zaide and directed me to sit with Mrs. Lacey, who immediately undertook to apologize for her employer's behavior at dinner. Behind his apparent gruffness, she assured me, Lord Rhodes was the sweetest, most even tempered man in three counties.

"He has his fixed ideas, it is true, which it is politic not to chal-lenge. But what gentleman has not? My own father, for instance, was an ardent Predestinarian. On any other subject he was amiable, tolerant, imperturbable, but let there be mention of Election and Free Will. . . ." She bit her lip and shook her head, as if quailing before that remembered wrath.

"My uncle Jerningham is something like that, too. It does not distress me."

"But Godfrey *ought* to have known better. I fear that he was deliberately baiting him. Darwin!"

"Who *is* Darwin?" I asked, really not knowing, so perfectly had the Jerninghams protected me from even the rumor of his doc-trines.

"Oh, Miss Reeve, please don't ask. He is a great troublemaker, and my nephew is another. After all, as Lord Rhodes pointed out, it is not a matter for *us* to meddle in. Let the gentlemen have their arguments and their port. We have other concerns. Do we not, Contessa?"

Mrs. Lacey leaned forwards, smiling and pantomiming her approval of Renata's *broderie anglaise*. Since an example of her own needlework lay in her lap, I cannot believe this display was quite genuine. Renata's muslin was warped and buckled by too hasty stitching. The pattern was askew. It would never see any finer use as a handkerchief than to wipe away the tears of frustration that its working evidently inspired. The young noblewoman acknowledged Mrs. Lacey's praise with a wan smile and toiled on at her appointed task.

Experience, whether of the cruelty of the world or its delights, had not yet marked the fine oval of Renata's face with any certain signs of character, and so she did not "show" to good effect by candlelight, which too much softened features that wanted the emphasis of direct sunlight. One word inevitably sprang to mind as one studied her—*weak*. She had a weak chin, a drooping, weakish cast to her lips, and a way of letting her head hang weakly so that her eyes were usually fixed on the lap of her own skirt. Weakest of all were her eyes, yet she refused, I suppose for the sake of vanity, the assistance of spectacles. She would weep all night over a piece of embroidery before she would resort to wearing her glasses. In daylight, though, and out of doors. . . . But an adequate account of that transformation would take me too far afield, and I must reserve that tale for a later chapter.

"How old would you say she is, Miss Reeve?" Mrs. Lacey asked, pouring herself a second cup of coffee. My cup rested on its own little tripod table, tasted once and set aside.

"Who?" I asked.

"Our foreign companion here. Though I am told she is not a day older than you, I find that difficult to believe. There is as little of freshness in her as in last week's spray of cut flowers. Perhaps it is true, as I have heard, that girls gain their bloom more quickly in southern lands—and lose it, too."

I regarded Mrs. Lacey with some consternation. She met my look with a complacent laugh.

"She cannot understand us, after all, Miss Reeve. So long as we don't use her proper name, she can't suspect that she's the subject of our conversation. Poor thing. Her husband and her mother-in-law, I've noted, take the same liberty. All that we say must sound like so much noise to her."

She sipped her coffee and studied Renata with a kind of twinkling good will over the gold-edged rim of her cup.

"It is remarkable, is it not," she observed, "how very fair she is? If one did not know otherwise, one would almost suppose she were English."

"True."

"Now you, Miss Reeve—if I were told that *you'd* been born in Sicily, I would find that much easier to believe."

"I have not her blond hair, certainly."

"Nor her eyes. I remarked upon it at dinner to her husband."

"Indeed. And what did he say?"

"That her type is quite common in the south of Italy. There was an invasion there some time or other. He said the same people had invaded England, too. I must remember to ask my nephew about it. Godfrey is a great authority on invasions and old coins and such as that."

Anxious to divert Mrs. Lacey from any further discussion of Renata, I asked an entire catechism of questions about Mr. Mainwaring's education, his travels, his career in the church. The subject was entirely congenial. She doted on her nephew, indulged him, and worried over him as though he were an only son.

Mrs. Lacey was detailing the virtues of a fine chestnut stallion that Godfrey had bought at an auction in Horsham, when Zaide, wearying of my aunt's company, crossed the room to ask if I would like to take a stroll with her on the terrace. I complied with reluctance, not being used to regard nocturnal rambles as a source of pleasure. By her sigh of relief the moment we had stepped out of doors my companion demonstrated a contrary disposition. The night air, so oppressive to me, acted on her as an elixir, quickening her spirits and enlivening her talk.

"The heart, my dear, is an amazing organ. No matter how well we think we know it, it will surprise us. I approached this visit with a firm conviction that Blackthorne would yield me nothing but vinegar and gall, and truly, till this moment, that would be a fair description of its flavor. There is not a room I have passed through today but that it has awakened some bitter memory. Tomorrow, if you like, I shall give a shilling tour of all the rooms, and point out the crimes and outrages associated with each, as they do at the Tower of London.

"But this"—she spread her thin arms as though to receive the night's embrace—"this is worth a mile of family portraits, a month of my brother's jeers. It is lovely, is it not? At once such calmness and such mystery. I could almost believe that my feet are treading the gravel of twenty years past. Twenty? Nay, twice that! I was no older than yourself the last time I walked down this path and watched the night damps gathering in the hollows of the land. So lovely and so long ago. Time, my dear! Time is the tyrant who conquers us all."

I was touched by this speech. No one had ever spoken to me candidly on the grand themes of Time and Mortal Decay. I knew them only as a subject matter of sermons and poetry, not of social discourse. Age indeed knows much that Youth does not suspect, but one of its most closely guarded secrets is this: that there is a chitchat of the soul, distinct from but akin to the small talk of society. Perhaps at one time Zaide had felt poignantly all she spoke of in our walk through Blackthorne's moonlit gardens, but she was too much in the habit of expressing these fine sentiments to feel them any longer with much keenness. I have caught myself in the same fault too many times to blame her greatly. I cannot believe she was taking deliberate advantage of my inexperience and youthful hunger for the Ineffable. What motive would she have had? Like any artist, she took more pleasure in her own accomplishments when they could be displayed before an appreciative audience, and that I certainly provided. Had her words flowed from the very Helicon of poetry, I could not have listened with a more breathless attention, a more solemn delight.

"Do you see," I remember her saying, "those cypresses? Many has been the night I watched them from the window of my room, their tops bending and trembling in the wind. They seemed then, as they seem tonight, to be immense candle-flames, but flames of blackness rather than of light. The movement is just the same, is it not?"

"I can barely see them, it has become so dark."

"That's why, I fancy, it is easy to imagine them being what they're not. In daylight, they would be cypresses and nothing else. Night alters the world."

"It obscures it, certainly."

"Does not your own imagination set to work on such a scene as this?"

"Yes, though I would rather it did not." Though I'd meant this as a joke, it came out with a much too earnest ring. I began to feel annoyed with myself for seeming such a fearful, trembling ninny.

Zaide, however, seemed to find this an appealing quality, for she drew nearer to me as we walked and took hold my arm in a protective, soothing way, stroking my sleeve as a nurse might stroke the fevered brow of her patient. "What begins in fright," she continued in a kind of ardent whisper, "can grow into the finest, clearest, ripest beauty. The trick is all in surrendering one-self to the Sublime. And the Sublime is, notoriously, a nocturnal animal."

She stooped to pick a rose from one of the bushes that lined both sides of the path. "These white roses, for instance. Confess that they are lovelier now, by moonlight, than in the glare of day. They have become phantoms of themselves. Inhale their perfume —even that is richer now."

At that time, I had yet to see them by day, and so reserved final judgment. "Usually I love roses best quite early in the morning, beaded with dew."

"I see I can't persuade you. Well, perhaps it is more suitable at your age to prefer whatever is bright and definite. Renata is just the same. It will be many years before either of you will re-quire the flattery of dark corners and midnight promenades, as many years, perhaps, as it has been since even by such artifices I could play the part of an enchantress. But still one clings to the illusion."

"To what illusion?"

"In this case, to the illusion that illusion is still possible. There was a lady of my acquaintance in Naples—she has long since joined the Great Majority—who, even at eighty years of age, took such pains in painting herself each evening, whether she was receiving company or no, that Cellini himself would have envied her her art and zeal. Whenever, meeting her, I bent to kiss the crackling varnish of her face, I would say to myself—'Take warning, Contessa, or you will one day be such another as this.' But it is hard. People will praise the ruins of the villa where they once spent a pleasant holiday, but the unfortunate owner of those ruins must learn to stop issuing invitations."

"Really, Contessa, you are too hard on yourself."

"Well, that is one of my pleasures, too. But you forget—you must not call me Contessa now. The title has been usurped." She laughed lightly and squeezed my arm where her hand had rested, to show that this was meant in jest.

When we returned to the drawing room, the gentlemen had finished their port and cigars and joined us. My aunt was persuaded to play, and I was relieved, after the first faltering bars, to observe that her performance did not suffer to any notable degree from the effects of her medicine or the wine. A largo was rather broader than usual, a scherzo less brilliant, but I am sure I was the only person in the room to remark this. Niles seemed especially taken by her playing, assisting as her page-turner, and demanding encore after encore until Lydia quite fairly could claim to be too exhausted to continue. Even Lord Rhodes joined in the ovation. As she rose from the spinet, her eyes met mine, and I read in her glance avowals more candid and confessions more intimate than a month of Contessa Visconti's best rhetoric could have yielded. She *had* suffered throughout dinner from a sense of not acquitting herself creditably. The more she had striven, the more deeply she had mired herself in a painful inadequacy. "Now," her eyes declared, "I have redeemed myself, and *you* need no longer be ashamed."

I blushed then, as I do now, for I had been ashamed of her at dinner and was proud of her now. At that moment, I discovered myself to be a snob, and the discovery was as unpleasant as it was surprising.

CHAPTER TWELVE

Intoxication

AFTER MY AUNT'S PERFORMANCE, Lord Rhodes bade his company
a cursory good-night. Taking our cue from this, we disbanded to
our several rooms. Though I was brimming with much as yet un-
told and unshared, Lydia wished to retire at once, and I was
obliged to let this frothing mixture of first impressions still ferment
through the long hours of a sleepless night. Sleepless that night
would be, for its excitements were only beginning. No sooner had
I quitted my aunt's room than I heard myself addressed in soft
yet urgent accents. I turned to discover my cousin Niles advancing
on me with comically exaggerated stealth. Though the hall was
well-lighted, he bore a burning candle in a sconce.

"I'm glad to find you here," he whispered, drawing close to me.
"It spares me the impropriety of knocking. My mother would not
let me alone till I had come to ask if you would like to visit with
us a while in her rooms. I said you would be fatigued, but she
refuses to believe that the English can retire so early. At the
Palazzo Albrizzi, one only begins to be coherent at eleven. *Are
you still fresh?*"

"Not fresh, perhaps, but wide awake."

A strange invitation, I thought, but as it had been issued on
behalf of my kinswoman, I surrendered my scruples and accompanied Niles on a journey as devious and winding as any
labyrinth could boast. Sadly, I lacked the wisdom of Ariadne and
did not provide myself with any means for retracing my steps.
But of that, hereafter. At each new twist and turn, the level of
illumination became more dim, until at last Niles' candle was our
only source of light. I began to suspect my cousin of playing a
trick on me. Had his mother said something to him about my fear
of darkness?

But no, the Contessa had indeed been quartered here in the remotest corner of the northern wing, apart from all other guests, including her son. It was evident from the moment I entered her room that our host had not intended any compliment to her by this arrangement. The room in which I found myself was cramped and spare, furnished with a motley jumble of odds and ends. May be some of these pieces were of historical interest—many, by their design and the scarred and wormy character of their wood, must have dated to the Tudor era—but they did not otherwise recommend themselves to the senses.

"Clara! I am happy you could be persuaded. We shall not after all expire of boredom here if we three can make up our own little secret society. Niles, you draw up a chair—No! Not that one! The least strain and its arm pops off. You see!—and Clara shall sit beside me, here." She patted the threadbare upholstery of an aged ottoman. "I can't imagine where Douglas discovered this furniture. He must have scoured the attic to prepare this little bower for me. Bless his black heart."

"Now, Mother," Niles remonstrated, drawing up a rickety ribband-back chair which surely would have collapsed under the weight of a more substantial young man. "It is not our place to complain."

"No, you're right—it is Douglas's place. We are but his guests. If he wishes to keep some of us in quarantine, it is his house, he has the right."

"Pish!"

"In any case, I am not complaining. I jest."

"Then try to do so more merrily."

"You must get us in the mood for that. Tell us what the gentlemen spoke of once we had been swept out of the room. Did that young clergyman take up the oriflamme for Darwin again?"

"He could not be got away from it. I thought my poor uncle would have an apoplexy."

"Good. Good." Zaide nodded her approval.

"I like him, you know."

"Whom? Your uncle?"

"Him, of course. But I meant Godfrey Mainwaring. He's a manly, outspoken fellow. He has a high-flown way of speaking some times, which he may get from sermonizing, but he never cants."

"I gather, from his aunt, that he delivers most of his sermons at the dinner table. His curates do the work."

"Only," Niles retorted, "to free him for harder work. Did you know he has been excavating in Pompeii? That makes him almost our neighbor."

"Oh, you may have him to dinner, if that's what you're driving at. Other than his being a Muscular Christian I have no *real* objection to him. I even approve of his diggings in Pompeii, since necessarily they will prevent him from digging concurrently at Blackthorne."

Niles' laughter was the echo of his mother's. I had already noted at dinner that Niles became a different person in Zaide's presence, quicker, more playful, and more self-assured. It was not only that they were veterans of many games of verbal shuttlecock and so could always keep the words bandying back and forth neatly. It went beyond their having perfected a common style. They loved each other, and in a manner unusual between a son and a mother, in a way that was comradely rather than filial. Niles loved Zaide, and Zaide loved Niles, and the bond between them would have been nearly as strong had it been based on nothing but this mutual affection.

"And of what else did you speak?" Zaide asked. "Was Godfrey able to place *both* feet in his mouth?"

"To the top of his tall boots. My uncle complained of the progress of the American war, and Godfrey began a positive anthem in praise of Mr. Lincoln."

"What did *you* say?"

"Something diplomatic about how I could not wish ill to our relations in Virginia."

"That was clever."

"May be not clever enough. My uncle didn't seem *quite* satisfied, but I could not go so far as to defend slavery and all that. Godfrey would have given me my choice of weapons then and there. He's that fierce on the subject, a regular Abolitionist."

"On that subject," I ventured, with tremulous bravado, "I think I could become very fierce, too. I think slavery is quite terrible."

"It's shocking, my dear," Zaide agreed, "but you'd best not say so to Lord Rhodes. He's invested rather heavily, I understand, in Confederate bonds. But I'm happy to hear that Godfrey is standing up for *his* principles. He will not endear himself to his benefactor by it, and his loss is potentially our gain."

"I wouldn't want to profit by another person's loss," I protested.

"Nor, I am sure, would we. But, willy-nilly, it is the position in which all presumptive heirs find themselves. Fortunately, in my brother's case, there is more than enough to go round, if, that is, Douglas intends to spread it round. I long ago relinquished any hopes on my behalf, but I would be chagrined to see my son, my brother's nearest male relation, entirely passed over, especially if Mr. Mainwaring and his good aunt were principally to benefit from his neglect. To hear them talk, you'd think she was his cousin, not a servant in his house. One must trace her ancestry back to Noah to establish the degree of cousinship that exists between her and Lord Rhodes. But she thinks, because she lives here, because her nephew has the livings of Rodmell and Glynde—"

"Mother, it makes no difference what she thinks. I doubt not that she shall receive a comfortable annuity. But really! Has my uncle ever neglected me? May I ask who paid my expenses at Oxford? And his generosity since then has been worthy of a Maecenas. Clara, do not listen to her. It is all a result of her being quartered in this dismal pantry and being stared out of countenance by all these periwigged gentlemen."

Niles was referring to a number of portraits that formed the principal adornment of the room. They were not a cheering assembly as they glared out from their time-darkened canvases. Each face expressed a different degree of apprehension or distrust, as though it had been selected as a juryman for some particularly notorious and reproachful crime.

"They *are* an unsavory lot," Zaide said, "but at least they keep me company. I see already that Douglas has no intention of inviting any of his neighbors to Blackthorne for that purpose."

"Mother, you know very well that, except for sponsoring his share of the meets, my uncle does not entertain."

"If I did not know it before, I have been made aware now. You are right, Niles: he does not entertain. And Clara, I beg your forgiveness. Please do not think that any of my complaining has been directed at you. Lord knows, you have more cause to rail than I. In a juster world you would be mistress of Blackthorne, not its guest."

"I assure you, Aunt, I have never thought so."

Zaide, by her smile and a sigh, seemed to question this, but my protest was sincere. As well might I have questioned the policies of the Home Office or the Bank of England as to suppose that my claims might be placed in the scales of justice against the awesome weight of Lord Rhodes and all he possessed. *My* claims? I had none.

"Mother, this is scarcely hospitable. You speak of justice. Pray, do justice to yourself. Clara, you must pay no attention to her in these moods."

"The mood is past, and Clara, I promise not to embarrass you by another such display. I asked you here, indeed, so that we might understand each other. More exactly, so that you might understand us, since I flatter myself that I already understand you."

"Mother, for heaven's sake!"

"If that sounds presumptuous, forgive me. I'm so unused to being straightforward that I make complications where none exist. Niles, you speak for me. I shall see if there is enough brandy left for three small glasses."

"It is quite simple, Clara. You and I have been placed in the uncomfortable position of being rivals for my uncle's fortune, and this before we have had the opportunity properly to establish a bond of real friendship. I am anxious, as my mother is, that the accident of our rivalry—"

"Which is all that it is, my dear," Zaide added from across the room, "an accident."

"That it should not stand in the way of the possibility of a lifelong friendship."

"Then rest assured, cousin, that I have never regarded you in any other light. I appreciate your candor, but . . . well, that is to say. . . ."

My confusion was entire. I was flattered by such confidence and shocked by such lack of reserve. I felt obliged to reply to his candor with an equal openness—and, though this sorted ill with my other intention, to dissemble my shock as best I could.

Falteringly, and with no little embarrassment, I conveyed the substance of my own meditations while riding to Lewes that afternoon. I spoke of the resolution to which those thoughts had led me. I concluded by expressing the hope that Lord Rhodes' good health would continue to keep all his heirs in a wholesome state of suspense for many years to come.

"Amen to that!" said Niles, while his mother, with no less warmth, favored me with a kiss that made me realize, by its dryness relative to the damp of my brow, how unsettled my little speech had made me. Any more candor, and I think I would have had to faint. Perhaps Zaide sensed this, for she would not allow me to refuse the brandy she had poured.

"Just taste it, my dear. There is no restorative like a prime old cognac. My own physician swears that I owe the last decade of my life to it."

"If not the last, Mother," Niles said, raising his glass in a mocking toast, "let us hope the next."

I touched my glass to theirs and cautiously raised it to my lips. Even before I wet my tongue, the potent aroma of the brandy had rushed to my head. One sniff, and I had persuaded myself I was inebriate.

Truly, I did become drunk that night, though the brandy played only a small part in it. Between them, Niles and Zaide intoxicated me with the wine of their wit and worldliness. Even when their matter was shocking, as when they had advised me to dissemble my opinions before Lord Rhodes, their manner smoothed away my misgivings, enchanted me into moral complaisance.

Zaide returned ever and again to her brother, no longer to complain, but because he was her favorite subject of satire. His foibles and follies inspired anecdote after anecdote, all tending to one central thesis, which she at length stated outright: "*Enfin*, he is a misogynist, a woman-hater of the most uncompromising bitterness. It accounts for everything: his boyhood cruelties towards myself; his passion for riding and hunting pastimes from which women are generally excluded; the ludicrous denouement of his courtship of the long-suffering Miss Middlecott; his abuse of any woman who so much as opens her mouth, much less a book, as a bluestocking; even his dress and comportment at dinner tonight. It is all part of a pattern. He fears and despises our sex, and

persecutes it with the patience of Job and the zeal of an In-
quisitor.

"You are probably too young, Clara, to remember the scandalous Mrs. Bloomer. She was a kind of lady Prometheus from America who visited these shores in eighteen-hundred-and-fifty-one
with the purpose of exposing the evils of wide skirts and hoop
petticoats. By these means, she reasoned, women had disenfran-
chised themselves, and I think it is true that when one wears wide
skirts there are many doors one cannot enter. Mrs. Bloomer proposed to remedy these evils and to make English women rational
by putting them into a baggy sort of trousers she had designed for
them. May be you have seen pictures of ladies so dressed?"

I shook my head vigorously. Her first mention of the name of
Bloomer had started a blush to my cheeks. Nowadays, when we
may see young ladies bicycling everywhere in a costume almost
identical to what Mrs. Bloomer advocated, it is hard to understand
the degree to which decent people were outraged by a campaign
to put women into an article of clothing which many of them
would refer to only by a euphemism. Women in trousers! And I
must listen to my great-aunt jesting on the subject!

"Douglas was in Westminster then, lending the luster of his
presence to the House, and when Mrs. Bloomer appeared, as she
had promised, with her troupe of pant-legged Amazons in the
broad daylight of St. James's Park—you will find all of this re-
ported in the *London Charivari*—he was on hand to lead the jeering and generally discourage their immodesty. Most of the ladies
retired to a carriage waiting for them in Waterloo Place, but Mrs.
Bloomer, bolder and with a reputation to uphold, strode up and
down the paths, affecting not to notice her aristocratic hecklers.
Douglas, baffled by such *sang-froid*, was driven to ever more
desperate extremes. He barked and whistled, to the amusement of
his onlookers, but won from her not so much as a glance. He stood
in her path. She turned on her heel. He threatened, and, when she
ignored the threat, *did* throw her into the pond."

"Positively *ducked* her!" Niles added gleefully. "Have you ever
heard of anything like it?"

"Clara, you will note, does not share your amusement. Indeed,
it is a sordid and unhappy little story, and I only mentioned it to

illustrate the depths of Lord Rhodes' aversion to our sex. Not that I think *we* need fear being thrown into the Ouse, if only because Douglas is not so vigorous now as he was a decade ago."

"The truth is that my mother is a wicked gossip who likes nothing better than to make my poor uncle look ridiculous."

Zaide conceded this with a wave of her bony hand. In the course of defaming her brother, her voice had become rather hoarse, so, settling back with a replenished glass of brandy, she allowed Niles to divert the conversation to other subjects.

His talk took a rather skittish course for a while, but once it lighted on Italy I would not let him digress. Since I had learned only hours before that I had almost been spirited away to that faerie realm as a child, Italy had come to seem much more interesting than when it was only an empty boot into which schoolgirls fit the wriggles of its principal rivers and the dots of its major cities. Its popes and kings, its battlefields and cathedrals, and all else that goes to bulk out history books seemed trivial measured against these first-hand accounts of real Florentine fogs that had given Niles the grippe, of squids eaten in sauces made from their own ink, of day-long tramps in the Alban Hills and boat rides in the Bay of Naples. By his account of it, one would have thought our English sunlight a very inferior article compared with the authentic, *golden* sunlight of Italy, our countryside raw wilderness, our cuisine barbaric.

Though half-believing these slanders, I felt patriotically obliged to counter them. "Then, why, if Italy is so superior in every way, do you spend any time here at all?"

"Why? Because we don't want to be shot in our beds or strung up from lamp-posts."

"Is there any present danger of that?"

"My dear girl, Italy is undergoing a revolution," Zaide said languidly. She had ceased for some time to take an active role in the conversation. Indeed, she had slumped down so comfortably in the ottoman, she seemed in danger of drifting off to sleep. "It has been going on for some time. Did you not know?"

"I have heard of someone called Garibaldi, but I can't remember what. Is he a kind of Napoleon?"

Niles and Zaide had a laugh at the expense of my perhaps too calculated ignorance. This soon I was learning to be the innocent foil of their worldly wisdom, to play the *ingénue*.

"Not a Napoleon, no," Niles said. "The Italians are not likely to sweep across the whole Continent in so millennial a style, but they are pretty effectively demolishing their own country at the moment. Italy, as you know, is only Italy on English maps. Politically, it is divided up into a dozen states or more. Almost everybody wants to unify these many into one, except, of course, the rulers of those dozen states. Garibaldi has lately been presenting some of those rulers with the accomplished fact of their unification. It is a fact they resent."

"I can't tell from your account whether you're in favor of these revolutionaries or in fear of them."

"That depends where I happen to be. At the Villa Visconti, in Ischia, I am a partisan of Garibaldi, as he has taken over the government of all of southern Italy. In Venice, however, at the Palazzo Albrizzi, where we were living till this spring, it is high treason to hold the same opinions, so I loyally support my Austrian masters, till such time, at least, as they too have been unified into oblivion. I suppose at root I must be in favor of unification, since nothing else can enable me to unify my own opinions."

"Then you are in favor of your own comfort, and have no larger principles than that?" I asked, with an edge of undisguised sarcasm. His proclamation of willingness to bend whatever way the wind was blowing struck me as a shameful piece of cynicism.

"In Italy, that is the only rational principle. Is that not so, Mother?" Niles turned to Zaide for confirmation. "Will you look at her? Sleeping like a baby. Our journey fatigued her more than she knew. We two had best remove to the inner room. She will waken by-and-by, but if *we* should rouse her there would be the devil to pay."

Reluctantly I accepted my cousin's hand, and he led me into the Contessa's bedchamber. The contents of two battered trunks were distributed over every level surface of the room. Niles plucked a nightgown from the back of one chair, whisked three filmy shawls from another, and bade me be seated. I felt, amid the intimate disorder of Zaide's wardrobe, that I had trespassed into some secret region of her nature.

Niles sensed my unease or felt one kindred, but his way in such difficulties was to tackle them head-on. "Now," he said, pulling his own chair so close to mine that his right knee touched my left, "let's have a proper *tête-à-tête*. While she can't hear us, tell me— what do you think of my mother?"

"That she is quite the most distinguished lady I have ever met."

"And brilliant?"

"Yes, certainly. Though not," I hastily amended, "not what my uncle said."

"Not a bluestocking? I am afraid she is reputed one of the worst, or best. What is the wickedness, after all, of a lady knowing something?"

"None at all," I murmured, wishing desperately that Niles had settled on any other topic than his mother's character and reputation. Though it had never been directly stated that the Contessa Visconti had led a profligate life, I had gathered, from hints dropped, that there was some secret in her past that could not politely bear mentioning. Yet, as this remained a secret, the mere shadow of a scandal, I feared that some remark of mine might be misconstrued so that I would seem, all unwittingly and unwillingly, to be scornful or sarcastic.

Niles knew no such compunctions. He loved his mother, and he loved to talk about her. He would as eagerly anatomize her faults as praise her virtues; for to the true lover, the beloved's imperfections (as distinct from her sins) are one with her beauty, a source of interest rather than pain.

"Before we came in here, you had accused me of being a Machiavelli." He waved aside my protest. "No, the observation is just. I dare say I am. I dare say my mother is, too. Or any person who regards the exercise of intelligence, like the exercise of his limbs, as good sport. You are just the same, though you don't know it yet. I've seen it in your eyes, that little flash of understanding what is happening."

"One cannot help what one understands. What I objected to, if you'll recall, was your readiness to express whatever opinion is most convenient. Nor did I involve your mother in my accusation."

"No, not by name, but there it is, that little flash again. You thought so. And it is perfectly true. Indeed, she's a much worse weather-cock than I. I have known her to advance an opinion one night, and the next, in the same company, to adopt an attitude diametrically opposed, just to provide herself with an agreeable sense of controversy. Some times she insists on the most die-hard Toryism, declares that the entire object of statecraft must be to keep the nation in a pacific and prosperous condition so that the fortunate Few may advance the cause of Civilization by leading their own comfortable, civilized lives. The next moment she is a Democrat; nay, a Utopian, ready to put the whole world to the torch in the sacred cause of liberty. For either position she can adduce the most compelling reasons; to neither is her heart committed. That she reserves, exclusively, for herself. And, some times, perhaps, for me, so long as I don't cross her, which, believe me, I am careful not to do."

"What a frightful character you do give her. You make a person perfectly afraid to be known by you. My hope must be that you share this failing you describe so well and that tomorrow night you will prove to me that she is exactly the opposite of what you said tonight."

"Bravo! A neat escape. You have the makings of a master diplomat. But I've said no more than a week's acquaintance with my mother will convince you of, in any case. Her character is common knowledge; her secrets—Ah-ha! I've touched a nerve!— those are locked fast within my heart." He laid his hand upon the appropriate area of his waistcoat, adding to this gesture the signature of his thin smile.

(Ah, that smile! What fine words and tender meanings have I not seen enfeebled or denied by the quick, unwitting tensing of his lips. This habit of irony was almost reflexive in its nature, like the pucker that comes of biting into a lemon. Often, I think, when Niles wished to say something quite unequivocal—no more perhaps than to thank a stranger for some exceptional kindness— that smile would come unbidden to his lips, seeming to mock where no mockery could be intended.)

There was a knocking at the hall door. Niles signalled me to remain seated and went to answer it. As he left the door communicating with the outer room ajar, I was auditor to the following conversation.

A man's voice, breathless with hurry, addressed Niles. "Please to excuse the liberty of seeking you here so untimely, Sir, but your wife is in some distress. We none of us know how to deal with her."

"She is ill?"

"I am not sure, Sir. A scullery maid found her in the back stairwell, moaning, Sir, and crying and clutching to the newel post so that there's no way to lead her to her room, Sir, supposing that she's lost, which is what Mrs. Lacey thought at first."

"Does she talk, as well?"

"Yes, Sir, but all in her own language. I was dispatched to find you in your rooms, Sir, and when I couldn't find you there—"

"Very good. I'll be with you directly. But first I must inform my mother of this."

I heard the door drawn shut. A moment later he had rejoined me in the bedroom. I rose and studied his features anxiously.

"It is nothing, Clara, but I must go to her before the whole house has been roused. She shall recover directly she sees me." This reassurance lacked conviction, so much that I dared to ask:

"Has this happened before?"

"Something like it. She suffers, on occasion, from somnambulism. There is no real danger in it, for I have seen her maneuver staircases in this condition without harm. Shakespeare's description of Lady Macbeth, that her eyes were open while their sense was shut, turns out to be quite just. Once she is wakened from her dream, she is quite well. But this means I cannot escort you back to your room. Do you think you can find your way alone?"

I nodded.

"Good. We ought not subject the staff to *two* maidens wandering the halls in a single night. If Mother wakes, explain my absence, but do not waken her especially. I regret that I must take my leave of you so hastily."

I offered my hand. He pressed it between his own, and paused, his body inclined toward me in a half-stooping posture, as though he were debating whether to place a kiss upon my captive palm. Then, foregoing that courtesy, he left me alone in his mother's bedroom.

CHAPTER THIRTEEN
Who Held Me?

THE WIND HAD ENTERED the outer room where the Dowager Contessa Visconti still slept, slumped upon the ottoman, smiling and serenely inanimate. All but two candles were extinguished. In their dim light, the worn gray velvet of her dress shimmered like the first thin crust of sullied snow that mantles winter fields. Far from her, those night-terrors which even then were coiled about Renata's breast; far, too, that insomniac turbulence of spirit which was to keep me awake long hours of every night during my stay at Blackthorne. The sleep of the just? If not, it was as deep, as still, as sweet. The features of a sleeping face, the rhythms of a sleeper's breath, cannot dissemble.

I stood beside the outer door, alert for any sound that I might associate with Niles or Renata, but thanks to the remoteness of the Contessa's quarters, I could hear only the ordinary nighttime creakings and squeakings of old timber; that, and the quick pulse, as in a shell, of my own fearful heart. I dreaded making the journey back to my room alone; I dreaded equally the Contessa awaking and the embarrassment of explanations.

A little event decided me. I sensed a stir about the Contessa's person. I have roused her, I thought—but no, it was not she: a fat gray fieldmouse sat on the smooth knee-taut plateau of her skirt. He eyed me alertly, head cocked to one side, then to the other. When he was sure I posed no threat, he busied himself with the stuff of the Contessa's dress, using his forepaws to brush the nap of the gray velvet this way and that, as though he were grooming the pelt of some rodent vast beyond all reckoning.

I lifted my hand and hissed at him, but the mouse, instead of leaping from his velvet perch, burrowed deeply into it. He scampered up the waist and, where a deep collar of a darker gray fell in flat folds from the low neckline, vanished from sight. I stared in disbelief at the tiny bulge the mouse had created just above the hollow under the Contessa's left armpit, and my hand rose unbidden to press the same area of my bodice.

I could not endure to remain in the room. Wisest and kindest to leave at once: the mouse would emerge from his hiding-hole, and the Contessa could sleep on in happy ignorance. I slipped out into the blackness of the hallway, without a candle and without my shawl.

At the far end of the hall, a few vagrant rays of starlight crept in at the narrowest of Blackthorne's three-hundred-forty-eight windows. Setting this as my goal, I advanced inch-meal along the carpet. Gradually, I was able to make out rectangles of greater and of lesser darkness—a recessed doorway, a tarnished mirror. Reaching the window, I touched the chill pane for reassurance. Nowhere could I see another glint of light. I feared that the candles had been snuffed throughout the house by now. Even if I retraced exactly the windings and twinings by which Niles had led me to the Contessa's rooms, even if I stood before my own door, I would not be able to recognize it in such darkness.

I remained beside the window for some time, reluctant as any moth to venture from my little wedge of dimness. Though my aunt Jerningham had often advised me of the dangers of breathing the night air, I was already so far advanced in folly that I recked nothing of that. I lifted the sash and let the cooler outside air lave my brow and calm my distress. If need be, I could keep my vigil there through the remaining hours of the night, a companion of the cricket and the owl. It was mid-June. The sun would rise before the servants, and I could make my way to my room unobserved.

Before my anxiety had mounted high enough to overwhelm this brave resolve, I heard, quite close at hand, the tread of footsteps descending an uncarpeted staircase. A door opened not five feet from where I stood, and bright, sudden candlelight spilled out from the unsuspected stairwell. Without considering from whom I would conceal myself, or why, I pulled the window's thick drapery about my white dress.

Mrs. Lacey stepped into view, followed by her nephew, God-frey Mainwaring.

". . . whether it were epilepsy," I heard the latter say.

"No," Mrs. Lacey replied to him. "Miss Ditchitt in Rodmell has the falling sickness, and I've been by her when the fit was on her. This was nothing like."

Mr. Mainwaring turned round to close the door to the stair-well, and for a moment we stood, as it were, face to face, not three steps apart. Wrapped in my silly curtain, I could not believe that he could remain oblivious of me. Just the force of my own mortified attention was enough, I was sure, to notify him of my presence. Yet when the door was closed, he turned back to his aunt without interrupting the flow of their discourse by so much as any eyeblink.

"It more resembles," Mrs. Lacey went on, "a very sudden and desperate bereavement."

"I expect it was no more," Mr. Mainwaring suggested, taking her arm and leading her down the hall, "than the fright of being left alone in a strange room."

"And in a foreign country," Mrs. Lacey added. "I'm sure I cannot think how her husband could leave her under such circum-stances. Especially if, as he says, she's had such spells before."

The same consideration had visited me throughout the evening, even before Niles had been summoned away. I blushed now to hear the matter stated so bluntly. I had indeed been in the wrong to keep Niles so many hours away from his bride. That his mother had co-operated in that wrong did not make me feel any less ashamed.

Guilt has a way of moving the guilty from one place to another. Cain and Ahasuerus are renowned almost as much for their travels as for their sins; their destination mattered not, so long as they escaped the spot where they first felt the sting of conscience. As they fled, so did I. But where? I could not follow after Mrs. Lacey and her nephew. I did not wish to return the way I'd come. Only the staircase remained as a possibility.

I entered a darkness absolute as the galleried chambers of the mole, and like that animal I made my way guided only by the sense of touch. In reaching the Contessa's rooms, I remembered having come down rather a greater number of steps than I'd gone up; accordingly I now ascended. The stairs rose steeply, twisting in a tight clockwise corkscrew. As in climbing a ladder, I mounted these stairs as much by the effort of my arms as by my legs, holding firmly to the wooden railing and hauling myself upwards at each step. By daylight, if daylight ever entered this cramped stairwell, the ascent would have been difficult; in darkness it was positively hazardous.

When I had climbed, as I judged, nearly to the attic, my hand, in advancing along the railing, encountered an object that was neither rail nor newel post. I gasped and, without thinking, drew back suddenly—an action that would have sent me tumbling to the bottom of the stairs had not the hand that I had touched reached forwards to circle my waist. Another hand pressed the side of my throat. I felt my body propelled forwards by those two hands, felt myself crushed against my rescuer. I felt his breath upon my cheek, his lips upon my throat. I may have screamed, but I do not remember. I know that I did restrain my impulse to struggle from his arms, lest in doing so I topple both of us down the stairs.

"Please," I said, unable to muster the wit to say more.

His reply to this feeble whisper of a plea was a staccato gibble-gabble of sound.

In the ordinary circumstances of society, incomprehension of another's speech can be unsettling, but to have one's most earnest heart-utterance answered in the meaningless syllables of a foreign language raises the sensation to a pitch close to terror. In this thick darkness, where neither gesture nor expression could speak for me, language alone could serve—and it did not. His rough caresses continued in concert with his urgent, incomprehensible words, which I now could recognize as Italian. I had my footing again and could use my hands to ward off his more intimate attentions, though his arms remained tight-locked about my waist.

"Sir! Please to release me—you are under some misapprehension."

He seemed to find this longer speech as unnerving as I had found his; certainly the man's insistence lessened. After a pause, and in a tone of questioning, almost of chagrin, he replied: "Madam?"

"Allow me to pass."

He drew back. A step creaked beneath his retreating weight. Then a second, and a third.

"Excuse me. I am mistaked. I have believed you another."

I was about to return the way I'd come when the darkness before me was parted. A door had been opened for me, and I hurried
through it into the lighted corridor.

From this safe vantage, I glanced back. The door stood open,
but of him who had opened it I could see only a hand, weighty
with rings, gripping the torus molding of the doorframe.

"Miss," I heard his voice addressing me again. "You will not. . . .
Tomorrow, if. . . ."

I sensed the meaning he could not find words for, and replied, "I
will not mention our encounter. Rest assured."

"Thank you."

The door swung shut.

I looked about me and discovered with relief that the little
staircase had debouched opposite one of the few guideposts I had
taken note of, a rather fierce hunting scene showing a wolf turned
to bay, surrounded by hounds. By this token, I knew that my room
was not many yards distant, and I reached it with no further incident.

The sun had climbed above the tops of the cypresses before I
was able to leave the seat by my window and retire, with many a
tinkling of the canopy's glass flowers, to my bed.

CHAPTER FOURTEEN
An Unwelcome Friendship

To BED, MAY BE; but not to sleep. The speculations that had occupied me throughout the dawn's choruses of birdsong continued to
revolve in my mind through the carillons of a wakeful repose: whom
had I encountered in the stairwell? for whom had he mistaken me?

It was an easy matter to show that the man must be a stranger
to me. Of a certainty, he had not been Niles. The mustache that had

bristled against my throat was a sufficient proof of that, assuming that I could be mistaken in the larger matters of the frame of his body and timbre of his voice. Just as certainly it had not been Mr. Mainwaring, whom I had seen with his aunt only moments before. Who then? Not my uncle: to suspect him would be as ludicrous as it was disrespectful. But these were all the gentlemen staying at Blackthorne. Perhaps not a gentleman then: perhaps one of the servants?

This theory, though usually a very comfortable one (if one happens not to be a domestic), did not entirely satisfy. Putting aside my own preferences, the question still remained—whose servant? His fluent Italian and broken English declared him not in the livery of Blackthorne. So, unless he had been out-and-out a trespasser, there remained but one possibility: he had come here in attendance on Niles Visconti.

So far my logic carried me without a qualm, but when I considered the related question of who this hypothetical valet had thought *I* was, ah, then my misgivings were rife. Again, the most comfortable supposition was that he had been awaiting another servant. This, though impermissible, was not unthinkable. Indeed, if there be such a thing as a "philosophy" of household economy, its first precept would be to regard the servants' hall and dormitories as another country, to whose citizens one may allow the same tolerant inattention that one would afford a similar group of Parisians or Neapolitans. I do not mean that one should be indifferent to the morals of one's domestics, but only sensible of the fact that the *system* of their morality may differ in some instances from one's own.

Well, that is all very worldly-wise, I am sure, but not, in this case, much to the point. Only a few hours before, I had listened to the Contessa lamenting that she had come to England without attendance, and to this complaint Niles had replied with a second, that among all Blackthorne's domestics there were none capable of serving his wife's simplest needs. In short, none of Lord Rhodes' female domestics could have understood any better than I entreaties or endearments expressed in the Italian language. In all likelihood only two women in that household possessed such an understanding —the two Contessas Visconti.

Just as I could not picture Lord Rhodes in the character of a *cavaliere servente*, so I could not imagine his sister in the role of *inamorata*. There remained but one plausible explanation, resist it as I might: my would-be ravisher had mistaken me for Niles' wife. *She* would have understood the words he had addressed to her; *she* was of a stature like enough to mine to make a confusion between us possible in the dark. There was, moreover, the curious matter of her discovery in another stairwell of the house in a condition of some agitation. Sleepwalking, Niles had said, with, I doubt not, entire sincerity. Yet I wondered (and hated myself for wondering) whether he had not been imposed upon, whether Renata, losing herself as I had done in the maze of Blackthorne's hallways and encountering, perhaps, a servant, had not dissembled the symptoms of somnambulism, only to find herself, like many another actress, trapped within the role she had assumed.

It was a terrible suspicion; sufficient proof, if any more were needed, that Niles had been justified in calling me a Machiavellian. May be there is some excuse in my naïveté. Though I could weave such a web of scandalous inference, I had little conception of the gravity of my imaginings. Indeed, the only point at which I felt some guilt for my too free speculation was in the matter of assigning to Renata an interest in her husband's valet, and this scruple was settled by the simple expedient of revising my first theory. The imagined *valet de chambre* became a Mysterious Stranger, and then, at last, I could sleep.

The very next morning (or, really, the same) this charitable fiction was confuted in the smiling person of the man himself, no gentleman nor yet a stranger, but as I had first supposed, Niles' manservant. My aunt and myself were leaving the breakfast room in the company of the Contessas Visconti, neither of whom appeared any whit the worse for their distresses or excesses of the previous evening. Zaide had prepared a surprise for us on the lawn of the lower terrace, and thither, to be surprised, we followed her. Just as we stepped out of doors, I saw him. Before I had glanced at his thrice-ringed hand, before I'd heard his voice, I knew him, but both these tokens were added by way of confirmation. He stepped back, bowing his head and lifting his eyes to meet Zaide's. She addressed a peremptory question to him, and he replied, as she had queried, in Italian.

At the first sight of him Renata had taken a step back. I must blush now to confess how avidly I sought a tell-tale blush upon her cheek, nor was I disappointed. The fair skin crimsoned before his level gaze. By this blush and by a dozen other minuscule but certain signs—the manner in which she opened out her parasol, a hesitancy in her step when she passed by him—I thought I recognized the confirmation of what I had suspected, a guilty love. Indeed, if I were right, the very guiltiest!

And when his dark eyes met mine? No doubt I felt some warmth in my cheek. No doubt there was a certain hesitation in my step, too. No doubt at all I knew a sudden pang of guilt, for by the heedless promise I had pledged to him the night before, I'd made myself the accomplice in his wickedness; or rather, as I now supposed, in theirs.

"Italian," my aunt Jerningham observed disingenuously as we walked along the gravelled path, "is such a beautiful language. I really think, whenever I hear it, that it's like music. It seems no wonder that so many operas are in Italian."

"If you should ever come to live there, Mrs. Jerningham," Zaide replied, "you may alter your opinion. Though, as for the scoundrel I was just speaking to, there is something distinctly operatic about him, I will grant you. He always puts me in mind of Mozart's Figaro. The same merriness, the same deep-laid schemes, the same engaging *diablerie*. For my own part, I would have relinquished him long ago, but my son, like another Almaviva, can't do without the fellow, so I am obliged to be amiable. It is terrible, is it not, to be under the dominion of one's own servants?"

"Ah, Countess, it is just the same in my own home," said Lydia. "You would not believe how I let myself be bullied by my cook."

"Ah, yes! A good cook in England has as much power over a household as, in Italy, the subtlest confessor. But look—Figaro has done his duty. There, before us on the lawn, is my surprise."

A number of wide iron hoops had been arranged on the grass in a broad, double diamond pattern. From each hoop depended, on a piece of ribbon, a small silver bell. My aunt and I exchanged glances of candid incomprehension. Renata, however, was beaming with pleasure, for she was no stranger to the game of croquet. Such, as my readers already will have guessed, was the surprise Zaide had prepared for us.

Nowadays, when young ladies have been initiated into so many sports and contests once the exclusive prerogative of gentlemen, when there are playing fields populated exclusively by the fair sex, it is hard to appreciate the excitement, approaching very nearly to scandal, caused by the introduction of croquet. Renata had already caught the fever, and my aunt succumbed within the afternoon. Zaide, having instructed us in the rules of the game (and, by croqueting my aunt's ball far, far from the croquet ground, in its spirit as well), left us to the madness of enthusiasm. My aunt's and Renata's inexhaustible appetite for croquet brought the three of us together regularly every afternoon. Blizzards and earthquakes could not have kept us from our game, and thereby began a peculiar and embarrassing intimacy.

Just as a mutual incomprehension had kept us from forming a friendship our first evening together, so now that same incomprehension prevented me from keeping any distance between us. The young Contessa showered me with little attentions, making gifts of her forlorn needlework and of cakes and biscuits stolen from the tea table. If I wished to stroll through the gardens, she would accompany me. If I played, she would stand by the pianoforte, humming the melody. I could not escape from her even in my own boudoir, for she would come tapping at the door, bringing a great ledger-book with her. While I sat on the settee pretending to take an interest in a history of the Netherlands that Mr. Mainwaring had strongly urged on me, she would scribble away in her ledger for hours on end: her journal, I supposed, dreading to think what intrigues and wickednesses she might be memorializing in its pages.

The worst of it was my conviction that she regarded me as a willing confederate in her misadventures. Implicit in the promise I had tendered to the valet was the understanding that my secrecy was pledged not so much on *his* behalf, but on behalf of the lady for whom he had mistaken me. I doubted very much that he had been as discreet about our encounter. Indeed, I was certain that Renata knew of it, and that this lay behind these sundry unsolicited proffers of friendship.

Yet how could I altogether refuse her? Putting aside my suspicions, in which (though I could not see how) I might very well have been mistaken, her situation was one that would have inspired sympathy in the least compassionate breast. Worse than the loneliness of deserts and oceans is the solitude of foreign countries, for there the visitor is constantly plunged into the society of strangers who must remain oblivious of all he thinks or feels, as surely as though he were invisible to them. Indeed, I have often thought that if there are ghosts, their condition may be very like to Renata's in England, or my own, at a later time, in Italy. No, if she could find any kind of comfort in my presence, I had not the heart to deny it her.

And so, unwillingly, and all the while believing her motive to be, in part at least, a desire to secure my continuing complicity, I became Renata's friend. Alas for her, and alas for me, she would never, in the months of life remaining to her, know a closer friend, nor any other who could decipher the painful tale set down in the arabesques and curlicues of her conventual calligraphy.

That journal she entrusted to me on the day of my departure from Blackthorne. As I was sitting beside my packed box, in that limbo of suspended activity that precedes any long journey, I heard the light rapping, timid as a child's, that I now recognized as Renata's. She entered draped in no less than three merino shawls; from beneath their copious folds she withdrew the ledger-book I'd seen her working at hour after hour all through the week. This she thrust at me, accompanying her uncharacteristically forceful gesture with a torrent of earnest, incomprehensible words. Having already made my own surmise as to the probable nature of what the book recorded, I was appalled. I made to press it back upon her, but this only strengthened her resolve to have me accept it. She gestured at my box. I shook my head. She tore at the knotted cord with her own fingers, doing no little harm to her fine nails in the process. At last, only to quieten her, I acceded and allowed her to stow her journal inside. Once this was done and the cords again secured, Renata became more composed, though she would still insist on clasping my hand and pressing kisses on palm and knuckle, kisses I found as inexplicable as the few whispered words and single tear that accompanied them. I wondered what strange byway of passion had prompted her to feel so urgently the need of a confidante. Would the contents of her journal explain her behavior? But soon as the question crossed my mind I resolved that, even should I some day find myself able to, I would never read what she had set down. Nor, though I might regret the consequence of my reticence, can I really blame myself for having kept so long to this resolve. Before I would understand Renata's desperation and anguish, I would myself have experienced the cause of it at first hand.

CHAPTER FIFTEEN
A Family Dinner in Bayswater

I RETURNED TO LONDON with a sense, not wholly gratifying, of having carried out my resolve and having made myself as little interesting to my uncle as I might. Not an enviable task under any circumstances, this business of hiding one's light under a bushel, but even had I placed it, as the Evangelist recommends, in plain sight, on a candlestick, I fear Lord Rhodes would have noticed at most only a faint and far-off glimmering. Whether he felt, as Zaide had suggested, a general antipathy towards womankind, or whether his distaste was more particular, I left Blackthorne with a conviction—which was borne out in the event—that my welcome was not to be renewed.

A welcome did await me, however, in a quarter where it was least expected. As we stepped down from the hackney-coach that had brought us from Waterloo Station to the familiar iron palisade of Worcester Terrace, my uncle Jerningham appeared on the front stoop to hail our return in a manner so expansive as to give my aunt some cause for alarm. Though this was Thursday, he was dressed in his best suit, but more unaccountable than this was the smile that scarred the ordinary granite of his face. With just such a smile would Pluto have greeted Proserpina on the occasion of their annual reunion; with just such a sinking of the heart as mine would Proserpina have acknowledged that greeting. He grasped my hand—he, who had never touched me except to administer a punishment—and a shiver of foreboding passed through me. Before my mind could take in his purpose, my flesh had understood: in the week of my absence at Blackthorne, Mr. Jerningham had arranged a marriage for me.

He did not blazon his purpose upon the doorstep then and there, but he did have the intended bridegroom on hand, together with his parents. Lydia and I scarce were allowed time to nod to these guests, however, before my uncle, with that semblance of good humor which bespoke an aroused appetite, bustled us up to our rooms to wash off the dust of the day's travelling and to change for dinner.

"And Clara, if you please. . . ."

"Yes, Uncle?"

"Wear your new frock, the same you wore to dinner at Blackthorne. Now hurry!"

"Wonderful," my aunt observed, helping me a moment later with my lacings, "and still more wonderful. We have not seen Julius in I can't think how many years. Living off in Ely and being but a minor canon, he has not shown his withered face in London since the elder Mr. Jerningham's funeral. 'Forty-three, that would be. Not that the office of canon at Ely Cathedral is without dignity. Take a deeper breath, Clara dear. *So!* Not at all. But of all Josiah's brothers Julius seems to have prospered least. His income is small, and his marriage brought him nothing, I think, but the blessings of increase. Besides this Geoffrey, there were eight more, all of them girls."

"The bald gentleman with them is their son?" I asked.

"Yes—Geoffrey Jerningham. Who did you think?"

"He seems nearly of an age with his parents."

"Well, the Canon is rather a youngish old man for his seventy-five years, and Geoffrey is distinctly an oldish young man. And not even that young any more. Some two or three years younger than myself, I should say. When last I saw him, at that same funeral, he had already lost *most* of his hair. And speaking of hair, I must fix mine."

Our toilettes made, we rejoined the party downstairs, staying in the parlor only long enough for Geoffrey to offer me, in a voice sere and sepulchral, a compliment upon my charms. My uncle insisted that I reward this kindness with my arm, and so, with a sense somewhat of assisting some very frail and feeble pensioner through traffic, I accompanied that gentleman to the table.

The sweep and mass of that evening's dinner surpassed in wonder the fact of its being given at all. There was a first course of tapioca soup, crimped skate with caper sauce, an entree of sweetbreads, and another of oyster patties; then a second course consisting of haunch of mutton, a boiled capon in white sauce, and three entremets; lastly, for dessert, a boiled batter pudding and a rhubarb tart.

Conversation interfered very little with the serious business of eating. Once the Canon inquired whether Blackthorne's dining table could boast such a profusion, and my aunt assured him, raising her voice so he could hear, that Lord Rhodes' dinners had been frugal by comparison with this.

"Yet he is very rich, I think," the Canon's wife noted.

As this lady sat directly across from me, I must have observed her features many times in the course of the evening, yet my memory preserves only one fact regarding her appearance. Whether she was pale or swarthy, as feeble as her son or as hale as her husband, I could not say. This only can I vouch for: that she wore, dangling from the brim of a bonnet of bright solferino silk, a fringe of false curls, seven in number, which no more resembled a natural human growth than do the neat little waves carved on the marble heads of Grecian statuary; curls so audaciously unlike hair that one could not but suspect that beneath that bonnet her pate gleamed as nudely as her son's.

When neither my aunt nor my uncle made any response to this lady's observation, I felt that courtesy obliged me to say something, if only to second the incontestable truth she had proclaimed. "Yes," said I, "Lord Rhodes is quite wealthy."

The curls bobbed up and down like seven steel springs. "Just so! Just so! And very old, too, I understand."

"Not what you or I would think of as old, Cecily," my aunt remarked coldly.

But even this rebuke was not enough to check the Canon's wife, whose obtuseness was equal to her avidity. "And his health, the poor man?"

" 'The days of our age,' " said my aunt, echoing her sister-in-law's tone of malicious melancholy, " 'are threescore years and ten; and though men be so strong that they come to fourscore years.' . . . How does the rest go, Cecily?"

"I can't at this moment recollect."

" 'Yet is their strength then but labor and sorrow,' " Geoffrey Jerningham prompted. Bearing the weight of no more than two score years and ten, he was not put out of sorts by these notorious verses.

"Just so," said my aunt. "Just so."

"Are we to gather from that," Mr. Jerningham asked, "that Lord Rhodes does not enjoy good health?"

"It is a wonder he is alive at all."

"Indeed!"

"I had no idea," said Geoffrey. "Did you, Papa?"

But the Canon had no reply to this or any other question addressed to him, being all but completely deaf.

"It was afflicting to see him brought in to the table. His palsy almost prevents him from feeding himself, and then, as deaf as he is, the company was obliged either to shout or to hold no converse at all."

"Strange that one so beset with ills should wish to have company," said Geoffrey. "Did you see him otherwise than at dinner?"

"No, his physicians would not allow it. He has three of them always on hand. According to his housekeeper, their attendance has more than once saved his life."

Lydia had grasped more quickly than I the purpose of our visitors' questioning; had apprehended as well her husband's share in their scheme. She disliked the notion heartily enough, but, even more, the overt manner in which they were pursuing their goal had awakened outrage and aroused contempt. This it was that lay behind her remarkable mendacities.

No one thought to ask my corroboration of these lies, and I did not volunteer to contradict my aunt. At the time, I appreciated her motives only imperfectly. Not until after dinner did the whole truth dawn on me—that *I* was the golden fleece, rumor of which had lured these three ancient argonauts all the distance to London —and even then my awakening took a peculiar form.

My uncle, upon the company's return to the parlor, had bidden

me play music. My aunt sought to take the burden of entertainment on her own shoulders, but no, my uncle insisted that I
should perform for his guests. Obediently, I took my place at the
keyboard and began to rattle off a little dance by Rameau, which
in addition to its brevity possessed the virtue of a wholesome dullness. Short of playing arpeggios, I could have chosen nothing easier
or less "showy." I tinkled away at my piece with a kind of mechanical competence for the first so many bars, but gradually, under
the concerted stares of father, mother, and son, my playing became erratic. I tried to fix my attention wholly on the keyboard,
with the predictable result that my discords multiplied. Yet, when
I looked up, I would see, not three feet from my nose, Geoffrey
Jerningham's bony finger wagging at me, in, as he must have supposed, time to the music. The Canon, too, for all that he was deaf,
taking his cue from his son's forefinger, nodded his venerable head
from side to side, while his wife kept time with the tapping of her
foot. No one of these three metronomes were in agreement, and
under their joint influence, which I _could_ not escape, my little
gavotte quite disintegrated. I broke off, meaning to start afresh
from the beginning, but the Canon had been waiting for this signal
and burst into applause.

"Very pretty, Clara," my uncle said.

The fringe of false curls bobbed vigorously in concurrence, and
the Canon expressed a hope that I would grace the company with
another display of my accomplishments.

"Let me add my voice to my father's, Miss Reeve," Geoffrey
Jerningham said, stepping forwards so as to prevent me rising from
the piano. "Your playing, like your presence, is a breath of spring."
He regarded me intently with his squinting eyes, and yet, for all the
fixity and earnestness of that gaze, I felt curiously as though I were
not present to him, as though when his eyes encountered mine it
was entirely without any acknowledgment of my existing as another sentient being, but rather as a small interesting object in a
gown of white book-muslin with blue ceinture, an object which he
might or might not wish to purchase according as he judged it cheap
or dear. Had he squeezed the muscles of my arm or bid me show my
teeth, it would not have struck me as out of keeping. Thus it was
that my first conscious realization of what he intended should take

the form not of "He means to marry me," but rather I thought: "He wants to *buy* me."

Under the force of that impression, I could not move, nor speak, nor look away from him. Africans set upon the catasta to be auctioned off as human livestock must feel a similar paralysis and horror: else would they not rebel?

"Clara, are you quite well?" my aunt inquired.

A nod was the utmost I could manage. Lydia's concern had prompted a second and still wilder fancy: that Geoffrey Jerningham meant to take me in his arms and kiss me. He did, certainly, bend a little closer and squint at me with more determination.

After I know not what interval, reason at last interposed and translated these first frightful formulations into their mundane equivalents. I realize that my predicament, though awful enough, was the commonest in the world, one which on any given evening in London an hundred and more young ladies must come up against: the shock of finding out that one is considered marriageable. For the majority, of course, this knowledge is a fulfillment and a delight, but for all too many of us it has been far otherwise—distasteful at best; at worst a terror.

In my own case, the prospect of marriage had seemed as remote as the dews of summer mornings during the furious winter's rage. An undowered orphan, living sequestered from any society but the Sabbath greetings of neighbors on the steps of our church, what could have led me to such imaginings? Embittered by her own experience of matrimony, my aunt had never fed me upon those fictions and fancies which have been the adolescent sustenance of so many other maidens in our time. I saw no plays; I read no novels; the whole complex apparatus of modern romance was unknown to me. On the whole, I have been grateful for this deprivation, but on this one occasion some girlish conception of romantic love would have served as buckler and shield against the idea that I was doomed, by my uncle's unswervable will, to be married to Geoffrey Jerningham.

I could not, I would not marry him; yet, under the pressure of his gaze, and his parents', and Mr. Jerningham's, I felt how infinitesimally little my own small "could's" and "would's" mattered when weighed in the scale of *their* desires; I foresaw how my own unexercised will would be bent, and shaped, and finally shattered by *their* confident, inexorable collusion.

"What say you, Clara?" Geoffrey Jerningham persisted. "Will you give us what we all are craving? Will you play for us another song?"

In reply I did what I have never done before nor since; I fainted.

CHAPTER SIXTEEN
Mortal Combat

WHILE I TOOK REFUGE in unconsciousness, the first skirmish took place in what was to be a long contention between my aunt and uncle over the issue of whether I was to marry my cousin Geoffrey. My uncle, soon as his guests had departed, had announced my engagement as an accomplished fact: dowry and date were settled, and nothing wanted but the formality of my consent.

That, my aunt assured him, he would never obtain, so long as she was alive. My uncle received this contradiction with surprising mildness, as one who, having summed up a row of figures, arrives at an implausible result. He repeated the operation, certain this time the figures would jibe with his stated wish—but they did not! Incredulous, he demanded to know how she thought she could prevent the marriage.

"And how did you answer?" I asked, incredulous as well, when next morning she told me of this unprecedented defiance.

"I said that I would use all my influence with you to prevent your yielding your consent. 'And if I tell her that she must?' said he. 'Then,' said I, '*I* will tell her she must not.' You would not wish it, would you? No, of course not. Forgive my asking, but I have often thought that, were I in your position myself, I would be tempted to make any imprudent match that offered, just in order to escape from *him*. But believe me, Clara, the tyrannies of a husband are worse than those of a guardian, however cruel, however arbitrary."

"But what shall I do if Geoffrey Jerningham returns here and makes an offer?"

"Refuse him, if that is what you wish to do. Refuse him politely as you can, and if he persists in asking, persist in refusing."

"But will he not complain to my uncle?"

"Undoubtedly. And your uncle will do his best to coerce you into accepting. You must refuse him, too."

"And if he asked my reasons?"

"It would be unlike him to do that, but if he does, do not try to justify your choice. Only say you are acting on my advice. If he dares demand *my* reasons, I shall tell him outright I cannot allow you to make the same mistake that I made. Merciful heaven, I think there is no limit to the vileness of men! You are eighteen? Geoffrey is forty-eight. What are they thinking of? It is, of course, Blackthorne they are thinking of, and the fact you were invited there. They smell money."

"Oh, I wish I had never gone there. I wish I were no relation to Lord Rhodes at all. I wish my grandfather had been the son of a . . . a costermonger!" I carried on with such a string of self-pitying wishes that I at last exhausted even my aunt's patience, and she left me to my ineffectual litanies.

Alas, Geoffrey Jerningham's patience was not so easily exhausted, nor was he ever content to leave me to a private misery. Three or four evenings each week he would appear at Worcester Terrace, wearing always the same grim frockcoat that glittered blackly like a great lump of anthracite coal, the same coal-scuttle of a hat, and the same determined, moribund smile that exposed a row of decaying teeth—which also bore a resemblance to coal, though of a lower grade than his coat. He would come, and we would sit to dinner, and he would squint at me, and I would watch the food grow cold upon my plate, for in his presence I could never force myself to eat more than the first symbolic forkful required by good manners.

Having no liveliness in conversation, lacking his own ideas, and slow to understand another's, Geoffrey Jerningham nevertheless fancied himself something of a quiz. His wit was all of a hand-me-down sort, got from miscellanies and magazines. No joke was too moldly, no riddle too old but Geoffrey would trot it out to astonish us. We learned that newspapers are black and white and *read* all over; that for some reason pickles are like parsons, and lemon tarts like toes. Even the rhymes of the venerable Mother Goose were considered a probable amusement for us, and I did find it droll to hear Geoffrey recite in his rasping, sing-songy way such old favorites of my nursery days as "Little Boy Blue" and "Diddle, Diddle, Dumpling." I have never been to Ely, but to this day I believe that the citizens of that town occupy the long winter evenings regaling each other with lullabies and chuckling at counting-jingles. A simpler and likelier explanation is that from his vantage Geoffrey saw little difference between eighteen years and eight.

Three weeks were devoted to these preliminary flourishes of courtship, three weeks needful to each of us for mustering sufficient courage—he to ask, I to refuse. How both my uncle and aunt must have suffered in that interval! There were times when I verily believed Mr. Jerningham meant to assume his nephew's responsibility and propose to me himself. As for Lydia, her hostility to my suitor soon reached such a pitch of intensity that she could not trust herself in the same room with him. Yet neither did she dare leave us by ourselves, for she still doubted whether my distaste for my cousin's advances was pronounced enough to enable me to overcome my dread of my uncle's anger. I did not know myself till, one humid, hushed evening in July, Geoffrey asked for my hand.

We were seated on that same cast-iron bench off which so many years before I had witnessed Chloe tumble in the clutches of the jay. My uncle had contrived to leave us alone together, and Geoffrey, in a less antic mood than usual, had limited his discourse to a very terse appreciation of the sunset and an enumeration of its various colors; namely, red and yellow, for its streaks of pink and wisps of lavender were invisible to his weaker eyes. Then, swivelling round so as to be able to peer, albeit with his customary squint, into my eyes, he pronounced my name and clutched at my hand, which rested on the arm of the bench.

"Please," I said, attempting to disengage.

"Clara!" he repeated, with a kind of effortful ardor.

"My hand," I replied, in a tone of mild reproof.

"It is a beautiful hand, my dear Clara, and I would like it to be mine."

"Pray, then do not crush it so."

He released my hand but held fast to the arm of the bench, thereby preventing my retreat indoors. Indignation slowly gave way to dismay, as I realized that my weak little jest might be construed as a tacit consent.

It might be, and was. Like a lesser sunset, scarlet suffused the saffron of Geoffrey's hollow cheeks. Unsteadily he lowered himself to the ground; tentatively he arranged his limbs into a posture of kneeling. "Dearest Clara, you have made me the happiest man in. . . ." He paused, as though considering the exact dimensions of his happiness: in Bayswater? London? the British Isles?

I interrupted, and so will never know how far he might have flung his net. "Please do not misinterpret me, Mr. Jerningham. I am always pleased, of course, to know a near relation of my aunt is happy, but it cannot be within *my* power to increase or diminish your happiness."

"But surely your consent gives me liberty to rejoice."

"I have consented to nothing. I *will* consent to nothing."

The flush of triumph deepened to a blush of shame. "My dear Miss Reeve, let me put the matter to you so there can be no mistaking. I am asking for your hand in holy wedlock."

"And I am refusing."

"Well." Still he made no move to rise. "Perhaps you require more time to reach a decision?"

"I have reached my decision, Mr. Jerningham, and I have stated it."

"I see." Geoffrey lifted himself from the grass without mishap and took leave of me with no more ado than if I had been one of the garden's ornaments.

I was grateful to be left alone on any terms, for my spirit was in such a moil of dread and elation that for the moment I was incapable of rational action or coherent speech. I had done that which I had believed altogether beyond my power: I had set myself against my uncle's will. My cousin Geoffrey's chagrin would have been trebled had he known how little part *he* had played in the drama of his own proposal. Him I feared not at all; or rather, feared only with that milder apprehension, tinged by guilt, such as a certain rough sort of beggar may inspire, whom we pity even as we haste away from him. Throughout these first weeks of courtship, he had been as little present to my consciousness as I to his. At the very moment of his proposal, I had heard my uncle's stern command, like an insistent figure in the bass that drives the melody along, behind Geoffrey's hoarse and tremulous request. The request I could easily refuse, but that I had resisted the command—that was wonderful!

Worse would come, I knew. At any moment I expected to see my uncle sweep out of the house, borne up by the whirlwind of his rage. I expected to be reviled, threatened, humiliated, even cursed, but now I was confident, or nearly so, that I could bear all this in silence without yielding on the essential point. I would *not* be frightened into marriage.

I did not think to ask myself where I had come by my sudden access of strength and independence of judgment. My uncle, when he confronted me with my deed, was more acute, for he saw at once that my integrity was borrowed, and from whom.

"Your cousin has left," Mr. Jerningham announced, advancing towards the bench, from which I had not had the courage to stir, though the dusk had quite definitely graduated to darkness. "He informs me that he has made an offer for your hand and been refused. Your incivilities to him have been so many and so blatant that I cannot claim to be surprised."

"Whenever I am uncourteous, I hope you will correct me, Sir. I would not want to give my cousin needless pain."

"Your refusal of his offer is needless. The match in every way commends itself. You could not want a more respectable husband, or one more solidly placed. He is certain to have the canonry when his father leaves it."

He broke off, as though challenging me to contradict him, but in this he mistook my temper, for I would have endured hours of the most uncomfortable silence, my hands folded, my gaze fixed to the waistcoat looming before me as firmly and primly as the very buttons sewn upon it, before I would volunteer to contradict him.

"Well," he insisted, "am I to understand that you have changed your mind?"

"No. My conscience does not allow me to consider marrying my cousin Geoffrey. I feel no affection for him."

"Conscience! Affection! Twaddle! What can you know of conscience or affection at eighteen? Your aunt has been meddling in this. Can you deny it?"

I remained silent until my silence itself had amounted to an admission.

"She has been urging you to resist me in this. Give me a yes or a no."

"No—not to resist *you*, Sir," I ventured. "But to refuse Geoffrey."

"You reject my advice."

"I shall always listen to your advice, Sir. I cannot promise always to follow it."

"Oh, splendid, splendid! You will listen but not heed! That is the new meaning of duty, I suppose. There is not much use my wasting my breath, in that case."

"I am sorry to disappoint you, Sir," I said, with a dawning sense of how lightly I was being let off. A criminal, catching the first faint gleam of mercy in the eye of his judge, must feel just this same trepidatory gratitude, and, like that criminal, I longed to be sentenced while the gleam was still in evidence.

"Tell me this, Clara. If your aunt should change her mind; if she were to tell you she has reconsidered and that in her best judgment you *ought* to marry Geoffrey; if she should urge you to that course and give you reasons why you should command your affections rather than be commanded by them: would you still be quite so unalterably opposed to acting as your duty dictates?"

"I should always try to follow my aunt's advice. Just as I have always tried to follow yours, Sir."

"I see that you have got the knack of making pretty speeches, but I must know with a little more definiteness whether, if your aunt's voice were joined with mine, you would be more willing to marry your cousin. To think of it."

"I do not know, Sir. I really cannot imagine her urging me to do so."

"Then I shall not place that strain upon your imagination. Lydia shall speak to you this night."

His threat was not to be fulfilled, not that night nor (though by saying so I forfeit any advantage of suspense my narrative may possess) ever. Lydia gave me her full, staunch, and unflinching support. The welkin roared, volcanoes spewed, Mr. Jerningham loosed his whole armory of thunderbolts against her. Still she refused. Often, I know, he hurled her to the floor, nor did he scruple against striking her with his doubled fist. Once her eye was blackened so that for two weeks she could not leave the house without a heavy veil. After the fiercest of its excesses, my uncle's rage would somewhat slacken, but though the storms might be intermitted, there was no relief from the perpetual oppressiveness of low, dark cloud, rank upon rank, day after day, as in the very drearest of Novembers. He lived in a constant state of baffled anger, the effect of which was fearful to witness. The lightest meals carried severe penances of indigestion; the slightest task, such as the turning of a log in the fire, would, by releasing his tensed frame, set his arms and hands into spasms of trembling. I could not help but pity him, and had he ever mounted a fresh attack against *my* resolve I cannot be sure I would not at last have yielded to him. But all his fury was turned against his wife. The matter of my marriage had become little more than a pretext in what was essentially the battle of their two wills: he would, she would not; he commanded, she disregarded the command; he declared what must be, she denied its necessity.

Yet, throughout the many marches and countermarches of their opposed purposes, Lydia always limited her resistance to the realm of discourse. When violence was used against her, she did not answer in kind. As a result, it became common for their arguments to end in blows, since only in this way could Mr. Jerningham be assured of having "the last word." I was not often a witness to such scenes, nor did I then suspect their frequency, for in all her afflictions my aunt maintained a stoic silence before her husband, a silence in striking contrast to the tears and moans she would indulge in solitude or when I was her only audience. Had I known at that time all that she was made to suffer, I would surely have sacrificed my own repugnance and married Geoffrey Jerningham to spare her from my uncle's unrelenting abuse. But I did not know, and at just the moment it became painfully evident, a new event intruded to prevent such a self-immolation.

It was the fourteenth of February of 1863, St. Valentine's Day.

Geoffrey Jerningham's courtship had persisted more than seven months—or above two hundred days. He had called at the house during that afternoon and, at my aunt's request, been turned away with the excuse that she was indisposed. My uncle, arriving home a little later, learned of this through the servant girl and began at once to storm at Lydia there in the parlor, where we had been passing the time reading aloud from a volume of Cowper. Whether she really was under the baneful influence of a megrim or whether she could not endure to have me witness her husband's assaults, the era of her meekness ended. When Mr. Jerningham raised his hand against her, she caught hold of his sleeve, and warned him in a voice shrill with wonder at her own audacity: "Josiah, do not strike me. Curse me to your heart's content. Rave, bluster, swear! But you shall not threaten me with violence again!"

Her prohibition excited his anger rather than curbed it. Tearing loose, he hit her with the back of his hand, a blow that would have struck her full in the face had she not turned aside its full force with her raised hand.

The sight of this buffeting (which did not end with the first deflected blow but was repeated with a horrid, almost mechanic regularity, as though my uncle had become the mere energumen of his own limitless rage), and even more the sound of it, his gasping imprecations and my aunt's piercing protests, affected me past all reason. I was beside myself with fear, less for myself than for Lydia, who alternately fled from her tormentor and, from behind the momentary safety of an armchair or a table, defied him to do his worst.

Then, in warding off one of his blows, Lydia delivered herself over to her enemy. Mr. Jerningham grasped the lace ruffle of her sleeve and held fast. With his free arm, he began to pelt her so furiously that I was roused from the stupor of my fear. I threw myself upon him. He pushed me aside. I pleaded for him to stop, even promised that I would marry Geoffrey if he would but cease to attack my aunt. But he was beyond understanding me. I doubt he even heard my words above Lydia's screams and his own incoherencies.

She broke away from him at last, and, fleeing to the mantel, took down from its mitred niche the pride of her collection, a teapot blazoned with the features of the Queen and the late Prince-Consort, their coats-of-arms, and a view of Balmoral Castle. This she brandished above her head and, when he refused to heed her warning and still advanced, hurled at him. The missile struck him square upon the chest, bounced off, struck the iron leg of the fire-screen, and shattered. My uncle stood stock-still in the middle of the Turkey carpet, clutching at his waistcoat where the teapot had touched him. Lydia, heedless that he had stopped pursuing her, whirled about the parlor in a frenzy of destruction, snatching down the various commemorative plates and pots and smashing these upon the glazed brick frontage of the fireplace.

When the last piece was shattered, Mr. Jerningham collapsed to the carpet with a groan. At this, Lydia quietened somewhat, but our fear was so strong that we neither dared approach him.

Looking down at her torn sleeve, she began to cry, and crying, she excused herself upstairs, promising to return as soon as she had changed into another dress.

As soon as she was gone, I busied myself with picking up shards of broken china, with the notion (which seemed at that moment rational) that I would repair them upon the morrow.

My task drew me closer and closer to the prostrate form of Mr. Jerningham, but, as he did not move, I ceased to fear him. My whole attention was absorbed in sorting out one set of fragments from another. I was startled therefore when, almost on top of him, I heard him address me by name.

"Yes, Mr. Jerningham, I am here beside you."

His eyes fixed on mine with a terrible intensity. Recessed so deeply in that long, lean face, gleaming in the reflected firelight, those eyes seemed like live coals that have burned sockets deep into a sheet of ice. I could not look away. I could not close my eyes.

"Clara, I must have your promise."

"Sir?"

"You understand me very well. Promise me you'll marry your cousin."

"In all conscience, Sir, I cannot promise you that."

"I am dying, my dear little Clara. Would you refuse my dying wish?"

"Please, Mr. Jerningham. Spare me."

He lifted his hand, still clutching that scrap of lace. Whether he meant to strike me, or bless me, or wave good-bye, I could not tell. Whatever he meant, my response was to feel a pity for the man. It seemed, after all, such a trifle to wish for on the threshold of eternity.

"I promise that . . . if I marry at all . . . it will be to my cousin."

"Swear it. Swear on your mother's grave. Swear by her love."

I closed my eyes, and swore.

He smiled and said no more. When I at length opened my own eyes, his were closed and he was breathing quietly.

He died the next day at four in the afternoon, without regaining consciousness. The china was never repaired, nor did I tell my aunt of the oath that had been extracted from me.

CHAPTER SEVENTEEN

Pleasures of Mourning

NEW YEAR'S DAY OF 1864 was a bright, bitter, sunshiny day, a day of rimed windows and black smoke billowing from every chimney-pot on Worcester Terrace, a day of numbed fingers and frozen feet, of long sermons and longer thoughts both addressed to those traditional New Year's themes of retrospect and fresh resolve. For myself and my aunt it was a day of such profound thankfulness and quiet, conscious content that we were no little embarrassed, since the source of that happiness had been our bereavement. Though we did not say so, though we even exchanged some few dutiful regrets on the subject, neither our silence nor our speeches could refute the fact that Mr. Jerningham's death had brought new gladness to our lives, nor all the crepe we wore during that first year of deep mourning obscure the hundred evidences of our new freedom and our delight in it.

Gone from the parlor were the twelve volumes of Dr. Casbolt's

Commentaries, and in its place a great three-decker novel lent by Mudie's. Rooms that had never known any animal visitant but some few generations of marauding mice were now the daily haunt of two frolicking spaniels, the ginger-colored Thalia and sable Melpomene. The furniture, without losing its thorny, Gothic ornament, burst into blossoms of new upholstery, and instructed by papers from Mr. Morris's famous workshop, the very walls were taught to smile. The china lost on that momentous February day had been restored, doubly and then fourfold, until the house took on something of the character of Westminster Abbey, whose original medieval stamp had been almost blotted from sight by memorial after memorial fashioned in the modes of other centuries. There was even, as one mounted to the upper story, a festive air to the crisp black bow that graced the daguerreotype showing Mr. Jerningham's gravestone in Highgate Cemetery—a feeling borne out by the text from the Sixty-eighth Psalm that my aunt had chosen for an epitaph: *Let the righteous be glad; let them rejoice before God: yea, let them exceedingly rejoice.*

My readers must not draw from this the conclusion that my aunt was neglectful of the proper observances, or that she harbored any lingering resentment against her husband. Her conduct as a widow was as exemplary as had been, by and large, her behavior as a wife, nor was her mourning "but the trappings and the suits of woe." As the memory of Mr. Jerningham became dim, it became in proportion precious, and his figure merged with another husband of that time, deeply mourned and fiercely lamented, whose death was yet so fresh that the first sod had yet to be turned in Kensington Gardens for the building of his great Memorial: I refer, of course, to Albert, the Prince-Consort. My aunt had always been fond of discovering parallels between her own life and that of her Monarch's. The Queen had been born on the twenty-fourth of May; Lydia on the twenty-sixth. The Queen had married on February 10, 1840; Lydia just a week later. Now the parallel was extended by her early widowhood, and Lydia shared with the Queen a sorrow almost insupportable, a sorrow which only the generous application of Macpherson's Sulphurous Compound could alleviate.

Between these vastations, however, which occurred at regular fortnightly intervals, we were quite unprecedentedly gay. Some

of the household aspects of our changed condition I have already
mentioned, and many chapters ago I referred to the evening of my
nineteenth birthday on which we attended Racine's *Bérénice*. That
was but the first of many adventures into the world of high
romance, low comedy, gas-lit illusion, and magnificent rodomon-
tade. Ah, how many handkerchiefs have I not soaked mourning
Cordelia with Mr. Macready or witnessing the sublime Madame
Celeste in *The Child of the Wreck*! In general, I know, I am much
given to deprecating the fusty old Past at the expense of our improved and brighter Present, but in this one respect my allegiance
is all to the long-ago. Let the critics have their *-isms* and their
-ologies, their Ibsens and their Shaws. Give me *East Lynne*! Give
me *The Frozen Deeps*! Give me *The Turn of the Tide*!

Give me, in addition, my vanished youth and my enjoyment
will be wholly restored; for that, I suspect, and not a general
decline in the dramatic art, is the chief difference between the
plays I can remember and those I see nowadays.

One other circumstance distinguished many of those evenings.
The pleasures of the pretended drama were mingled with the still
headier delights of society. My cousin Niles had a passion for
the theater to equal ours, and when his affairs brought him to
London, as was often the case that season, he would take a box
at the Adelphi or the Drury Lane and, resplendent in a long tail
coat with ruffles at the wrists, a white cravat and white kid gloves,
would act as our escort and cicerone, instructing us in the titles and
characters of such of the other theatergoers as were known to him
(and of more than a few, I am sure, who were not). The Dowager
Contessa, too, was often with us, though less for the immediate
pleasure of the spectacle than for the chance, during the intervals,
to scoff at the players on either side of the curtains.

Throughout that first year of mourning, beginning indeed on
the very day of Mr. Jerningham's funeral, when they rode out to
Highgate next after the hearse and our own hired carriage in a
brougham borrowed from Lord Rhodes and bearing his crest,
Niles and Zaide had been visitors to Worcester Terrace as regularly
as they had come down to London from Corme Hall in Cumberland. This was one of Lord Rhodes' minor properties, and they
had it from him on a kind of extended loan for the length of their
stay in England. At first the continuing unrest and sporadic fight-

ing in Italy had kept the Viscontis from returning to that country; later there was a happier source of delay. Renata was blessed with the promise of motherhood, a promise that had been fulfilled in October of 1863, when she was delivered of a daughter. This child was christened Clara Maria Visconti, and to the honor of having my little cousin named after me was added the dignity of being chosen her godmother. I was not, however, present at the baptism; Zaide acted as my proxy and answered in my name.

The period of confinement had been unusually taxing on Renata's health, and the severe winter of the Lake District, following hard upon her delivery, had left the young mother, accustomed as she was to a so much milder climate, in a condition of permanent invalidism. From the moment of her arrival at Corme Hall, she had not once, so her mother-in-law claimed, set her foot out of doors; if this was an exaggeration, it was certain, at least, that she had never accompanied her husband or his mother on any of their trips into London.

Recording these facts now, they seem singular enough, not to say ominous. My heart fairly breaks when I imagine the life Renata must have led at Corme Hall, but at that time my complaisance was unruffled and my imagination inert. After what had passed between Renata and me, I did not desire for our acquaintance to be renewed. If she wished to remain sequestered in her moorland cell while her husband visited London, I was content to accept my own good fortune without too closely inquiring into its conditions. Nothing makes us so insensitive to another's ills as when they are the foundation of our own happiness.

As well confess it now as later: I had come to find Niles Visconti attractive, and I was conscious of liking him past the liking proper to mere cousinship. Had he *not* been married, I might have been less ready to admit this to myself, but knowing his destiny indissolubly linked to another's, I found it easy to give my impulses free rein. Nothing in my experience or education had suggested that the knot of matrimony was less than adamantine or that any suspicion of impropriety might attach to an open and declared friendship with my married cousin. I required nothing of him but his conversation, and if with growing acquaintance our conversations had become a pleasure more delectable to me than any other, still, could I be blamed for craving what had never been forbidden me? He welcomed this state of affairs; his mother encouraged it; my aunt seemed not to notice; I knew no better.

Then, late on the evening of that bright, bitter, sunshiny New Year's of 1864, came news that threw these pleasant, nebulous, dangerous feelings into a new disequilibrium; news that, from the first moment of reading the telegram dispatched from Penrith, seemed tremulous with future consequence. Renata was dead. There was no mention how she had died; just that bare, fearsome fact and an urgent request that we come to Corme Hall.

CHAPTER EIGHTEEN
"The Horror of It!"

ZAIDE GRASPED MY HAND and bent forwards to place an icy kiss upon my forehead. My face was still warm from the heated railway carriage, but hers, from having waited so long in the barouche, was chilled to rigidity. Once our baggage was stowed behind and we were securely wrapped in furs and blankets inside, Zaide gave a rap to the wooden wall, and the coach set off into the darkness of a late, heavily overcast afternoon. On the journey northwards, I had rehearsed an hundred tactful condolences, but now I had not the wit to say one sympathetic word. The Contessa's own restraint had compelled an answering silence; her swaying figure, obscured by shadow, seemed to refuse even the attention of my glances. Accordingly, I fixed my attention on the lantern mounted outside the window of the barouche. Through its feeble sphere of light, the snow made an endless, slow, slanting descent.

Just after dark we stopped at an inn to change the horses, to warm ourselves at the fire and take some refreshment. As we returned to the barouche, Zaide broke her silence long enough to apologize for having involved us in such a journey in such weather.

"Believe me," my aunt insisted, "it is no inconvenience. If our presence can be any help, any comfort. . . ."

"The only help, the only comfort, believe me. I would not have sent that telegram otherwise. Niles is quite, quite desperate with grief. It is only natural, of course. One can never believe that one so young, and still in the very springtime of life . . . that Providence should see fit to bring an end to an existence barely begun."

"It is not for us to question His wisdom or His will," Lydia said from deep inside her own mound of furs, thereby forestalling me from offering the same doubtful comfort to our companion.

What *can* one say at these times? I have never known. To seek to assuage a present grief with professions of faith in the life hereafter is presumptuous: if those whom we would comfort share that faith, there is no harm, certainly, to speak of it, but no great need either; if they do not, then what we mean as balm will taste of wormwood. Faith is indeed the remedy for sorrow, but only if it is well-established in our hearts before we are afflicted. All that I knew of the Contessa's philosophy made me reluctant to inquire into the exact state of her feelings or her faith. Just as at our first meeting my impulse had been to step back rather than advance to meet her, so now my inclination was to stop outside the threshold of her heart, as though that precinct were some dark cavern or chthonian temple wherein rites were performed that would be too painful, too awful to witness. I had enjoyed her company often; I craved it still; but I shrank from an entire intimacy.

Add to this that my own feelings were obscure to me. I had been more shocked than grieved by the news of Renata's death. I had known her but slightly, and even that slight acquaintance had been shadowed by doubts as to her true character. Further, I was in possession of a document that would, I was certain, confirm or deny those doubts. I had vowed not to read the ledger-book with which Renata had entrusted me at Blackthorne, and I meant to keep that vow, but now I had to ask myself whether I ought deliver it into the hands of my cousin. Properly, I told myself, any writings of his deceased wife belonged to him, yet how could I, just for my own mental relief, choose to inflict a pain which might be worse than the pain of mourning? The pain, that is, of knowing Renata had been faithless in her love.

So, like the lantern on which my wearied gaze was fixed, my thoughts wavered this way and that. Probity demanded that I surrender the ledger; then compassion would say—No, spare him, burn the book. The lantern swayed again, and the carriage moved on, creaking and straining, through the fresh snow, and my mind passed restlessly back and forth between one alternative and the other. So preoccupied was I with my own dilemma that when Zaide again addressed us I was quite startled.

"You have been so forebearing, both of you, and I am grateful." Her tone was as light as a sigh. "I owe some larger explanation to you, I know, and yet . . . it is so difficult. My daughter died—I say 'daughter,' for she'd come to seem my own child—she died in circumstances which were—there is no other word—grotesque."

"She did not die, then, of an ague?" Lydia asked. "You spoke, when last you were in London, of how poorly she'd adapted to our English weather. So I had assumed—"

"Her health was as good as it had been any time this last twelvemonth; not blooming, as you know, but tolerable. We would not have stayed on at Corme Hall otherwise. Yet our English weather, as you style it, has been—yes, and in the most fearful way —responsible for her death. Renata died of exposure. She was found frozen in the snow."

Incomprehension gave way to horror; horror contested against incredulity. My aunt made some hushed protest.

"I know, I know," Zaide continued. "I cannot, to this hour, believe it myself, and yet I saw her corpse taken from the cart that brought it to the hall. She was huddled into a ball, her arms wrapped round her ankles; beads of ice sealed shut her eyes, and as they thawed they turned to tears again."

"But how had she come to be outside?"

"Well may you ask, Clara. We do not know for sure. That she was gone from her bedroom on New Year's morning, that the hall door was found unbolted—these are our only certainties. She'd had a croup all last week, and so Niles had slept in an adjacent room to avoid the possibility of contagion. No one can blame him, but he does blame himself, and bitterly."

"Do you think, then, that she unbolted the door herself, that she was, as at Blackthorne, walking and sleeping at the same time?"

"Did she do such things at Blackthorne, too?" Lydia asked. "I had not heard of it."

"Yes," said Zaide quickly. "It is something which, in general, one chooses not to advertise. Yet Niles carelessly made some reference to the matter in Clara's presence, and then it seemed best to impart the bare fact of the malady, though we did conceal, as much as we could, the dangers that beset her in consequence of her illness. Unless you have seen someone in a somnambulistic trance, you cannot imagine the strangeness and horror of the sight. I have stood before Renata, laid my hand upon her shoulder, shaken her, as one would shake a heavy sleeper, and all the while her eyes were open, though what they saw I could not surmise. I was invisible to her, yet doors did not bar her way, nor stairs, nor did she stumble against even the lowest footstool. Once I saw her walk by a fire, oblivious of the sparks that lighted on her shift, and since then my greatest fear has always been that she would set herself on fire. Who could have conceived this—that she would venture out of doors clad only in a flannel chemise during the worst blizzard of the year? Such a storm as makes this tonight seem mild to benevolence. Or who would think, venturing thus, that the first icy blast would not wake her from her trance? But no! She walked three miles across the snowy moors. We have already passed the spot where her body was discovered, half-buried by the drifts, in a ditch beside a thorn tree. It was seeing that tree roused me to speech, and knowing we would soon be at Corme Hall. Yet even by coach it is no slight journey—and she, with no shoes upon her feet! How can the mind be so sundered, the will from the senses? Yet such must be the case; there is no other explanation."

"The horror of it," Lydia said, after we had ridden for some time in silence.

"The horror of it," Zaide agreed. "Exactly. But we must try not to dwell on that. It should not make such a difference, the manner of her death. That would be a way of questioning the Divine Providence, too, would it not? I would not have inflicted such a tale on you, but I did so advisedly, in order that, knowing all now, you would not inquire more of Niles. Since she was found, he has been beside himself. We must encourage him to mourn his loss, but not to abandon himself to a despair that feeds upon his mistaken sense of guilt. All the household knew of her affliction, and to that degree we share a common guilt in not having foreseen this and acted to prevent it."

"But how could anyone foresee such a thing?" Lydia asked.

In answer, Zaide was silent.

The coach turned sharply to the left and ahead I could see, beyond the lantern's little circle of shining, the lamps of Corme Hall ranged on the horizon, like a single constellation in a sky else devoid of light.

CHAPTER NINETEEN
Corme Hall

I REMEMBER BLACKTHORNE as I saw it first, thrust into the daylight like the great Dover Cliffs, its myriad windows blinking at the sun; I remember the glow of its gardens in the dawn, or, as I stood at my window, the soft sweep of the surrounding hills and the glory of the sky above; the various brilliances of the summer light; the slow, solemn majesty of coursing cloud.

But Corme Hall? Though I was to spend eleven long weeks there, I remember it only as a great darkness segmented into a hive of lesser glooms; I remember a smell of tallow that mingled unpleasantly with the lingering traces of the Contessa's musk and a damp that penetrated every curtain, every cushion, every table-cloth, items that exist in my memory only insofar as they were capable of absorbing the moisture perpetually condensing from that mephitic air. Perhaps, had I made my first acquaintance under more auspicious circumstances, my mind would have summed up its elements differently—perhaps; and yet I doubt it. It was an ugly, ill-built, inconvenient house, which my relations had the use of only because Lord Rhodes had long been unable to rent it.

I can see my cousin's face peering from that all-pervading darkness. Oh, as clearly as if it were limned on the very page across which my pen moves at this moment! As clearly as if Niles were here in this room, lecturing me in his fine, fluent voice; or, may be, only looking at me. For he *would* look. Minute upon minute his eyes would rest upon me, and then, when my own gaze would meet his, he would turn away: here, there, feigning to ignore me. Oh, that was the essential Niles! That quick little wandering movement of the eyes, back and forth, back and forth, as though reading, while he sought out some pretext, any trivial object in which he could pretend to take an interest; and then, when I had returned to my book or my needlework, the slow, inexorable drift of his attention back to me—to my shoes, to my mourning-dress, to my own face, tense with expectation. Niles' pale countenance, and his restless eyes, dark as the darkness of those narrow rooms—that is what I remember of Corme Hall.

He did not speak of his loss. Some times he would include his wife's name in a reminiscence, but these were never the grief-stricken reveries of a widower dwelling obsessively upon the scenes of an irrecoverable past; only inadvertencies, lapses, forgettings. Formerly, at Blackthorne and in London, he had spoken so freely of his own affections and aversions, joys and sorrows, that I was often taken aback by his candor, and my aunt quite shocked (not unpleasantly); now he never referred to the state of his feelings, except, like many another gentleman newly isolated in some rural and snowbound solitude, to complain of his boredom, his hunger for sunlight, his impatience for the spring. Yet I was certain, though he said nothing, that he felt that loss deeply and mourned Renata dead with a singleness of attention that (I feared) he had rarely devoted to her alive. He would sit, for instance, with a book in his lap, hours at a time, and though he made a pretense of reading it, he lacked the energy to make this imposture convincing by cutting the pages as he progressed from front to back.

Little Clara Maria, with her wetnurse, had been dispatched to the home of her maternal grandparents in Amalfi for the sake of her own health and of her father's peace of mind. From the moment of her departure, under the care of Niles' valet, it was as if she had died together with her mother. Niles did not speak of her, nor did Zaide, and in a short time the servants had removed every painful reminder that the child had ever been born.

If he was silent concerning his own feelings, he was a perfect magpie on every other topic. If he was not brooding, he was talking, and it seemed only natural, in order to keep him from brooding, to keep him always talking. This was his mother's policy, and I followed her example all too willingly.

He talked of the great issues of the day: of the Schleswig-Holstein question, over which hostilities had just commenced; of the tragic war in America, whose outcome was evident now to even the blindest partisans of the Confederacy; of the Russian occupation of Poland; of anything, indeed, the newspapers saw fit to mention. The whole world seemed to be at war, or on the brink of war, and Niles took a delight, inexplicable to me, in calmly, judiciously, implacably explaining why the several parties to these diverse conflicts wished the annihilation of the other parties, and by what tactics of war or diplomatic threat they might attain that goal.

That was one of his themes; the other, I am thankful to say, recommended itself much more to my attention, though I could never contribute more myself, in all the hours of discussion, than a few rather tentative questions. This was the theme of Art; of the Italian painters in particular, and especially the painting of Giotto and his followers. I had never heard of Giotto, much less seen examples of his work, which were all (Niles gave me to understand) firmly bonded to the walls of some seven or eight churches scattered throughout Italy. Niles was able to show me engravings made after some of the best-acclaimed of these frescoes and four small sketches he had painted himself in gouache. I marvelled mightily at these. Not, I must add, at their beauty, but precisely at what seemed to me their entire lack of it, at their positive, their flagrant, their incomprehensible ugliness. To my eye, trained on the scrupulous renderings, jewel-bright colors, and narrative delicacy of contemporary painters, Giotto seemed scarce to be an artist at all, a mere barbarian of the paintbrush—his drawing inferior to that of any practiced schoolmistress (and very likely to that of her pupils), his colors muddy, his compositions unnatural and absurd. How any churchman could allow such childish scrawls still to blemish the temples of his faith I could not conceive, and what was *more* wonderful was that my cousin, whose own hand was capable of creating sketches of really remarkable loveliness, that *he* should bow in fealty to this clown, this nincompoop, this Giotto!

Well, since that day, I have learned how to respect, if not quite to admire, those first pioneers of Art's rebirth. My preference shall always be for the decorous, polished, and perfected form, but I can see that there is *something* to Giotto, and for that much enlightenment I am indebted to my cousin Niles. He it was, there at Corme Hall and later in churches all over Tuscany, who instructed my taste and taught my eyes to see what erewhile they had been blind to.

A strange way, you may think, to pass a time of mourning. No doubt it was. I often thought so then, and yet one cannot sit covered with ashes week upon week. Life will rise up in us, will tingle in limbs made leaden by inanition, will drive us out of our curtained rooms to drink in the great and still-continuing pageant of the earth underfoot and sky above. I knew a widower once who, losing his only daughter, gave himself up utterly to horses; every day he would be up at dawn and in the saddle, nor would he be back at his stable till it was quite dark. I knew a boy of twelve who, from grief for a beloved uncle, became uncannily accomplished in classical Greek before the grass had taken root on the mound above that uncle's grave. And I have known grief myself, the very bitterest, and known, as well, the bittersweetness of an activity in which were united my grief and an unbounded appetite for living. But of that, in its place.

Lydia and I, in departing London, had had no notion of settling at Corme Hall for a term of eleven weeks, and if we had, the dismal nature of the place and of the event to which it had been witness would quickly have dispelled such a notion. However, on the very day of Renata's funeral, Lydia was stricken with a megrim of exceptional severity, which her usual remedy did little to alleviate. The next day she was feverish and suffered alarming spasms of coughing. The fever rose, the spasms became more violent, and nothing was effective against either. Add to this that these symptoms were identical to those which had so much wasted Renata in the months following the birth of Clara Maria, and you may imagine the anxiety that I experienced on my aunt's behalf. A physician was called in, and instead of ordering us back to London, as I had hoped, absolutely forbade any movement, even from her bed, till she was fully recovered. To this latter end, he applied a great quantity of leeches and prescribed a medicine, which my aunt (wisely, I think) refused to take. Day after day she languished in her damp, drafty room, too listless to talk, to read, or to sew.

Gladly would I have attended my aunt through every hour

of her illness, but she had no use for me. Indeed, my presence positively interfered with the one pleasure available to her, the dreams engendered by her laudanum. Thus it came about that I had so much leisure, for so long, to spend with my cousin.

The Contessa (there was once again no need to qualify her title with "Dowager"), out of respect for my aunt's sense of decorum, tried to be present at these *tête-à-têtes*, though she rarely took part in them, preferring a novel or her own thoughts for company. I got the impression that Niles had long since despaired of reforming his mother's tastes, which he considered, so far as they touched on the fine arts, as invincibly vulgar. I recall one occasion when Zaide did join the fray to champion the Pre-Raphaelite Brotherhood, whom Niles had maligned by some passing remark.

"I should think," said she, in a tone at once melodious and acerbic, "that one who professes to admire the barbarities of the *trecento* might have a word of kindness for Rossetti and Morris, who, when all is said and done, share your perverse taste for the archaic and the superannuated."

"Don't talk to me about the Pre-Raphaelites. You know I can't stomach them." As often before when his rhetoric had outstripped the bounds of ordinary good breeding, Niles made a little grimace of apology towards me.

Zaide was not so lightly put off. "Oh, if the modern painters could find a way to have worms eat through their frames, and for half the paint to flake from their canvases, you would find them quite congenial. It's their being alive in *your* century that you resent. You critics are all the same—all mean-spirited, grudging assassins!"

"Well," he said, with an approving smile (for Niles relished his mother's insults), "an ounce of criticism is worth a pound of Dante Gabriel Rossetti."

"Seriously, my boy, they *do* have that same ethereal, wispy idealism one so much admires in, say, Botticelli."

Niles threw up his hands. "Botticelli! Oh, Mother, have done! Idealism? Botticelli, an idealist? Or for that matter, that crew in Chelsea? They are about as *spiritual*, the lot of them, as the seraglio of the Sultan of Turkey! You have been to the Uffizi; you have seen his Venus, that serpent-goddess of the Philistines; you've seen his Graces, with their twining fingers, their draperies of billowing gauze, their transparent sensuality. You call that idealism? Mother, for shame!"

"And Raphael?" I asked, somewhat at hazard, for my motive was less to draw out Niles on this subject than to divert him from his anger. "Do you include him in your condemnation?"

"You've put your finger on the very spot, Clara, where my judgment sprouts horns and impales me. I can never decide about that courtly gentleman. Shall I lump him with those other libertines? Or shall I allow him, as Rome did, a place in my Pantheon? I look at the Fornarina, and the choice seems clear; I regard the *School of Athens*, and I am just as certain of his supreme sublimity."

"Sublimity?" Zaide repeated, with calm contempt. "Pish! A limp, silly piffler, the arch-bore of a hundred galleries—that is Raphael."

I again endeavored to add oil to these troubled waters. "Except for engravings, I know only such paintings as I've seen on my three visits (two of them with you) to the National Gallery. But I remember from those visits a very beautiful painting by Raphael, a picture of Mary with the Infant Jesus in her arms." I paused, conscious of having introduced an image which might have quite painful associations. The last time I had seen this Madonna and Child it had put me distinctly in mind of Renata.

But Niles passed over my remark as if it had been as harmless (and uninteresting) as a cage of rabbits in a menagerie of exotic carnivores. "I know the painting, and the ascription to Raphael is doubtful. Still, the type is his, of course, and I must allow that it is beautiful, or pretty, anyhow. There *is* an ideal element, but it is so entangled with the carnal. Never more so, I think, than in the case of his Madonnas. It is the same dilemma, always."

"If you are in that much indecision, I shall go on liking him with a good conscience. If a painting is beautiful—or even, as you say, 'pretty'—I ask no more."

"And I shall like Raphael with a freer conscience, too, knowing, dear coz, that he is a favorite of yours."

"And will you like Botticelli any better," Zaide asked, "knowing that he is a favorite of *mine*?"

"On the contrary, Mother; whenever you express a taste for

a painter whom I like as well, I begin to question *my* liking. By that means you have taught me to despise Greuze, Boucher, and whole hecatombs of French pastry-chefs. You're a dear old girl, and I adore you, but you might as well be blind, for all the good it does you to look at paintings. With Clara it is another matter. Her eye is still fresh, and her taste . . . redeemable."

"If you mean to educate her into such another connoisseur as yourself, then I would rather be deaf than blind. To have both of you carrying on like this would be as bad as living with Methodists! Beware, Clara. Don't let him make an enthusiast of you. Learn from him what you can, but then conceal that knowledge, lest you be accounted a bluestocking. It is almost as bad as losing one's reputation, as I know to my cost."

"I can't believe you are serious, Aunt."

"In fact, I am. For a young lady to become known as an intellectual is as much as she is worth. She may as well forfeit at once any hope of marriage."

"Then I may safely let myself be educated to the hilt, for I have no intention of marrying."

"*Stai attenta*, my dear! *Stai attenta!*"

"Or," Niles translated, "as our whilom Chancellor of the Exchequer wrote in one of his popular romances: 'What we anticipate seldom occurs; what we least expect generally happens.'"

CHAPTER TWENTY

Niles Proposes

As though to confirm Mr. Disraeli's epigram, Niles, on the day before we were to leave Corme Hall, proposed for my hand.

"The calendar says it is the equinox," he announced cheerfully at breakfast, "and verily one can believe it is, for look what has lit upon the jam pot—a ray of sunshine! What say you, cousin, to a

walk upon the fells? From our doorstep, at a very little expense
of walking, we can enjoy a splendid view of Helvellyn. Its pic-
turesqueness is vouchsafed by Gilpin himself, and if his authority
is not enough, my mother will add her own testimonial, for she
saw it last July, and I dare say it has not changed much in the
meantime."

"In July," Zaide remarked, "the path was dry."

"Foreseeing that objection, I was up betimes, with the first
glimmering of the dawn, and I can assure my cousin that the path
was as dry as, well, not a bone, may be, but dry as toast." Popping
a great wedge of the same into his mouth. "Allowing for a little
butter."

"The weather may change, and then what will you do?"

"I shall take along an umbrella and a good stout mackintosh.
But it won't rain. The gardener is absolute on that point."

"Go then—admire your mountain. Clara has had precious little
benefit of our famous scenery. If she wishes, I shan't stand in her
way. Though, mind you, I won't let you drag *me* along."

"Well, Clara? It rests with you."

"I should love to walk anywhere at all, with or without
scenery. But it is not up to me. I must ask my aunt."

Straightaway I betook myself to her bedroom, to which,
though our departure was set for the morrow, Lydia was still con-
fined. I had little hope of obtaining her consent. An unchaperoned
excursion across the empty moorlands was just the sort of morsel
her Goddess Propriety loved to devour, and on that divinity's
altar, I was certain, my wishes would be sacrificed like so many
Cumberland lambs. Fortune, however, was at odds with Propriety
that day and helped me have my way. My aunt had taken her
morning dose of laudanum some minutes before I came into her
room. If I had asked leave to run away with the Gypsies, she
would have given it, provided only that I did not ruffle the faerie
tissues of her revery. With half-closed eyes she bade me to "do as
I liked," and, when I returned to Niles, I had already changed into
a stouter pair of shoes and a cape of black corded silk. Niles
handed me my muff, Zaide tied the strings of my bonnet about
my chin, and we set off (Heyday!) for the view of Helvellyn.

The sky was a brilliant blue, the grass all bursting with the opulence of the spring, for Corme Hall was situated on the higher fells, which had not yet been grazed. Here and there, tufts of heather and matted fern accented the pastures with broad swaths of russet and brown, and as we climbed, these colors predominated over the hopeful green below. Just so, as we grow older, do the memories of our yesteryears return in ever-greater multitudes, while that future which we populate with our daydreams so abundantly in youth scarcely figures in our thoughts at all.

Reader, forgive the vagaries of an old woman! I shall proceed with my story. I shall even dispense with all the fragrant particulars of that March day, though it be a duty as painful as emptying one's home of a lifetime's legacy of sachets and pomanders. How precious it is, though—spring and sunlight and the wasted, golden hours of our youth!

My chief sensation in that particular golden hour, however, was not of the loveliness heaped all about me, but of a great heaviness in my legs, and a heaving of my lungs, and a desperate weariness in general. "A very little expense of walking," indeed! thought I, as I sank to the stone bench that looked out across a wide valley to the gentle grandeur of Helvellyn.

While I recovered my breath and tried to do justice to the view, Niles paced back and forth restlessly between the bench and a cairn of immense stones. His eyes, never more nervous, refused to be fixed on anything, least of all on the vista that had been our purpose, as I thought, in coming here. He looked at me, and looked away impatiently, and wiped at his forehead with a handkerchief, and brushed aside a cluster of curls made curlier by the dampness of his exertions, and sighed, and kicked at stones, and generally showed himself to be in a fret. At last I had to ask him what was wrong.

"Wrong?" he asked, in the falsest tone imaginable. "Have I not solemnly declared that I want nothing more of my life than that spring should come again? And here it is, and here *we* are. So nothing can be wrong, can it?"

What was I to suppose from this but that he was angry with me? Though why, I could not think. Then his mood changed round, quick as the shuttle of a Jacquard loom, and he seemed all melting and melancholy.

"I shall tell you what is wrong, Clara. It is wrong that you are going back to London, and it is still more wrong that I should so wish to have you stay on in this gloomy wreck of a house to keep company with a gloomy wreck of a man."

"You shall be visiting us in London as before," I protested. "You have promised to."

"As before, yes."

"If you are gloomy, Niles, Corme Hall may be blamed for that, and the dreariness of winter." I hesitated, before adding: "And your bereavement. That too must be a source of deep unhappiness. But as to your being, on these grounds, a wreck, I say—Humbug! I am ashamed to hear you speak so! *I* should not have to tell you how fortunate you are, how very much you have to be thankful for. Youth, health, rank, the expectation of great wealth, and a mind formed—as I had thought—so as to make the best of all these great advantages."

"All that, I will grant you; and yet—if you could see within my heart, Clara. . . ." His eyes met mine with an unusual steadiness, as though he meant to give me an opportunity to peer into that dark region; but all I descried therein was the shadowy sense of some pain so long hidden from the light that, like some poor nocturnal beast startled from its lair by the approach of torches, the least glint of recognition would make it flinch and flee to deeper darknesses within.

At last I turned away. "Well," said I, with some small bitterness of my own, "I cannot."

"Then let me tell you what is there."

"If you will."

"I must. I have kept it pent up long enough—too long. Clara, I love you."

He awaited my response. I should have risen from the bench and demanded that we return at once to Corme Hall. Either I lacked that presence of mind or (which I think likelier) I wanted to know all he would say. By my silence I invited whatever would follow from his declaration.

"I have loved you since the June evening when I saw you again at Blackthorne—and, may be, before that. It seems I have loved you since my soul was formed. And yet, I will be honest: it is no fiery passion either. My ardors are not a Romeo's nor an Othello's.

I stand here utterly adoring you, but I would not, for all that, so much as steal a kiss from your lovely, frowning lips; no, nor disarrange one strand of that ravishing black hair. I might paint it, though, if you would allow me; I might do that."

"Why are you saying this?"

"Because I love you, Clara, and lovers eventually *must* speak. I would not, believe me, have breathed a word of this while Renata was alive. I even hoped that I might keep silence till I did not have to perjure my soul by the hypocrisy of draping my body in mourning."

"Niles! Think what you are saying!"

"I have thought it an hundred times over. I have lain awake night after night, thinking what I would say when the time came finally that I would say it. I love you, Clara. I have never loved my wife. Oh, there were times I felt a kind of affection for her, a little *liking*. That came and went. But there was no *bond* between us. As there is already, without our even willing it, between the two of us."

"There was the bond of matrimony!"

"The bondage, rather. Would you know how I came to marry her? What part my own preference played? My father and hers were fellow-officers in the army of Naples. They shared a friendship of the fanatic kind that loves to swear vows and mix blood; and not content with scarring their own forearms, they decided to attack *our* flesh while we were yet unborn. My father, you may know, was dead at the hour of my birth, while Renata's father had still to marry. And yet—we were already betrothed!"

"Surely, though, you were both free to refuse. In the eyes of your families, there may have seemed an obligation, but not before the eyes of God."

"Perhaps, but I was not instructed in such distinctions in my early years. I only knew that if I did not marry Renata, she would end her days in a convent, and I, like as not, would be the victim of an assassin's knife. Family honor is an important consideration in the south of Italy. But let me not paint myself in too noble colors: there was a dowry, too. Renata's father, when he did marry, married well. Oh, I had every possible reason to marry her, except the only one that matters. I did not love her. To do Renata justice, she was not such a fool as to love me either."

"At first, perhaps. But surely, as you came to know each other . . . ?"

"You think a daily proximity blossoms naturally into love?" A smile disarmingly sweet touched his lips and made them for a moment fuller. "I'm glad *you're* of that opinion. But in fact, it just as often happens that more knowledge only leads to deeper misery."

I started, quite as though he had accused me directly of secreting such knowledge from him. Had he known of that ledger-book? Did he suspect I had it? Often during my stay at Corme Hall, I had been tempted anew to turn over Renata's journal to Niles, but now my worst suspicions were hardened to conviction by all that Niles had said. I was determined never to show him those pages, certain they would prove to be a record of her shame.

"You are repelled at this glimpse into my heart," Niles said, misinterpreting my reaction.

"No. I honestly do not know what I feel, except surprise."

"You do not blame me for Renata's death?"

"Do you blame yourself?"

"Yes. Because I have been grateful for my liberty."

"Truly, it was got at a terrible price. But if you never wished, beforehand, that such a price be paid. . . ."

"Yes, that must be my excuse. All the same, I feel no less guilty than if I *had* willed her death. I was not with her on the night she died."

"I know. Your mother told me."

"What she told you was in part a fiction. I mean, all that night I was away from Corme Hall altogether, not simply in a room nearby. I was carousing with the local gentry at the very hour of Renata's death, roasting my feet at a fire, and toasting the New Year in steaming pints of negus. What do you say to that?"

"Only that you spent the evening like a majority of your countrymen, and that I think you are being ridiculous. You have been farther away from Corme Hall than to a neighbor, and for a longer time than one night. Are you prepared to feel guilty for every visit you have made to London?"

"If I had not made those visits, Clara, I think I should have died."

I labored on in his exoneration, regardless of a blush. "Did anything in Renata's behavior make you think she might begin her sleepwalking again?"

"No. But then there never was any warning when she might do that. In any case, that is not at the root of my doubts. I know I could not have been by her perpetually. Has it never occurred to you, though, that Renata may have been quite conscious what she was about? That she did not unbolt the door and leave the house in a state of trance, but perfectly wide-awake, and consenting to the deed? That she was, forgive me for suggesting this —that she was a suicide?"

"No. No, I have never thought that."

"I have, Clara."

For a time we pursued our own thoughts in silence. Mine, naturally, reverted once again to my possession of that ledger-book. If Renata had so much as mentioned suicide. . . . Here was still another reason for keeping the existence of that document a secret.

"Isn't it time," I suggested, "we began to set back? We can still converse on the way, as it is all downhill."

Niles smiled, and not constrainedly, but with genuine good humor. "Back to the tomb, is it? Back to the smoke-house? I would rather we took up a wholly new life as vagabonds here among the Lakes. I could fancy you burnt quite nut-brown, like old Dotty Wordsworth."

"And I think *you* would do very handsomely got up like the old leech-picker in 'Resolution and Independence.' We would make a brave couple then!"

"I would be willing. *They* did, you know—William and Dorothy. I'll wager they've stood on this very spot of ground on a spring day very like to this. They did go all about England, you know, as freely as the wind."

"England was different in their time. People were more free in general."

"People are free the minute they decide to be, Clara."

"However one accounts for it, they set a fine example—I grant you that."

"Clara, let us follow it. Let us be such another pair."

I shook my head sadly. "One cannot choose to be brother and sister. That gift is in God's giving."

"Clara, we can! In every essential way, we can! Do you know his great poem on Tintern Abbey? There is a passage that has always stuck in my mind, though I have made no effort to fix it there. Now it seems almost a prophecy. Can I say those lines?"

"I cannot imagine taking offense at Wordsworth."

" 'Oh! yet a little while,' " he recited, though there was nothing in his delivery of a lesson learned by rote. Rather the poetry seemed to flow from his heart, which seemed, now, no shadowed place at all, but a very meadow flooded with the noonday light.

> *"Oh! yet a little while*
> *May I behold in thee what I was once,*
> *My dear, dear Sister! and this prayer I make,*
> *Knowing that Nature never did betray*
> *The heart that loved her; 'tis her privilege,*
> *Through all the years of this our life, to lead*
> *From joy to joy . . ."*

He paused, as though the last phrase were too delectable to pass over without special emphasis. " 'To lead from joy to joy,' " he said again, in just the lingering, caressing way I have seen him lift his wineglass in homage to some particularly rare vintage.

> *". . . for she can so inform*
> *The mind that is within us, so impress*
> *With quietness and beauty, and so feed*
> *With lofty thoughts . . .*

" . . . that . . . that. . . ."

" 'That neither evil tongues,' " I prompted.

" 'That neither evil tongues, nor. . . .' No, I have lost the thread. But, please, if you can pick it up, do."

"For a little way, I think." I continued:

> *". . . that neither evil tongues,*
> *Rash judgments, nor the sneers of selfish men,*
> *Nor greetings where no kindness is, nor all*
> *The dreary intercourse of daily life,*
> *Shall e'er prevail against us, or disturb*
> *Our cheerful faith, that all which we behold*
> *Is full of blessings."*

As I came to an end, Niles knelt before me. He took my hand between his own, nor did I withdraw it. I had no will, no wish, no mind of my own, but all of me was transmuted into poetry. I do not blame Wordsworth, nor can I excuse myself.

"Clara! Dearest, loveliest, mildest, brightest, best Clara! We *must* be married: nothing is so certain as that. Clara, I see your consent in your eyes. Let me hear it on your tongue!"

Though touched by his eloquence, I retained enough good sense to be mute.

"Clara, just think how splendid it all could be. The world is simply spread before us like a feast. In all its beauty! In all its richness! In all its charm and wit and excellence!"

"Niles, I cannot."

"There is no *reason* you cannot. You can! If you want to, you can. *Do* you want to?"

"I am in such confusion, Niles, I honestly don't know. So much has happened, so much has been said. I must consider."

"Grant me this, then: that if you won't say yes, at least you won't say no. Flatter me that my offer is worth a week's consideration."

"It is worth much more than that," I protested.

"A week, a month, a year, as long as ever you like."

"I didn't mean 'more' in that sense, Niles. I meant—"

"I knew what you meant, and I took a mean advantage. You must be careful, for I can be a shrewd lawyer in my own interest. But I was serious as well. If you are still uncertain in a week, I would rather remain in a blissful suspense than force the balance. We cannot be wed, in any case, until I am out of mourning. I cannot promise, of course, that I will not mention the matter from time to time."

"But please," I begged, "do not refer to it again today. I feel . . . I can't say what I feel. Only that I would be grateful if we could return to the house."

He bowed in his gravest manner, which even so was tinged with a kind of mockery. He could not help it, and he did not intend it. It was built, I think, into his bones.

Offering me his arm, without another word, Niles led me back to Corme Hall.

CHAPTER TWENTY-ONE

Irresolution

As soon as we were back at Worcester Terrace, I told my aunt Jerningham of Niles' proposal, not omitting what he had said concerning his marriage with Renata.

Lydia was whole-heartedly in favor of my accepting him. "Though, of course," she added, "this has been quite shockingly premature. But then you say he is prepared to wait for the full term of his mourning to expire before posting banns. If he has been somewhat over-hasty, I can find it in my heart to forgive him. He could see that a young lady as charming as my little Princess of Bayswater would soon have other suitors."

"Aunt, I wish you would forget that old name. You shall some day use it when we can be overheard, and we shall both be mortified."

"Whatever you say, my dear. After all, 'Countess' is nearly as good."

"Aunt! Please. I have not accepted Niles. For you to speak as though it were quite settled is *most* disconcerting."

"Quite right, Clara. You must make up your mind yourself. Far be it from me to urge you against your own considered judgment. You have my permission. Beyond that, I have no interest in the matter, and shall not mention it again."

Though she was as good as her word, it was clear that she regarded my betrothal as wanting only a formal announcement to be official. Her attitude towards Niles, which had never been less than cordial, warmed to a family feeling, and she often trusted me alone with him in the drawing room or in the little walled garden behind the house, such times as he would call at Worcester Terrace.

This, however, he did neither more nor less frequently than before. Niles never took advantage of our moments alone to further his siege, nor did he suggest that a time be set for my decision. In all he did and all he said he was congenial, blithe, and withal so easy-mannered and affectionate that we might really have been, as he had wished, brother and sister.

In one respect only did he evince any immoderation of passion or appetite, and that was for the things of the mind. I have known three or four gentlemen in society who, though lacking vanity for themselves, took evident and exorbitant pleasure in bedizening their wives in whatever gauds and baubles the modes of Paris dictated. Niles seemed to find a similar, reflected glory in the process of my education. He lent books to me and questioned me about them. He took me to galleries and made me study the pictures there as though they were so many lessons in a cabalistic science of mass, line, proportion, and (the favorite of all his catch-words) emphasis. It was never enough, with Niles, to praise a likeness, or to say that a thing was interesting; he would want to analyze the likeness down to its component atoms and discuss whatever was of interest till it had become quite dull. Yet, strangely, despite that we talked so many fine things to death, the world at large began to seem more various and livelier. Odd little facts that I had had to learn at my aunt's knee now took on a significance I had never believed them capable of possessing. Once, for instance, when my cousin had taken me to the Tower of London to see its Norman chapel, my fancy leap-frogged one whole millennium back to the very dawn of British history. I remember staring down into the dry moat that rings the outer walls and thinking how its shape had first been marked out by Julius Caesar; thinking this with such vividness that I would not at all have been surprised to find that gentleman's sandal or his rent toga beside one of the tulip beds planted there. Until that moment, I had never really believed in Julius Caesar, other than as one of Shakespeare's less memorable characters, and but for Niles' tutelage, such he would always have remained. That is a single example; I could give, may be, a thousand more, and the sum of them all would be that Niles touched the wand of his knowledge to the old pumpkin of the everyday world and it became a golden coach; he touched it to the dithering mice of an hundred ill-assorted books and they became a stately cavalcade. And when he touched his wand to me? I enjoyed it, of course. Is there a woman alive who has not fancied herself, some time or other, as another Cinderella?

Thus equipped, and thus caparisoned, and companioned everywhere by Niles, the Princess of Bayswater enjoyed a blooming spring, a regal summer, and an autumn overbrimming with tickets to concerts and plays, with never a thought of the hands of the clock.

The highest point of this range of pleasures was a fortnight spent at Brighton in August of that year. My aunt had never wholly recovered from the illness that had detained us at Corme Hall, and her physician had urged the air of Brighton as being the best medicine for her weakened lungs and qualmy digestion. Lydia so far entered into the spirit of her cure that she adventured out into the ocean water. Being Lydia and worshipping Propriety, she did not, of course, expose herself to the common gaze (as, it was rumored, some ladies at Margate had lately done) but entered the water from the privacy of a bathing-machine.

It was farther than I dared go. For me it was enough to regard the ocean from the esplanade, to smell its fragrance on the pier, and taste it, diluted, from an oyster shell; but most of all I loved to hear it sucking at the shingle, lapping on the shore. My hotel room commanded a view of the sea, and there I would sit, through many quiet hours when I was supposed to be asleep, and listen, and be lulled.

One evening towards the end of our holiday, taking the air with my cousin on the terrace of our hotel, I very nearly did consent to be engaged, and not for any reason that he gave (for, as I say, Niles never urged), but in almost the same spirit in which one might close one's eyes the more luxuriously to enjoy the soothings of the night-breeze. Very nearly; but I did not. The moment slipped away from me. Niles said good-night, and I retired to the seat beside my window and the gentle, riddling murmur of the sea.

Even when I was not there to listen, the waves wore away the hours of the night, and the nights lengthened, and the year, which had seemed to stretch before me quite without end, now stretched behind me as vastly. The period of Niles' mourning was very nearly expired, and still I had not given him an answer, being still undecided what answer to give.

CHAPTER TWENTY-TWO
A Visit from Mr. Mainwaring

TWICE SINCE WE HAD MET HIM at Blackthorne, Godfrey Mainwaring had paid visits to Worcester Terrace. Following the
announcement of my uncle's death, my aunt had received a black-
edged letter of condolence from that gentleman, to which she had
replied with a card returning thanks for his kind sympathy. Shortly
after this, he appeared at our door, looking much altered from the
young man of fashion we had been acquainted with. His Dundrearies were trimmed down to a mere whisper, and there was a new
stiffness to his collars and his manners that contrasted vividly with
my recollection of a "heavy swell." There seemed an almost
Quakerish air about him now, an impression heightened by the
many times we lapsed into silence on that first visit, and indeed, on
the second, which came hard upon the anniversary of the first, just
after our return from Corme Hall.

Some element of awkwardness was inseparable from what we
had to speak of on that second visit: the tragic circumstances of
the young Contessa's death and, on Mr. Mainwaring's side, his
appointment as an officer to, and his work with, the Magdalen
Mission Society, a very worthy charity devoted to the rescue of
degraded women in Lambeth and Southwark. He seemed filled
with a zeal for his new calling, which one could not help but
admire, despite that one could not express as inquiring an interest
as if his work had been among foundlings or pensioners. My aunt
was visibly relieved, when, after the bare quarter-hour that courtesy
demanded, Mr. Mainwaring took up his hat and his walking-stick
and brought his visit to an end.

Then, in the week before Christmas of 1864, on the afternoon
of a "London particular" so dense you would have supposed our
back windows looked out across the Styx, Godfrey Mainwaring
called for a third time at Worcester Terrace. I was sitting by
myself in the drawing room, bent over my embroidery frame and

working with that depleted energy which a week of sunless days
will inspire, when the bell sounded. A moment later the serving-
girl brought in Mr. Mainwaring's card, across the top of which
was scrawled the brief message *P. P. C.* Before I could instruct
the girl to tell our visitor that my aunt could not receive him, he
had himself entered the room. He stopped short, realizing that we
were alone, and blushed deeply; a blush that seemed all the more
vivid from his having shorn off the last trace of his whiskers.

"Miss Reeve—pray, forgive me! I would not have intruded upon
your privacy but that I was given to understand I would find Mrs.
Jerningham at home."

I remained seated—what else could I?—and extended my hand,
which he accepted—what else could he?—with some little pretense
of reluctance, as if repeating his apology in dumb-show.

"Please be seated, Mr. Mainwaring. My aunt has retired with
one of her megrims, which always seem to afflict her most cruelly
in foggy weather like this. Dorothy must not have known, and I
cannot find it in my heart to blame her, since by her mistake we
are allowed to talk. Really, do sit down. My aunt shall see your
card, and will be concerned to know that you're making plans
pour prendre congé. You must stop long enough, at least, to tell
me where you are going and how long you mean to be gone."

"Back to Italy, and for several months. As long, really, as the
Mission Society can spare me. I have been invited to work at
Pompeii under the director of the new excavations, Fiorelli. For
an amateur like myself, it is an unheard-of honor. Fiorelli has transformed archaeology from being a mere rapacious scramble for
treasure and trophies into a science. The knowledge that man can
wring from a few bones and a broken pot! From the dust itself, I
dare say!"

"Somehow, Mr. Mainwaring, while I envy you your trip, I
can't quite share your excitement for broken pots. Will Pompeii
really be no more exciting than *that*? I fancied, from reading Lord
Lytton's book—"

"A romance, all a romance! Not an ounce of science in it; not
a centigram!"

"Is a centigram much or little?"

"Do you know, Miss Reeve, I can't remember. A kilogram is

about two pounds English weight. But centigrams? I can't tell you. As soon as I cross the Channel, it will all come back. But here I am, riding my hobby-horse a mile a minute, and your poor aunt is suffering. I am really very sorry to hear you say so. Please convey my wishes to her for her better health."

I said I would, and Mr. Mainwaring fell to studying the enamel case of his watch, which, with its heavy chain and pendant seals, remained the one extravagant "touch" in his new darker and more staid style. I must have shown rather too intent an interest in this article myself, for Mr. Mainwaring slipped it from its chain and offered it me for a closer inspection.

A lady in a loose, blue gown held an infant in her arms: more than this I was too embarrassed to note.

"It is Italian, of course," Mr. Mainwaring said, when I gave him back his watch. "Mrs. Lacey worries that it represents the first step down the path to Rome. Next, she fears, it will be graven images, incense and candles, and finally a tonsure."

"And are you never tempted? My cousin Niles tells me that he has been much affected by the beauty of their churches and their rituals. He says that our Protestant services are like London fog compared to the sunshine of the Italian mass."

"The Italian vineyards are beautiful, too, but I'm not liable on that account to revert to the worship of Bacchus. No, you shall never see me go the way of Newman and Manning and their cohorts. My conscience, both as a Protestant and as an archaeologist, would prevent that."

"How, as an archaeologist?"

"Rome wasn't built in a day; nor was the Papacy. As the first began to fall to pieces, the other began to rise—using those same pieces as its building blocks. As an archaeologist, the literal truth of that is evident in half the churches of Rome. As a Protestant, the figurative truth is just as clear. In the worship of the saints and their relics, in the veneration of the 'Queen of Heaven,' and in an hundred other details, the imprint of pagan practices is discoverable. It can be, as your cousin says, quite charming and colorful. Awesome, even. But cannot the same be said for the surviving shrines of paganism? There is a temple not far from Pompeii, built by expatriate Greeks seven centuries before the birth of Christ and

dedicated to Neptune. One cannot look at it without a profound
sense of its majesty, without wondering at the miracle of its enduring through so great a span of time. But is one tempted, on that
account, to offer a sacrifice to Neptune?"

"Dear me, I didn't mean to suggest—"

"Of course not, Miss Reeve. Forgive me. I have been too
vehement. It is a matter upon which Mrs. Lacey and I have had
some disagreements. My sore point, as you might say."

In the course of this diatribe, my visitor's manner had become
much easier. His hat and walking-stick were set to one side; his
vertebrae had loosened perceptibly; even his collars seemed less
stiff. Such were the reasons I gave myself then (though now I
wonder whether my impulse may not have sprung from some
deeper source) for asking Mr. Mainwaring if I might speak to him
in strict confidence, in his capacity as a minister of the Gospel. In
the history of any friendship there must come such a moment,
when one or the other party exceeds the bounds of polite discussion,
and who can "reason" his way to such an impulse? It is enough
to say that, in a metaphorical way, I stretched out my hand and
that Mr. Mainwaring, most cordially, clasped it firmly in his own.

Considering the many nights I had lain awake, mesmerized by
my dilemma as by the spinning of a top, I astonished myself at
how succinctly I was able to state my case, and ask my question.
I told of Geoffrey Jerningham's unwelcome courtship, of the
promise I had made to my uncle, and of the second courtship and
my year-long waverings and vacillations.

Mr. Mainwaring considered the little enamelled lady on his
watch-case for a long while; then, just as intently, he regarded me.
"My dear Miss Reeve—with the best will in the world, what can I
say? You seem to understand the elements of the situation clearly
—all, it would seem, except what is in your own heart."

"But what of the promise I made to my uncle?"

"By your own account, that promise was obtained by coercion."

"And yet it was made."

"If it would be any comfort, I could show you a score of cita-
tions from the most potent authorities, all to the same effect—that
an oath sworn under duress is not binding. If that is all that prevents you from accepting Count Visconti's offer, do not trouble
yourself more."

"Oh, I'm afraid I haven't made myself clear at all. It's just the other way. You see, what I promised my uncle, the exact *wording* of my promise, was that I would marry no one *but* my cousin. At the time, I thought I had committed myself to perpetual spinster-hood, for I had no notion then of marrying any *other* cousin than Geoffrey. But Niles is a cousin equally with Geoffrey. Rather more nearly, in fact."

"Miss Reeve, you amaze me. If I did not know better, I would think you had been brought up in a college of Jesuits."

"I gather, then, that you think my promise should have no weight, one way or the other."

"Absolutely none at all."

"Thank you. You say what I've often thought myself, and yet over the past year, with no one to confide in—for I could never bring myself to tell my aunt that all her efforts had been in vain, and that I'd finally given in to Mr. Jerningham's will at the last—that scruple seemed to swell and swell, until it had displaced every other consideration."

Mr. Mainwaring smiled. "You put me in mind of the story of the princess and the pea. I trust you'll be able to sleep easier, now the pea has been removed?"

"As you say, it is a matter now of knowing my own heart. That ought to be the one subject on which any person would have expert knowledge."

Though I did not complete my meaning, Mr. Mainwaring apprehended it readily enough, and he spoke to me, in a tone of quiet sympathy, as though I had stated in so many words that I did *not* know my own heart, that, in fact, my feelings were in a perfect ebullition of contradiction and uncertainty.

"If it is any comfort, Miss Reeve, I can assure you that from the vantage of thirty-one years it is no easier. One's heart can be as indecipherable as Hebrew and as opaque as basalt."

"But isn't that a reason in itself for refusing Niles? I mean, the fact that I have any hesitation at all."

"I think it does you credit. The kind of love that takes one look and then a headlong leap. . . ." He trailed off oddly, consulted the lady on his watch once again, and resumed, not quite sequentially. "*That* is the man's part. Niles has acted with admirable decisive-ness. He deserves congratulations."

I could not help but think this was meant sarcastically, and that it concealed a reproach for the hastiness with which Niles' offer had followed his bereavement. Poor Mr. Mainwaring! He had intended no such slight, yet for all our great effort to be confidential, there was no way he could speak what then was on his mind. Nor can I allow myself, in this instance, the liberty of interpreting his secret thoughts to my readers, for they were such as can never be paraphrased.

In order, partly, to relieve this moment's awkwardness, I brought forwards the other scruple that had been troubling me: the matter of my possessing Renata's ledger-book. No sooner had I begun this tale than I regretted my lack of reticence. Naturally, as I could make no mention of my doubts regarding Renata, Mr. Mainwaring was unequivocal in recommending that I turn over the volume to her widower.

"It is strange, though," he went on, in a reflective tone. "Let me return you confidence for confidence. The young Contessa tried to make me accept that same journal, during that same visit, and I had some difficulty refusing her. She was quite intemperate in her insistence. I suppose the fact that I could speak, however poorly, her own language made me the first choice as audience. It is impossible not to be curious as to what she wrote in that book, but equally impossible, I'm afraid, to gratify that curiosity."

"Even if I could read Italian, I had no thought of so much as opening the book. But I have thought the best course might be to burn it. If it should contain anything that would be a wound to her husband's feelings, I would always blame myself for having been the source of his hurt."

"Yes. I see your difficulty. I'm afraid this is a scruple I cannot so easily relieve you of. Yes, it's very awkward. And that now he should have proposed for *your* hand. . . . My own conviction is that when the choice is between prudence and one's principles, one should prefer the latter. And it is a very ancient and well-established principle that honesty is the best policy. So I would say—give the book to him. Yet a more careful or worldly adviser might well counsel you to the opposite course. In fact, fifteen minutes from now I might counsel the opposite course myself."

However, he did not. Our conversation moved on to matters

of a more general interest, and Mr. Mainwaring reverted to what I had come to think of as his "missionary" manner. He denounced the weather, asked more particularly after my aunt's health, and joined with me in praising the Metropolitan Railway, which still, a year after its opening, possessed the gloss of novelty. At last, with a promise that he would write to tell me of his excavations at Pompeii, he took his leave.

That night, I decided not to marry Niles. The reasons that buttressed this decision were as indefinite as the forms that loomed outside my bedroom window, but I was as certain of their substantiality as I was that the various spectres of that fog would resolve, with the morrow's sunlight, into trees and gables and chimney-pots. Chief among those reasons, though then the most obscure, had been the example of Mr. Godfrey Mainwaring: his earnestness, his diffidence, his stiff collars and stiff manners, his strength.

I had been nine months arriving at my decision; it took me almost as many days to write my letter of refusal. When at last it was finished, and blotted, when it had survived three careful readings and been tucked away into an envelope, and that envelope addressed and sealed with wax and stamped and then tucked inside my beaver muff so that I should not neglect to post it at my first opportunity, Niles himself arrived at Worcester Terrace, in a state of nearly hysteric excitement, to announce that my great-uncle Douglas, fifth Baron Rhodes, was dead.

CHAPTER TWENTY-THREE
The Reading of the Will

THE ANNOUNCEMENT OF LORD RHODES' DEATH, the invitation to his funeral, and an urgent letter from his solicitors requesting my presence at their offices in the Old Buildings of Lincoln's Inn, together with sundry other letters of less import, were discovered, unopened, under my aunt's pillow. Lydia was so thoroughly under

the influence of her medicine that there could be no thought of
rousing her to accompany me to the offices of Sharples and Hautboy; it was just as unthinkable, therefore, that I should go there.

"But you must, Clara! Mr. Hautboy refuses to proceed with
the reading of the will until you are present. My poor mother is
in such a state of pique and impatience that she will very shortly
begin to chew off her leg in sheer aggravation."

"I'm sorry to be a cause of her upset, but what am I to do?
I cannot set off with you in a carriage to the other end of London,
unchaperoned!"

"Oh, if that is all!" He reached into his hat, like a conjuror, and
flicked out a silk scarf.

Within ten minutes, we were rattling along Bayswater Road at
a furious clip, in that same borrowed brougham in which Niles
had ridden in my uncle Jerningham's funeral procession. There
were three of us—Niles and myself and our cook, Mrs. Minchin.
That good woman was wrapped in my aunt's second-best mantelet,
with her face and bonnet both veiled in such abundance that she
must have had very little benefit of the scenery, which was, itself,
lurking behind its own veils of fog.

When not jolted into silence by the carriage's pell-mell progress, Niles gave me an account of the manner of his uncle's death,
which, briefly was this: for quite two decades Lord Rhodes had
been resisting improvements in the illumination of Blackthorne.
He maintained that the only sources of light not positively injurious
to the human eye were the sun itself and good beeswax. In any
case, so far from any city, gas was out of the question. For a long
time, however, with an instinct for good management commendable
in any housekeeper, Mrs. Lacey had been urging the use of camphine
lamps. At last Lord Rhodes had yielded to her persuasions and a
new brightness irradiated the dusky rooms and murky corridors
of Blackthorne. Then, in one of those accidents so characteristic
of the use of camphine, Lord Rhodes was blown up. Whether by
tipping his lamp, or dropping it, or simply by lighting it improperly
shall never be known. The resulting explosion destroyed, as well,
most of the furnishings of the oval drawing room.

By the time this appalling accident had been explained twice
over (for Mrs. Minchin would not be content with less than a
complete review of all the facts), we had reached the great bare

plane-trees and brown wintry gardens of Lincoln's Inn Fields. We rattled under the archway that gave entrance to the buildings of the Court and over the immemorial cobbles to a second archway, where we alighted. Up a half-flight of stairs, a few yards down a stony corridor, a rap upon an imposing carved oak door, and we found ourselves in the presence of a multitude of well-bound books and a great mass of gleaming mahogany in the form of wainscotting, desks and chairs, all of it, including the ranks of books, fashioned on an heroic scale, fit for a race of giants.

Of the people there assembled, only the Contessa Visconti seemed to live up to the demands of the furnishings, her height augmented by several inches of black brim and crepe bows, her slim figure magnified by a gown of terrific proportions and sumptuous trim. Both bonnet and gown were new, and it struck me as ironic (though not really strange) that she should mourn so extravagantly on behalf of a brother for whom she had had so little affection. Mrs. Lacey was also at hand, more modestly attired, and greeted me, as had Zaide, with a cordiality rather chilled from having been kept, as it were, so long on ice. I made a general apology for my tardiness, glossing over my aunt's indisposition and laying the blame on the negligence of a servant.

A short, round, intense gentleman with prominent eyes and prominent teeth and uniformly short, bristling hair, looking like (as Niles said later) a feral species of teddy-bear, appeared and was introduced to me as Lord Rhodes' solicitor, Mr. Sloane Hautboy. Mr. Hautboy concerned himself with seating me neither too close to nor too far from the fire, but he could not prevail upon Mrs. Minchin, who was terrified of him, to budge from the stool next to the door, upon which she had stationed herself.

When we were all settled, and neither too hot nor too cold, Mr. Hautboy took up in one hand a sheaf of papers neatly tied up in green ribbons and in the other a tiny silver scissors. A moment later, the ribbon was lying, curled in serpentine folds, between two of the brass paw-feet that supported the fine dark wood of Mr. Hautboy's desk, and Mr. Hautboy, behind that fine dark wood, was reading the opening paragraphs of the last will and testament of Douglas, fifth Baron Rhodes.

Though I tried to pay strict attention, it was a lengthy document padded out in the highest legal style, a style designed expressly to baffle the layman's interest and comprehension. I might copy it out in full from the transcript I have at hand, but I shall let my readers off with the barest of summaries. First, a great number of mourning rings and mementoes of doubtful worth were distributed among whomever Lord Rhodes had ever had occasion to resent. Then the servants were provided for, which involved a great parcelling out of waistcoats, stickpins, saddles, hounds, and freehold in various cottages and small properties. Then Mrs. Lacey was bequeathed, besides an annuity of some hundred pounds, the five-merk land of Coppleswith, together with "all its towers, fortalices, houses, biggings, yards, orchards, tofts, crofts, mills, woods, fishings, mosses, muir, meadows, commonties, pasturages, coal-heughs, tenants, annexes, connexes, parts, pendicles, and pertinents of the same whatsomever." A very brave catalogue for a very modest little manse at the edge of the village of Rodmell. Her nephew, Mr. Mainwaring, inherited the parsonage at Glynde, his uncle's four favorite horses, Sparkler, Dashaway, Phantom, and Lady Jane, the continuance of the two livings in which he was already established, and a sum of one thousand pounds. Once this portion of the will had been read, the Contessa, having been spared the realization of her worst fears, gave an audible sigh.

Since the bequests seemed to be arranged in an ascending order of magnitude, I expected to hear myself mentioned next. Instead, my cousin Niles was named as heir to the Cumberland estate of Corme Hall, with, once again, all its towers, fortalices, houses, biggings, yards, et cetera. (With a great many grim memories, too, though the writer of the will left these off his inventory.) Niles and his mother were then designated as co-annuitants according to a complex formula of contingencies that would yield, at the utmost, an annual income of three thousand pounds.

Mr. Hautboy paused, cleared his throat significantly, and directed his regard more particularly toward me. "To my grand-niece, Clara Reeve, daughter of the late Robert Reeve, Esq., R.N., and his wife, Dora Elizabeth, only daughter of my elder brother, Howard Spottswood Rhodes, and his sole heir-at-law—"

"No!" Zaide had risen from her chair and stood opposite the solicitor, fierce in her defeat as any Amazon. "Spare yourself, Mr. Hautboy. I shall hear no more."

"Contessa Visconti, I beg you to compose yourself. There is only a little more to read."

"No doubt. *All* need not be inventoried at such tiresome length; it is the little nothings that must be enumerated and drawn out." Even in the fury of her vituperations, her voice was musical, nor did her aged hands tremble as she tore apart a mourning handkerchief of Maltese guipure lace. Though my only real desire was to run from the room, I could not help but admire the style and breadth of her defiance. When she cast these scraps of torn lace at the solicitor, he flinched as though they had the power to harm. "Oh, I am no fool," Zaide went on. "I've seen it coming. When we were obliged to wait the whole morning for my niece to be at hand —excuse me, Clara, I mean no slight to you—I knew then, quite well, what was to be. I did not foresee—who could have?—quite the scale of the insult my brother had prepared. The furthest extent of his malice, that I imagined, was that he might name my son co-parcener with the bastard's grand-daughter."

"Your Ladyship! Please!" Mr. Hautboy entreated.

"Again, Clara, I mean no slight. I speak only of facts. Facts which, as Mr. Hautboy well knows, have been established as such by law. By the very Court of Chancery in which he serves. Be assured, Sir—and be warned, Clara!—that my son and I shall keep you very busy in this case. We shall make *Visconti versus Reeve* a legend in Chancery. You are a fortunate man, Mr. Hautboy, for I should think a contest of such dimensions should make a millionaire of you, if you are not one already."

"Mother, please control yourself," Niles admonished, but without conviction, as though he had no more hope of being heeded by Zaide than if he had addressed himself to the wind or the sea or a boulder bouncing down a mountain slope.

"If your Ladyship will allow me a few words of explanation?"

"It would require more than a few words, Sir, to legitimize what has been proven illegitimate."

"Not as many as you may suppose. What you will no doubt be surprised to learn is that Lord Rhodes' will, far from being the 'insult' or caprice that you imagine, represents an act of reparation of most awesome proportions."

"As to its size, I agree."

"If you will but listen."

With a wave of her hand Zaide resumed her seat.

"Thank you. Now, since her Ladyship has already alluded to the matter, and since a clear understanding of it is necessary not only to an appreciation of Lord Rhodes' justice and generosity, but as well"—raising his hand to circumvent Zaide's protest—"but as well of the folly of attempting to oppose that justice and generosity; since all this is so, I should first apprise Miss Reeve of certain unpleasant events connected with the disinheritance of her grandfather, Howard Spottswood Rhodes. May I ask, Miss Reeve, what is the extent of your knowledge in this matter?"

"Only that his father disapproved of the marriage he made, and of his politics, and that in consequence he was disinherited."

"In a better world, Miss Reeve, I would never need sully your ears with a more particular account than that. In fact, it is a rather difficult undertaking for a peer to disinherit his eldest son. In fact, it is impossible, that son's right of inheritance being indefeasible, provided only that he outlives his father. Even then, the heirs of his body maintain an indefeasible right, both of succession and inheritance. I trust I have made myself clear?"

I smiled.

"Very well then! How came it that he *was* disinherited? And that his younger brother succeeded to his father's title and estates?"

"The answer to his question, Clara," the Contessa interposed, "is as simple as it is unsavory. It was proven, before the highest court of Chancery, that Howard was not Lord Rhodes' son. Lord Eldon himself was judge in the case."

Mr. Hautboy darted a look at Zaide more expressive than an hour of the smooth, concessive flow of his speech; a look that effectually silenced her so long as she remained in his offices; a lightning flash of animosity.

"Your Ladyship is most concise—and in this case, like the court itself, most mistaken. The evidence by which Lady Rhodes was stripped of her reputation and her son stripped of his birthright was forged; the witnesses suborned; and, though it pains me to say so, there is a strong possibility that Lord Eldon himself was aware of some of these irregularities. Douglas has left a document, dictated and signed before witnesses, which can leave very little doubt of the facts. I will not read it now, though I may, by Lord Rhodes' instruction, offer your Ladyship a copy of it. It is a confession, and a very painful one. At the time of his father's death, it seems that Douglas obtained possession of that gentleman's avowal of the wickedness he had accomplished. Douglas was then thirty-six years old, and newly possessed of a great fortune and high title, both of which would be forfeited by making public what he had discovered. He destroyed his father's confession, and in doing so inherited his guilt. Later, he found an identical document in a folio of sporting prints he'd taken down from one of the highest shelves of his library; this was destroyed like the first..

"The fourth Lord Rhodes had had some intuition, it would seem, of how Douglas would deal with his confession. Why, you will ask, if he wished to repent his crime, did he not do so more simply? Well, it is always easier, for one thing, to make amends posthumously. As for drawing up a new will that would incorporate these revelations, he may have feared to, for his solicitor—who was, I'm sad to say, my father—had been deeply involved in the original falsification. He was therefore as little to be trusted as Douglas.

"May be, too, Lord Rhodes meant the successive discoveries to be a kind of torture to his son, a kind of sword of Damocles suspended over him. But such speculation, though interesting itself, lies outside the sphere of law. So, to continue: to the second confession there succeeded a third, discovered in a corked bottle in the rosebeds; and to that third, a fourth; and so on, to the number of fourteen. There may still be more of his confessions to discover, but if so they will be superfluous, for the fourteenth confession was not destroyed. For its preservation we owe thanks to the good woman who discovered it and whose urgings helped waken Lord Rhodes' slumbering conscience. Mrs. Lacey, we are all indebted to you for acting as your employer's good angel and leading him, by little and little, towards this act of restitution."

"Please, Mr. Hautboy. You are much too kind. I did what the situation required, no more."

"As to that," Mr. Hautboy said, "I think it will interest your Ladyship to know that Mrs. Lacey has acted very much against her own, and her nephew's, material interests. Before Lord Rhodes' change of heart, their portion in the inheritance was considerably larger. I am not, of course, at liberty to say *how* much larger, but there can be no question of Mrs. Lacey's selflessness. It was majestical."

"You go too far, Sir. You will make Miss Reeve think that I have some claim on her, and it is just the opposite. All these years that I have enjoyed the distinction of serving Lord Rhodes, she has been obliged to live in . . . well, not poverty, of course, but under the shadow of false accusation. I did not want to say anything on this occasion, but since the question has been raised, and my name mentioned, I feel obliged to inform Miss Reeve—and Mrs. Visconti, too, though it ought not to concern her—that, in all conscience, I cannot continue in my former position at Blackthorne. It is as painful to forsake old duties as to throw away old clothes, but some times it must be done. I have never had a vacation. I intend to have one now. As soon as my services can be spared, I mean to join my nephew in Italy."

I must have made some reply to this, if only to assure Mrs. Lacey that *I* did not require such a sacrifice. But could I, so quickly, have assumed my new authority as mistress of Blackthorne? A day before, the world's opinion, and my own, would have assigned Mrs. Lacey a much higher place on the social scale than it could have allowed to a resident of Worcester Terrace in Bayswater. Yet we all behaved—she, and I, and Mr. Hautboy, and even Niles and Zaide in their way—as though this reversal of so many expectations were no more momentous than my winning a rubber at whist, which they, perforce, had lost.

I say "all," but there was one exception. Poor Mrs. Minchin, at her post by the door, had at last pieced together what had happened, and she began, at first discreetly, but soon very earnestly and audibly, to cry.

"You had better look to your aunt, Clara," Zaide said sourly. "I think she is in need of her medicine."

While Niles explained to his mother who had been present all this while swathed in my aunt Jerningham's veils, I attended to my chaperone's distress. Mrs. Lacey's grand renunciation of her post as housekeeper had affected Mrs. Minchin past all reason, and she felt called on to offer, again and again, her own resignation, nor would any amount of reassurances serve to stop the steady flow of her tears.

"It hurts me, Mum, as you may believe. It rightly breaks my heart to leave you, but there can't be room for such as me in a great place like Blackthorne. Your aunt has told me how it is there, how even the lowest scullion of the kitchen talks like the gentle-folk, and how all the food is French, which is a kind of food I have never cooked. I couldn't do it, Mum. I wasn't born so high."

In soothing her distress, I found myself more and more sharing in it, and I was grateful when first Niles and his mother, and then Mrs. Lacey, took their leave. Once Mrs. Minchin had been calmed, I spent an hour, at Mr. Hautboy's earnest request, signing those papers which most urgently required my signature. It was a steady-ing task, and I was grateful for it, though I might have wished that Mr. Hautboy had been less conscientious in seeking to impress on me the one fact that was certain always to renew my disquiet— the fact, namely, that I had become quite ridiculously rich.

Will you laugh at me, reader, if I should say that the thought of this wealth was a source for me of no little distress? When I conceived of the great gray mass of Blackthorne looming above its acres of parkland, when I thought of its three-hundred-forty-eight windows and its labyrinthine halls, its legions of servants and battalions of tenants, all of them looking to me to carry on in the grand tradition to which they were accustomed, my only impulse was to close my eyes, like a child, and wish the house and all its inhabitants out of existence. Useless! When I opened my eyes, Blackthorne was still there, immense, incontrovertible and mine.

Fa-la! you may say. If she does not feel equal to that weight of wealth, no matter! It is hers, and she must shoulder it. What a silly, over-delicate, and hypocritical creature to complain of her excessive good fortune.

So you might say, and I would, by and large, agree. People speak of the curse of Midas, but, in practice, no one is pitied for having been placed under that curse. Indeed, why should they be? My misfortunes did not come from my being an heiress, but rather from my failure to rise to the occasion and accept, gratefully and gracefully, the bounty that Providence had showered upon me.

CHAPTER TWENTY-FOUR
I Give My Hand

NILES WAS WAITING, slouched against the brougham, when Mrs. Minchin and I emerged from the Old Buildings. Though it still wanted some minutes of two o'clock, the day was grown so dank and dark that the lamps of the quad had already been lighted. Mr. Hautboy, who had seen us down the stairs, gave me a questioning look, as though in doubt whether I welcomed my cousin's presence at this moment or shrank from it. There may have been some doubt in my mind, too, but if so, Niles immediately dispelled it. Taking his hands from his pockets, he swept off his hat and bowed in so grand a manner that I knew he was in good humor, for Niles was never more agreeable than when he was ironic.

"Just as I was to drive away with my mother," he said, addressing himself to Mr. Hautboy, "I bethought myself that by doing so I would be leaving my cousin without any means of returning to her home. So I have taken the liberty of waiting for her."

"You are too scrupulous, Count. I would have summoned a fiacre for Miss Reeve."

"That is how I disposed of my mother. She must get used to them, in any case. This vehicle, after all, was lent me by my uncle. Now I must return it to my cousin, with thanks for the use of it these many times."

"If you'll do me the favor now," I said, "of accompanying me home, you may continue to enjoy the use of it for as long as ever it may be useful. And if you would do me the additional favor of helping me convey to my aunt all that has happened, I shall owe you a greater debt than I can easily pay."

"Ah, Miss Reeve, it would not be the thing to do—involving you in debts now, the instant you've come into a fortune. In any case, I've promised to return to my mother, whom I mean to console, as best I may, with some philosophy. There is, though, a favor I would beg of you, and that is a moment of your time. I have that to say which it were best I said at once and, if it is possible, in privacy. If your companion"—smiling the very sparsest of smiles at Mrs. Minchin—"could allow us a bare five minutes? And if you, Miss Reeve, would care to accompany me on a circuit of the quadrangle?"

I let him take me by the elbow and steer me off along a gravelled path. Mr. Hautboy, with an air of prescient understanding, had bidden us good-evening, and Mrs. Minchin had helped herself into the brougham.

"Well, Clara," Niles said, when we were a little way from the coach, "the world is a wonderful place."

"In the sense that it is full of surprises, I agree. And really, I wish it weren't. I've never liked surprises."

"Even today's, dear coz?"

"Especially today's."

"Do you know—I believe you!"

"I should be very hurt if you did not. I have never coveted any part of this fortune. Never!"

"I know that, and Mother should have known. When we were alone, I gave her such a raking as she will not forget for some time. She is penitent now, and begs to be forgiven for whatever she has said that may have given offense. For so many years she has been convinced that Blackthorne would fall into my lap, and this today has been an acute disappointment. Not that that is any excuse."

"If any excuses are to be made, I think it should be for me to make them."

"Nonsense, Clara." He released his grip on my elbow, for we had reached the farthest corner of the quad. The brougham, with Mrs. Minchin in it, was invisible. "One need never apologize for winning at a lottery. If the losers complain, that is their own disgrace. To complain of ill-luck is as absurd as to be vain because the dice have come up in one's favor. But dear me, I begin to sound like a confirmed gambler."

"Oh, you sound wonderful, Niles. And I don't mean in the sense of your being full of surprises. I mean you sound just like yourself."

"You must allow me one surprise, cousin. I know you have already had too many, but in all conscience I couldn't let another day go by without saying . . . what must be said. Indeed, I came within an ace of bursting in upon your conference with Mr. Hautboy, I was that anxious to have the nastiness of it behind me."

As he spoke, my fingers, unseen within my beaver muff, creased and re-creased the letter I had signed and sealed that morning, the letter of my refusal.

"Clara, you must allow me to withdraw my offer. No—hear me out! The match that I proposed to you last spring was one that might be judged, in a worldly way, as advantageous to you. The same match, today, represents a very poor bargain indeed. You are at this moment one of the wealthiest women in England, and I am one of the poorest and pettiest nobles in a country legendary for the impoverishment of its nobility. As for my title, it is worth no more than five thousand pounds on today's marriage market, and that is a generous estimate. My chief virtue, aside from my being acquainted with a good tailor in London and one or two clever people in society, was that I had expectations, and now I do not. You have heard how Mr. Hautboy addresses me, the way he lingers on that 'Count.' If I were to propose for *his* daughter's hand, you can be sure he would refuse me. He knows what I am worth."

"Niles, don't disgrace yourself! I have been very much remiss in having delayed this long in reaching a decision. But believe me—" I could feel a tear forming, and turned away my gaze. Within my muff, I ripped the letter in two—and the tear dried up within me. "Believe me, Niles, if I have been vacillating, it was not from any consideration of how much or how little you would eventually inherit. It was entirely from my not knowing my own heart."

"You may not, Clara, but I think I do, and that is one more reason I must ask you to release me. Because it is a tender heart, and altogether too apt to mistake pity for love. I have been disappointed in the matter of Blackthorne. What would seem more natural to such a heart than to restore the old balance by marrying me and, as it were, making good my losses? No, Clara—I insist."

"Very well then. I'll let you take back your offer, but on one condition only."

"And that?"

"That you allow me this one chance, first, of accepting it. No, you must hear *me* out now! This morning, before you came, I had reached my decision, and had written to you of it. When you appeared at the door, I was of half a mind to hand you that letter then and there." (This much, at least, was not a fiction!) "But then your news was so startling, and you were so urgent for our setting off."

"Do you have that letter now?" Niles asked, and I could scarcely blame him for seeming suspicious.

"No."

Nor was this entirely a falsehood, for it existed now only as a litter of bits, shredded infinitely small.

"But I can tell you what it said," I added.

And still I had not spoken an outright lie, though I had gone so far towards it that, if Niles had thought to ask, I would have given way and said that I had written my acceptance. But he did not ask: he leapt.

"Clara. My very dearest love. Give me your hand."

As I withdrew my hand from the muff, a scrap of the letter that had been caught under my nail became dislodged and fluttered to the cobblestones. If Niles saw it, he seemed to assign no significance to it. He never did revert, at any later time, to the matter of the letter.

First he placed a kiss upon my finger, and then a ring that he had taken from his waistcoat pocket. His lips were cold; the ring, from having nestled close to his body, was quite warm.

I could not yet look Niles in the face, so I pretended to be fascinated by the ring, turning it this way and that so the facets of the diamonds flared in the rays of the hissing lamp.

"It's quite beautiful," I said, and remembered having said the same words to myself when first I'd seen that ring upon Renata's hand.

Perhaps the same association crossed his mind, for he said that the ring had belonged to his mother.

"But I couldn't wear it if it is *hers*!" I insisted.

"She will think it a very fair exchange for Blackthorne, my dear, reluctant heiress. Lord, yes!"

Silently, I waited for Niles to seal our betrothal with an embrace and a kiss, for I had learned enough of such matters by now to know that this was considered a formal necessity, like a roast goose at Christmas and fireworks on Guy Fawkes' Day. But Niles was no traditionalist, or else he sensed my reluctance. He released my hand, and I returned it to the muff. Taking me again by the elbow, he guided me back towards the brougham.

A year, a week, and a day after Renata's death, we were married at St. John's, Clerkenwell. The Contessa Visconti and my aunt Jerningham signed the register as witnesses. That same afternoon we all four set off, by rail, for the Continent.

BOOK
II

The married state is one of the trial of Principle rather than the fruition of Hope.

—MRS. ELLIS,
The Wives of England,
Their Relative Duties

CHAPTER ONE
Bride and Groom

THE PALAZZO ALARI-UBOLDO stands on the right bank of the Canalazzo—as the Venetians style their principal highway—between the Palazzo Bembo and the Palazzo Manin. Its façade has been deplored by Ruskin as representing the first decadence of the Gothic spirit, but even so, the sheer exuberant loveliness of its traceries and polychrome marbles seduced him into a paragraph of grudging admiration. Though I was to reside there for many weeks, I saw only the gnawed bones of that loveliness, for the Palazzo, due to its peculiar situation, had suffered exceptionally during the Austrian bombardment of the city in 1849. Those traceries that Ruskin had so reluctantly extolled were now rubble in the silt of the Canalazzo; the fragments of marble had been gathered up by urchins and sold to artisans who fashioned that precious rubble into a thousand gaudy trinkets and souvenirs; even the brick thus laid bare was pock-marked from cornice to waterline by the cannons' relentless barrage. A sorry monument to the martial arts, and yet one must be thankful, after all, that the balls fell short of their purposed targets, which were the Doges' Palace and the Basilica of St. Mark's!

My introduction both to Venice and the Palazzo Alari-Uboldo came on a night of cloud and bitter cold, and so I did not remark either the general resplendence of the one or the particular damage that war had wrought upon the other. My first overwhelming impression was rather of absences—absence of light, of warmth, of all accustomed city sounds. There were no lamps to illumine the watery streets of Venice; once the gondola had drawn away from the embankment outside the railway station, only the faintest glimmerings, filtering through the curtains of private chambers, flecked the darkness over which we glided and glinted from the blocks of ice that floated about us. These, as our craft knocked against them, would grind and rasp upon its wooden sides; other than this, all was silence. Like a wood seen across an expanse of meadow, the shores to either side of us were visible only as blacknesses more massive than the water and more dreadful.

Yet am I entirely candid in this? It was dread, surely, that I felt as we were rowed through the little Arctic of the Canalazzo—a dread that deepened perceptibly as the gondola's iron beak passed under a low archway to enter a kind of aquatic antechamber to my new home. But a dread so abstract? So merely mysterious? What the wayfarer fears, peering into the dark wood, is the Unknown, while I had a perfectly clear conception of what I feared, even as, in another sense, I hurried towards it. Like any other bride, I feared to cross the threshold of the nuptial chamber.

For the first time since I had been married, I was alone with my husband. At Niles' own insistence, we had delayed this inevitable moment until our arrival in Venice. Upon the train, as well as upon the boat crossing the Channel, we had never been quit of our travelling companions. I had shared a sleeping compartment with my aunt Jerningham, Niles with his mother; no other arrangement seemed practicable. We might, I suppose, have interrupted our journey, but we were all, for our several reasons, committed to the idea of a headlong, headstrong haste; nor did the weather, which had been uniformly unpleasant from Calais till the Euganean Hills, invite us to linger in a touristic way. Yet, at last, our foursome was split in two. My aunt, after watching me be seated within the gondola, had refused, in the most absolute terms, to follow me, and insisted that she would reach the Palazzo Alari-Uboldo without leaving dry land though it meant hiking the whole length and breadth of the city. The Contessa, to my astonishment, did not join Niles and me in trying to dissuade her from such folly, but rather pronounced it a capital suggestion and offered to accompany her on this ramble. It was an obvious conspiracy (as both ladies were later to admit), but there was no combatting it.

The boat had stopped beside broad steps that led straight down into the water, as though making no distinction between that element and the air. A pair of smoking lanterns hung from iron rings to either side of the entrance.

"Here we are, then," said Niles, who had not spoken so long as we were moving across the water, "at our palace. Be it ever so humble."

With the oarsman's help, he rose and stepped from the unsteady boat onto the lowest step. He made a grimace as a wave of our boat's own making washed over his shoe. "Carefully," he advised as I took his hand. The boat swayed, and rocked, and then I stood safely upon the slimed stone step; and then, before my own boots could be soaked, I skipped up to the next. The oarsman laughed and made a remark in his own language.

"He says that was done like a native," Niles explained.

He made a second remark, which Niles rewarded (without translating) by tossing the fellow three silver zwanzigers, which he picked from mid-air as deftly as if they had lain in a saucer. Then, with a single flick of its long oar, the black gondola, with its black-cloaked gondolier, was assumed into the completer blackness without.

The door of the Palazzo, a cumbrous affair of well-weathered oak, had been left unlocked, though no servants were at hand to welcome us. I felt Niles' eyes upon me. I felt his expectation. Wrapped as I was in my winter clothes, I blushed as though I had stood before him like Eve, in shameful nakedness.

Niles sought to dull the edge of these first keen moments with humor, a remedy he applied with the same reckless, random faith that my aunt invested in *her* panacea. Perhaps there was, in Niles' case as well as Lydia's, an element of addiction, of craving the medicine for its own bittersweet sake.

"I would lift you up, my darling, as a bride ought to be, except I fear I'd slip on these confounded steps. I know that at our first meeting I managed the task well enough, but our relative dimensions have changed since then, and I mistrust whether I *could* lift you now, bundled in all those furs. In any case, I think the custom smacks rather strongly of a more barbaric time, when brides were borne off willy-nilly like the poor dear Sabine women."

"As for that," I said, taking the arm he offered me, "I feel that you have borne me off as much as it may be done. Here I am—"

"Here we are," he corrected, pausing at the threshold of the open door that I might precede him.

"—having hurtled across the whole length of Europe without

pausing for breath, in what must surely be the strangest city in the world—"

One glance within silenced my nervous chatter. Even in that first quick survey of my new surroundings they struck the note which more acquaintance would only sound with more intensity —the note of decay. There must be some special agent in the damps of Venice that acts on wood and stone and plaster so as to accelerate the ravages of time. Rome is older, yet there is a crisp- ness to her most tumbledown ruins that makes them seem juvenile by contrast to a Venetian *sala* of the eighteenth century, such an one as we entered after mounting to the *primo piano*, or first floor (as Italians style the second floor of any building): a high, sprawl- ing hippodrome of a hall, its walls thronged with all the inhabitants of Olympus, while its tessellated pavements stretched out acre upon acre as bare as any Sahara. Admittedly, there was a little oasis in this wasteland where a few scrawny, cane-bottomed chairs huddled round the painted warmth of a *trompe l'oeil* fireplace, but their presence could not combat the oppressiveness of so large a vacancy. The wonderful thing was how with such sparseness of means the room managed to convey, so intensely, its air of desuetude and tottering dilapidation.

I regarded the *sala* mutely, leaving it to Niles to set the tone, whether of satire or forced admiration. He advanced to the hollow center of the room, his footsteps magnified and multiplied as though proportioned to the multiplicity and size of the shadows that he cast in passing before six or seven newly-lighted tapers disposed at intervals along one wall.

"It is just as I remembered it," he said at last, his breath turning to steam in the unheated air. "Neither more nor less."

"It is very grand," I said, in a tone less reverential than reprov- ing. I did not want to seem displeased with what was, after all, a palace, but I could not see quite what direction to take towards liking it.

"Oh, grand as a continent. But a little wanting, may be, in some of the usual amenities—such as furniture?"

"It might," I conceded, "be warmer."

"And it will be, come May or June. The Venetians rely on Divine Providence to right the balance, rather than spend good money on wood or coal. The months of insufferable heat make up for the months of intolerable cold. Oh, but such a look, my dearest, coldest darling! You don't think, with all our millions, that I shall let you suffer a single chilblain? I've insisted that the rest of the place be heated up to an English standard of comfort. As for this old barn here"—Niles waved at a faded goddess above the false fireplace—"there is no way to heat *it*, short of setting the whole Palazzo on fire. Best regard it as a kind of roofed-in avenue along which we have, each of us, our own little *residenze*. And now, if you would like to be shown to yours?"

I took the gloved hand he held out to me. "Don't you mean . . . to ours?"

"Yours, ours—that's all one now."

So saying, he opened a door onto what seemed, at first glance, an impossibility. What I beheld was the parlor of my former home on Worcester Terrace. There was the well-known pier-glass with its crocketed canopy, the mitred armchairs, the mahogany table bristling with buttresses, the brown velvet drapes; every detail, even to the disposition of the china ornaments, just as I remembered them. A hearty coal fire blazed within the fireplace, and gaslight suffused these wonders with its own steadying sense of probability. Had Niles led me into the cave of Aladdin, my astonishment could have been no greater, for nothing is so strange as the familiar encountered in an alien context; here that contrast was strained to its utmost limit. What was I to think but that the Jerningham parlor had taken wing, like the palace in that same legend of Aladdin, and crossed Europe ahead of us? How otherwise could it have preceded us to Venice, when we had accomplished that same journey with all possible dispatch?

Niles was too proud of the surprise he had prepared to answer these questions at once. In fact, he rather teased me, till my bewilderment began to verge on real distress. Then he revealed how, with my aunt's help, he had enlisted the services of the Jerningham manufactory to discover, where they existed, and to duplicate, where they did not, the entire contents of our home on Worcester Terrace. This was, besides "some odds and ends of jewelry" he'd given me in London, his wedding present to me. I did not know whether to berate him for the extravagance of the deed or to join him in laughing at his own enchanting foolishness. I laughed, and gave him, for thanks, a kiss on either of his rosy cheeks.

"You're pleased, then?"

"Yes—so long as I don't think of what it must have cost. Then I'm aghast."

"I hope you won't make me ship it all back."

"Niles! Don't terrify me. Even in jest."

"Well, I have one more surprise for you."

He indicated a door of verdigris green, looking quite burlesque among so much imported sobriety. Behind this quintessentially Italian door was a bedroom identical to the one I'd left on Worcester Terrace. Here, however, Niles had taken some liberties with the original. This bed, though of the same design, was nobler in its proportions and in the stuff from which its hangings had been fashioned. Where formerly my walls had displayed two little prints of Mulready's charming *Noonday* and *Midnight*, Niles had supplied the original paintings! Further, some few pieces had been added unobtrusively to fill out the loftier space: a little rosewood writing table, a chiffonier stocked with the recentest English books, and one of Dimoline's *papier-mâché* pianofortes. All in all, this blend of homely comfort and delicious novelty was so agreeable that I quite forgot to be anxious. I could do nothing but laugh and admire.

"Tell me again that it suits you," Niles insisted.

"As though there could be any doubt!"

"But tell me. It will be my whole business now to please you, which I can only do if you are candid about your pleasures."

"Dear husband, what more can I say? If you should want to mure me up in these two rooms, like one of Bluebeard's wives, I would be happy. To have come so far and still to find myself at home is wonderful."

"I *am* your dear husband, am I not?" Niles repeated.

"Does it seem as strange to you as it does to me?"

"I hope Clara, it shall never seem anything else."

"Well, I suppose there is no helping our getting used to each other. Perhaps that will be even nicer."

"Than what is nicest? Impossible! But are you hungry? Shall we sit down to our first supper *à deux*?"

I nodded, and he tugged at the bell-pull that hung beside the bed. Niles helped me off with my winter wraps, and when we returned to the outer room a little table had been set up there that gleamed like some jewel of the domestic arts, so brave a display of silver and crystal had been compacted into so small a field of napery. When Niles uncovered the central dish, a pasty of game and venison, I knew at the first puff of steam that billowed up that this represented another, and still dearer, link to the life I had thought I had quite abandoned in coming to this far-away land. Without needing to taste it, I knew this pasty was the work of Mrs. Minchin, and that the job she had left for so precipitately, three days before our own setting-off, had been none other than to come to work in the kitchen of the Palazzo Alari-Uboldo. I thanked Niles with none of my earlier, uneasy hyperbole, and sat down to eat with a much heartier appetite than I would have supposed myself capable of.

CHAPTER TWO

Husband and Wife

WE HAVE REACHED THAT POINT in my narrative, dear and faithful reader, when I must ask myself whether you exist; whether, that is, these many sheets of foolscap shall ever be seen by any eyes but my own. However delicately I continue this tale, the fact remains that to be telling it at all must amount to an impropriety of the gravest order. No doubt I should have given warning of this earlier, before involving you in what I now declare to be a suspect venture. The reason I did not is that, like most unpracticed writers, I really did not think when I took up my pen that I should hold to my first purpose so far as this. But I have, and now I am faced with the dilemma of how, without offending against decency, I may go on. To speak only of those events that society recognizes as seemly would be to tease my readers into a state of utter bafflement. There is no way I can convey the real substance of my "Italian experience" without parting that veil with which other writers customarily have screened the innermost privacies of the nuptial chamber.

Perfect modesty, then, would require that I keep silent altogether, but no one who is perfectly modest would embark on such a task as this at all. Should I be debarred from telling the story of my life because its essential facts might bring a blush to young cheeks? It is the only life I have had! Forgive me, then, if I tell the single story that I know, and judge, if it distresses you, how much the blame for that is mine.

All through the long year of Niles' courtship I had speculated on what it would be like to be married to *him*, and those speculations had been more than ever vivid during our journey hither. Now my theories, like so many fragile toys, collapsed beneath the brute weight of my ignorance. Of a wife's duties to her husband I knew only that though reputed to be unpleasant they must be accomplished in respectful silence. That—the importance of silence—had been my aunt's chief admonition. She had also stressed the necessity of vigorous hair-brushing and good lace. The latter item she had seen to herself, and it was of the best. While we had supped, my maid (her name was Rose, and that was as much as I knew of her, except that she was remarkably pretty) had laid out my night-clothes on the gray silk coverlet of the bed. There they gleamed like hoar-frost on a pane of glass, a prodigy of whiteness, the delicate monument of an hundred patient hours' ceaseless toil, a garment fairer and costlier than the modest dress in which I had been wed. I changed into this gown without assistance, then sat down at my dressing table and began to brush my hair. Wave upon dark wave dashed upon the whiteness of the lace, and with a toss of my head, fell back, and advanced again with another stroke of the brush.

I did not hear Niles entering the room. He appeared within the oval of the mirror, reduced by perspective to a manikin no bigger than one leafy sworl of the silver frame. How vast this room is, I thought to myself; but that thought did not interrupt the steady motion of my hands. Had the Austrians still been shelling Venice with their artilleries, had the Palazzo begun to sink into the Grand Canal, I dare say I would have gone right on, stroke for stroke. It was my only certainty, the supreme act to which my life had led me, my destiny and my hope. Heavens above, such a hair-brushing as it was!

Niles came towards me. His figure took up more and more of the mirror until, had he wished, he might have touched his own pale image in the glass. Years after this event, I was to be present at a seance, a threadbare theatrical business, in the course of which the medium's assistant, a spindly girl scarce fifteen years old, had dressed up in a bedsheet and pretended to be a celestial spirit. Though I was not taken in by this imposture, I was deeply affected by the sudden sight of her suspended, so it seemed, slantwise above the table: she had put me in mind distinctly of Niles' appearance on our wedding night. There was in her demeanor the same mixture of playfulness and desperation, the same restless glance, the same fixity of the smile. Like that later spectre, Niles was all in white, and like her, he said nothing and moved soundlessly, until I almost doubted that he was there beside me, in the room, in the mirror.

At last he reached forwards to stop my busy hands, as one might reach into a clock to still the pendulum.

"You must feel very tired," he said.

I agreed that I was fatigued, supposing that this was to be desired in a bride, though in fact nothing could less aptly have described the state of my feelings. I was as wakeful as a parliament of owls.

Having doused every light but the candle that he carried, Niles led me to the bed. "There is one large matter we have still to settle, Clara."

"And what is that?" I asked, with just such a flutter as ruffled through the candle-flame.

"Whether you prefer the right or the left side of the bed." He placed the candle on the table by the bed.

I chose the left, that being nearer, and Niles helped me in, then walked round the foot of the bed, drawing the hangings close as he went, creating thereby a darkness so absolute that I knew he had come to lie beside me only by a shifting and creaking of the mattress-springs. I lay quite still, and Niles, beside me, was as still as I.

I had never been so aware what an unquiet mechanism are the human lungs. Indeed, one's whole physical being is in an incessant commotion, which the usual circumstances of life obscure, as the ordinary bustle of a street muffles the plash of a nearby fountain; but let the traffic clear away, let the two last strollers cease from talking, and what a rattle and prattle of water then is audible! So with ourselves: we are, the very daintiest of us, whole orchestras of groanings and rumblings, of wheezings and poundings, of noses sniffling, ears popping, and teeth rasping on other teeth. Really, it is a wonder that sleep is ever possible, and certainly, so long as we are conscious of this great orchestra's performance, it is not.

After the equivalent of a moderately long overture of wakefulness, Niles addressed himself to me in a whisper: "Clara, are you asleep?"

I admitted that I was not.

"Nor am I. It's hard, at first, to get accustomed to another presence. But after a while it's just as though one were quite alone. Are you a light or a heavy sleeper, usually?"

"My aunt says I sleep like a stone."

"Myself, too. The bed is comfortable for you?"

"Oh yes, very."

"It's an English bed. The mattresses indigenous to this area are intolerably soft. One stifles in them."

"This is just of the firmness I am used to."

"Good."

After a considerable pause, he resumed. "I watched you, earlier, while you were brushing your hair. For quite a while, in point of fact. I had never seen you before with your hair let down. It is beautiful hair."

"I've always wished it were less dark."

"Oh, no! You're much nicer as you are. Indeed, I wish that mine were just as yours. This is so mousey and ragtaggedly plain. I often regret that wigs have gone out of fashion. I could quite fancy myself under a great tower of black curls, like our great-grandfather Clarence, in Ramsay's portrait of him."

"Oh, *you're* much nicer as *you* are."

"Hoist by my own petard! But you're right—we can't help being who we are, so there's no use in regretting the fate in the mirror."

I shifted round under the bedclothes so as to address myself to Niles rather than to the canopy overhead. "*That's* a pretty conceit," I said, with a kind of affectionate mischief.

A hand touched my forehead, brushed back some stray hairs. "So long as you find my conceit pretty, so long, dear Clara, am I safe."

"How can you see to touch me? It's so dark."

"My mother told me, ever so long ago, that you don't like the dark." His hand strayed down the side of my face, following the long curve of cheekbone, jaw, and chin. "That you're afraid of it."

"I was tonight, a little. It wasn't the dark only; it was encountering so much, all at once, that was unfamiliar—the boat, and Venice itself. Even the novelty of being . . . alone. . . ."

I broke off, abashed at what I had been about to say. Darkness may engender fears, but it is just as capable of tempting us into rash confidences, for we imagine, when our auditors become invisible to us, that they follow the drift of our candor as easily and acceptingly as we do ourselves; an error that clear observation of their features would correct. In short, we are apt, in these circumstances, to be talking to ourselves.

Even uncompleted, my meaning had been caught by Niles, and he pursued it. "And why not?" he asked. "To you I represent the Great Unknown, and one is never quite sure of oneself, confronting *that*. It is just the same for me, you know. For me *you* are the mystery, the conundrum, the riddling Sphinx."

"Me? I am the least mysterious creature that ever was!"

"You are Woman and Woman is the very source of mystery."

"My own sense of it is that I am Girl. By *your* account of it, I don't think I shall ever be Woman. I don't like what is dark and hidden; I don't like riddles and enigmas, and I hope, if I seem to pose any to you, you'll tell me, so that I may solve them for you at once."

"*Brava*, my darling! Argued like a judge. Shall I put your principle of perfect candor to the test?"

Immediately he had asked, I recalled the ledger packed away in a box of my old lesson-books and felt a chill constriction of the spirit. I had reason to be grateful for the obscuring dark, for I am sure I must have winced. But I brazened out the challenge. "Whatever test you care to apply."

"Then I would merely ask—what are you feeling now?"

"This very moment?"

"Yes—now."

For the life of me, I could think of nothing but that ledger-book; not with any particular misgivings, only with the sense that it existed, that I possessed it, and that Niles did not know.

"Well?" Niles insisted.

"You must give me a moment. It's all a fluxion, like the waves when we watched them from the Brighton pier."

"But what is the prevailing color?"

"Oh, there's such a flicker of contradictions. On the one hand, I keep thinking that this is a momentous evening, unlike any other in my life; that, in a way, my future hangs in the balance. Then that seems exaggerated. I think: I am still Clara Reeve, the same shallow creature that I was a week ago and that I will be tomorrow."

"There I can prove you wrong. You're no longer Clara Reeve. You are the Countess Visconti. And will be tomorrow."

"I'm afraid that's just what I can't lay hold of. But I will keep trying."

"It will come, but not by reaching for it. You'll just be ambling along some day, and *Ecco!* the fact will confront you, like your own face when you glimpse it going past a shop window."

"My fate in the mirror."

"Just so. And then you'll know you're a married woman, just like all the other married women."

"It all sounds very probable and pleasant, and not a mystery in the least."

"Mysteries needn't be nasty, you know. Take, for instance, the annual miracle of Santa Klaus. Isn't that the height of mystery? Or take angels—such an angel, my darling, as yourself."

"Don't suppose I am an angel, or you will be very disappointed when you learn that I am not."

"Never let me discover it. Blind me with the brightness of your wings."

"I have none."

"But I have seen them! Here." Invisibly, his hand slipped within the collar of my nightgown and traced the lines where, in most paintings, wings are jointed to an angel's human-seeming back. "And here."

To this I had no wit to make rejoinder. My body seemed, in the same instant, weakly to tremble and rigidly to clench. I knew that if he went on teasing me I would break into tears. Instead, he matched me silence for silence, until I began to wonder if he had fallen asleep.

"Angels," he said at length in a more deliberate tone, "if they do exist, must communicate more largely than we do. They must be able to take in the minds of their fellow angels as easily as we take in a face—at a glance. While we poor mortals must make do with our eyes . . . and ears . . . and hands."

I thought this would be a cue for his tickling me again, but he was too deep into philosophy for that.

"And that, our being limited to these *surfaces*, that is the cause of all mysteries. The essence of the other person is always locked away within, like the man in the iron mask, whose identity is always in doubt."

"Surely he can *say* who he is," I objected, "and then there is no mystery."

"But will what he says be the truth? Eh? Suppose he swears; he may be perjured. Or suppose *he* does not know; suppose he has been *misinformed* on the very question of who he is?"

"There is one matter, at least, on which he can't be mistaken, and that is the question you asked of me: what are you feeling? And I think I know what he would answer."

"Really? Then you know more than I."

"He would say: I am *so* uncomfortable. Please, would you remove this iron mask."

Niles laughed. There was a premonitory shifting of the mattress-springs, and then his lips touched against my cheek, which seemed to take their imprint so exactly that I could discern the crisp circumflex of his smile.

CHAPTER THREE

Lady Elizabeth Towton of High Wycombe

As IF THAT KISS had been a sleeping draught, no sooner had Niles lain his head back on his own pillow than I knew by the altered rhythms of his breathing that he was asleep. Not so for me. I wore out the long hours of that winter night with a wakefulness that the necessity (as I regarded it) of never stirring a limb rendered peculiarly irksome. Yet for that very discomfort I felt an odd sort of gratitude. My aunt had urged me so often and so direly to steel myself against the shock of the first days of marriage that I was quite relieved to be undergoing, as I thought, the first of my conjugal trials.

Though I did not sleep, these hours of wakefulness had the quality of a dream from which one awakens with a sense of having brushed shoulders with . . . something quite dreadful. But what? The face is gone, and even the uncertain and unsatisfying sense of *something* having been there fades before the guileless light of day.

When that light began actually to glimmer at the edges of the curtains, I rose from the bed by infinitesimal gradations of stealth. Slipping a peignoir over my night-clothes, I advanced towards those heavy draperies with the same suspenseful eagerness I would have felt in a theater before the curtains part upon a scene that has promised to be particularly imposing—Valhalla, perhaps, or a ballroom *en pleine—valse*. What the parting of these curtains discovered was no less wonderful—the Deluge itself. Facing me across the breadth of the Canalazzo, and facing the dawn, were the palaces of Venice, stretching southwards as far as I could see and bounded on the north by the sprawling step-ladder of the Rialto Bridge; century upon century of wealth and pride and beauty rising up sheerly from the element that had made that wealth, and nursed that pride, and was, in itself, incarnate beauty. The old bricks and tattered marble absorbed the morning light as though it were their nourishment, and, even as I watched, they seemed to glow a richer pink, a deeper gold, like invalids whose cheeks are flushed by their day's ration of port wine. So lovely, and with each advancing moment lovelier. Soon there was traffic upon the Canal, lithe gondolas and squat, slow-moving market-boats plowing lanes of blackness through the silvery fields of the water. Figures went up and down the Rialto Bridge or loitered on the *fondamenta* opposite. No one hurried, as people hurry in London, for Venetians are alive to a sense of the beauties about them. More simply, they are alive— clamorously, brilliantly, ever-presently alive. It is the quiet brilliance of this energy that is the central paradox of Venice, and indeed of Italy, for there is everywhere a juxtaposition of the most intense liveliness and the most moribund decay. Imagine a ruined abbey all overgrown with columbine, every fissure, every gaping window aglow with the encroaching blooms, and then imagine not just one such ruin, but a whole continuum of them, endless landscapes of crumbling, golden, elegiac loveliness.

There! I have had my say about Italy, and I shall not go on about it more. It would not, in any case, be possible to do justice to *every* noble prospect, *every* venerable masterpiece, *every* majestic cypress that casts a meditative shadow upon the vanishing glories and the grand old tombs.

So, closing the curtains upon that larger view, let me chronicle the more humdrum splendors of my new condition. In every external it had been altered out of recognition. As swiftly as the money had come to me, I had been surrounded with its regalia. Dressmakers measured me, and a small army of seamstresses labored night and day to create a trousseau that filled, by my wedding day, twenty-six travelling closets. My aunt and my mother-in-law were also amply provided for, and Niles' wardrobe underwent an expansion slower but in the end just as extensive. I spent an entire afternoon selecting from the jewels I had inherited those I wished to bring with me to Italy. In every way that money might fashionably be disbursed mine was. Once begun, the mighty expenditure seemed to proceed, like another Niagara, of its own volition, and my own part in the process consisted only in standing comfortably back from the spectacle and admiring it. Some times, when Niles or Mr. Hautboy had asked me, I would put my signature to a piece of paper, but now that I was married I could be spared even that much trouble. These were the days before the three successive Married Women's Property Acts, and so, having declined to have Mr. Hautboy draw up a special settlement, my chattels were vested absolutely in my husband. I speak of "my money," "my jewels," even "my dresses," but from the moment I had married Niles I had transformed all that was mine to his, and the great mass of it had become, thereby, a much more supportable weight.

I have likened Venice to the Deluge; I might extend that and compare our residence to the Ark, for each day we stayed on at the Palazzo witnessed the enlargement of its menagerie of furniture. Whatever could stand on legs or hang on walls was summoned aboard, and the Noah of this summoning was Zaide. She bought a good many of the pieces that filled out the great hollow hulk of the palace, but a greater number came from Blackthorne. Niles had given his mother her pick of its furniture and pictures. How she must have savored the task of going about her childhood home, from which she had been so long an exile, and informing the usurping Mrs. Lacey (who had stayed on just long enough to witness this spoliation): "That desk, and the Constable, and both these Aubussons, and of course I shall want the mirrors, too." A steady procession of the plunder kept arriving at the Palazzo, and, for weeks, a blaze of firewood from the dismantling of the crates brightened the faded flesh of the various Junos and Jupiters, Dianas and Apollos floating about in the high, allegorical ceilings.

Of course it is nice to have one's wishes gratified, once one has got into the way of *having* wishes; even if they are not one's own, exactly, it can be nice. I delighted to see everyone around me so happy and bustling and splendidly got up. Even the servants—and there were aboundingly many—seemed transfigured by our prosperity, as though the very aroma of the wine they poured into our cups had made them drunk. Yet, in a curious way, *I* felt untouched by the great transformation. Pumpkins had been changed to coaches, mice to footmen, my rags to the latest mode, but mentally I had not moved from my post beside the fire, and somehow I managed to convey this attitude to those around me.

Perrault was wise to conclude his celebrated fairy tale at the instant of matrimony, for a sequel would show that Cinderella was as much bullied after her apotheosis as before. Once it had been her step-sisters who had forced the role of servant upon her; later it would be her servants who would insist that she act like a lady. That jest I have worn out with too much telling, but it has its grain of perdurable truth. To this day, I tend to implore, or cajole, or cheer on my domestic staff—anything rather than command them, and I know I am regarded as something of a laughingstock in consequence. I have learned not to care, but in those days it vexed me to tears (albeit, secret tears) that I could not more adequately represent the character of a Contessa. Not that Niles or his mother ever seemed to require any unusual grandness of me, but the servants, oh my!—*they* could be tyrannical!

The most ruthless of them all was Rose, my waiting-maid. Zaide had found her through an agency in Mayfair, and she came with unimpeachable references from Lady Elizabeth Towton of High Wycombe, the American wife of the financier Lord Towton. This lady and her husband had been, by Rose's account, paragons of comportment and *ton*, and it was against a standard of the legendary Towton excellence that my own performances were measured, particularly in the item of dress. Like a child with a single doll and endless leisure, Rose dressed me and undressed me four or five times a day, lacing me tighter and tighter as the hours advanced and tire-lessly combining and recombining my own hair with the false hair and padding and beaded nets that Fashion, in the person of Lady Elizabeth Towton of High Wycombe, remorselessly dictated. When Lady Elizabeth herself was without an opinion (which was seldom), Rose would have recourse to the latest number of *La Mode Illustrée*, against whose authority there was no appeal.

While she dressed me, she would talk, alternating between English and French as naturally (and almost as rapidly) as a skater would alternate his right foot with his left. Thanks to the curious accident I have already mentioned, my command of French was so imperfect that I was grateful for the example she set me. If the sub-jects she chose to discourse on were some times trivial in the ex-treme (I remember in particular an hour's debate she conducted with herself on the merits of a "peg-top" sleeve relative to a Gabrielle, the while I was being trussed up for a dinner party), did not this allow me to concentrate all the better on the perfection of her vowels and consonants, the richness of her Parisian idioms, and her enviable knack of expanding the littlest notion into a great deal of sociable chatter?

In fairness to Rose, I must say that it was not only her manner that was instructive, but her matter as well. More than any con-vent girl, I had been brought up innocent of the Beau-Monde, and through Rose's sharp eyes and quick tongue I began to discern the shore-line of that fabulous country, to which, as I supposed, my marriage had transported me. Rose had lived in the fashionable world and knew its "ins and outs"—its intrigues and outrages—quite as well as any of that world's acknowledged citizens, includ-ing, certainly, the great Lady Elizabeth Towton. In time, I even

began to wonder whether that lady had not been, as much as myself, the mere creation of her servant, a doll that was decked out in
necklaces and placed at dinners, driven through parks and conducted down garden paths, entirely in obedience to Rose's whims.
But such heresies belong to a later stage of our relations. In the
Venetian chapters of my life, I accepted Rose, as I accepted every
other alteration in my habits and habitation, as a natural consequence of my metamorphosis from a Miss into a Ladyship.

CHAPTER FOUR
The Opening of a Door

THERE WAS, HOWEVER, one member of our domestic establishment
whose presence I could not regard with such equanimity. This was
my husband's valet, Manfredo. I trust my readers will not need to
be reminded how I had made this person's acquaintance at Blackthorne. As he had not been in evidence at Corme Hall during the
eleven weeks of my "visit" of condolence, nor during the ensuing
months of Niles' courtship, I had assumed what it had suited my liking to assume—that he had been dismissed from Niles' employ.

I discovered my mistake on my second morning at the Palazzo
Alari-Uboldo. The rest of the previous day had been passed with
my aunt Jerningham in a haze of wonderment, as Niles had escorted
us through the city from splendor to splendor. It had been all I
could do to remain awake at dinner that evening, and more than I
could do to share in either its food or its conversation. I went to
bed at nine and slept round the clock, waking alone in a strange
room that seemed all the stranger for being inhabited by so much
familiar-seeming furniture.

Alone: that was the keystone of my distress. Till that moment I
had taken the well-known verse from Matthew—"They twain shall
be one flesh"—as a virtual warranty against solitude now I was a
married woman. No matter that such an expectation defies common

sense—I had believed it. I have known, since then, many young women, and a few gentlemen, to subscribe to this foolish article of faith, and to suffer no inconsiderable pang when they are un-deceived. Having not grown up amid the reassuring bustle and busyness of a large household, I ought to have been better forti-fied against the shock of this first large *absence*. Indeed, the wonder is that with so little experience of married life I should have noticed it at all; but I did, and with some alarm. Else, could I have acted so unthinkingly?

My bedroom communicated by a kind of private corridor to Niles' rooms. When I woke, the odd little door opening onto this corridor stood ajar. (I say "odd," though its oddity—that it had been painted, in lighter and darker shades of olive-green, to *resemble* a door—is a commonplace of much Italian architecture. Where else in the world would a perfectly substantial wall be made to look like the painted canvas of a theatrical set?) I looked down the corridor; I entered it, conscious of each footstep along its chill, tessellated floor. As I approached the farther end, I heard Niles' voice, rippling in Italian. Without understanding a word, my own spirits were borne up by the music and buoyancy of his speech.

Another olive-green door separated us, but I had second thoughts about rapping on it. Niles would not be speaking to him-self, and whoever was with him would not find it edifying to have me burst in upon their conversation *en déshabillé*. But still I lingered by the door, listening to the familiar voice speaking in an un-familiar tongue. At intervals, the flow of Niles' talk would be inter-rupted by deep-throated laughter or a curt remark, which might elicit, in turn, Niles' own more silvery mirth. At first I did not think to accuse myself of eavesdropping, since the substance of this dialogue remained as obscure to me as the doctrines of the Free-masons or the operations of the differential calculus. Then, in the midst of this pleasant meaninglessness, I thought I made out my own names—"Clara"—pronounced first by that darker voice, then taken up by Niles. It was enough: I bethought myself of the full gravity of what I was doing. As I turned to leave, there was a burst of laughter in the next room—and the green door was thrown open.

I would have died of shame if the simple shock of the con-frontation had not been so much greater. There stood Manfredo, his laughter stopped, as it were, in mid-stride. One hand rested on the handle of the door; in the other an opened razor. Our eyes met, and, despite the briefness of that meeting, there passed between us a multiplicity of meanings: first, the recognition, on each side, of the other's presence, and the mutual acknowledgment that it was no welcome presence; then, most strangely, a kind of challenge, an almost formal casting down and taking up of gauntlets. Never, but for the suddenness of this meeting, would such an overt declaration of enmity have escaped from either of us. From the candor of that look, we both took a step backwards—I, quite literally; he, by turning to his master.

"Clara! Awake at last?"

Niles addressed me from behind a mask of stiff white lather. He had been lying back on a divan, but on seeing me he'd pushed himself upright, dislodging, as he did so, a towel that had been tucked into his dressing gown.

"You must excuse me. I didn't mean to. . . . That is to say, I was looking for you and—"

"And you have found me, in the likeliest place."

"I was just going away, having heard your voices, when—"

"This is Manfredo, darling. My valet. I'm afraid he rather gave you a start. He didn't mean to. He was after the strop. Manfredo, I'll ring when I need you again."

"No, no—I'm leaving. I didn't mean to interrupt." I fled down the length of the corridor without heeding Niles' further protests. Once in my own room, I closed the door without turning round, for I could not have endured such another glint as I had seen in the eye of Niles' manservant.

I rang for Rose, hoping that the novelty of being dressed by her hands would help to settle my mind, which, to a degree, it did, if only by giving me time to consider what had happened. In fact, very little. At the moment of discovery it might have appeared that I was eavesdropping, but to what purpose, if they spoke Italian? It was distressing to learn that Manfredo was still wearing the Visconti livery, but any suspicions I had had about him might now properly—nay, *must* now absolutely—be laid to rest.

One little misgiving lingered on, like a fine sliver embedded in my fingertip: a suspicion that Niles, in defiance of all ordinary observance, had allowed his manservant to refer to me as "Clara," had even echoed the fellow's familiarity. Nor could I forget that this exchange had ended in laughter. Necessarily, I wondered if that laughter had been at my expense.

Not that I thought myself too high and fine to be made sport of. Indeed, I knew that my position was peculiarly liable to seem ridiculous. What satirist can resist a smile or sneer at the expense of the *nouveau riche*, to which class I belonged as certainly as the Archbishop of Canterbury is a member of the clergy. I knew this, and I thought I was prepared to bear the expense of whatever smiles or sneers I met with. But that the jest should be between my husband and his valet!

Well, reader, you may share in this supposititious laughter if you like—not, in this case, because I am a parvenu, but for the much commoner failing of my being a silly nit. My whole case against Niles was toppled that same afternoon when I took tea with my mother-in-law in her rooms.

After ascertaining that Venice, in general, and the Palazzo, in particular, had met with my satisfaction, she suggested that I might wish to begin learning Italian. I assured her that I felt a passionate desire to do so, and indeed a moral obligation.

"Good. Then, to begin not at the beginning, for there is no beginning to any language (St. John to the contrary), and no end either. Let us begin with *you*, shall we? That is, with the word *clara*. Did you know that your name is an adjective here?"

"No. What is its sense?"

"As pretty a sense as you could wish for. It means 'bright,' or 'clear.' In Tuscany, *clara* shifted to *chiara* some centuries ago. There is a lovely poem by Petrarch that begins '*Chiare, fresche e dolci acque*'; that is, 'Clear, fresh, and sweet waters.' In general, Italy has followed Tuscan usage, but in *our* home—in Ischia, among Ischiotes—the older form lingers on, and your name is as common, I'm afraid, as the sunshine."

"How delightful." (And, I reflected to myself, how confusing. The Contessa's philosophy of education was evidently of the sink-or-swim variety, and I already felt myself sinking.)

"I'm glad you think so. I'll try to come up with as agreeable a word for tomorrow's lesson."

"Dear me. Are we to proceed as slowly as that—a word a day?"

"You'll be surprised how fast the words, and the days, can mount up. But if you're in a greater hurry, we might dip into a verb or two after we've attended more immediate needs. Now, tell me, for I forget—how do you like your tea? With milk, or . . . ?"

I laughed. "*Clara!*"

By this inadvertent means, my suspicions, so far as they touched Niles, were confounded, and all was made "bright and clear"; or nearly all. One solitary shadow lingered on, in the person of Manfredo, whom I would encounter at odd times of day, within the Palazzo or without, assisting Niles or employed on his own business. By contrast to the other servants, he seemed to lead a very leisurely life. Except when he was helping Niles to dress, I never saw him stir a limb at any ordinary task. This apparent idleness was, Niles once assured me, exactly the measure of Manfredo's excellence, since the object of the upper, as against the lower, servants is to convey an illusion that all the work of the world can be accomplished by the mere tug of a bell-rope. The more, therefore, a servant was in evidence, the less he should seem to do; by this criterion, Manfredo was a nonpareil.

I could never be comfortable in his presence. Sensing this, he never let an opportunity go by for conveying the satisfaction he took in my daily discomfiture. His eyes would seek mine, but the instant that I noticed him, his thick lashes would droop and he would bow his head, indicating by this gesture and by the hint of a smile that we shared a secret understanding.

However vehemently I might deny to myself these suggestions of complicity, they did, in fact, suggest a truth. The uneasiness Manfredo caused me was nothing more uncommon than guilt. It is the nature of guilt that the more we try to escape it the more pervasive is its growth. There came a day when the bare possibility of Manfredo's presence, or a glimpse of a bald head associated with a certain squareness and squatness of figure (I should note here, if I have not already, that the man was ten years his master's senior), would be enough to deflect me from any purpose I might be pursuing. I would not enter Niles' rooms on whatever provocation, since they were the valet's virtual domain. When I saw him on the street,

I would take any detour that offered itself, however inconvenient, to avoid confronting his obsequious, accusing smile.

He had mastered, parrot-like, some dozen or so formulae by which he could act as Niles' emissary. "My Lady," each of these set speeches would begin, but there would be a kind of twinkle in this simple preliminary, as though he had seen through the imposture of "My Lady," as though these little courtesies were a little joke that we shared. "My Lady, your husband wishes you to know . . ." And it would always be bad news—that Niles must be absent from dinner, or would be unable to go along on an outing we had planned, or simply that he was out-of-sorts and wanting to be left alone. Necessarily I must listen; necessarily I must make some reply. Each time it was as though I must relive that incident upon the staircase at Blackthorne, must listen to his faltering request for my silence, must yield again to his extortion.

In short, I was being haunted. Not by any ghost or *revenant*, but by the least other-worldly creature imagination could conceive —a portly, half-bald, mustachioed *valet de chambre*, who could not speak without putting one in mind of a comic opera. But let him knock upon my door, and the needle in my hand would tremble, my knees weaken, my throat become of a sudden so dry that any reply that I made came out rasping and harsh. An unreasonable response? Yes, nightmares do not listen to reason, and there is no remedy for guilt, except a thorough and heartfelt confession.

CHAPTER FIVE

The Chevalier of Malta

THE TRUE OWNER of the Palazzo Alari-Uboldo, Danilo Alberico Alari, had spent the last fifteen years of his life as a prisoner in the notorious fortress of Olmüz, in Austria, in consequence of the part he had played in the uprisings of 1848 and 1849. Alari's family fled to Savoy, abandoning their home, which served for several years as a barracks for the victorious Austrians. It then passed into the possession of Contessa Visconti by a shadowy process involving the payment of a very trifling annual rent to the exiled Alaris ($£120$ by the Contessa's account—$£50$ according to her son!) and the friendly intervention of a general in the Austrian army: Rudolph, Count Wrbna and Freudenthal.

Count Wrbna (a Bohemian name, pronounced *Verb-na*) has figured, often quite prominently, in the many recent books chronicling the Italian peoples' struggle for national independence. As most of these books are written to celebrate the new nation, I regret that Count Wrbna's reputation has not been enhanced by the attention being paid him. At the time I knew him, he was *aide-de-camp* of the Military Governor of all Lombardo-Veneto, the Archduke Albert. Since the Archduke was a careless administrator, whose preferred post in the ship of state was rather the head of the table than the helm, the greater part of the everyday business of governing fell on the shoulders of his A.D.C. I shall not pretend to know better than so many excellent historians, who are unanimous in denouncing Count Wrbna's policies, but when they go on to revile his character, I must, somewhat, demur. When Professor Minghetti charges, for instance, in *Miei Ricordi*, that Count Wrbna "joined to the vile carnality of a Caligula the cunning of a Jesuit, the avarice of a Jew, and the ambition of an American," he is guilty not only of rhetorical excesses but of downright untruth. Cunning Count Wrbna may have been; but if he harbored any of those other vices, they took so rarefied a form as to be imperceptible to my eyes. You may counter that my eyes had, by my own testimony, seen very little of the world and its vices; I would reply that they saw a great deal of Count Wrbna, while Professor Minghetti relied on the unsupported conjectures and pasquinades of a turbulent era.

It is neither my task nor my wish to be Count Wrbna's apologist. Since the Count's large destiny and my own smaller one were for a brief but crucial time intertwined, I am obliged to introduce him to these pages, but I would not have my readers think that I was acquainted with such a monster as Professor Minghetti and the rest have described. Indeed, the peculiar interest of his character was that such immense power and authority should co-exist with such jolliness and gentility. A Caligula? Say, rather, a Pickwick!

Now I am flying to the other extreme. Perhaps Niles' summing-up of the Count did most justice to the whole man. He first told me of the Count as we were being rowed up the ice floes of the Canalazzo to his headquarters in the Palazzo Grimani. It was my third evening in Venice.

"So long as you do not express a serious opinion, you are safe," Niles advised. "He'll pick a quarrel with you, for the sport of it. He loves to argue with the English, particularly with English ladies, though properly he ought not to, because of his vows."

"Vows?"

"Poverty, chastity, and obedience: not speaking to ladies comes under the second head."

"He is a priest, then?" I asked.

"No, something stranger—a Chevalier of Malta. From an honest English point of view, that is as much as to say he's the Beast of the Apocalypse. Or, at any rate, one of the Four Horsemen."

"My goodness! If he is as bad as that, why are we visiting him?"

"In effect, my dear, he is our landlord, which makes him, when you think of the rent we pay, our benefactor as well. Furthermore, Mother adores him, *has* adored him for years, and that makes it our duty to be pleasant, which after all, is quite possible, for he's thoroughly amiable."

"And apocalyptic, too?"

"Your uncle Jerningham would have thought so. The Order of Malta, in which the Count possesses a commandery, has a fairly sinister reputation, even among Catholics, though to my mind it is nine-tenths sheer flummery got up to compete with the antics of the Freemasons. The young initiate has to lie down on the floor of a cathedral, and a requiem mass is said over him. Then he's given a new suit of black clothes and a white Maltese Cross to pin on the suit and told that henceforth he's dead to the world. He swears his vows and—hey presto!—he's a Chevalier. That is to say, he can continue a bachelor to the end of his days in good conscience and enjoy some very choice prerogatives meanwhile. It's like belonging to a very select London club. For no one is invited to join the Order unless his blood is of the intensest blue. Christianity nowhere takes a more aristocratic form. Even the Papacy is less select."

"You make it sound harmless enough."

"When you meet him, you may judge for yourself. He will try and convert you, of course, but in Italy that is only a polite attention, like offering a plate of cakes at tea-time. You're at liberty, of course, to refuse to be converted. He will tolerate any heresy, religious or civil, so long as you don't insist on proclaiming it in public."

"I am not about to."

"Nor am I, and so we are safe within his den."

"Then it *is* a den?" I insisted.

"Oh yes, beyond a doubt. That's just its interest for the likes of us. Venice is a city under siege, you know. Every morning there is another corpse fished out of the canals. But don't be alarmed. It won't affect us. Thanks to my mother we have a safe-conduct among the Austrians, and thanks to myself the republicans will do us no harm. Not that I flaunt the tricolor cockade—that *would* be imprudent—but in my own home I am a subject of the *Galantuomo.*"

"Garibaldi, you mean?"

"No—Verdi."

"Verdi!"

"You must have seen it scrawled on a hundred walls about the town in big block letters—VERDI! *Victor Emmanuel, Re d'Italia* —King of Italy!"

"I've seen it, but I'd only supposed that people were more passionate about opera here."

"Some of the corpses in the canals have found their way there for no greater crime than writing that word."

"But that's awful!"

There was some real anger in my protest, but not against the Austrians. I was offended at Niles for telling me such tales. Not for a minute did I believe that Count Wrbna could be a murderer and a despot and that *we* were, in blithe indifference to these facts, about to pay him a social call.

With such a reputation for contrariness, I did not look for the veritable Count Wrbna of the Grimani drawing room to have any surprises in store. Niles' account of him had prepared me, I supposed, for anything, however mild or mad. Yet Niles had left the single most striking fact out of his account—and not willfully, that I might be made to gape, but because neither he nor his mother had ever noticed what at a first glance quite floored me: Rudolph, Count Wrbna and Freudenthal was the twin of my late great-uncle Douglas, fifth Baron Rhodes. Nothing less can express the closeness of the resemblance. The same bald head and heavy white mustachios; the nose, the jowls; the same weary, witting eyes; the stance, so upright and yet so suggestive of the props supporting that uprightness. Indeed, in Count Wrbna's case there was an audible creaking of stays, for, like most older Austrian officers, he had adopted the vanity of tight lacing.

I was spared the necessity of concealing my astonishment. Once we had been introduced, the Count concentrated his attentions on Zaide, who was as cordial to this double of her brother as she had been frosty to the original. Almost at once they settled into a comfortable coze, speaking a form of French peculiar to the Grimani Palace, a French rich in English and Italian idioms and topped with a *schlagobers* of German in the softened, sibilant dialect of Vienna. Had they spoken the first language of prelapsarian man I would have found their talk just as unfathomable.

I was not, by any means, ignored. Though there were few ladies present at that gathering (after fifteen years, the families native to Venice still refused, on the whole, to mix with their oppressors on a social basis), any number of colonels and captains exercised their English on me, or allowed me to exercise my French on them, until I had quite mastered a little speech on the beauty of Venice and my own susceptibility thereto. My colonel or captain would then inquire whether I had seen this or that landmark until he had discovered (it did not take long) one that was unfamiliar, which he would then praise as representing more than any other the true genius of the place. Invariably, such praise would be preface to an invitation to escort me . . . wherever: to the Accademia, to the Mocenigo Palace, to the statue of Bartolomeo Colleoni in the square of San Zanipolo, and to churches near and far, each one reputed the repository of one or another painter's supreme work. One officer in the uniform of the Hungarian Magnates, gold and silver passementerie upon a ground of pale-blue silk, even proposed an excursion to the Lido, to watch the waves of the Adriatic breaking on the barren dunes, but I never again encountered this romantic young man at the Grimani, nor would I ever see the Lido in its rudimentary wasteland character.

Foreseeing these invitations, Niles had instructed me to accept any that I found appealing. All were appealing, and in equal degree, and thus it was that almost with my arrival I was caught up in a whirl of sightseeing by day and dinner parties by night; a life so full of sheer eventfulness and "pleasure" that I could scarcely recognize myself at the center of it; no better could I understand how it had come about. That a great wind had sprung up, I knew; but not from which quarter of the compass. Now it seems quite clear to me that all these attentions were a kind of simulation of "society" produced, like an evening of amateur theatrics, for my special entertainment and diversion. The colonels and captains were acting under orders when they escorted me from palace to shrine, from shrine to vista, and their orders came, necessarily, from Count Wrbna, who, in collusion with Zaide, had devised this method of putting me more fully at my ease by sweeping me up off my feet.

CHAPTER SIX

What Is Right and What Is Proper

EVERY MARRIAGE ENTAILS an act of betrayal. That great bond cannot be formed except that other ties be loosened and made less. The firmer the knot, the more acutely do we feel the pain of its unravelment. All parents know this, but the knowledge is useless to them in this abstract form. The betrayal, when it happens, is unforeseen; else it were no betrayal. Its shape and size will vary, from the first eloquent hesitation in what had been an unbroken smoothness of confidences to the unequivocal declaration of a

Cordelia to a Lear. My betrayal of Lydia was in the middle range of being neither too subtle nor too stark.

In the days immediately before and after my marriage, I could not conceive that there ever could be any conflict between my old affections and my new duties. Lydia herself had encouraged me to accept Niles, and when the trip to Italy was suggested she heartily entered into our plans with no suspicion at first that they included her. Once it had been suggested that she accompany us abroad, even her physician had added his voice to the chorus of persuasion, for Venice's climate was still accounted salubrious at that time, its very mud valued as though it were a medicine.

Travel, whether to the Pole, the Amazon, or Venice, can indeed effect wonderful cures. Like most entrenched Londoners, my aunt Jerningham had settled into too torpid a way of life. The novelty of a foreign city was immediately efficacious: her megrims vanished, her appetite improved, and a general mild contentment settled over her spirit, which took the visible form of a smile, causeless and unconscious, that waxed and waned a dozen times each hour.

Though it shamed me to think so, I often reflected during that first month that *she* had been made happier by my marriage than I! However she might pretend to make light of her ambitions for me, they had been real. I suspect they had come to her as a trust from my mother, who had kept them alive through many a long and disappointed year. If so, Lydia had had the good sense not to pass on such a bitter inheritance. Thus, the little imposture of my nursery days, that I was the Princess of Bayswater, had had a larger significance for my tutor than for me. Only the most fervid and hardened gamblers could have appreciated such desperation of wishing, such splendor of good luck. I am myself so little a gambler that, really, I must relinquish the attempt to enter more deeply into these feelings. In any case, her fortunes were to alter rapidly enough, and with them the supreme comfortableness of living among wishes that have come true.

The first rumble of the approaching storm came from the nether regions of the Palazzo Alari-Uboldo. Poor Mrs. Minchin was at sixes and sevens with everyone and everything about her. The lowest scullion in the kitchen ignored her orders or, what was likelier but no more useful, did not understand them. The ovens baffled her, the pots and pans played tricks on her. She judged the water of Venice not to be potable, and regarded the produce of its markets with horror or contempt. Local ingredients would not combine into the dishes she was noted for. She complained that the flour was too coarse, the eggs stale, the milk sour. She could not do her own marketing and distrusted the servants who might have helped her, suspecting them of being in a conspiracy with the tradesmen. In short, she was in a condition of passionate home-sickness.

For this malady there is only one known cure, short of return-ing to the longed-for land—the medicine of reminiscence. My youth as well as my new title and wealth prevented her from approaching me, but my aunt was visibly the same Mrs. Jerning-ham as before. Perhaps, too, Mrs. Minchin could detect in my aunt's manner hints of the illness that had so vanquished her. In either case, whether the seeds were already there or whether Mrs. Minchin herself planted them, Lydia soon was griped by the same discontents. Each day she and the cook would closet themselves in Lydia's boudoir and there, in secrecy, surrender themselves to the vices of complaint and comparison.

I do not mean to suggest that Venice may not be complained of, or that London is not, in a great many ways, the fairer and more rational city. Yet, are we not obliged, if we set foot on foreign shores, to be a little tolerant of their foreignness? I did not blame poor Mrs. Minchin for feeling lorn and lost; indeed, I pitied her. Nothing in her past had prepared her to be uprooted from the soil in which she had always flourished. I did, however, blame my aunt, though I forebore from saying so. That this was wrong of me, I now can see. I *ought* to have extended as much charity to Lydia as to Mrs. Minchin.

Instead, I became contentious. When Lydia would disparage St. Mark's on account of its darkness and the crudity of the mosaics, I would defend it with a raft of half-remembered argu-ments from Mr. Ruskin's admirable books. Similarly, I might defend, though without Mr. Ruskin's help, the Venetian way of serving shellfish or eels, all the while I secretly shared my aunt's preference for Mrs. Minchin's honest English cookery.

To Lydia's credit, I must say that she never took offense at the airs I gave myself of being, all at once, a cosmopolite. Indeed, she regularly professed her pride and satisfaction in my adaptability, which she chose to regard as a "gift" that had come to me, along with my brown eyes, from my grandfather, a part of the general Rhodean heritage. This being so, she felt herself under no obligation to come to terms with Venice, nor did she. The persistence of Italians in speaking Italian and worshipping in Catholic churches never ceased to be sources of affront, and their other improprieties and inconveniences, such as the way they heated their palaces ("Though I *don't* see why they call them palaces, when the better part of them, as I understand it, are no more than rooming houses!") or the way the kitchen help were allowed to see callers any evening of the week ("Mrs. Minchin says it's a scandal, nothing less")—these came to seem part of an all-embracing Italian *system* of perversity.

It reached the point, within a month of our arrival, when Lydia would scarcely venture out of her own rooms, unless she were required as a companion on an excursion with one of my captains or colonels. "I am happy right here," she would tell me, when I came with an invitation to dine at the Palazzo Grimani. "I like a warm fire and a good book. Later on, perhaps, I'll have Mrs. Minchin make me a nice cup of tea. Really, I have appetite for nothing else. In any case, that general with an impossible name has no use for me."

"But Count Wrbna particularly insisted you should come."

"He may *appear* to insist, but you may be sure, my little Contessa, that he does so to be nice to you. Which is as it should be. Don't think for a moment that I am being fretful. In my own quiet way, I am as happy as one of these bellowing gondoliers, who wake people up here in lieu of roosters. Mind you, I don't complain, since they would have no other way of getting up, under the circumstances. Happy—and snug as a mouse in my little nest by the fire, which, I dare say, is a better fire than any I'd be likely to find at the Grimani Palace. It has been so thoughtful of your dear husband to insist on supplying me with proper English *coal*. But then he is always thoughtful. My dear Clara, there is no reason for you to cry."

"I'm not crying!"

"And *I'm* not crying. Because, as I have said so many times, I'm perfectly content."

I determined to leave well enough alone, trusting that warmer weather and an over-plenty of Mrs. Minchin's company would do more than my arguments to draw Lydia forth.

The latter days of January were, in any case, so piercingly unpleasant that none of us cared to venture out of doors, excepting Zaide, whom the elements in whatever awful combinations could not prevent from her evening's *tête-à-tête* with Count Wrbna. Niles, under the influence of daily, deep potations of Tintoretto, had set about doing my portrait, a full-length picture very much in the grand manner. Fully a week went by before he had satisfied himself as to costume, coiffure, and backdrop, and then—dear me, what fussing and finicking each morning while he and Rose would arrange me into an identical pattern of curls and draperies! How he would scowl, and mutter, and squint, and shake his head, and sigh! At the end of a whole day of such ardors he might declare that all his efforts had been in vain, but however much he complained I could see that the contest had stirred his blood.

Though I was not allowed to view the progress of my portrait, my own experience was by no means limited to the mere passive tedium of keeping my eyes open and my hands still. There is a kind of tension that develops between a painter and his model (I have observed this other times as well) that is unlike any other social relation. The painter seeks in the mute lines of another face the mystery of an alien existence. He contemplates a pair of eyes which in turn are fixed on him (for I regard profiles not as portraits but only as an elevated form of paper-cutting); he senses, behind those steady eyes, a flux of thoughts, a spirit, a *being* like to his own and yet as riddling as the Sphinx. If these are the painter's thoughts, what are the model's, as she studies, hour upon slow hour, the painter's activity divorced, as it were, from its issue?—

But what is all this impersonal talk of painters and models? It was Niles who painted, I who sat there and watched his deepening bafflement, his mounting exasperation; who felt, with him, the start of some new hope as a "solution" occurred; who saw that hope slowly crumble. It was not that his hand failed to execute, but rather that his eye could not solve the riddle that my face and figure posed to him. I thought some times the fierceness of his scrutiny would send me up in flames, but, hard as he might stare, he could not take me in. Heaven knows I was not trying to elude him. No vase of summer flowers could have offered themselves as freely to his gaze. *Here I am*, my face cried out. *Look at me! Paint me! Make me your own!*

At last—it was late in February; the days were lengthening; the air grew warm—Niles threw down his brushes and turned the portrait round for me to see. Then he stalked out of the room, as though my face had become a Gorgon's head, which with another moment's witnessing would petrify him to despair.

It was not, superficially, a bad painting. Many details had been rendered with *brio*, and in its conception there was real boldness. One could see that he had been to school with Tintoretto. Considered either as a pattern of light and dark or as a conglomeration of pretty bits, one could not have found fault; only as a portrait did it miscarry. Within the well-drawn oval of my face, a stranger's anxious eyes peered out from a rolling plain of pale flesh, and lips of too raw a carmine swelled in a smile that seemed, somehow, pinned on. Nothing hung together. Beneath the broad bell-shape of my pagoda sleeve it was very doubtful that there was an arm, and even doubtfuler whether that arm connected to a shoulder. The whole effect of the picture was of a very excellent dress trimmed in the latest fashion but so constructed that no actual human being could have worn it. It was wrong—that was clear—but how it had gone wrong I couldn't tell. No wonder Niles had been so perplexed. The day after he had thrown down his brushes the painting disappeared, never to be seen again. Very likely it helped to heat the Palazzo.

February brought spring to Venice, and with spring came the season of Carnival. Formerly, the entire span of time from Christmas through Ash Wednesday had been devoted to masking and merry-making, but such was the ill-feeling between the city's populace and its Austrian rulers that hostility rather than gaiety was the keynote of the season. Maskers could still be encountered throughout the city in the traditional black and red costumes, their faces disguised by the traditional black dominoes and long noses. They carried sacks stuffed with the traditional bon-bons and oranges, which they would offer with the old Carnival phrase, "*Resta servita, Signora!*" But everyone knew that these maskers were supplied with their costumes and candies by the Austrians, who hoped to give the city at least the semblance of its old *allegria*. Their scheme met with no observable success: the paid maskers dared not venture into the more populous quarters of the city for fear of the jostling, hooting crowds, and were to be found instead haunting its lonelier streets, trailed by bevies of urchins with wooden whistles. (Whistling is regarded throughout Italy as a mark of derision.) Everywhere the gutters glittered with bright-wrapped bon-bons, and oranges were almost as common a sight in the canals as ice had been a month before; this, despite that many of those same whistling urchins lived on the edge of starvation.

Into this sullen Carnival did my aunt Jerningham set forth one day towards the end of February, accompanied by the indispensable Mrs. Minchin. Her object was the uncharitable one of revenging herself upon the Jerninghams by buying lavish presents for them, which were to be symbolical of how much better a match had been made for me than if I had succumbed to my cousin Geoffrey's offer. Her natural parsimony made this a more difficult task than it need have been, but after having visited many shops she had supplied herself with two lengths of Venice chain (neither long enough to span even the narrowest waistcoat) and a very little bit of very fine lace.

While my aunt was consulting with Mrs. Minchin as to the directest route home through the maze of *calles, campos*, and *salizadas*, they were approached by two maskers. Mistaking their intentions and not comprehending their words, the two English-women refused to take candies from the proffered bags. The sweets were offered with more urgency. Mrs. Minchin, like the majority of her countrymen, was of the conviction that English spoken loudly with sufficient distinctness was intelligible anywhere in the world. She told the maskers that she Did Not Wish To Buy Anything from them and insisted that they Go Away. All the while the poor woman, and my aunt, too, were in terror of these bizarre creatures in their long-nosed masks and antique costumes. Repulsed, the maskers began to pelt Mrs. Minchin with their bon-bons. Mrs. Minchin shrieked; the maskers laughed at her. Having exhausted their supply of bon-bons, they used oranges as their missiles. Outraged, Mrs. Minchin whirled about to strike at her enemies with an umbrella. She lost her footing, for she had been running on the slimed stone beside a small canal, the Rio dei Miracoli. My aunt, foreseeing the worst, let loose a scream loud enough to rouse the whole neighborhood—but her scream could not prevent the worst from happening. Mrs. Minchin plunged into the canal. The maskers ran off, and no one thought to offer pursuit, since the business of fishing an Englishwoman out of the canal promised to be a larger entertainment. Such, though here much reduced in scale, was the story my aunt Jerningham related to me that afternoon, once she had changed from the clothing she had drenched in assisting Mrs. Minchin back to the Palazzo.

My reaction struck my aunt as cool to the point of being cold-blooded. She accused me of harboring a secret amusement at Mrs. Minchin's expense. I denied this, protesting that I was appalled at what had befallen her. Even as I protested, the tremor of a smile betrayed me. I could have bitten my lip in self-reproach, but the damage had been done—Lydia had her evidence.

"It astonishes me, Clara, that you can sit there and calmly smile at such a matter, when the poor woman—I say nothing of what *I* may have felt—very nearly drowned."

"Believe me, Aunt, I am concerned. If I see it in a less serious light than you do, it is because I was present only at the aftermath. The sight of Mrs. Minchin dripping all across the *sala*. . . ."

"A shame you missed seeing her hurled into the canal, in that case!"

"It is wrong of me, I know. I would not be tempted to smile at all, except for my relief that there were no worse consequences."

"That remains to be seen. I shall count it a wonder if Mrs. Minchin does not come down with a pleurisy. And there can be no question of inducing her to stay on in Venice. *That* is a bad enough consequence, I should think."

"Dear me, Aunt, one may encounter ruffians in London as well as here. It was an unfortunate accident, certainly, but I don't think all Venice should bear the blame."

"It was no *accident* that Mrs. Minchin was thrown into the canal. It was a deliberate *attack*."

"Well, yes . . . in a sense."

"In the most malicious sense possible. I did not mean to speak of this, but you compel me. When Mrs. Minchin struck his mask off with her umbrella, I saw the face of one of those scoundrels. I recognized his face, and so did she."

"Why did you not say so earlier? If you know who he is, he can be brought before a magistrate. He shall be!"

Lydia fell unaccountably silent, and her eyes avoided mine. I did not urge her to speak. Indeed, I felt myself cringing from what she was about to say, having during this space of silent accusation foreseen whom she would name.

"It was your husband's valet," she brought out at last.

"Are you quite certain?"

"I am, and Mrs. Minchin is. But I wished to spare you, and so I made her promise to say nothing. Now I've let it out myself. I'm very sorry, Clara."

"But good heavens, Aunt—I must tell Niles at once!"

"I do not think that would be wise."

"There can be no question. He must know at once."

I had arisen from the divan with a sense of being veritably lifted up by my purpose. A strange gladness mingled with my indignation. Though I regretted what had happened and dreaded the necessity of being the bearer of such news, I knew that the consequence of my doing so must be Manfredo's dismissal, and for this I could only be grateful. His presence in the household was a source of daily oppression to me; how great an oppression I had not realized till just this moment, when I could see my way clear of it at last.

My relief was short-lived. Quick as I had sprung up, Lydia was beside me. Her hand grasped my arm firmly, detaining me.

"Niles already knows. I told him, and he has persuaded me that I am mistaken. The fellow was with him throughout the afternoon. He was using him as a model. He showed me the sketches he had made. Naturally, when I learned this I assured him I would not mention the matter to you. It was wrong of me to do so. If you speak to him now, he'll be angry with you, and angrier with me."

"But you said that you were certain."

"I was, and I am."

"You don't believe Niles, then?"

"It is hard to disbelieve the evidence of my senses. I saw the fellow's face. Those gross mustaches slicked with oil. That beak of a nose. It is not a face one would easily confuse with others. But you must promise me, Clara"—tightening her grip—"that you will not speak of this to Niles."

"How can I, if you insist so positively that you cannot be mistaken?"

"Anyone, I suppose, can make mistakes."

"It was, after all, only a glimpse," I said tentatively, as though negotiating the terms of a truce from a position of very little strength.

"Exactly," said my aunt with conscious magnanimity. "And now, if you'll excuse me, I must look to Mrs. Minchin."

I kept my word, though not without misgivings. I said nothing to Niles, preferring the comfort of believing him to accepting Lydia's so much more distressing account of the matter. For his part, Niles showed a plausible degree of indignation, while his mother was positively fierce in denouncing the maskers. She took the matter up that very evening, as she was later to inform me, with Count Wrbna, who was ultimately responsible for hiring the maskers and sending them about the city. He, in turn, promised to discover their identity and have them punished.

I no longer entertained any doubt of Lydia's being in error when, a week later, a policeman appeared at the door of the Palazzo, accompanied by two rough-looking fellows who had confessed to the deed. As Mrs. Minchin had already returned to London and my aunt refused to see them, I was obliged to go downstairs and receive their grudging apologies. Though their words meant nothing to me, I noted that the elder of the two did bear some resemblance to Manfredo, especially with regard to the two features my aunt had made particular mention of, his mustache and his nose. The likeness was rather that of cousins than of twins, but . . . it was enough.

Lydia did not question me on the matter. She took in at a glance that I had made the choice which, some time or other, every wife must make. Though I cannot be certain, I think she secretly was proud of me. It was the *proper* choice, and for Lydia Jerningham that mattered more than whether, merely, it had been the right one.

CHAPTER SEVEN
Suppose a Gallery

PAINTERS DEVOTE A MUCH LARGER PORTION of their energies to recording the pleasant, perishable side of things than do writers. Entire careers have been given over to depicting vases of fresh flowers, and there are artists who have won considerable renown for capturing the shifting, intricate glint of watered silk. The evanescent glories of how many summer days now grace the walls of galleries half a world away and, may be, centuries after the veritable leaves and grasses have withered quite to dust. By contrast, how few writers take such moments as their central theme, or even make an earnest attempt to introduce a representative amount of sunshine into their productions. It is hard. When one is happy, one's natural impulse is to be still. Nothing is likelier to dissipate the sensation than to insist on its dimensions or to attempt to catalogue its variety.

That March was the happiest month of my marriage. Having stated this much, I find myself at a loss what else to add by way of corroboration, unless to suggest what pictures might be hung to represent my brief, golden consummation. To wit:

First I would fill one fair-sized museum with oils and water-colors of Venice itself: Venice in its majestic, monumental modes and Venice in its harum-scarum aspect, filled with ragged bravos and cherubic urchins; Venice drenched in the rose-pink of dawn and Venice stark against the broad blue noonday; Venice resplendent as an empress with the plunder of the centuries and Venice stripped by those same centuries down to the bare beauty of its brick; a Venice, above all, wedded to the sea—a swirling, shimmering, watery Venice that could dissolve into a vast cartouche of silvery shining as the western winds efface its image from the mirror of the lagoon.

I would fill another dozen museums, as they are filled already, with the works of the great Venetian painters—Vivarini and Bellini; Giorgione, Titian, Tintoretto, Veronese; Guardi and Tiepolo. During that March, I feasted with that great company and an hundred masters more. Niles was ever at my side, sharing in my pleasure, instructing my taste, and joining in my praise. Praise and pleasure greatly preponderated over instruction, for the paintings of the Venetians are seldom theoretical. Rather, like the city itself, they offer themselves immediately to the delighted senses, and like those other famed sea-creatures, the Sirens, they enchant and captivate all who accept the offer.

Then, on a more modest scale, there might be a little gallery of genre studies, in the manner of a latter-day Longhi. These would represent the Palazzo Alari-Uboldo in its refurbished condition, canvases alive with anecdote both high and low, the whispers of servants and the gossip of guests. Attached to this gallery, I should deck out a hall with portraits jostling each other shoulder to shoulder. It would need to be a large hall, for now that Zaide had furnished the Palazzo to her satisfaction, she must entertain. A fair number of those portrayed would be shown in the various uniforms of the Austrian army, but by no means all.

Despite the uncertain political situation, the warmer weather had brought the usual influx of foreigners to the city. Some of these portraits might still be recognized by my readers, for among them there were celebrities whose fame has not entirely faded with the years. I doubt, however, whether any of these good people would welcome the publicity of being named in these pages as visitors at the Palazzo Alari-Uboldo. So let there be dust-covers draped over all except those whose names are indiscerptible from my tale.

My readers will recognize those that remain on view, though they may be a little taken aback to see the lot of us so much more richly dressed than when we were first introduced. (But isn't that always the way with portraits?) There is, perhaps, a bit more

gauntness to Zaide's figure, a bit more opulence to my aunt's. I
have advanced to the brink of one-and-twenty, while Niles has
just concluded his third full decade of life. He often insisted, in
those days, that thirty was of all the ages that one might attain to
the rosiest, jolliest, most comfortable, and best-tempered. I doubt
that an objective portrait would bear him out in all these particulars. From the time I knew him at Blackthorne, the years had
rather subtracted from than added to his figure, and it had never
been so large a figure as to bear much subtraction. Still, his expression had not changed, and that is what one looks for in a
portrait. One would have known him by his smile alone.

CHAPTER EIGHT
Zorina Stanley's Confession

ON THE AFTERNOON OF THE FIRST OF APRIL, Lydia and I had been
escorted by one Colonel Koestritz to the Armenian monastery on
the island of San Lazzaro. As his reward, the Colonel was asked
to stay on to dine *en famille* at the Palazzo. Count Wrbna was
also to be present at that dinner, but by this time his face was so
usual at our table that he quite counted as "family." The meal was
uncommonly good, and at its end Zaide proposed that, rather than
adjourning to the drawing room, the ladies should remain behind
with the gentlemen while they enjoyed their cigars and their port.
I was delighted, and Lydia did not object.

Without special prompting, the servants set glasses before all
six of us. I watched Niles light a long black cigar and sniffed at
the fumes produced thereby. In those times, tobacco was used
far less restrictedly on the Continent than in England, but I
had never before been *in a room* when cigars were being burned.
There was for me a distinct sense of being inducted into the
mysteries of adult life. This once I welcomed novelty rather than
shied from it, and my reckless mood was not subdued by the port
wine glowing in my glass and (very soon) on my tongue.

Count Wrbna rose, and proposed a toast: "To our dear Countess." Zaide affected to believe that the company had been asked to drink in my honor rather than hers, so a second, more explicit health was drunk. Niles lifted his glass and declared: "To my mother, on her anniversary."

"Do you still celebrate your anniversary?" Lydia asked, always ready to applaud the more heroic acts of widowhood.

"Today is an anniversary more to be regretted, I'm afraid, than celebrated, though these gentlemen by their grinning would seem to suggest that the day is a kind of Saturnalia. Colonel, I except you from my reproval."

This ostensible rebuke was delivered with no very ill humor, but even so Zaide was no more forthcoming on the subject. She parried the Colonel's and my own curiosity with some polite questions as to our sightseeing.

Lydia, who had been my invariable companion on these expeditions, related our adventures at complaisant length. She described the printing machines at the monastery, displayed some beads of Venice glass she had bought that morning at a shop nearby to Florian's, and concluded with a remarkably complete inventory of the goods of the Mocenigo Palace, to which the Colonel had accompanied us on an earlier outing.

"I am astonished at you, Mrs. Jerningham," Niles put in. "Next I shall be told that you took my wife to a wineshop to drink muscat with the gondoliers and *facchini*. The Mocenigo Palace, indeed!"

"It seemed as respectable as anywhere else we have visited," my aunt replied. "There *was* a painting—did you say it was by Titian, Colonel?—that perhaps should not be publicly displayed. But I did not linger before it; nor, rest assured, did Clara."

"Niles is making sport of us, Mrs. Jerningham," Colonel Koestritz said. "The Mocenigo Palace is a perfectly proper object of interest."

"It is the Madame Tussaud's of Venice," Niles retorted. "Count Wrbna, will you bear me out?"

Count Wrbna considered his cigar carefully before replying: "I would not say it is notorious." (Though by his tone he *did* say so.)

"Then why," Niles asked, "on any fair summer day do ten troops of Englishmen ask to be admitted? Not, you may be sure, because the Mocenigo has been the family seat of Doges. Lord Byron passed half a year on the premises and made them, by his conduct there, an imperishable scandal."

"Niles, Niles, Niles! It is mean of you to bait a poor old woman in this manner. Whatever have I done to merit it?"

"Mother, I protest! If I have said *anything* that might offend the most delicate sensibility—"

"You see, my dears, as Niles and the Count well know, I was acquainted with the gentleman in question. Though it was a brief acquaintance, the tale is long and tedious, and I shall not burden this company with the hearing of it."

"It is never a burden to listen to you, Contessa," replied Count Wrbna, "but *comme tu veux*. If you prefer, I will tell *you* a story on this same theme. You will remember that I was in Paris last October on a mission for the Archduke, in the course of which I became acquainted with one Marquis de Boissy. The business that had brought us together is of no importance, except that it required a certain show of friendliness between us. When the Marquis asked me to call upon him at his home, I did so. I was shown up to a room that had somewhat the air of a museum. That is, a great variety of very common-looking objects were disposed about the room, in cases and on shelves, so as to suggest that they were treasures. At the center of this ossuary, displayed on a gilded divan that would have done justice to a Cleopatra, was a very old, very frail, very tired lady whom my host most solemnly introduced as: '*La Marquise de Boissy, ma femme, ancienne maîtresse de Byron.*' "

"Not the Guiccioli!" Zaide exclaimed.

"Herself."

"And still alive?"

"Most forcibly," Count Wrbna assured her.

"Really, Mother, it is not such a prodigy. She cannot be so very much older than you."

"As for that, I'm sure there are people who are amazed to learn that *I'm* still alive. It *has* been some forty-two years since I met the woman."

"You did meet her, then?" Count Wrbna inquired. "I wondered."

"Oh, to be sure. She was that jealous that she would follow him about from room to room, like a spoilt lapdog. There was no question of her being hidden away. She wouldn't have allowed it."

"I don't think I understand," my aunt said, in a tone that indicated she had begun, at least, to suspect. The point of the Count's anecdote, being in French, had eluded her at first. "Who are the . . . Guiccioli?"

"There was but a single one that I met," Zaide answered. "Teresa. Her husband, Count Guiccioli, lived in Ravenna. I was told he was an invalid. There were the Gambas, of course—her father and brother. One saw a good deal of them, the brother especially—Pietro. It was he, I'm told, who put the bee into Byron's war bonnet about going off to liberate the Greeks."

"What I think Mrs. Jerningham wishes to know, Mother, is the nature of that lady's relationship to Lord Byron. Am I correct?"

My aunt nodded.

"I can only say that it was not one to do credit to either party. It was the Countess Guiccioli, together with Byron, who gave the Mocenigo Palace its present reputation as an object of scandal."

"But if we had known—"

"As to that, my dear Mrs. Jerningham," Colonel Koestritz said, in what he intended to be a reassuring tone, "you need not concern yourself. Count Visconti has pointed out that everyone who comes to Venice pays a visit to the Mocenigo. The English especially."

The Colonel went on to excuse the weakness of the man by proclaiming the greatness of the poet, but my aunt was not prepared to accept this time-honored alibi. She developed a sudden, reproachful indisposition and excused herself from the table.

"I am afraid we have offended your aunt, Clara," Zaide said, as soon as she had left the room. "I'm very sorry. I did try to steer our talk away from areas I knew would not agree with her."

"The blame must be mine, in that case," Count Wrbna said, with equanimity. "It is droll, though, that I should be called to account for one sin all the while I knew myself guilty of quite another. The story I told concerning the Marquis de Boissy, though

I firmly believe it to be true, is not my own. I thought that surely you, Zaide, would twit me for adopting so common a scandal as my own discovery."

"My dear Rudolph, where I have been these past two years, there are no scandals but the weather. But that is not my chief complaint against the country. I could endure any degree of pastoral dullness so long, *mein alter Schatz,* as I could share my tedium with you."

"Then the next time you set off to some rural seat you must secure my presence there."

"It is less than candid to cadge an invitation you know you'll not accept. Do I not ask you almost daily to come down to the Villa for a part of the summer?"

"I shall go there with you, and gladly, as soon as ever these Garibaldini relieve me of my duties here."

"Now it is my turn not to understand," I said. "I thought Garibaldi and his followers were your enemies?"

"And so they are, my dear Contessa, but I have no illusion that they must, simply on that account, surrender. It takes no gift of prophecy to see that sooner or later—*heut' oder morgen oder der übernächste Tag*—Venice shall be joined to Italy. The army's task, and mine therefore, is only to tip the balance in favor of 'later,' and we have succeeded for many more years than I would have thought possible. Did I not predict, Conte, when you were leaving Venice, years ago, that we should not meet here again?"

"You did, which only proves that you are a better administrator than a prophet."

Encouraged by Niles, Count Wrbna delivered a long encomium on the city he had ruled so many years, an account half lyrical and half humorous. All of us, listening to him, were soothed into a mellower mood, and when a little later the conversation again came round to the matter of Zaide's "anniversary" she did not demonstrate the same reluctance to unfold this tale.

(Formerly I have believed that my mother-in-law had set out that evening on purpose to corrupt my morals. Now, in the calmer perspective of the years, I can see that her motive was the commoner one of being unable to bear a secondary role. She had, at all costs, to keep Count Wrbna from usurping all our attention and applause. Finally, a good session of gossiping was one of her favorite pleasures, and the port she had drunk encouraged her to seize the pleasure then and there in a mood of genial and uncritical self-approbation.)

"Since you have all so cleverly conspired to have me tell my tale, you must allow me to do so at my own poky pace, beginning at the very dawn of time, which is to say, in 1822, the year that poor Lord Castlereagh committed suicide. I was then newly hatched into the life of society. Like most events too long prepared for, my *début* had been a disappointment. At sixty there is no harm in being tall—we call it stateliness—but at seventeen it can be a curse equal to leprosy. A squib was circulated, which to this day gives me a distinct twinge:

> *Ah, what avails the sceptred race!*
> *Ah, what the brightest talk!*
> *What mounds of heirlooms, miles of lace!*
> *If Z_____ be such a gawk!*

I began to refuse invitations, to take solitary walks, and . . . *to read books!* Literature was my undoing. If I had had a daughter, I'd have made it a principle never to teach her to read. Nothing is so dangerous to the young female mind as a three-decker novel, unless, perhaps, it be poetry. Now of all the poets that a girl might read in 1822 the most approvedly seditious, the most notoriously ardent and romantic was Lord Byron. I read *Childe Harold* and swooned. I read his *Sardanapalus* and fell in love. I committed both cantos of *The Bride of Abydos* to memory and would wander through the halls and gardens of Blackthorne, muttering stanzas like a Bedlamite.

> *He lived—he breathed—he moved—he felt.*
> *He raised the maid from where she knelt.*

Rhyme after rhyme, line upon line—it was heavenly. That was the sublimest moment of my life, I dare say, for my imagination had yet to be corrupted by experience.

"Well! Experience was to come. I wrote to him, to my god, to the great Byron. I remember the exact words, since I recited them to myself quite as often as any of his poems. 'I tremble,' quoth I, 'in addressing you, yet I cannot remain silent. To you I am indebted for almost all the happy hours I have spent, my daydreams have been full of you—how romantic you would think me, did I tell you all the projects I have formed of which you were the hero.' I signed my note with an alias, Zorina Stanley, and consigned it to the mails.

"I had given a post office in Fitzroy Square as Zorina's address. It was the Season, and I'd accompanied my father to our house in town. In order to have a reason to return to that post office every day, I entered into correspondence with half of Sussex. I waited, and fretted, and sighed, and despaired, and in a month there was a letter for me. From Italy! From Him! Never mind that he counselled me to seek a worthier object on whom to lavish my feelings; no matter that he called my passion an illusion: he had answered me! I wrote back at once, confessing that my name was not (as he'd suspected) 'Zorina' but 'Isabel,' which seemed a more probable sort of name to me than my own, which I detested. Because he had emphasized the disparity in our ages, I addressed him as 'My dear Papa,' and told him that I wished I were indeed his child, that I would gladly have been *his slave* (which I underlined three times). This, too, received a reply, rather warmer than the first. In my next letter, my feelings overflowed into French. '*Je vous aime*,' I wrote, '*avec tout mon coeur et pour toute ma vie.*' I think that '*toute ma vie*' must not have been to his taste. In any case, there was no reply.

"Meanwhile, however, my father had arranged with his friend, Lord Blessington, that I should accompany that gentleman and his wife upon their intended tour of Europe. This was meant to act as an antidote to the poetry from which I had been suffering and to remove me from the marriage market till I had acquired a more polished presence. Lady Blessington had been reputed one of the great beauties of the Regency, despite that she, too, was taller than beauties have any right to be, and it was hoped that a few months of bouncing about the Continent (there were no railways then, of course, and one *did* bounce dreadfully) in Lady B.'s company would make a similar kind of goddess of me. An Amazon instead of a gawk.

"Whether that purpose was accomplished, I wouldn't venture

to say, but I did enjoy myself mightily. We saw Paris, Vienna, the Alps, the Lakes, an hundred sights and a thousand genial faces. I had complained in London of the insipid conversations one must endure if one enters Society. I found that the same conversations, if conducted in French or German, were thoroughly entertaining. But that is by the by. *My* great purpose in all this junketing was that of approaching at last the shrine of my idol. The Blessingtons seemed bent on going everywhere, and somewhere in that everywhere *he* awaited his Zorina. Or, rather, his Isabel. Finally, on the night of March thirty-first, we arrived in Genoa, and the next day—"

"Forty-two years ago today," Niles observed, lifting his glass in a mock salute.

Zaide paid him no heed. "The next day we drove out to the villa Byron had rented in the suburb of Albaro and introduced ourselves. I was the least conspicuous of his callers, and I was grateful not to have much notice paid me. Enough that he had glanced at me! Enough that I could gaze at him!"

"What was he like?" asked Colonel Koestritz. "I mean, to gaze at."

"As well ask Semele the color of Jove's eyes as expect my mother to describe Byron."

"On the contrary, I observed him with that sharpness which only lovers possess. His nose was the work of Praxiteles. I meditated a great deal on the perfection of his nose, since in other respects his features varied somewhat from the way I'd seen them represented in engravings. For one thing, he was beginning to go bald. That was something of a shock, at first, though within a week I had persuaded myself that Byron's degree of baldness represented an ideal of masculine beauty. I observed that his clothes were shabby and out of fashion, but could there be any fashion, after all, but what *he* might set? In the crucial respect of representing my *idea* of Byron, the reality actually improved on my earlier fantasies. He had a delectable quality of manliness just beginning to droop with overmuch wisdom; of beauty pathetically poised on the brink of its decline."

"It seems," Count Wrbna commented, "that your infatuation has abated very little from its first force."

"A little loyalty is always in order on anniversaries. Besides, I was never allowed the opportunity of a gradual disillusionment. Shortly after we arrived, Byron decided he must go and rescue Greece from tyranny."

"Where he died," Colonel Koestritz solemnly informed us.

"Where he died," Zaide agreed, sipping at her port.

"And did you never tell him who you were?" I asked.

"Oh yes, Zorina Stanley could not keep in the shadows for ever. It was no easy matter, though, to find an opportunity. If Lady Blessington had not collared him, then our companion, the Count d'Orsay, was at his ear. Byron's thirst for gossip was unquenchable. Also, the Guiccioli had him under her very keen surveillance. I'd begun to despair of ever having him to myself, when one evening late in April he quite spontaneously took me aside, under what pretext I shall never know, for immediately I had my chance I seized it. I told him who I was and declared my deathless love. I shall never forget his response. Before I'd finished pinning my heart to my sleeve, he burst out laughing. He sat down on a bench in his garden and quite exhausted himself with laughter. I died, my dears. Then and there, I died."

CHAPTER NINE
Insolence

I HAD DISGUISED MY REACTION to the Contessa's tale so effectively that I could not be sure, later, what my own true feelings were— the mild amusement I expressed (in imitation of the other listeners) or the revulsion I concealed. This evening's talk had been my first intimation that misconduct and impropriety may be excused on the grounds of youth and inexperience. Zaide seemed to regard what she had done with amusement rather than with shame, as though her infatuation with Byron and the actions to which it had led were just a harmless joke against herself, not essentially different from my own story, recorded earlier in these pages, of going to see

Rachel in *Bérénice*. By contrast, I had been brought up to believe that young ladies must be especially sensitive to appearances, especially careful, especially good. Was I now to be initiated into a larger wisdom? Were such expectations a kind of moral fiction, like tales of Santa Klaus, invented to keep young ladies in ignorance of the actual dimensions and operations of the social sphere they inhabited? This seemed to be the moral of Zaide's tale. Even as I shrank from such a lesson, I pondered it, in much the way, I imagine, that Eve turned the proffered fruit round in her hand, admirous of its shape and color, curious as to its flavor.

The company did not linger for ever in the dining room, and when they removed to take their coffee I excused myself, claiming, which was quite true, that I was suffering from a headache. In my own quarters, I rang for Rose, and when she was not forthcoming I decided to take the air in the little enclosed garden behind the Palazzo.

With the first breath of the mild airs suffusing the garden, my spirits rose and the pain grew duller. In spring, the canals of the city are not sluggish as in summer, and so the atmosphere that night was enlivened by the salt aroma of the sea. Only the farthest corner of the garden received any light from the moon, which, some few days short of the full, hung low in the west, looking unnaturally large beside the ranked chimneys of the Palazzo. I sat down upon the rim of a small, dry fountain domed over by a giant scallop shell of crumbling stone. There, folding my hands and composing my thoughts, I meant to imitate the stillness of the plants about me, hoping by my outward quiet to induce a more significant peacefulness within. I was not many minutes established inside my shallow cave when I was joined by a companion. A fat brindled tom dropped, like a ripe peach, from the iron scrollwork of the garden wall and came to sit by my feet. Not that he sought company, for after a glance to satisfy himself that I was harmless he commenced to lick his wrists contentedly, paying me no more attention than if I had been a statue recently installed. This dusty fountain was his regular haunt, and he was not about to change his habits on *my* account! Cats are the decayed gentry of the animal kingdom: they know precisely what is due them and they insist on receiving it.

There we sat, the brindled tom and I, while the shadow of the

Palazzo crept towards us, mantling the young leaves of the bushes and the scrawny stalks of the borders in a deeper darkness. Some of the tom's complaisance had rubbed off on me, and I remember having a pleasant daydream on the pastoral theme of how, in the weeks ahead, I would deepen my acquaintance with these shrubs and flowerbeds; how I would be witness, soon, to the promise of buds forming, the fulfillment of blossoms; how I would revisit these paths, in daytime, with my shears and my basket and my wide straw hat to gather the choicest blooms and make of them a posy for the breakfast table; finally of how delighted Niles would be and how he would praise my little offering of flowers.

This idyl was interrupted, for both of us, by a sudden fierce outburst, half shriek, half muffled laughter. The tom darted into the shrubbery, while I, supposing that the voices I heard had their source outside the garden walls, tried to unravel the sense of their whispered words. A wicked thing to do, and even wickeder had I succeeded! However, without following the sense, without even certainly knowing what language was being spoken, it was possible to discern the dramatic outline of this exchange. He pleaded; she refused. Then, more urgently, he would offer reasons—reasons she rejected, though with no real sense of finality, but rather in such a tone as to invite the renewal of his importunings. Gradually, two facts became clear—that this dialogue was part of a courtship (a courtship fairly well-advanced), and that the speakers were on the hither side of the garden wall. Perceiving the impropriety of remaining longer concealed in my scallop-shell cave, I rose, and cleared my throat, and scraped my shoes on the gravel of the path.

Despite every fair warning that they were not alone, the couple paid no heed. The shrubs formed a single avenue of approach towards my corner of the garden, and it was onto this path their steps had strayed, nor was there any other path by which I might leave and still avoid them. They came within a dozen yards of where I had placed myself, in plain sight, in the middle of the path. Dark as it was, it was not so dark that they could not have seen me. I saw them clearly enough, though I wished I might not have. Even if the blackness had been so entire as to blot out the immodesty of their actions, the evidence of my ears would have been sufficiently shameful.

Again, with a more desperate ostentation, I sought to make my presence known. I confess that at that moment no larger or loftier motive stirred me than a desire to avoid a "scene." Yet there was a limit to how long I could stand by, an unacknowledged spectator of their guilt, a limit to the magnitude of the sin I would witness unprotesting. When that limit had been reached, I stepped forth— not boldly, to be sure, for my hope was still that they would take alarm at my approach and, at the least, if they would not flee (it was perhaps too late for that), they would desist from their raw indecorum. They did not, and each footstep required a fresh resolve.

When I was quite upon them, Rose sprang up with a little cry of "Madame!" I continued past her without acknowledgment, but *he* had the effrontery to catch hold my sleeve. I sought to pull loose, but his fingers were an iron shackle round my wrist, and I was obliged to turn round. He accorded me a bow, mocking in its exaggeration. The taunt that had been latent in his civilities he now permitted full expression. "My Lady, you must excuse us. We did not know . . . that you"—he paused, as always, before the subjunctive—"were here."

"But you *did* know, didn't you!" I burst out, without considering.

"My Lady?" Oh—in such a cool, insinuating tone!

"You *must* have heard me. You surely saw me."

I broke off, as the first blaze of anger was succeeded by the first flush of embarrassment. I realized that, in effect, I was reproaching Manfredo not for the wrong he had done but because he had not taken the trouble to conceal it from me.

"My Lady? If you will please—"

"Let go my arm!"

He complied at once, and salvaging what I could of my dignity, I turned my back on the two servants and fled (I might almost say "flew," so mightily did my feelings of fear and outrage bear me along) towards the door of the Palazzo.

Rose, lacking the valet's arrogant assurance, followed me upstairs to the dim-lighted *sala* as far as the door to my own room, pleading her innocence even as she tried to repair the more salient disorders of her dress. Angry as I was, I still pusillanimously sought to defer the inevitable moment, the moment of Rose's formal dismission.

I had another motive, too, for lingering outside my room pretending to listen to these lame excuses. There were traces still of tears at the corners of my eyes. I did not want my maid to know how much I was distressed.

With a predator's quick instinct for a prey's weakness, Rose sensed my reluctance and tried, by taking a more bullying tone, to re-establish our relationship on its former basis. I was upset, she declared. I had stayed up beyond my usual hour. Tomorrow I would see matters in a different light, and now—

"I will undress myself, if you please."

She seemed to consider whether to take up, still more emphatically, the tone of a scolding nanny; whether, for instance, to push past me into the room and disrobe me by force. Thankfully, I was not put to the test. She adopted, instead, a tactic of supplication. All her excuses, pleas, and accusations were reducible to the simple contention that all men are scoundrels and Manfredo a larger scoundrel than most.

"I will not discuss the matter any further," I declared.

"Thank you, my Lady. I promise I shan't give you reason to."

"Please hear me out. At the first opportunity, I shall take up this matter with my husband, and I trust that he shall take it up in due course with you." With that, I entered my room hastily, cursing my skirts for being so wide and requiring a proportional amplitude in the opening of the door. But Rose did not offer to pursue me within. Evidently my last words had given her pause.

Alone at last, I closed my eyes and waited for . . . I knew not what. Vastations of tears and trembling? Kindlings of a righteous indignation? I am told that in Bermuda, at the first shock of an earthquake, the populace abates its work, then pauses, as though entranced, waiting for the blow to fall or pass them by. So I paused, and so, when the feeling did well up within my breast, it seemed to have the force of a revelation: *I needed Niles.*

I needed him! I could not breathe unless he were beside me. I could not bear to open my eyes if by doing so I should not see him. It was all I could do to keep from calling out his name aloud, as though I were in immediate peril of my life.

My first thought was to go to him at once, but even as I stepped towards the door, I checked that impulse. Was it not all too probable that Rose would still be standing where I had left her? A similar consideration prevented me as I was about to tug at the bell-rope, for Rose would almost certainly be the servant to respond to such a summons. I could not go to him, and I could not send for him. I sat down, facing the door, *willing* Niles to come to me and compressing all my confusions and my single, certain need into the one whispered syllable of his name.

CHAPTER TEN

In Defense of Insolence

THE DOOR OPENED. I could not comprehend, at first, it was not Niles, coming in response to my dire need of him.

"My Lady must excuse me I do not knock."

Only when, without averting his eyes from mine, Manfredo had closed the door and leaned his body's weight against it, did I realize my true position. Even then I was not able, all at once, to take it in. Certain rules of social behavior are so inviolable that their first violation leaves us unbelieving, as though a law of nature, rather than a rule of etiquette, has been betrayed.

"My Lady must understand, please. I have much regret for this evening. In the garden we have believed that we"—he hesitated before the subjunctive—"would have been alone. It is my habit in the evening to walk in the garden. But it has not been my lady's habit, I think, and so tonight I am not careful. I am most regretful, and my Lady's maid, too, is most *deeply* regretful. My Lady must accept this apology."

I could only stare at him. He had not bothered, before entering, to brush the dust from his trouser-legs, and I noticed, also, that his waistcoat had been improperly done up, so that a little wreath of gray linen was exposed at his waist. Quickly as I perceived these details I thought—*he is doing this on purpose to offend.* The simpler explanation, that he was in his cups, never occurred to me at all.

Drunk or sober, Manfredo was not to be defeated by my disdainful silence. Assuming that My Lady had accepted his apology, as per demand, he went on: "It is not necessary, I think, to speak of this to Conte Visconti. My Lady will no doubt remember, some years since, another time when I have asked her not to speak of . . . I do not know the word in English. Another *sconsideratezza? Indiscrezione?* You understand me."

"I do not!"

"But my Lady must surely remember. . . ." The jewelled hand made a lazy circle in the air, a gesture that, taken in conjunction with a certain, somnolent smile, had to be interpreted as suggesting our complicity. The suggestion was made almost tenderly. The tone of his voice was identical to that I had heard him adopt earlier in the garden with Rose, a sinuous mingling of entreaty and veiled threat.

"I choose neither to understand nor to remember."

"My Lady has reason to be angered. Yet if she will think one moment of her position—"

"You had much better think of yours! But I will *not* discuss it! Leave this room."

"As my Lady wishes. But first I should like to know what my Lady will say to her husband."

"Now!" I pointed to the door, against which he was still indolently slouched.

He did not move, not by the blinking of a lash. Once again, as when he had surprised me behind the door to Niles' room, our eyes locked in a kind of psychic combat, but this time there was nothing inadvertent in the struggle. If the look that passed between us in those moments had been made of wire, one might have played music upon it, so tautly was it drawn, so tightly stretched. And the music's theme? That he meant to subdue me to his will, and I refused to be subdued. Physically I did not fear him, for it was the nature of the combat that it should be *only* between our wills. For him to have taken a step closer, for me to have spoken another word, would have amounted to an admission of defeat.

The contest ended in a draw. Niles entered by the door com-municating with my bedroom. "Ah, there you are!" he called out cheerily, and the wire snapped. We neither of us knew whom Niles had intended by this greeting, and both turned to him like soldiers called to attention.

"Clara! My dear, what is wrong?"

My eyes had spoken the distress that my tongue could not. Niles hastened towards me, impelled by the magnetism of my need. I could only clasp the hand he offered me—no longer, now that he was here, afraid to show my helplessness before Manfredo.

The valet, who had defied my most peremptory command, was dismissed by a nod of his master's head.

"Are you quite well, Clara?"

"Yes." It was a small untruth. All that was weak and womanly in me craved for the release of tears, longed for the brute comfort of being stroked and soothed and held and spoken to. If Niles had embraced me then and there, I am sure I would not have had the strength to resist the luxury of an incoherent grief. Yet I was glad when he did not, for I knew that the only enduring remedy for the pain I felt lay in a full and free confession.

"But your hand is trembling so."

"I have had . . . something of a fright."

"Well, let us sit down and you shall tell me of it. Here, or in your bedroom?"

"This will do quite well."

He helped me to a mahogany chair, the twin of one in the Jerningham parlor. Gripping its prickly arms, I seemed to draw a kind of strength from the old seat, as though it were the witness chair in a courtroom and I, a witness, sworn to speak the truth, sustained by my oath. I told, first, of how I had gone into the garden; of how, when I had realized I was no longer alone, I had tried to leave; of how I had been baffled in that purpose. What my testimony lacked in exactness on this last subject it made up for with a heartfelt indignation. Nevertheless, I sensed that Niles, while still sympathizing with my distress, regarded it as immoderate. At my account of Rose's efforts to justify her fault, he only nodded, as though this had confirmed some failing already known to him, and already forgiven.

"And Manfredo?" he asked. "Was that why he was visiting you just now?"

"Yes. He dropped in to tell me that I must excuse him. Mind you, that I *must!*"

"It shows a deplorable impudence in him, of course, but a deplorable innocence of English grammar as well. I don't think we can hold such nuances against him. That he should address you at all, without solicitation, is bad enough, and really you ought not to have listened to him."

"I didn't *want* to listen to him," I replied, with some heat. "He entered the room without knocking, and he refused to leave when I asked him to do so."

"Oh, now *that* can never be allowed! He'll get a proper dressing-down on that score, have no doubt. I'd do it this minute, except. . . ." And he stroked my hand, clenched to the arm of the chair.

Earlier that might have been enough to mollify me. Now my indignation had been rekindled. "You will punish him for being discourteous—but not for being immoral!"

"There are some things it's best to overlook, Clara," he said, continuing to stroke my hand. "Or if not 'best,' then wisest. Servants are human, and if Rose wishes to set her cap for Manfredo, I don't see how we can prevent her. Or him, for that matter. It's the common Italian philosophy of *Lascia star'*. Leave be." He spoke in a tone of such calm and kindly good sense that, without accepting the philosophy that he proposed, I did begin to mistrust my indignation.

"Of course," he went on, "they shall have to find somewhere else for their rendezvous than the garden. The winter months have probably accustomed them to regarding it as their private deer-park. I'm sure they had no idea you were out there. You must have given them quite a start."

"So Manfredo claimed, though I don't for a minute believe him. But even if they *didn't* know, doesn't the fact remain?"

"What fact, my dear? I must say you haven't made that quite clear."

Reader, I cannot express the confusion of my feelings—the bafflement, the shame, the anger, the pain of betrayal, and, withal, the dawning doubt.

"I'm sorry, Clara," Niles resumed in a gentler tone. "Truly, I don't want to wound your feelings more than they've been wounded already. Manfredo is mightily at fault, and he shall answer for it. Rose, too. But the fault lies, as I see it, in their behavior towards you. In their discourtesy, if you insist. What they may have done together. . . . *Lascia star'*."

The pain of hearing Niles so demean himself had become unendurable, and I determined to tell him that which he could not shrug off. "I have not told you everything. There was another occasion . . . at Blackthorne . . . the evening when I visited your mother's room and you were called away—"

"You needn't say more, Clara. Manfredo long ago told me what happened that night, how you discovered him with the serving-girl."

I felt as one who, rushing towards water, discovers he has been cheated by a mirage. In my effort to speak the simple truth, I was being enveloped in a new and more complex deceit.

"What . . . exactly . . . did Manfredo tell you?"

"Only that you stumbled over the two of them in the darkness of the stairwell, and how he begged you not to speak of the matter for fear that Lord Rhodes might expel him from the house, which almost certainly would have been the result if you *had* said anything. Believe me, Clara, I've always respected your silence on the subject. A promise kept is not a cause for blushing."

Was I blushing? Then chagrin, not shame, had brought the color to my cheeks—chagrin at the ease with which my burst of candor had led me directly into a new morass of lies. If I were now to speak of my suspicions, Manfredo had an alibi prepared. The woman he had been awaiting in the stairwell had been one of Lord Rhodes' domestics—not his master's wife. Such new facts as I might add would only serve to give Manfredo a character for chivalry. The difference between our stories would be imputed to his wish not to compromise *me*! Indeed, what reason did I have to think that this was not his motive? That, in fact, *all* my suspicions had been baseless?

My resolve to speak out the truth had exhausted itself in the maze of these misgivings, and I allowed myself to be led into the bedroom. Then, before I could prevent him, Niles tugged at the bell-rope.

"Niles, no! I can't possibly—"

"Sleep is what you need now, Clara."

"Yes, but you have just summoned—"

"Your maid—to undress you. You can't very well sleep in that gown, now can you?"

"I'd rather sleep beneath the Rialto Bridge than have her here, touching me, tonight."

"Tonight—that's just the point. To behave differently tonight would be putting yourself into her hands. Remember—*you* are the mistress. Her feelings are of no consequence."

"I wasn't considering her feelings. I was thinking of mine."

"One doesn't have feelings about one's domestics. Or thoughts, for that matter. One rings for them, and they come and do what is required. What is required now is that you get some sleep, my dear. *I* can't very well help you to undress. Can I?"

"No. You're right, and I shall do whatever you say."

"That's a dear little wife, and a wise little wife, too. No more discussion, eh? Rose will hear us and get a swelled head. I shall go now and change into my nightgown."

There are a multitude of milestones along the road to any catastrophe. Most go unobserved in our haste towards what we still fail to recognize as our appointed end, but one moment necessarily stands out from the common ruck—that moment when we first recognize that we are on a downwards course and can discern the awful, inescapable shape ahead. For me that moment came as I sat before the mirror of my vanity, waiting, benumbed, the humiliation of my maid's attentions.

CHAPTER ELEVEN
A Question Is Posed

"I HOPE," LYDIA SAID, after she had laid her music aside, "that you have been thinking of names."

We were alone in my bedroom. Lydia occupied the bench before the Dimoline, while I was still *en déshabillé*, sitting up in bed, propped by pillows. Since the evening of April the first, a week before, I had developed a convenient malady that had prevented me from leaving my room—or summoning Rose into it.

"Names? No. There wasn't a thought in my head. I was listening to you play."

"I don't mean now—I mean in general. It is never too soon, you know."

"Too soon for what, Aunt?"

"For thinking of names, of course!" When I persisted in regarding her with puzzlement, she burst out: "Of your children, Clara! For goodness sake."

"No. In fact, I haven't."

"Then you ought to."

For many weeks I had wanted to broach exactly this subject with my aunt, yet now that it had arisen I felt unsure how to pursue it. "Am I . . . likely to have a baby soon?"

"Well, Clara, that is not for *me* to say. This is, of course, generally the time when one would begin to . . . speculate."

"Do you mean, then, that it's for me to say? Because I'm not certain I understand what signs I am supposed to look for."

"Niles hasn't spoken about . . . ?"

"Not a word."

Lydia heaved a sigh. "Isn't that just like a man? Josiah was the same. Never once in all the years that we were married—not a word, not a syllable."

"So you don't know either?"

"As to the signs? Not a great deal. You would have been too young to remember when Mrs. Minchin was expecting."

"I think I do remember. She swelled up, did she not?"

"Yes, of course."

"But that, I have gathered, comes only in the final months. Before that . . . what happens?"

"I can't say from my own experience. Mrs. Minchin complained a great deal of her digestion. That seems to be quite usual. In fact, it was your own queasy appetite this last week that set me to wondering."

"But beyond that, Aunt—"

"Beyond that, Clara, I know nothing at all."

"I mean, as to the cause."

CHAPTER TWELVE

A Hasty Departure

BY THE DEATH OF MY UNCLE JERNINGHAM I had been left at liberty
to marry Niles; by Renata's death he was enabled to ask for my
hand; finally, the death of Lord Rhodes had tipped the balance in
favor of my accepting his offer. Now Death, who had been such
an industrious matchmaker, acted once again, and by a fourth
fatality secured the ruin of the marriage built on those dark
foundations.

On the twelfth of April, 1865, an old widow-woman, one
Signora Ricci, a lace-maker from the isle of Chioggia, entered the
Grimani Palace under the pretense of delivering a basket of eels
to its kitchen. Once inside, she assumed the character and costume
of a chambermaid. With broom and dusting cloth she moved from
room to room—as it were, invisibly. She seems to have proceeded
directly to the Grimani's chapel (whether by a fatal intuition or
advised by a member of the domestic staff could never be determined), where the gray eminence of all Lombardo-Veneto was
privately celebrating the Mass. There, with a stiletto she had concealed beneath her clothes, she took the life of Rudolph, Count
Wrbna and Freudenthal. Then, before the guards, summoned by
her victim's outcry, could disarm her, the old lace-maker killed
herself as well.

In *Miei Ricordi*, Professor Minghetti celebrates this act as a
blow struck for liberty and acclaims the murderess as "another
Judith, the spiritual sister of Charlotte Corday." As to the political
consequences of Count Wrbna's death, I would not dispute
Minghetti's shrewd analysis: Venice did, indisputably, slip loose
from the grasp of the double-eagle shortly thereafter. Whether
Signora Ricci was motivated by the high and selfless purpose that
Minghetti attributes to her is more doubtful. Rather, like Lucrece,

her hatred of tyranny sprang from a more personal source, and one which (though I was not to learn this till some time later) was not unconnected to the events set forth in these pages.

It seems that the good widow's son Paolo had been the same fellow whom the police had brought round to the Palazzo to confess to persecuting my aunt and Mrs. Minchin with bon-bons and oranges. Following that forced apology, he had been packed off to the island of San Giorgio Maggiore, which the Austrians had converted into one vast prison. Signora Ricci petitioned Count Wrbna to release her son, swearing that at the very hour of his supposed crime he had been with her in Chioggia, at the other end of the lagoon. The petition was refused, and worse, the guiltless prisoner was transported to the Spielburg, where he died, within a week of his arrival, of the cholera.

Paolo Ricci was an agent of the Austrian police, and as such he had gone about the city as a masker. It was his misfortune that of all the agents so employed he had borne the closest resemblance to the true culprit. My aunt had *not* been mistaken in her identification, and Niles *had* lied to her. Further, through his mother, he had begged Count Wrbna to supply him with a scapegoat—solely in order to allay my suspicions against Manfredo! The Count had complied. Why he insisted, once the false apology had been delivered, to imprison Ricci for his fictitious crime I shall never comprehend. It was an act of the most arbitrary tyranny, and like many a tyrant before him, he paid for that tyranny with his life's blood.

At the time, I knew no more than that Count Wrbna had been assassinated by a political fanatic. This was dreadful enough, but very soon it became clear, despite Niles' efforts to keep his own forebodings from me, that the Count's death was to be a source of great vexation as well as great grief. His murder acted as a signal to a population seething with discontent. There were riots and disorders throughout the city. The barracks of the army, the offices of the government, and the homes of any persons known to be sympathetic to the Austrians became potential targets of the people's rage. Five times during the next week rocks shattered the windows of the Palazzo Alari-Uboldo, and the revolutionary acronym of VERDI! was scrawled in crimson letters five feet high on its poor war-battered façade.

But the persecutions of the Garibaldini were not the bitterest. The Archduke Albert proved more than ever reluctant to govern in fact as well as name. Refusing even to set foot within the turbulent city, he appointed the Ritter von Toggenburg as the Luogotenente, or deputy-governor, of Venice. Toggenburg had hated the man whose authority he had inherited. One of his first acts of office was to notify Contessa Visconti that the Palazzo Alari-Uboldo would once again be required as a barracks for a regiment of Croatian infantrymen. We were to be allowed one week in which to pack up our possessions and surrender our residence to the army.

Zaide had cloaked her mourning in a mantle of solitude; she expressed the bitterness of her exile in furious activity and in execrations against not only Toggenburg and the Austrians but against Count Wrbna as well, for having allowed himself to be murdered. She did not scruple even to inveigh against the Order of Malta for having inherited (in accordance with the Count's vow of poverty) the whole of his considerable personal wealth, excepting only his horse and his sword. These, indeed, were bequeathed to Zaide, but so vast had her pique grown that she ordered the horse to the slaughter-house and threw the sword into the Canalazzo after first having seen it snapped in two.

Measured against events as grim as these, my own recent grievances seemed very small indeed. Swallowing my pride, I co-operated with Rose in the urgent business, for which a week seemed scarcely sufficient, of packing my clothes back into their twenty-six travelling closets. Rose displayed her usual competence in combination with an untypical reticency. Only once, when I was dealing in a rather peremptory fashion with a bonnet that had outgrown its bandbox, did she take up her former, domineering tone, remarking on Lady Elizabeth Towton's great respect for, and tenderness towards, *her* bonnets.

"Rose," I said, stopping my work and regarding her very levelly, "I never want to hear of Lady Elizabeth Towton again. Do you understand me?"

"As my Lady pleases."

"Or High Wycombe. Or how things have been done better or differently in the county of Buckinghamshire."

She bowed her head in acquiescence, and so long as she remained in my service, however strained our relations might otherwise become, she never again reverted to this proscribed subject. In a curious way I think that the Lady Elizabeth Towton had been Rose's nemesis no less than mine and that she welcomed her exorcism as much as I did.

On the twenty-fifth of April the Palazzo Alari-Uboldo was surrendered to the Croatian infantry, and its former residents set off, by rail, southwards for Ferrara, where it was intended that we should divide into two parties: Zaide proceeding alone directly to the Villa Visconti on Ischia, while Niles, my aunt, and I were to pass the summer touring the cities of Tuscany. At Padua, however, we learned that the Austrian engineers had taken down all bridges crossing the Po and were now making preparations for inundating the surrounding countryside. The train was switched to a westbound track, its engine was unhooked, and for four hours we were left, bereft, in the middle of a field of young maize plants, to bake in the afternoon sun and wonder what would become of us.

At last the engine was restored, and we set off for Verona, where, at midnight, all the passengers were obliged to step down to the platform for the examination of their passports. While the examination was under weigh the train backed from the station and vanished, like Don Giovanni, into a cloud of smoke. Zaide made strenuous protests to the gendarme in charge of stamping our passports, who responded by calmly refusing to honor the visas we had received in Venice, noting (quite validly) that they specified Ponte Lago Oscuro as our point of exit from Lombardo-Veneto. It was useless to object that Ponte Lago Oscuro, together with the other bridges across the Po, no longer existed.

We spent that evening and the next in Verona's best hostelry, La Colomba d'Oro (which means, in English, "The Dove of Gold"). While Niles returned to Venice to secure a new *lascia passare*, permitting us proceed by rail from Verona west to Peschiera, we were eaten alive by the vermin who lived under the wings of The Golden Dove.

The remainder of the journey to the border was accomplished with more convenience, thanks to the personal intervention of our old companion Colonel Koestritz, who had returned with Niles from Venice. Even with the Colonel's help, the delays to be endured and indignities to be silently suffered were enough to have made Italian patriots of every passenger on the train.

In the very shadow of the black and yellow signboard proclaiming that we had reached the *Grenze*, one last unpleasantness awaited us. A customs officer, examining one of Lydia's trunks, discovered her supply of Macpherson's Sulphurous Compound. Lydia, anticipating a long sojourn in Italy, had come prepared with a copious supply of quart-bottles of her panacea, and the customs officer refused (as we understood through Niles' translation) to believe that she was not engaged in commerce. Niles tried to slip the man a bribe, but my aunt, having less flexible standards of morality, made an outcry against this. In retribution, the customs officer declared that she could take only three bottles of her medicine across the border. Lydia, at this point, was prepared to take the matter to court, but Colonel Koestritz suggested a compromise that satisfied both my aunt and the customs officer. Each member of our party (with the servants, there were eight of us) re-packed three bottles of the medicine into his or her own luggage, and with that we were allowed to take our not very regretful leave of Austrian territory. My heart joined in the great shout of *Viva Italia!* that went up from my fellow passengers as the train rolled past the signboard welcoming us to the newly reborn Kingdom of Italy.

CHAPTER THIRTEEN
A Contemporary Miracle

EAST OF SPOLETO, AT A DISTANCE of a day's journey by coach through the Umbrian Hills, upon the summit of one of those hills, the town of Cascia crumbles to dust. Too poor to be beautiful and too old to be ugly, Cascia lies becalmed above its terraced vineyards like the Ark on top of Ararat. One day a year it comes to life again, the twenty-second of May, when its narrow streets (there are four) are filled with pilgrims who have come to venerate the relics of its patron saint, Blessed Rita of Cascia, as those relics are transported in solemn procession from the Augustinian convent where she died in 1456 to the little church of San Galgano, the scene of her most significant miracle.

Niles loved these spectacles of homely piety, but an additional motive had impelled him to Cascia. He had read in Vasari that the church of San Galgano possessed a chapel painted by Piero della Francesca, whose work had become, since our stay in Perugia, Niles' new infatuation. Entering the city on the day before the feast, it was hard to believe that such a ruinous tumbledown little town could be the repository of even the most modest masterpiece, but in three weeks of travel about Italy I had learned that the old saw about books and their covers applies equally well to paintings and their frames.

Niles was baffled in his first attempt to see the Piero fresco, for San Galgano was being decorated for the morrow and no one, not even a visiting Conte Visconti, was to be allowed within. So we settled into a suite of rooms that possessed a narrow balcony overlooking the route of the procession, and added the dust from our clothes to the more abundant residues carpeting the tiled floors and spread in gossamer coverlets upon the spindly furniture.

I slept poorly that night and was up at the crack of dawn. Already the street below was lined with devotees, gossiping, fingering their beads, intensely patient. All were women; most, apparently, were widows.

During breakfast, which consisted of tea of my aunt's own brewing with some Abernethy biscuits out of a tin, Niles explained why the *cultus* of the Blessed Rita had an exclusively feminine following:

"In Spain, whence half of these good women have come, she is known as *la santa de los imposibles*, which refers, one surmises, not to all impossibilities in general, but to the single commonest impossibility, a bad marriage. Rita herself suffered through one of the worst, despite that she'd wanted nothing but to be a nun. But her parents wouldn't hear of that and made her marry a terrible scoundrel. He abused her for eighteen years, and then, when Rita was thirty—"

"Pardon me," my aunt put in, "but that would make her twelve when she married."

"And so she was. The same is said, you know, of Shakespeare's Juliet."

"How barbaric!"

"Rita, I'm sure, would agree with that. In any case, after those eighteen years her husband was murdered. This, though, was only the beginning of her greatest trial, for her twin sons swore to avenge their father's death. Rita appealed to Heaven to prevent such a sin, and Heaven answered her prayer by taking off both sons in the plague. That is the miracle commemorated in the chapel of San Galgano—Rita's prayer, and the boys' deaths."

"A desperate remedy," I ventured to comment.

"But a popular one, if we are to judge by the numbers who've gathered here on her feast day. But do you hear the music? We had best go out on the balcony."

The procession was led by a waif with a shorn head and a raggedy cassock, who carried a large, tarnished crucifix atop a wooden pole. Our balcony was so low and the pole so long that the crucifix passed right before our faces. Behind the cross-bearer came a whole tribe of little boys, carrying pictures on pillows and swinging censers. After the children, the nuns of the Augustinian convent, in dark violet habits, passed before us in double file, singing a most lamentatious hymn, to which the pilgrim women in the street added a polyphonic accompaniment of sighs and groans, mounting in intensity and volume as the object of their devotion drew nearer.

Standing upright in a kind of *chaise à porteurs*, which was supported on the shoulders of four elderly priests, the polychrome figure of the saint advanced along the line of frantic worshippers. She was represented in the habit of a nun carrying in one hand a rose, in the other two green figs. In the middle of her forehead, redder than the rose in her hand, she bore one of the wounds that the Roman Church regards as a sign of highest sanctity, the stigmata.

Just as the statue was passing our inn, one of the old priests supporting the palanquin stumbled. Vainly his companions tried to keep the platform from capsizing. The women, witnessing the lurching, inexorable progress of the accident, began to scream in good earnest. Rita's torso smashed into the balusters of our balcony; her head snapped off and rolled across the floor. My aunt Jerningham rose to her feet and joined in the general chorus, while I, who am usually ready to take fright at a squirrel in the park, stooped down and retrieved the carved head. I looked about for Niles, but he had chosen just this moment to be absent and so I was myself obliged to snug the head back upon the peg projecting out of the statue's neck. A deathly still had succeeded the earlier hubbub. I felt the eyes of all the pilgrim women upon me and lowered my gaze to my lap. Imagine my dismay to see that my dress, both overskirt and, where that opened in front, the underskirt beneath, covered with gouts of a viscid, deeply vermilion fluid. I sought to blot up these stains with my handkerchief only to besmirch both my hands with the same substance.

"It is the statue," declared Niles, who at the first outcry had hastened back to the balcony in time to see me restoring Rita's head to her body. He touched a finger gingerly to the spreading stain. "They have daubed fresh paint on the wound."

"Fraudulently? Oh, surely not!"

"It is that or, as all the women in the street seem to believe, a proper miracle. Dearest—and Mrs. Jerningham—I think we had better go back into our rooms. We are drawing rather too much attention here."

While my aunt sought, with the help of some turpentine supplied by the innkeeper's wife, to clean my hands and my skirts, Niles went to San Galgano. He returned within minutes to declare that Vasari was either a mountebank or a fool.

"If Piero ever so much as *looked* at those frescoes, then I am the King of the Hottentots."

"Are they very bad?" I asked.

"Atrocious. You would think them modelled on the woodcuts from broadsheet ballads. All in all, I'm afraid, Cascia has been a great disappointment. The sooner we depart the happier we all shall be. I've commandeered the diligence, and it can take us back to Spoleto this afternoon. Never mind fussing any more with that dress, Mrs. Jerningham—it's spoiled past saving. You shall only stain your own in the attempt."

The diligence was at the door of the inn at noon precisely.

Usually in Italy, especially in its smaller towns, the population hides within doors during the hours of the day's fiercest heat, but the crowds were, if anything, larger now than they had been in the moments before the procession. Taken one by one, I had to pity them. What unhappiness must each of these stoic, wrinkled faces be hiding! What desperation to have come so far to pray to the patron-saint of impossible causes! But taken all together, it was fear that they inspired—fear of their massive, communal appetite for the miraculous. They had come to Cascia for prodigies and been given only a parade. Their hungers, baffled, turned to rage.

When I left the inn to step into the diligence, they set upon me with shrill cries. Some had scissors ready; others needed only their hands, hands made strong by years of labor. Wherever my dress had been stained by, as they believed, the blood of their saint, they snipped and tore. The borders of ruched ribbons were first to go; then, piecemeal, the overskirt's scalloped hem. I cried out, but I feared to contravene more actively from a rational regard for their busy shears.

Niles, the coachman, and my aunt all endeavored to push the fanatic women back, but they were too few against too many. The women encircled me, desperate not only to have a relic of the saint but intent, as well, to touch *me*. In their minds, I had become by that morning's accident a kind of semi-sacred personage, the avatar of the Blessed Rita. "*Sanctissima!*" one very aged woman cried, falling to her knees and clutching the boots on my feet. "*Guardami! Ascoltami!*" ("Holiest One! Look at me! Hear me!")

I was in terror. It seemed they wanted to tear me, quite literally, limb from limb. In a sense, it was the accomplishment of just this purpose that saved me. The old woman who had been tugging at my boots caught a grip on my overskirt and two other women took hold of her. I was being dragged to the ground, but Niles, and then the coachman, caught me up. The stitching gave way in one lightning rip.

While the women were engaged in partitioning their prize, Niles managed to get me inside the coach—an easier task than usual with my now much narrower skirts. Lydia took the seat beside me, Niles the facing seat. Even as the coach lurched into motion hands appeared at the open window. Niles rapped at the swollen knuckles with his walking-stick and swore an English oath.

We arrived in Spoleto an hour after sunset. My fright at noonday, followed by the hours of taxing travel in the hot coach, had been too great a strain. As soon as Rose had brought down a mantle so that I might decently enter the hotel, I went to my room and let Lydia put me to bed.

I did not leave that room for a fortnight.

CHAPTER FOURTEEN
An Illness and Its Remedy

I DID NOT LEAVE THAT ROOM for a fortnight, and rarely did I rise from the bed. That same evening an illness, mild and obscure, enfolded me in the warm wings of a fever to which I succumbed with conscious gratitude.

It had not been the fatigues of that single day that had brought me to such a pass that a sickbed looked welcoming; for a month I had been hurtling about Italy in railway carriages, or jolting along its roads, or mounting up interminable staircases to take in the views recommended by those indefatigable authors, Messrs. Murray, Baedeker, and Bradshaw. I felt I had achieved in that one month what it had taken fully four hundred years of feast-day journeyings back and forth, between her usual niche in the convent and her place of honor at the church, for the Blessed Rita to achieve—a condition, namely, of resistless prostration; of perfect, blissful collapse. Had my own head rolled off my shoulders and across the clean, caressing sheets of my bed, I would not have been much surprised.

Emotion recollected in tranquillity may be a satisfactory formula for poetry, but disease recollected in good health is a certain bore, especially if the least taint of hypochondria be sus-

pected in the sufferer's constitution. I do not say that my illness
was illusory; still less that I feigned it in order to gain a reprieve
from sightseeing. My symptoms were real, and if in one sense they
were convenient, they were also very unpleasant. I shall not, however, chronicle every movement of the mercury in the thermom-
eter, nor shall I attempt to paint in anything like their natural
brilliance the pains that would flash and flicker, like summer
lightning, through the inner hemispheres of my brain.

Those pains were actual, and yet I cannot believe, in retrospect,
that they were unrelated to distresses of a mental and moral nature,
which must receive some notice here. Perhaps the two realms, of
spirit and of matter, are not so distinct as many would believe;
perhaps for every sorrow and disappointment that we feel, there
is, deep within us, in those secret regions that only surgeons have
explored, an answering metamorphosis of our flesh. In my own
case, it is certain that my fevers and headaches were accompanied
by a persistent and morbid anxiety, a notion that I had offended my
husband in a manner at once unmentionable and unforgivable; or
that I was about to. Just as dissensions long developing in secret
may burst out in quarrels over trivialities, so this anxiety of mine
took the form of worrying how well or ill I had measured up to
Niles' expectations as to the re-forming of my tastes. Each time we
entered another church or gallery, I braced myself as for an ordeal,
miserably certain that my first instincts, whether of admiration or
repulsion, were likely to be incorrect. Niles would never tell me, in
advance, what works of special merit or significance we had come
to see, preferring (he said) "to let it be a surprise." I must, therefore, *choose* at each new halt on our itinerary, those elements that
had earned the village, church, or palace its stars in our Baedeker.

It seems absurd, I know, and yet I went through agonies as I
was marched past the ranked madonnas and the hundred thousand
saints frowning down from their gilded panels and their worm-
eaten frames. There was Ambrose, with his wide-brimmed crimson
hat. There was Jerome, looking like his twin, unless, may be, he
were fondling his pet lion. There was the ghastly Lucy with her
two eyes on a dish, and the even more gruesome Agatha. So many
—and I knew them all! These discriminations are, of course, the
easiest. Every urchin in Italy is acquainted with the saints and

their emblems, as well as with those stories (and only those) in the Bible that lend themselves to pictorial representation. To become a connoisseur after Niles' own heart it was needful that I discern the difference between an Ambrose by Giotto and another Ambrose by his pupil Giottino, between a Jerome by Giottino and another by Taddeo Gaddi. Giotto had a dozen pupils, and *they* had pupils, and so on down to the present day. No one, not Niles, not the great Baedeker himself, could know them all. But certain mistakes were tolerable, while others were egregious, and all too often it was the latter sort of mistake I would fall into. In a church in the village of Sansepolcro I walked on past the renowned Resurrection by Piero della Francesca to admire an anonymous nativity scene. In Arezzo I admired the façade of a church which had been carved by no other hands than the wind and the rain. Niles never showed any annoyance at these errors of taste; indeed, he professed, each time, to be amused. But I was mortified, and each new gaucherie would deepen the wound and keep it smarting. I considered each new error, compounded with those already behind me, a mathematic proof of my unworthiness, as though Cinderella, within a few weeks of her wedding, were to discover that her foot had grown too large for the glass slipper.

So, wretched as it was to be sick and bed-ridden in a provincial hostelry, I was spared by that sickness the greater wretchedness of being shown up as a fool. My aunt, too, thrived, in these altered circumstances. As a tourist she might be querulous and unappreciative, but as a nurse she was a proper angel of mercy. She held my hand when my hand needed holding, and cooked my meals, and talked to me through the long, dull, restless hours of the Italian afternoon. She told of her own girlhood in the rectory of St. John's Clerkenwell, of games she had played with her brother Robert and girlish quarrels she had picked with him and how she had cried when he went off to become a midshipman. She told me more of her own past in these long reminiscences than in all the rambling soliloquies of the past, when it had been I who sat by her sickbed; more of my own past as well. Like another sibyl, she summoned up the spirits of my dead parents and bade them rehearse for me the brief poignant drama of their courtship, marriage, and too early deaths. When her own memory flagged, she resorted to the first volumes of Mrs. Oliphant's comfortable *Chronicles of Carlingford*, which had the special virtue for an invalid of never provoking too heady an interest.

Such were my days, and they were bearable. As the shadows lengthened across the landscape and the light in my hotel room thickened to dusk, my real torment would commence. Like some nocturnal creature stirring in its nest, my headache would re-assert its dominion over me, growing from a mild, monotonous throbbing that could be endured with only a little stoicism into a fierce fusillade of pain against which it was impossible to main-tain a façade of impassivity. I *would* whimper; I *would* cry out; I *would* twist my limbs about in unavailing efforts to find some position that would bring surcease.

My aunt viewed my sufferings with alarm and sought to al-leviate them with a dose of her own tried and trusted remedy. I was too wretched to resist. The dose she administered each even-ing, two large spoonfuls of Macpherson's Compound, would have sufficed me for a week of illness, unaccustomed as I was to the effects of laudanum. My headache vanished at once, and I could close my eyes upon a blessed blankness. My aunt would leave me then, bidding me, as she went out the door, to sleep soundly and have sweet dreams.

The peace that the opium brought, though profound, was not attended by sleep; and yet I dreamed. Paradoxically, I seemed to cross the threshold to that other phantasmagoric world without taking my leave of this one. A breeze stirred the white muslin hangings of the bed, and they became the banner in the hand of the dead and resurrected Christ that I had seen in the town of Sansepolcro. This was the masterpiece by Piero that I had scanted so disgracefully two weeks before; now I saw it again as clearly as if it had been placed at the foot of my bed flooded in the light of the brightest camphine lamps. Nay, *more* clearly. The Christ of the painting now looked straight ahead with that strange, passionless expression at once so distressing and so persuasive, a look that seemed to pass through me like a dagger of infinite thinness. Yet there was also a kind of mercy in his regard, but a mercy so lofty (or rather, a mercy proceeding from such terrible depths) that it was harder to support than the spite of lesser beings

—that unwavering glance, and the gentle ruffling of the banner that was also the muslin drapery of my bed, and at Christ's foot, sleeping sprawled beside the sepulcher, the inert faces of the soldiery, and in the pale flesh of His side the lance's wound, whence the action of His rising had caused fresh gouts of blood to trickle forth. Like another Thomas, I doubted what I saw, and in my dream I stepped towards Him. With interminate slowness I would lift my hand towards the wound, and touch the wound, and take my hand away. A gout of red paint glistened on my fingertips. At that moment of awe my dreaming mind made no distinction between the two realities, that of the blood and that of the paint.

How swift in telling, yet how slowly the dream unfolded in my drugged consciousness. Ordinarily, dreams are remarkable for a super-abundance of events compacted into a narrow space of time. This was as though I had entered not so much into the world of dreams but into the related world of art, where time is no longer of significance because all meanings have been condensed into a single, all-sufficing moment. I looked at the unchanging scene before me with an untiring sense of wonder. What did it mean? I could not answer to that, then or now, except to say that the beauty and the strangeness of it afflicted me quite as if the terrible pains that I had suffered, minutes or hours before, had been transposed, by the action of the opium, into this phantom shape, into these calm, supernal eyes; as if this image from the well of memory were those same pains rendered in a form that I could comprehend and so accept as what was due me.

And yet, if this be so, was it not a kind of cheating to experience my suffering in this diluted form? If instead of swallowing those two spoonfuls of laudanum each night I had seen my headache through to its natural conclusion, perhaps it would not have returned as it did, day after day, with the dull persistence of a bill collector. So long as one neglects to pay one's bills, one will be dunned for them; it is as simple as that.

Niles seemed as embarrassed by my illness as if it were one of the mysteries of my sex which he ought not too closely inquire into. He came to my room in the morning more in the character of a visitor than of a husband, bringing great posies of summer blooms and resting his hat upon his knees with an exaggerated delicacy, as though instead of his gloves it had contained a dozen eggs. Sitting several feet back from the bed, he would address me in a tone of subdued melancholy on matters of no conceivable interest, under the impression, apparently, that I had lost my wits as well as my health. Having thus carefully avoided exciting me, he would set off for a day-trip on the railway, venturing as far north as Assisi and as far south as Rieti. When my illness persisted into a second week, Niles' excursions took him farther afield, and twice he was unable to return in the evening, due to the vagaries of the Italian rail schedules. On the second of these occasions he returned to Spoleto with his eye swollen and blacked.

"Now, Clara, you are not to fuss, and you are *not* to get out of your bed. I appreciate your solicitude, but there is nothing you can do. In her own time Nature will repair the harm that's been done."

"But it looks so—"

"Unsightly. Yes, but the worst of it is that people will suppose I'm some kind of pirate or pugilist, whereas in fact I happened by it in the most innocent manner imaginable. But really, my dear, if it is going to get you into a fret—"

"No, I'm quite composed now. Witness." I picked a scarlet crowfoot from the posy of mixed blooms beside my bed and sniffed at it in a somewhat satiric display of my calmness.

"Take care," said Niles. "That is just how I got my black eye. You'll recall I was meaning to go to the Fonte Colombo Monastery outside of Rieti. I did go, and arrived at dusk. I was shown into the cloister garden, the walls of which are covered with jasmine. The vesper-bell was ringing, the monks were chanting, the flowers were opening—for jasmine, you know, blooms at night—and the whole world seemed to be one great delectability. In minutes, the scent of that jasmine had become overpowering. Feeling a momentary kinship with St. Francis—the cloister was a favorite spot of his—I went over to Sister Jasmine and was declaring my love to her when Brother Bee, who must have fallen asleep in a convolvulus close by, woke up and declared his love for me."

"You were stung?"

"I'm lucky that I wasn't blinded. It looked much worse than this last night, but the good brothers applied a simple made from the ashes of the *melanzana,* and the swelling came down considerably."

As Niles was leaving, Rose appeared in the doorway with an air of more than usual importance. She presented Niles with a telegraphic dispatch. In his haste to open it he ripped the message down the middle.

"Oh." He sounded disappointed and at the same time relieved. "It is from my mother."

"I hope that nothing—"

"No, she's quite fine, and sends her love. It seems that Godfrey Mainwaring—you remember him from Blackthorne?"

"Oh yes."

"It seems that he is in Florence with his aunt. He wrote to us in Venice, and the letter was forwarded to the Villa Visconti. If you recover in time, we may be able to coincide with him for the last part of his stay. That is, if you care to renew his acquaintance."

"I should love to. His aunt, after all, was directly responsible for our good fortune. But really, Niles, it is for you to decide."

"Then it's decided. We'll see him. The best medicine for you now would be honest English faces and honest English talk."

"For all of us, I think. I'm sure it will do my aunt good to see Mrs. Lacey again. And there is all of Florence, too," I added, lest my enthusiasm appear immoderate, "which I am desperate to see. It is all very well to save the best till last—"

"You're right, and I'm much to be blamed for having worn you down jaunting along all these side-roads and by-ways. I never considered how taxing it would be."

"If you continue in that vein, Niles, I shall begin to reproach myself for being an invalid and a burden. And indeed, I *do* reproach myself. But it can't be helped. I shall try to get better as soon as ever I can, and really, these last three or four days I feel I *have* been mending."

"I'm glad to hear it, but I can't let you feign good health to please me. We must wait and see."

We waited two days more. My headache, which had been haunting me like the most vengeful of revenants, evaporated in the warm glow of my expectations, and the two weeks of rest had been more than enough to replenish my supply of high spirits. I was hungry for Italy once again. For the moment, even my anxieties about measuring up to so much high art did not trouble me. Florence would be stocked with such an abundance of master-pieces that I was certain I would not be lacking in appreciation.

So, on the morning of the sixth of June, we were assembled, with all our bags and boxes (as many as had not been sent on ahead to the Villa with Zaide), on the platform of Spoleto's railway station waiting for the train, which was late. We would have served *La Mode Illustrée* for a fashion plate that day. At Niles' insistence, I had adopted the new style of daytime dress hitched up above my ankles so as to expose tall boots of rose-colored silk trimmed with crimson tassels, and instead of a bonnet, a Bergere hat with a brim so wide I scarce had need of a parasol to keep my face from the sun. Niles, no less contemporary, was clad in the "ditto" style—his coat, waistcoat, and trousers all cut from the same bolt of dove-gray superfine, the whole topped off by a pearl-hued bowler hat. My aunt was dressed in mourning as sumptuous as the Queen's. Even Rose, in a paletot of violet plush, cut a fine figure, though she suffered even more than the rest of us from having misjudged the Italian climate. Already at nine o'clock the sun was beginning fairly to render us like so many pieces of suet; by the time the train arrived, I could have wished to be dressed, like young ladies indigenous to Italy, in less fashion and more comfort.

As Niles was handing me up into the carriage, I paused on the step. "Are you sure we have thought of everything?" I asked him.

"What has been forgotten?"

"I don't know if he has been forgotten, or if he's late, but I did not see your valet on the platform."

"Oh, then I forgot to tell you. Manfredo's gone on to the villa ahead of us. Mother needed someone to help her put the place back in order, and on the way he'll be fetching little Clara from her relatives in Amalfi."

Niles helped me to a seat by the window, the train began to move, and I fixed my eyes on the landscapes fleeting past in an Umbrian blur of greens and tawny yellows; my thoughts were elsewhere. As surely as I had been witness to his blush, I knew that Niles was lying. In general, my spontaneous intuitions into the

mysteries surrounding me had not been remarkable for their pene-
tration, but in this one instance my suspicions were correct:
Manfredo had departed from his master after they had quarrelled,
and in that quarrel Niles' eye had been blackened. That was my
theory, and it was scarcely a pretty one, yet I was not altogether
displeased with the turn I thought events had taken. Even more
than I wished to be rid of Rose myself, I wanted Niles to escape the
influence of Manfredo. I was not precise, in my mind, as to the
nature of that influence, except that it was no healthy one. Long
custom had blinded Niles to the actual degree of his subjection,
but now (I hoped) those scales were fallen from his eyes and he
would be able to obey his own better nature. So far (and so
fondly) I reasoned, but no farther; nor did I think to ask myself
what might have provoked such strong contention between man
and master. Had I asked, the answer would have been no farther
to find than in the nearest mirror.

CHAPTER FIFTEEN
Eros with a Dolphin

FLORENCE IS A CITY ALL OF STONE. It is paved with great blocks
of cut stone and encircled by stone walls, and it has been the special
glory of its architects to erect buildings so massively and in-
sistently stony that, like the Kaaba, they seem not to be hollow
like buildings elsewhere but stone throughout. There is no
greenery, not so much as a window-box, nor do the stones of
Florence permit themselves to be carved in those floral shapes
which are Art's traditional concession to Nature; instead they
have been rusticated and vermiculated to create a heightened
impression of their stoniness. Its residents, necessarily, are made
of flesh and blood like the rest of us, but the Florentine genius
has sought to circumvent this inconsistency by populating its
public places with an host of giants carved from its preferred

material. The largest single assembly of these stony people is in and around the Loggia dei Lanzi, which faces the Palazzo Vecchio in the Piazza dei Signori, and it was here, in the late morning hours of Wednesday the seventh of June, that Niles and I awaited Godfrey Mainwaring and Mrs. Lacey.

My aunt Jerningham had stayed behind at the Hôtel Royal de la Grande Bretagne, in deference to the heat, which is, indeed, the most rational response one can make to the fierceness of the Florentine summer. I was glad she had stayed behind, for if the heat had not prostrated her, the indecorous display of the Loggia's statuary would surely have done so. Nowhere in Italy had I yet witnessed such a profuse and brazen display of all that elsewhere is screened for the common sight. Always, till this day, Niles, as our cicerone, had been able to guide our steps through the palaces and galleries we had visited so as to spare us the embarrassment of being confronted with such productions, but in the Piazza dei Signori it was useless to avert one's eyes—they were everywhere. Moreover, they were beautiful and possessed the power of all beautiful things to command one's attention.

Unwillingly I looked, reluctantly I admired, but I could not, finally, approve. By the canons of formal beauty and craftsmanship these statues were, doubtless, masterpieces, but these criteria cannot be divorced from moral considerations, and morally these masterpieces made a rather questionable assemblage, even a downright reprehensible one. I do not say this on the grounds my aunt would have (that is, because they were all, or most, of them naked); it was rather their actions I deplored, and their creators' apparent intention to glorify these actions. All these statues seemed to commemorate murderers. They were shown either contemplating a murder, like Michelangelo's squinty-eyed David or Donatello's Judith, sneaking up to behead the sleeping Holofernes; or committing murder, like the repulsive figure of Hercules bludgeoning an opponent; or else glorying in the accomplished crime, like Cellini's insolent Perseus holding up the head of Medusa. Besides murder, another popular theme was rape. It was as though in removing their creations' clothes, the sculptors had unleashed every irrational and wicked impulse in human nature, and in doing this had reduced the dignity of the human form to that of the brute creation (which was, in fact, another favored subject of these sculptors, for the Piazza also boasted a large number of lions, who gazed with petrified wistfulness at the slaughter and rapine surrounding them). All in all, scarcely an edifying spectacle to place in a city's major thoroughfare, and scarcely an auspicious omen for the new state of Italy, whose capital Florence had become and whose Parliament building was to be this same Palazzo Vecchio.

It was with a sense, therefore, of being rescued that I greeted Mr. Mainwaring and his aunt. Niles, too, showed himself to be extremely cordial, and he agreed to Mainwaring's declaration that our first order of business must be to escape from the heat. Niles took Mrs. Lacey's arm, Mr. Mainwaring took mine, and we directed our steps to the imposing doorway of the Palazzo Vecchio.

"I must apologize to you, Contessa," my escort said, as we passed by David's shapely marble feet, "for having made you wait for us in such unprepossessing circumstances as these."

"Nonsense, Mr. Mainwaring," I replied. "You are punctual to the minute. It was Niles insisted on coming ahead of time so we could study the statues at our leisure."

"And did you find them worth your study?"

"I found them rather startling. But our guide-book, which is never wrong, says it is impossible not to admire them. Niles was in ecstasies over the Perseus."

"For my own part, though I would never gainsay a guide-book, I question whether so much exposed flesh, even when the flesh is marble and bronze, belongs on the street. It would never do in London."

"I dare say. But as my husband often reminds me, this *isn't* London."

"And he is right. Indeed, as I remarked to my aunt as we came across the Piazza, these statues have adopted the one mode of dress suited to the furnace they inhabit."

I laughed, and shook my head in mock reproof. Truly we were not in London, for I could not imagine Mr. Mainwaring making such a jest or I laughing at it in Trafalgar Square!

We had entered into the courtyard of the Palazzo, where a fountain emitted a jet of water as feeble as the Arno in that dry season when it is reduced to a sluggish creek meandering through civic marshes. This fountain took the form of a cupid attempting to hold on to a large, playful fish while balancing with one foot on the lid of an urn. After the throng of criminals we had seen outside, this so charmed us that we temporarily abandoned our purpose to explore the upper rooms and settled for a chat on the benches disposed round the fountain. One might even imagine, by listening to the trickle of the water into the basin and ignoring one's other senses, that it was cooler in this courtyard than it had been in the Piazza.

Mr. Mainwaring was extravagant in his praise of Florence, and Mrs. Lacey was cautious in her disparagement. Her principal objection to the city was that she had been to a restaurant where she claimed to have seen undressed, roasted sparrows served to the diners.

"Sparrows!" I exclaimed. "I find it hard to believe."

"When Godfrey asked the waiter, the fellow insisted that they were quails, but I can still tell a hawk from a handsaw, and sparrows from quails. They think because we are English we will believe anything. But I do not mean to give you a false impression. I am delighted to be here. So many lovely churches: I often think it is a pity one cannot pray in them. And though the people are so poor, they are much happier on the whole. Godfrey says it is a lesson for us all. As Shakespeare observes somewhere, 'I'd give my jewels for a set of beads, my gorgeous palace for a hermitage,' and it is very true."

She said this with no ironic emphasis, but even so I flinched inwardly, since it was hard not to apply the moral she pronounced to her own situation and to her nephew's. During our first greetings I had been conscious of an alteration in Mr. Mainwaring's person and bearing—and to a lesser degree in Mrs. Lacey's—that had puzzled me at first, not through any effort on their part to conceal the fact, but rather from a reluctance on my side to admit an uncomfortable truth: Mr. Mainwaring had come down in the world.

I recognized his trousers and waistcoat as being the same that he had worn when I'd first seen him coming down the steps of Blackthorne. Then he had been the very picture of a heavy swell; now there was something distinctly seedy about these same clothes. The waistcoat had been brushed too many times and its snuff color had a coppery tinge to it. The trousers had been altered so as to conform to present taste, but they could not quite escape looking like the "peg-tops" they had been. Worst of all, nothing fit. In the intervening years Mr. Mainwaring's figure had somewhat shrunk; not so drastically that he no longer seemed robust, but enough so that the once perfect tailoring hung on his thinner frame with the proximate imprecision of clothing bought from the rack.

Niles had seen these evidences and summed them up much faster than I. Though nothing in his manners or speech could be interpreted as condescension, I nevertheless felt that Mr. Mainwaring had lost his claim, in my husband's eyes, to be considered altogether a gentleman. I am sure Mr. Mainwaring himself was oblivious of this unspoken judgment, for he was of that happy disposition that believes the world accepts us at our own valuation. Mrs. Lacey, however, with sensibilities sharpened by years spent in the ambiguous situation of being treated turn-and-turn-about as either upper servant or poor relation, sought to excuse her nephew's "reduced" appearance by belittling what she termed his "eccentricities," by which she meant the study of archaeology. In a sense, this was true. Mr. Mainwaring did not neglect himself with regard to the polish of his boots or the cleanliness of his linen, but in the disposing of his income he clearly preferred spending what he had on his research rather than on his wardrobe.

Niles, though he noted the difference, was no less cordial on that account; perhaps even a little friendlier. Often it is easier to strike up an intimacy from the vantage of conscious inequality: one does not so carefully consider the risks of unreserve. Within minutes of shaking hands, Niles and Mr. Mainwaring were acting like schoolmates at a reunion. Lacking a common past, their conversation had naturally to concern itself with a common present, but being tourists in Florence this was no great liability. Wherever one might glance, some artifact asked to be appraised and admired, and Mr. Mainwaring was quite as vain as Niles about his powers of appreciation.

Mrs. Lacey and I were not enjoying a comparable success, and were relieved, therefore, when Niles, to include us in their livelier conversation, asked what *we* thought of the little figure on top of the fountain.

"It is lovely," said I, nor could I extend this weak tribute by a single word. Strain as I might, "lovely" was as far as imagination could carry me. So concerned was I with not seeming a ninny that I had become quite oblivious of Verrocchio's statue.

"But it is rather odd, don't you think?" added Mrs. Lacey. "Why is the little boy carrying that great fish? It is much too large for him to have caught it."

"Perhaps," Niles suggested facetiously, "he has stolen it from a fish-vendor and is running off with it. There would be some probability in that, given the character of little boys in Italy."

"But he is not a little boy exactly," Mr. Mainwaring objected in all seriousness. "He is Eros. Dan Cupid, in our own tongue. His wings tell us that."

"Next you will tell us that the fish is not a fish," Mrs. Lacey said.

"Nor is it. It is a dolphin, and dolphins are mammals, like ourselves."

"Now, Godfrey, I beg you not to start in on Darwin and his monkeys. You know how that upsets me."

"Ah, but he's right!" said Niles. "Not Darwin, I mean, for I know nothing of that, but your nephew's right about this statue. They are *both* beings of a double nature. The cupid is a creature of the land and of the air; the dolphin of the land and of the sea. That *is* clever."

"I don't see its cleverness," Mrs. Lacey persisted. "Even if it is so, what does it mean?"

"There you have me," Niles answered. "If it is an allegory, I lack the key. My wife has said all one may really say about it—it is lovely."

"How is this for a meaning, Aunt?" Mr. Mainwaring ventured. "The winged boy represents the Ideal, which lifts up the rest of creation and redeems it from the gross reign of Appetite."

"It is a fine meaning," Mrs. Lacey replied, "but it doesn't make me care for the statue any better. I continue to see a naked boy, who quite clearly stands more in need of redeeming himself than any fish. Why they don't put clothes on these statues I shall *never* understand."

"Now, Aunt, I warned you when we spoke of coming here—"

"And I warned you, Godfrey, that an old dog doesn't learn new tricks. I do not say that all of Italy is indecent, and I don't say it isn't. I am a visitor, so it is not for me to judge. I only said that I thought it was odd, and I do think it odd, and furthermore I think that by any standard, English or Italian, it is time for lunch!"

To this we all feelingly agreed. At once we set back to the Hôtel Royal de la Grande Bretagne, where, over four leisurely courses, Niles engaged Mr. Mainwaring in a lively discussion of neo-Platonism and its influence on the Florentine Renaissance. By the time the basket of fruit had been placed before us, they had become, to all appearances, the closest of friends.

CHAPTER SIXTEEN
The Question Posed Again

WE BAKED FOR TWO BLISSFUL WEEKS in that most austere and beautiful of cities, which was a week more than we had intended. At last a date was fixed that could not be postponed. Rose began to pack away all the pretty, needless bibelots I had been acquiring with no other aim, really, than the abstract pleasure of their acquisition. Though in London I had never regarded spending money as a recreation, if the sign in a shopwindow said *Calzoleria Per Le Donne* instead of "Ladies' Shoemaker," I could not resist the lure of adventure. Any merchant shrewd enough to puzzle out my eight or nine words of Italian instead of seeking to display his own twelve or thirteen of English was certain to be able to sell me . . . anything at all.

Niles, on our last day in Florence, had to call upon the Papal Nuncio to have our passports visaed for Rome (through whose dominions, then still distinct from the Kingdom of Italy, we had to pass on our way south to Ischia). I, meanwhile, set off for one last fling of spending. Such, at least, was my stated purpose. Outside the church of San Lorenzo, whom should I chance to meet but our good friend Mr. Mainwaring? Mr. Mainwaring volunteered to be my escort for the rest of that morning, and Rose was dispatched back to the hotel with three Leghorn straw bonnets, an alabaster figurine, and the well-founded suspicion that my path had not crossed Mr. Mainwaring's entirely by chance.

"I am sorry," Mr. Mainwaring began, "that I could not offer to receive you at my hotel, but our lodgings lack the amenity of a sitting room, and as for the public rooms of the hotel—they are just that. For the purpose of a private conversation I thought that San Lorenzo would be fitter."

"It is ideal," I replied somewhat hastily. Though secure in my own conscience, I could not escape some anxiety at the construction Mr. Mainwaring might have placed on my request to speak with him in private.

Mr. Mainwaring drew back the tattered, tasselled curtain that on summer days took the place of more substantial doors, and I entered into a space so fairly shaped, so luminous, so luxuriously congenial to every sense that one could not draw breath there without feeling at one with the world; with, at least, this particular harmonious corner of it.

"In all Florence," I confided, taking the arm Mr. Mainwaring offered me, "there is nowhere I like better."

"It is my favorite, too, though I confess that I have misgivings about it. It is so little like a church. The equipment for worship is all here—the altars, the pulpits, the funerary monuments—and yet I am never aware of anything but pure, bare architecture. I come inside and feel that I've turned into a theorem in a geometry book."

"I shouldn't think that would be an agreeable sensation."

"Oh, the most agreeable there is, for me. At school I treasured my ragged Euclid above my cricket-bat. But you, Contessa—what are your associations?"

"It puts me in mind of a restaurant. Not any I have ever been to, but if there are restaurants in Heaven, this could serve as their model. It is the potted palm-trees, I suppose, that make me think that."

Mr. Mainwaring suggested we sit down by one of these palm-trees at the back of the nave, where neither worshippers nor tourists would be likely to intrude on our conversation; we did so.

"Let me repeat, Mr. Mainwaring, what I have already said in my note. While I value your friendship dearly, it is not as a friend that I wish to speak with you, but rather as a minister."

"I appreciate that, Contessa."

I wanted to tell him not to call me Contessa, that I always felt like an impostor when addressed by that title, but this admission would hardly square with my insistence that our meeting was to be suprapersonal. I would only say what I had planned to say, the words I had been rehearsing night after sleepless night in the Hôtel Royal until, like lines of poetry mechanically recited, they were drained of their power to disturb or embarrass.

"Mr. Mainwaring, you will remember one other occasion when I asked to speak with you in confidence. I have often reproached myself for having imposed on you then—"

"On the contrary, Contessa."

"Please hear me out. I reproached myself, but I am glad I established that precedent. Else I do not think I would have had the courage to approach you on a matter as delicate as . . . as this. Even so, it is difficult. I understand now why Catholics have dark boxes to hide in when they make confession."

Mr. Mainwaring had begun uneasily to finger the seals on his watch-chain, and I hastened to add: "Not that I have anything to confess—except ignorance. I have tried to ask my aunt these questions, but she has been evasive. She says I would do better to consult a physician. Well, there are no physicians here that I can consult; none who speak English; none, anyhow, whom I have met. My aunt said that lacking a physician I might speak to a minister."

"Well, here am I, a minister. I speak English, you have met me, and I am, believe me, Contessa, anxious to be of assistance in any way that is in my power. You say that this is a matter of some delicacy. I gather that it concerns your marriage."

"Yes. Yes, it does."

"Something that you have found . . . distressing."

I nodded.

"If it is any comfort, Contessa, I can tell you that I have often been consulted by young married women. The first months of even the most accordant marriages can be a trial for anyone."

"That is what my aunt has said."

"You must bear up under it, Contessa. That is the best advice I can give, and really, the only advice. When it seems most difficult, that is when you must strive to remember your love and feel the force of it."

"That is just what I don't understand, Mr. Mainwaring. You speak of the need of bearing up and of enduring trials, but the only trial I've had to endure is that I am some times unable to sleep, except for an hour or two in the morning. That, and being sick those two weeks in Spoleto, but I suppose I might have been just as sick without having married."

"Perhaps, though very often the initial shock does produce a kind of debility."

"I had severe headaches."

"That is common symptom, I understand. Though really you would do better to consult a physician on those matters."

"But as for feeling, as you say, shock—I haven't. Not at all."

"And you are upset because you haven't? Really, Contessa, you should consider yourself fortunate."

"But you see. . . ."

"Yes?"

"I don't understand what is supposed to be so shocking. How, exactly, am I to bear up? What is the trial I must endure?"

"My dear Contessa, that is not something . . . that I can easily discuss."

"I realize that. But whom else may I talk to? My aunt refuses even to listen to me now. She leaves the room if I bring it up."

"And your husband?"

"He says it is all humbug and tries to make a joke of it. When I asked how, precisely, babies come to be born, he insisted they were all delivered down chimneys by storks."

"No one is quite comfortable discussing what our greatest poet calls 'the rites mysterious of connubial love,' and such whimsys are a common subterfuge. Of more importance than what he may say is, how does he treat you? Is he gentle and considerate? From what you have said already I have gathered that he is."

"Oh, he is gentleness personified. The last thing I should want to do is complain of him. All I seek is to *understand*."

"To understand"—Mr. Mainwaring cocked his head to the side and regarded me warily—"what?"

"What Shakespeare calls—how did you put it?—the mysterious ritual."

"But my dear Miss Reeve—forgive me!—my dear Contessa, what you are asking, I scarcely know how to answer. However, as I see you are in earnest, I shall try. When a man and a woman come together, they begin to feel. . . . Or rather the man begins to experience a certain . . . a very intense desire. And they embrace, of course. And . . . and there you are!"

"And after they have embraced the woman will have children? I understand, naturally, that they grow in her stomach. But I don't, you see, I don't know. . . ." Quite spontaneously, I threw up my hands, imitating a gesture I had seen repeated all over Italy, a gesture expressive of complete and hopeless bafflement. "I don't know *why*."

Mr. Mainwaring screwed up his face in an expression of solemn deliberation. I think he must have let a full minute pass in silence before he spoke again, but now when he spoke it was with none of his previous hesitancy.

"Contessa, if you would return with me to my hotel, my aunt may be able much better than I to offer you the explanation that you seek. She has been married, and has assisted at childbirths, and is a woman of sound common sense and great sympathy. Whatever you care to ask her, I'm sure she will answer directly and straightforwardly. I will say a word or two to her in advance, in order to spare you the awkwardness of another lengthy explanation. If, after you have spoken to Mrs. Lacey, you have other questions to ask of me, I shall be at your service."

I assured him I was grateful for his taking so much trouble, and together we made our way through the empty noontime streets to the Piazza Santa Trinita and Mr. Mainwaring's hotel.

CHAPTER SEVENTEEN
Cruelties

THE DRAFT CREATED BY THE FLINGING OPEN of the door snuffed out the candle in Niles' hand. "Clara?" he asked in a whisper.

Though I had been awake, I lay motionless in my bed and made no answer. No doubt there will be souls on the Day of Judgment who will feign not to have been wakened by the trumpets' blasts; who will cower in their graves and hope to remain unnoticed and unjudged; whose hope shall be as ineffectual as mine. Niles closed the door, and called my name again, more loudly, more angrily.

"I am awake."

"You went to see Mainwaring today," he stated.

"Yes, in a sense. I encountered him outside San Lorenzo's, while I was out shopping with Rose."

"It was not by pre-arrangement, then?"

In the ensuing silence Niles crossed the room, a shadow among shadows, and reached behind the drawn curtains to close the casement window.

"You went with him from San Lorenzo's to his hotel. Rose saw you."

"To say good-bye to Mrs. Lacey."

"You had not thought that they would see us off at the railway station?"

"I had bought a small present for her, a remembrance. Having it with me, it seemed a natural thing to do."

"Do you know, Clara, that your voice alters when you tell a lie? It develops a kind of tremolo. The effect of it is pleasing, but it does tend rather to defeat your purpose. In short, my dear, I don't believe a word of it."

"I'm sorry, Niles. I spoke to Mr. Mainwaring in confidence, as a man of the cloth."

"In confidence?" His voice had become quite shrill.

"Yes, Niles. If I did wrong, I am sorry, but I am sure Mr. Mainwaring would not—"

There was a sound of shattering. Next morning I discovered the pieces of an old majolica candlestick on the stone floor. Whether Niles hurled it in anger or broke it by stumbling in the darkness I do not know.

"Oh, Clara, Clara! For shame! If you had branded me as they do malefactors in the lands of the Turk, I could not have felt a deeper humiliation than you have made me feel tonight! If you had jeered at me in a public assembly because I am short and slightly built! If you had spit in my face in the dining room of this hotel! You have made my heart, that loved you, into a nest of snakes. Do not be surprised, my dear, if one of them should strike at you. I am not answerable now."

I sat up in alarm and sought to scan the darkness. Before I had seen him I felt his hand. It brushed across my forehead and tangled in my unbound hair.

"What did he say to you, Clara, after you'd told him your sorry little tale?"

"Believe me, Niles, I told no tales of any sort. I only asked a question. Blame me for ignorance. Blame me for indiscretion. I intended no ill."

"And have you been cured of your . . . ignorance?"

"Mrs. Lacey explained to me about . . . that is. . . ."

"Oh, don't be ashamed, my dear! Say it aloud. Publish it through the city. We shall find a troupe of dancers somewhere, and you may get up a proper entertainment with bawdy songs and skirts hiked up over your knees."

He let loose my hair abruptly, and I fell back upon the pillow; as suddenly his tone changed from one of passionate invective to a whisper as cold and neutral as the words on the sign of a shop. "What did he say to you after? I must know."

"After I had talked to Mrs. Lacey, I said nothing more to Mr. Mainwaring, except a very curt good-bye. I was upset. I still *am* upset, Niles. I do want to talk to you about this. Indeed, I think we are obliged to, but—"

"About our annulment, you mean?"

"No. Of course not. You know that is not my meaning, and never could be."

"Are you crying? Let me feel your cheeks. Oh, that's adequate. That's worth two handkerchiefs."

"Niles—please! I cannot bear such cruelty; you cannot mean it!"

"You'd be surprised what *meanings* I am capable of, if you provoke me to them, Clara. Now say—what did he tell you? Did he say we aren't truly man and wife? That is what he said to me. Not in so many words, of course. He is much too well-spoken for that. He came to call on me at ten o'clock. I received him in my smoking jacket, and he was very cordial and smiled and was well into his second glass of Madeira before he mentioned what had brought him by the hotel. I had been thinking, guileless as I am, that he had come by only for the pleasure of my company. He said that of course it was none of his business but his conscience required that he speak—as my friend. These moral bullies with their meaty faces and their fine intentions! Oh, I understand his intentions well enough. Better, I'll wager, than he does himself. My friend!" He paused; then, as quietly as before, he asked: "Clara, what did he say to you?"

"Nothing, Niles. Nothing you could have taken exception to. He advised me to be submissive to you, and I have been, and I am now, and I shall be, Niles—I shall be!"

"Only you will gossip afterwards with whom you please, is that it? I expect you plotted all this with your aunt."

"I have been as little successful in getting her to speak in candor with me as in getting you to do so."

"Then please, Clara, as you are submissive to me, continue not to distress the poor woman with this kind of sordidness."

"Niles, I do not think it is sordid. If I have not been a proper wife to you, it is my own fault. I had no notion what was involved, and you, quite naturally, did not want to shock me."

"Oh, yes—quite naturally."

"But now Mrs. Lacey has explained the matter to me, and you need not be over-careful of my feelings."

"I'm sure that between them they've given you a proper

education, my dear. A minister who concerns himself especially with the raising up of fallen women and an old midwife. One could not ask for better authorities."

"Niles, don't be unjust. Poor Mrs. Lacey found the whole thing an ordeal."

"I'm sure she did. It isn't every day that a matron of her years is asked to give young ladies a guided tour of the gutters."

"Niles, I refuse to consider the most sacred act of our married life as . . . indecent. I can understand that it may be distressing some times, especially if there is no love. If you and Renata—"

"Is that what Mainwaring suggested?"

"It is what I have been thinking to myself as I lay here, trying to understand your feelings."

"You're curious about my feelings for Renata? Then let me enlighten you. I hated her. I considered my marriage as a kind of spring trap that had its teeth clamped into my tenderest tissue. I writhed, Clara."

"But you must have loved her, too."

"You mean, because she had a child by me? It is much easier, you know, to cohabit with a woman one does not love. The degradation of it is not then so painful."

"But need it always be degrading and painful?"

"Yes, for the woman, always. Why do you think the back alleys of every city are filled with women who sell the night's employment of their bodies to men? Many, if not most, of those men have wives—whom they love, and whom they would spare from their lusts. As I have spared you."

"You make it all seem so ugly."

"Because you insist to know."

"Is it wrong to want knowledge?"

"That was Eve's question, and you will recall what answer she received."

"But how is it a sacrament if it is so wrong?"

"Wedlock is called holy, but so are most wars. There is more of enmity than of real love in the marriages I have seen. Your aunt Jerningham has more affection for her Josiah dead than ever she felt for him living. You can't deny it—I remember him. Can you imagine the act of love, so-called, between *them*?"

"May be their marriage was an exception."

"It is ours, Clara, that has been exceptional. But now you would end that."

"It has not been a marriage. You say so yourself. It is what you said that day, looking at Helvellyn: we are like brother and sister—not like husband and wife."

"Am I to understand that you have not been satisfied?"

"I have been very happy, Niles, but I have been . . . uneasy, too. Without understanding why."

"Well, my dear, it is easily cured. Bend over."

"What?"

"Get up on your knees and bend over. Now, lift your night-gown—so! Spread your legs apart. Did Mrs. Lacey tell you nothing? Close your eyes. It hurts, you know, but you ought not to cry out if you can help it."

I felt a stab of pain, but it was not so sharp as the pain that had come with my headaches and it was over in a moment.

Niles had gone to the night table, whence came the sound of water poured from pitcher to basin.

"I'm afraid it is too late, Clara, to ask for a bath to be drawn. There is a sponge over here, however, and I can help you clean yourself, if you wish. As for the nightgown and the sheets—and, I'm much afraid, my cuffs—they are soiled past saving. In some countries, you know, they hang the sheets out on the morning after the nuptials as a kind of trophy."

"Niles! I beg you—do not use me so!"

"You can't have it both ways, Clara. Either I shall use you or I shall not."

"You speak to me as though I had become hateful to you."

"What I feel, Clara, is regret. I did not wish to do what I have done, but you obliged me. But let us have no more discussion of it. We must be up early tomorrow."

I heard the latch lifted, and saw Niles silhouetted in the open doorway.

"Niles, don't leave me like this."

"I! Leave you?" He laughed theatrically. "That was never the danger. Quite the opposite, I should have thought."

"Niles, I have never—"

He overrode my protest. "But that doesn't matter now. If you want to leave me—try! Display yourself to the doctors and the lawyers. You bear the true stigmata now of marriage."

"You know, Niles Visconti, and I know, that is not true. What you've done to me in this hour—any *surgeon* might do."

"Good-night, Clara."

"Niles!"

But the door was closed.

I could not bear it. The pain could be endured. All pain is borne, somehow. But not this blackness, not this utter dearth. I tried to remain there, tried to cease from thinking, but nothing, no one can demand of us that we accept despair. I rose from the bed, heedless of the hemorrhagy that each step renewed, and followed Niles into his own room.

He had taken off the soiled shirt and was searching through his travelling closet for a clean one. In the light of the single lamp his thin, bare arms seemed almost as white as the linen of his undergarment.

"Niles?"

He affected to ignore me, undoing each button of the shirt he had taken from the closet with an exaggerated niceness. Then, standing before a pier-glass, he put on the shirt and tied his cravat. All the while I stood silently upon the threshold of our two rooms, persuaded that my mute presence must finally awaken and compel the pity that my words could not. A hope as frail as foolish, for when, turning from the mirror, he did regard me, it was with a glance so withering, so unrecognizing, that I might as well have been a mendicant among a dozen others, exposing my deformities on the steps of a church for his careless disdain.

"Niles, do not *hate* me! I'm sorry if what I did today, or said tonight, has given offense to you. Truly I am. I did not mean to reproach you. Only . . . you made me desperate. I need you, Niles, so badly, and I love you so much. If you will but let me!"

"What you *need*, Clara, is sleep. We leave Florence early in the morning. You must be fresh."

"Won't you sleep with me, Niles? I should feel so comforted if you were beside me."

"Sleep? Impossible. We should neither of us sleep a wink. In any case"—putting on his hat—"I should have thought it was evident that I am going out."

"And I beg you—do not!"

"I'm sorry if it distresses you, but that is what *I* need."

"Niles," I replied, with (as I supposed) a logic not to be resisted, "I do love you."

"It's all very well to talk of love, but you know you've sworn to honor and obey, as well. The honor I have forfeited, I suppose, for the time being, but as for obedience, on that I really must insist. Good-night, my dear."

"Niles—no!" I ran towards him, determined, if by that means I might prevent his leaving, to throw myself at his feet and cling to them. "I will do anything! I promise you—anything you ask of me. Only don't leave me alone, here, tonight."

"Please, Clara—the carpet." He touched the silver tip of his walking-stick to the hollow of my chest, keeping me from coming closer to him. "You shall stain the carpet."

I stood before him, close enough to have reached out and touched the hand that repulsed me. But I did not.

"Go, then," I said.

"Tears, Clara? Is that to be the weapon of last resort?"

I wiped at my face with the sleeve of my nightgown. I did not know when I had begun to cry. Their flow did not have its source in my will; scarcely, it seemed, in my feelings. Niles regarded me reprovingly, as if my weeping were an indecency like the blood that stained my nightgown. Then, taking the lamp, he left me, and I was alone in a darkness that seemed emblematic of my whole life, past and to come. I felt like a traveller plundered and left by the wayside, wounded but still alive, too wretched to resent the hurt that had been done me, too forlorn to seek its remedy. The night enveloped me and filled my heart with blackness; I did not believe the sun would ever rise again.

CHAPTER EIGHTEEN
"Within the Coliseum's Wall"

TRUE TO THE WISDOM OF ECCLESIASTES, the sun did rise upon the morrow, and I rose also, to bathe and dress and fill the odd corners of my luggage with whatever remained unpacked. I took my place at the breakfast table to eat a boiled egg and a buttered roll, and when the time came to mount into the hackney coach, I was at hand. Neither my aunt Jerningham nor Rose could have observed (I think) any difference in my behavior; yet the difference, inwardly, was entire. There was a bitterness in my heart amounting almost to despair. I could foresee no life for myself but an endless mockery like that of this morning, a parade of polite breakfasts and pointless journeyings, of misery dissimulated and pretended mirth.

Even Niles seemed to believe my outward bearing to be a fair representation of my intrinsic mood, for as he helped me up the steps of the railway carriage, he remarked in his mildest everyday style that the sky had taken my modiste's suggestion and decked itself in the same becoming blue as my travelling dress. There could be no question of his keeping up appearances, for my aunt and Rose were out of earshot; he simply thought that I could be counted on, without an explanation, to forget and, with not a word of apology, to forgive.

I regarded him levelly with a smile too cold to be misunderstood. "I have something of yours," I said, reaching into the pocket of my skirt. "You forgot it on my night table."

I saw him feel, through the leather of his glove, for his wedding ring, which he would often remove at night and leave upon the bedside table.

"Not your ring, Niles. This." I handed him the penknife, which had become glued to the scrap of cotton I had wrapped it in.

By that gesture I secured for myself a day of uninterrupted thoughtfulness. My aunt, in preparation for the long journey south, had taken a dose of her medicine, and so made no conversational demands but sat and nodded over the landscape that fleeted past as though it were a particularly dry stretch of Mrs. Oliphant's *Chronicles*.

I heeded the sequent glories of Tuscany, Umbria, and the Campagna no more than she. My thoughts turned inwards, and I regarded, with no less awe than I might have accorded to some colossal ruin, the innocence I had preserved through twenty-one years of maidenhood and almost six months of marriage. Innocence? Call it blindness, rather. A denizen of Plato's cave who, believing in the reality of shadows, escapes to discover the larger reality of the sunlight could not have viewed the transfigured world before him with more wonderment.

How this knowledge altered everything! There were essential truths of the religion that I professed to believe which had till this day been no more to me than words, formulae I had repeated to myself with the pious incomprehension of Papists mumbling Latin prayers. Indeed, their dead language was a lighter veil, for beneath it they could all discern the solemn mystery of the Savior's birth, while I, more benighted, had never thought to inquire the meaning of this article of my faith. How was it possible? Passage after passage from both the New Testament and the Old which I had recited at Mr. Jerningham's knee rose up to haunt me like ghosts awakened from the dust by a libation of wine. What had I thought St. Paul to mean by all his comminations against the sins of the flesh, the filthiness and corruption of the flesh? What sense had I gathered from the stories of Abraham and Sarah, of David and Bathsheba, of Ruth and Boaz, and an hundred couples more, joined by wedlock or by a guilty love, generation upon generation in an unbroken chain since the day of Adam?

In later years, I have noted that most young people give credence to the doctrines of their religion and the tales of Scripture with as careless an attention, and are able for almost as long as I to maintain their innocence side by side with the knowledge that ought at least to tarnish it. Perhaps they regard the content of the Biblical tales as being, along with their language and geography, something exotic, fanciful, and far removed from the mundane circumstances of an English existence. Yet I think that there is more: I think that children sense—that *I* had sensed—a dark reality behind these ancient scandals and solemn adjurations, and that they deliberately keep themselves from knowing more. They walk to the mouth of the cave, see but a single beam of light, and retreat again to the comfortable darkness within, denying what they have glimpsed and trying most strenuously to efface the memory of it. Earlier in these pages I surmised that *the fear of knowledge* was an essential key to my character. Now I trust my readers will appreciate the extent of that fear and the degree to which it affected not my character only but, as well, my fate.

It is not, after all, an unfounded fear, and certainly not an uncommon one. I began to perceive how all the proprieties and marks of decorum in which I had been so exactly schooled were founded on the bedrock of a legitimate anxiety. There was a *reason* for the custom of chaperonage and for all those other rules that seek to abridge a perfect candor between the sexes. The whole concept of Scandal suddenly became real.

This new world opening to me was not only dangerous but cruel. I remembered an anecdote from Murray's *Handbook* concerning my new home of Ischia and the means employed by Alfonso of Aragon in securing that island's loyalty: he had expelled all its male inhabitants and forced their wives and daughters to bear children to his soldiers. I recalled the statue in the Loggia dei Lanzi of a Roman soldier struggling with his Sabine bride as he stood athwart his vanquished foe. I thought of my grandfather disinherited by the false imputation of his mother's guilt; of the perpetual warfare between my aunt Jerningham and her spouse; of how narrowly *I* had avoided being married to my cousin Geoffrey; of what that marriage would have *meant*, the violation it would have represented not merely of my wishes and feelings but of something so much more intimate I could not, even with this new knowledge, quite conceive of it: a violation, it seemed, of my very existence. One after another, like monsters of the deep rising up to the calm sea-surface, each of these matters, seen in this new perspective, would bring to my cheeks a retrospective blush, or to my chest a spasm of inutile dread.

How can people bear to live, I wondered, in such a world? Nor was this question merely a means of rhetorical emphasis. What else lies behind the decision, so common in Catholic countries, to abandon a world in which such wrongs are tolerated and to escape to the cloistered quiet of a convent or monastery? Had I been at liberty to make such a choice myself, I am certain that at that moment I would have taken the veil, and gratefully. Rita of Cascia no longer seemed a figure in an eccentric, slightly unsavory legend, but a living exemplar of true virtue; in short, a saint.

But this black, renouncing mood was not one that I could entertain without dishonoring my marriage vow, and so I warred against it. Mrs. Lacey, as an instructress, had emphasized the positive side of her subject, and I had been content through most of the previous day to accept matters at her own prudent but smiling valuation. As the new and so much darker day wore on and the valleys through which we progressed became broader and more verdant, I tried to return to this more cheerful attitude. I considered my parents: here, surely, was a case to contradict Niles' contention that all marriages, with regard to this central fact, were doomed to fail. But could I be sure? My memories of them were so few and so misty that I could scarcely pretend to have any intuition of their most intimate feelings. I had only my own experience to go by—that is to say, none at all—and a frail hope, which my own husband called unfounded, that the marriage bed might be an abode of love rather than a scene of woman's pain and humiliation.

We were to have stayed a week in Rome before continuing on to Ischia, but that week had been sacrificed to our longer sojourn in Florence. We did, however, break our journey at Rome for one night, putting up at the Hotel Costanzi, which was convenient to the railway station.

After a cold supper for which only Lydia displayed any appetite, and after my aunt had retired, Niles insisted that I come with him to view the Coliseum by moonlight. "For," he said, in that blandly amiable tone that had vexed me that morning, "if you are to have a single memory of the city, it should be that."

"Really, Niles, I am not disposed to go sightseeing. The hour is late; we have been riding all day; my mind is not in a state to be receptive to romantic ruins."

"You refuse to come—even to please me?"

"If you urge me to do so, I shall come."

"I do urge you, and you will be grateful that I did, once we are there. No need to take more than the merino shawl you have with you. Rome's summer nights are warmer than the days of London. I told the carriage that brought us from the station to wait for us at the door of the hotel. We can go there and be back in the space of half an hour."

And so I was borne off to view that grandest of all Time's wrecks, nacreously agleam in the moonlight. For all I cared, it might have been a row of offices anywhere in London. We were let in by the watchman through a small grated door and proceeded up the steps and through a broken archway to emerge in a kind of valley, at the far end of which a tall black cross rose up from the strange, tangled pasture.

"It is the valley of the shadow of death," said Niles.

The words seemed meaningless to me. My imagination had become inert; my sensibilities leaden. I saw only a more or less orderly slope of white stones, shadowed here and there by tufts of ilex and aliternus.

In all the world is there a monument that can make true sorrows less bitter? A church that can restore a shattered faith? I looked at the Coliseum; I looked at the bright moon; I looked at Niles, who seemed to share a common unreality with the scene before us, a lack of substance. I felt that we had been drained of every living possibility and left, the merest husks of our humanity, soul-less as stone.

Niles, whether blind to my feelings (or the lack of them), or else from an impulse to wound me by showing how little he had been affected by what had so crushed me, began to recite the famous verses from Byron's *Manfred* commemorating this same moonlit scene.

> "I do remember me, that in my youth,
> When I was wandering, —upon such a night,
> I stood within the Coliseum's wall,
> Midst the chief relics of almighty Rome;
> The trees which grew along the broken arches
> Waved dark in the blue midnight, and the stars
> Shone through the rents of ruin;
> . . . And thou didst shine, thou rolling moon—

And then—"Clara, do you know it from there?"

"Know what, Niles? Pardon me, I haven't been attending what you say."

"My dear Clara, it is no less a torment for me. But we must go on. What choice have we, really?"

"We can be *honest* even if we are unhappy."

"And talk about our wounds? They will heal faster if we try and forget them."

"In any case, I don't know the poem you were quoting. I could recite another, if that is what you think will make us happier."

"Is it an apology you wish, Clara? Then I am sorry for what happened last night. I was angry and a little drunk. I behaved like a beast. I repeat—I'm sorry."

Far away there was a creaking of iron against iron. The watchman, I suppose, was admitting other visitors, or letting them out.

"But do you know what I regret most, Clara? Not our discord, not our cruel words to each other, nor my brutal act, though these are all regrettable. Still, I am confident that our love is large enough that we may surmount these things. What I regret much more is that this has cost me a friend. When I showed Mainwaring to the door, I told him we would not be able to receive him or his aunt at the Villa. I was as rude as I fairly could be without offering him a pretext to strike me. And I almost broke into tears when I closed the door after him. I'd so much wanted him for a friend. Do you know, I'm thirty years old and I have never had a friend of my own sex? I don't know why it is, but I have not. Once, at Oxford, when I was little more than a child, but since then never."

I was oddly moved by this avowal, and tried to offer Niles some reassurance; yet, at the same time, I felt still emptier and more deeply slighted. In his unconsciousness of my feelings there was something deeper than cruelty. It was as though he had forgotten my name.

"Anyone would be proud to be your friend, Niles," I assured him. "I'm sure that Mr. Mainwaring, after a lapse of time, will come by to visit us in Ischia. You have heard him complain of the lack of companionship here in Italy. Also, as a Christian minister, he is obliged to seek a reconciliation. You'll see—it will be he who comes to ask your pardon."

"Yes, but it would never be the same. He will always be studying me, always a little suspicious. The door has been closed and locked and barred."

There were tears in his eyes. I took a handkerchief from the pocket of my skirt and wiped at them. Yet even this act, the very emblem of compassion, seemed somehow *neutral* morally; as if these droplets on his cheeks had been splashed on him by some passing carriage. At last his tears ceased, but he made no offer to leave. Where was there to go to, after all? We did not touch and seldom spoke, but still we sat upon the tumbled stone, like the last two corpses left from that stadium's ignoble games; unable, because we lacked the trust, or the understanding, to speak of what we felt or feared or longed for; unable even to unite our separate miseries into a bond of sorrow shared. For an hour of inarticulate pain we looked at the lifeless amphitheater, and then returned, on foot, to our hotel.

BOOK III

'Tis morning: but no morning can restore
What we have forfeited. I see no sun:
The wrong is mixed. In tragic life, God wot,
No villain need be! Passions spin the plot:
We are betrayed by what is false within.

—GEORGE MEREDITH,
Modern Love

CHAPTER ONE
The Island

I HAD A NIGHTMARE ONCE, in which it seemed I was pursued across Hyde Park by the driver of an omnibus, who accused me of having cheated him of his fare. It was a holiday; the park was thronged. As I fled, I sought to draw attention to my plight, but my screams elicited, at most, gestures of annoyance and disdain. Finally, on the bridge across the Serpentine, my pursuer seized me—and I woke. Waking, I discovered that the man I had taken for the driver of the omnibus was seated by my bed. He was my physician! Naturally, he sought to calm me, and gradually I let myself be calmed. Then I noticed that the knees of his white suit were stained green, from when he had stumbled in the park. I was afraid to scream, lest he take advantage of the moment to force down my throat the medicine he had prepared for me; which was not medicine at all. In fact, I had not awakened, but rather slipped from one nightmare into a second: deeper, fearfuler, and more insidious.

Such were my feelings with regard to Ischia. Since departing Venice, all Italy had been a waking nightmare for me, but now, at just the moment I had expected the horrors to be dispelled by the soothing regularities of domestic life, they thickened and became more definite.

This sense of living in a dream was heightened by the chimeric nature of my island world. For those born there, Ischia continues to be a source of wonderment throughout their lives; other mortals are doomed to disbelief. It is too paradisiacal. One touches its bizarre and nameless flowers with the expectation that they will vanish, just as, at regular intervals through the day, Mount Epomeo vanishes into the coursing clouds, which themselves dissolve as they are swept onwards across the Tyrrhenian Sea. And one is right to withhold belief, since this paradise, like all must be that are terrestrial, is infected. Latent fires of the inner earth heat the island's soil and sand, for Epomeo is a brother of Vesuvius, which it faces across the Bay of Naples. While the fires of Vesuvius are concentrated all within the volcanic cone, to be pent up and then spent in deadly eruptions, those of Ischia are dispersed through the island, issuing in perpetual springs of hot or boiling water or hissing up through fumaroles in fetid vapors. There are stretches of the beach where the sand will burn the soles of the best-shod feet, and one may catch a whiff of brimstone among the groves of palm.

Yet the approach is fair, even majestical. From the moment one steps onto the little packet-boat on the quay of Santa Lucia until one sails into the submerged volcanic cone that forms the broad cirque of Ischia's principal port, one witnesses a ceaseless procession of solemn beauty. Each successive sheer uplifting of rocky headland is a new and more thrilling marvel, until, rounding the isle of Procida, the mass of Ischia looms ahead, a single mountain rising from the sea. These are landscapes better proportioned for giants than for men, nor is this impression limited to those accustomed to our gentler British geography: Virgil himself makes Ischia the headstone over the watery grave of the rebellious titan Typhoeus, who, buried but not dead, causes by his groans and writhings those upheavals of the earth for which the island is still noted.

With seas smooth and the wind favoring, we reached our new home after a voyage of four hours. Lydia, who had crossed the Channel in January without a qualm, suffered acutely from the gentle motions of our boat. Niles, as a gesture (I thought) towards our reconcilement, was patiently solicitous of her comfort, walking her from bow to stern and stern to bow and rattling on the while, a whole Baedeker of information both real and fancied, in an effort to distract her. But Lydia, once she had set her mind on being ill, was not to be distracted, much less comforted.

Leaving the boat, we were greeted by a small delegation of beggars representing every type and condition of mendicancy, sickly and robust, pathetic and bullying, true and false. To each, Niles gave a coin. They replied with their blessings, then settled down to wait the next boat arriving from the mainland, due on the morrow. A burro harnessed to a crude cart regarded us and our luggage with resentful suspicion, as much as to say: "You can't expect *me* to haul all of that and you besides!" Except for these, the beggars and the burro, no one was at hand to welcome us.

Though it was past five o'clock, when one might hope for some abatement of the day's heat, the sun beat down with indiscriminate ferocity upon the quivering waters of the harbor, upon the whitewashed walls and closed shutters of the customs house, upon the burro and the beggars and ourselves. Except for us, and perhaps the walls (which were crumbling at the edges) no one seemed greatly to mind. The water shimmered gaily; the beggars had settled down to a game of cards; the burro, convinced we posed no immediate threat to his leisure, had returned to his old quarrel with some large flies.

"And to think," observed my aunt, "that this is but the second day of summer."

"Hush! Niles will overhear us and think that you are blaming him."

Niles at that moment had walked to the main roadway to see if there were any hope of our deliverance, while Rose and Antonia, my aunt's maid, were huddled in a scrap of shadow underneath a low, bristling palm.

"Blame him? *He* does not cause the sun to shine, nor the waves to toss, nor the road to be empty, nor his mother to neglect us." She wiped her beaded brow with a damp handkerchief, and sighed. "I'm sorry, Clara. I have been most unjust, but I feel a megrim coming on, and furthermore, you must admit that after the number of letters and telegrams we have sent on ahead of us—"

"Aunt, please."

"Just as you say, Clara."

"There is a bottle of your medicine at the top of that trunk. Rose shall help me with the straps and—"

"No, my dear—not here in the public gaze. I'd sooner die from a *coup de soleil* than of embarrassment. Only, next time your husband offers to hire a conveyance, oppose him with less determination."

I followed this advice, and within an hour of our debarking, the burro's worst suspicions were realized. Six of our most substantial closets were loaded on the little cart. Meantime, other of his relatives, no less sullen than he, were assembled and meted out similar tasks under the instruction and encouragement of three beggars who had lost their first stake in the card-game and were anxious to gain a second. At last our hired coach appeared upon the quay and received a general acclamation. It was a kind of berlin, very tall, very thin, and very ancient, drawn by one weary, philosophic mare notable for the same qualities. It seemed doubtful whether such a Rosinante could draw such a carriage even when empty, but in addition to the three of us inside, the maids were bidden to climb up on the box beside the coachman.

The beggars were rewarded once more for their good will, and we set off to the west followed by our long baggage train. It was now six o'clock, but the sun, taking no notice of time, continued to beat down with a special spite for closed carriages. The road wound close beside the shore. To our right, sea and sky blended in a bright, blue-white, horizonless haze; to our left, a profusion of flora blended into a single luxuriance of exotic shapes and colors. There were trees that had gone mad with flowers and others that had foregone every arboreal notion of flower, leaf, or branch and were nothing but pillars crowned, high up, with tidy Ionic capitals of green scrolls. Masses of crashing red and glaring violet bloom graced the walls and hung in festoons from the balustrades of the richer dwellings. Everywhere growth heaped upon growth, green upon green, life upon life; and yet nothing in all this vital super-abundance seemed quite *natural*. It was as though by crossing the Bay of Naples we had entered upon a second, alternative Creation, wilder and lovelier than the first, though unfriendlier as well; but of the *scorpions*, the *sand-flies*, the *hornets*, and the *mosquitoes*, anon!

At intervals, and those intervals ever more closely spaced, Niles and I, and the two maids, would be obliged to dismount from the coach so that the poor mare could draw its freight of gilded lumber to the top of the rise. I was grateful for these respites, as much out of pity for the horse as from relief at escaping the stifling heat of the carriage. Outside we could behold the whole sweep of the misty sea, the full majesty of Epomeo. Add to these the not inconsiderable spectacle of our caravan climbing the dusty road, like an allegory of Vanity impeding the Soul's progress towards Paradise.

During one of these periods of exercise there was an earthquake. As earthquakes go, this was the demurest tremor; one of Typhoeus' sighs, rather than a full-scale groan. First there was a rumbling, as of far-off thunder in a cloudless sky. The burros stopped and brayed reply, like trumpets answering to kettledrums. Then the ground shivered. The jolt was more to the balance of one's mind than of one's body. Niles took the hand I stretched out to him with tentativeness, less offering his protection than sharing in my apprehension.

It was over. The sea and sky and sun, the gray peaks of Epomeo and the white dust of the road were all as they had been. The foliage rustled as before in the languid southern breeze. The donkeys resumed their upward toil. The carriage with my aunt in it waited for us at the crest of the hill.

We neither moved. Our fingers, twined together, did not relax. Niles smiled a wincing smile, as though he had tasted a medlar of exemplary ripeness, bitter and succulent both at once.

"What on earth!"

"It is the island," said Niles, "bidding us welcome."

"Is it over, do you think?"

"If not, what then? If the earth means to come to an end this afternoon, can *we* stop it?"

Ahead, at the top of the hill, my aunt had come out of the carriage and was waving her furled parasol at us energetically in (we supposed) a semaphore of distress.

While Niles hastened up the road to soothe Lydia (with some solider reassurances, I hoped, than those he had offered me), I followed as fast as I might. For a single moment, alone in that unlikely landscape, with the dust that the burros had raised settling on my damp face, I wanted to turn back down the road: to the quay; to Naples; to England; to my home in the suburbs of Bayswater. Needless to say, I did not; not by so much as a glance.

My resolve was rewarded. Reaching the hilltop, I discovered that Lydia had meant to signal not distress (earthquakes were too foreign a phenomenon to excite her English imagination) but to announce glad tidings. Ahead of us, approaching on the same road, was the coach Niles had described to us, blazoned with his family arms, and beyond the slow-moving coach, on a spar of black rock at the end of a small peninsula, were the tiers and terraces of the Villa Visconti.

All Italy condensed into a single view of perfect loveliness.

CHAPTER TWO
The Villa

THAT VIEW EXISTS NO LONGER. The Villa itself is but a tumbled mass of masonry scoured by the action of the sea, a new bed of stone and brick for the unquiet slumbers of Typhoeus. The very rock from which it rose lies dismembered beyond the altered shoreline, a jagged shoal that fishing boats avoid. All gone. All ruined in the same vast ruination that swept to Judgment two thousand souls and more in one sweep of the scythe.

I remember still the morning that I learned of it, a Saturday in July of 1883, calm and bright and ordinary. I recall taking up the London paper from the tray and opening it to an account of the debate in the House on the Corrupt and Illegal Practices Act, when somehow I became conscious that this same page bore other news more appurtenant; and reading that news, and trying to conceive the might and scope of Ischia's vastation; and then encountering at the very foot of that long column of print, among the names of those already known to be dead, the familiar name Visconti; and weeping and having to lock myself in my room till I recovered; and the pain, the bitter pain of knowing that I could not express my grief by any show of mourning.

Yet can it be gone, while it is all still so distinct in memory? That staircase mounting from the entrance hall and its double file of satyrs holding up their lightless lamps and leering welcome; the great hall of scagliola—plaster painted to resemble stone but so faded as to seem the ghost of stone; the state-rooms where I sat imprisoned by the heat of Ischia's summer, too inert to lift a needle or to turn a page; my own more hated room, where my imprisonment was of a crueller kind; the broad tribune from which I would look down upon the close, indecipherable handwriting of the waves, waves that even then awaited their triumph over all these proud forms. The garden, too—dissolved; only its fountains and some shattered urns to testify that there had been a garden at all. Instead of vines, seaweed clinging to the trellises of the pergola; the carp in the pool, as many as survived the earth's upheaval, poisoned by the salt water of the sea; the broken limbs and shattered torso of Athena, mere marble once again.

I mourn, and always shall, the living that are dead; but for the rest I am glad. Yet, except, for the living, what loss is so affecting as the ruin or mutilation of a work of art, even the humblest? The Villa Visconti, while not perhaps one of the masterpieces of its time, was certainly of its place the noblest and best. By contrast, the Aragonese Castello at the other end of Ischia was a mere earthwork. Yet I am glad. It is foolish, to be sure, this resentment against inanimate objects. It was not the house that meant to do me harm, nor any *thing* of plaster, wood, or stone. Prisoners, however, are not to be reasoned with on the subject of fetters. The Bastille, for all I know, was a handsome piece of architecture, but I suspect that few who were immured there regretted that the Revolution razed it to the ground. I say it again: I am glad.

I had seen enough of Italy, its palaces and villas, to be undismayed at my first inspection of my new home. It was too grand, but I was a brave mouse by now and grandness could not stop me. What was disconcerting was not the stage itself, but rather finding it, when we entered, deserted and disordered. The Contessa Visconti was not in the coach that so belatedly had met us; nor at the gate; nor at the door; nor in the entrance hall; nor anywhere we looked for her. Niles sought to make light of her absence, pretending that we played at hide-and-seek, but the pretense lacked conviction.

"She must be napping," he decided. So we went to her boudoir, and Niles knocked upon the thick door, and called her name, and knocked again. Though there was no answer, we went in. If the Contessa were asleep, she had found some other couch for her repose than the musty behemoth of tarnished buhl sprawling before the shuttered window. Here, as elsewhere, nothing had been done to declare the rooms inhabited, except to remove the dust-covers from the most necessary items of furniture. There were no flowers, no candles in the sconces on the walls, no personal effects of any kind. A display in a shop would have been warmer. Indeed, the whole Villa had the air rather of a warehouse than of an habitation, an appearance heightened by the crates and boxes stacked against the walls and clustered in the hallways.

"I hope we will find her in good health," I said by way of extenuating these disorders.

"If she were not, we would have heard before this. Nothing is so certain to set the old girl to writing as a flutter of her bilious complaint."

"May be it has come on her of a sudden, or may be—"

"May be, but if you'll step over here, you may see the patient."

I joined Niles at the window and peered out through the slanting louvers of the shutter. Below us, on the uppermost of the garden's four terraces, reclining on a lawn-chair beside the carp-pool, was Zaide. Oblivious of us, she sipped from a wineglass, set it aside, lifted it again, languid as the sirocco that fluttered the ends of the Chinese scarf with which she had blindfolded her eyes against the declining sun.

"*My* diagnosis," Niles said, "is that she is drunk. But we can apply other tests. If you would rather not come down to the garden with me. . . ?"

"I'd much rather come *with* you, but if you think it would be more agreeable for her to welcome you first alone, then I can look after Lydia."

"We're safer together. But be warned: she parted from us in no good humor, and the condition of the Villa would suggest that she has not quite rallied."

"Then it's well that we're at hand to rally her."

And so, cheering each other on, we returned to the ground floor, and out onto the terrace. In a whisper, Niles bade me give no signal of our presence. Though only a few yards away, on the far side of the pool, Zaide remained unconscious of us, thanks to the scarf over her eyes.

Three dull-gold fish made sullen ripples in the stagnant water. I remember wondering how they escaped the Villa's cats. A minute elapsed, or more; I could not say. Niles studied his mother with a fixity of interest that I found disconcerting, a regard that was neither warm nor cold. It must have been this way of looking at her that put me in mind of cats—their calm measuring observance of even those whom they love.

Zaide tipped up her glass—unavailingly, as it was empty. Niles stepped forwards, took up the bottle from the stone bench, and filled the glass top-full.

Zaide smiled, and nodded. "*Grazie, caro mio.*" There was such naturalness in her smile and her thanks as to vanquish any preconception of mine concerning the proper uses of the afternoon.

Niles bent over his mother and placed a kiss on her forehead, as gently (it seemed from where I stood) as if the sirocco had placed it there.

The smile upon those wide, rouged lips grew broader, then collapsed into flaccid uncertainty. She pulled the scarf down from one eye, and exclaimed: "Niles! It's you!"

"Who else, dear Mother?"

"And Clara! My dear, come close and let me touch you. How well you look! It is wicked, though, to come sneaking up on an old woman like this. The slanting light shows every wrinkle."

"Wrinkles, Mother? Where?"

The smile with which she replied to this was so unlike the smile of the moment previous that the difference seemed rather between two distinct persons than between two shades of feeling. One was Niles' mother, the other my mother-in-law. It saddens me now to think that I never actually met the more amiable of these two women. Might we even have come to be friends? It is conceivable. Heaven knows, I was hungry for friendship. How strange a tale would have been mine to tell, how much stranger even than this, if that had come to pass! After all, it is just as well that I knew her no better than I did. I survived her enmity; her friendship might have destroyed me.

"And where is your aunt Jerningham, my dear?" she asked, after a loose handclasp betokening my welcome.

"We left her within to catch her breath," Niles answered for me, bending down to wipe the stone bench with his handkerchief.

"Fatigued by her journey, no doubt."

"Oh, she has stood up better than any of us. But we *are* tired, as we haven't stopped since we left Rome. And a little terrified as well. There was an earthquake on our way to the Villa." Niles gestured for me to be seated, and, when I was, sat down next to me.

"Indeed, yes. It made me stain my bodice. Here." She touched the blot on the gray *glacé* silk with a certain tenderness, as though it were a wound that still could smart. "Clara, I trust *you* were not frightened?"

"I scarcely know, it was so soon over. And Niles was there beside me."

"A great comfort, to be sure."

I must have been staring unconscionably, for she turned her head aside and raised her hand, visor-like, over her eyes. They were quite dreadfully bloodshot, the white veined with heavy streaks of crimson, like rose agates.

"Are you thirsty? Of course, you must be. Pour yourselves wine. If there are glasses. I was not expecting you so soon. It seems I dispatched the coach only a moment ago. Why *are* you goggling at me, Niles? I have been too much in the sun, and it has hurt my eyes. Here, let me spare you—I will bandage up again." Her fingers fumbled at the knot of the scarf.

"Mother, don't *fret* so! If I was looking at you too closely, it was prompted by nothing but the pleasure of seeing you again. It's been two months."

"It *seems* no longer than a week, but that is the way of it here where there are no events to announce the hours and mark them. The sun moves across the sky fast as any cloud. I am scarcely dressed before it is time to—"

"Holloa!"

Niles stood up, interrupting his mother, and held out his arms towards a wild waif of a child who had materialized before us beside an ilex shrub. Though her dress was passably genteel (a very pretty bib-and-apron of Paisley with a moss-green tippet), her face and limbs were so dirty, her stockings such a disgrace, and her manners so unlike those of any well-brought-up child I had

ever known, that I did not at once recognize her for who she was
—my step-daughter. Rather, I supposed her to belong to one of the
gardeners. She seemed to have been reared on the same *laissez-faire*
principles that had formed, or permitted, the weed-choked beds
and sprawling shrubberies about us.

Zaide turned her head and addressed the child in Italian. Clara
Maria shook her head emphatically and began to suck on a curl
of her own straw-color hair. She wore no hat, then or ever, which
is nearly as uncommon a negligence in Italy as it would be here.
Zaide repeated what she had said more sharply. The child replied
at some length in a complaining tone, but her words, like those her
grandmother had addressed to her, were so strangely inflected that
for all my continuing labors with the language I could not catch
their drift, except that a command had been made, and refused.

"Never mind, Mother. The mountain will come to Moham-
med." So saying, Niles approached his daughter, scooped her up,
and kissed both sullen cheeks. Returning with her to the bench, he
stood her upon it and explained in a clear Tuscan accent, which *I*
could understand if she could not, that I was her new mother and
that she must learn to love me for I already loved her very much.

Clara Maria was not visibly moved, nor, looking into my own
heart, was I entirely persuaded whether it was quite so amply
provided with love for this little stranger as Niles declared it to
be. I *wanted* to love her; I *meant* to love her; but *did* I? *Could* I?
In time, certainly, once we had learned to be friends, but Niles
seemed to expect the fruit before the blossoms. That was his
nature, and I respected it in him. For my own part, I could offer
my step-daughter nothing but my smile, as pledge against the rest
to come.

Clara Maria had her doubts as well, and was less hesitant of
expressing them. She began to cry. Niles took her on his lap; Clara
Maria pulled away; Niles insisted. There was a shout from both
throats simultaneously. First I thought the child had fallen off the
bench, but if so the tumble had done her no real injury, for she
was on her feet again and off pell-mell along the gravel path to
the terrace next below.

"The imp! Look!" Blood flowed freely down the back of his
left hand and dripped from the fingertips. "See what she's done!"

"Small wonder," Zaide remarked coolly, "the way you swept her up. I warned you when you met her to be circumspect."

"What ought I to have done? Bowed to her?"

"You are a stranger to her. We all are. How should she not fear us? If she is a little more at her ease with me, it is because we have had two weeks to become acquainted."

"Niles," I interposed, "don't wrap that handkerchief around the cut. You used it to wipe the bench. Here, let me."

Clara Maria's infant teeth had left four distinct punctures in the flesh at the base of the fourth finger. The blood soaked quickly through the scrap of lace I wound about his hand and recommenced to flow.

Niles cursed.

"You shan't ruin *my* lace," Zaide declared. "Go into the house and have Manfredo bandage your wound properly. Clara, meantime, shall tell me of her adventures in the Umbrian hills. When you have been made whole and are disposed to return to us, bring a fresh bottle of *nocillo* with you, and some glasses."

Niles departed, and Zaide began to work loose the knot of the scarf. Her more agile lips formed words of silent encouragement for her fingers.

I offered to help.

"No, I feel it loosening now. There!" She held it up and let the breeze unfold the silk and play with it.

"You will excuse me, Clara, if I am not quite myself."

"But you're perfectly yourself!"

"Yes?"

"I mean, there is nothing to excuse."

"Then I'm more drunk than I imagined. I had thought that I was rude to you."

"It escaped me, if you were."

"I didn't bite anyone; that's true. If your aunt had been here, I think I might have bitten *her*. She doesn't like me, you know."

"Nonsense. She thinks you're wonderful. She always has."

"As for that, one may dislike any number of wonderful things and never know it. Cheese, for instance. I've seen you picking dutifully at a sliver of Gorgonzola, and really hating it, but too polite ever to say so. Your aunt, though, has a great deal of character and knows what she dislikes."

"It is true that I don't like Gorgonzola *now*. But I mean to keep trying, and some day I shall."

"I am certain of it; and your aunt shall like me just as much. How did I ever pick such a comparison? Though it's apt enough for today, I am that rottenish." Zaide re-folded her scarf and used it once more to cover her eyes. This accomplished, her lower face grew slack, a sigh of relief parting her lips. After an interval, she resumed. "One can't be on one's best behavior always and forever, with never a *moment* of candid, human ill-temper. *I* can't, at least. Now that we are become mother and daughter, so to speak, you must allow me a few minutes to breathe. I shall die otherwise."

I did not know how to reply to this, but sensing that something was expected of me, I said, "What you are saying is not far, I think, from what Blake wrote in one of his epigrams. Perhaps you know it:

> *I was angry with my friend:*
> *I told my wrath, my wrath did end.*
> *I was angry with my foe:*
> *I told it not, my wrath did grow.*"

"My dear, I honor you. There is simply *no* occasion to which you can't find a polite response."

"Perhaps I should look for Clara Maria."

"Just as you please, Clara. I would appreciate a moment by myself."

A strange welcome, this, to my new home! Yet for all its abrasiveness I was not so put out of temper as Zaide, judging by her precautions and equivocations, seemed to expect. Who could say but that she, and William Blake, were right? Weren't we all straining much too hard at being agreeable to each other? Wasn't there something unfamilial in our courtesies and considerations? Might we not be happier if when we wished a moment of privacy we simply asked for it, like Zaide?

I dare say there is not one of us who has not, some time or other, laid these flattering unguents to his or her soul. How much easier our lives would be if we did not need to exercise tact, if our charities could all be those of impulse rather than of prudence and policy. Only consider how happy we are when no effort *is* required, when we are alone, or, better, at ease in that more perfect solitude of true soul-fellowship. All the world's utopias begin with such a dream of universal candor; they end, usually, in bitterness and recrimination. Still, in even the most foolish utopia, there are fine moments, and I was able to entertain the belief, for hours at a time, that my life was becoming larger and happier, too.

For I had become conscious of freedom; very dimly, to be sure, like a shore-line glimpsed in the shimmering distance. But even so, how lovely! I could stroll beneath an open sky, uncompanioned and unseen, through the whole length and breadth of the Villa's gardens; utterly at liberty to turn left or right along what path I chose; to take my bonnet off and lay my parasol aside and let the sun lavish its heat upon my face and dissolve my thoughts into a blessed blankness.

You must allow me a few minutes to breathe. I shall die otherwise. Though I could not have said those words myself, I recognized their truth.

CHAPTER THREE

Nymph and Satyr

NILES AND ZAIDE WERE LATE SLEEPERS, and so in the early mornings I would usually have the garden to myself. Such times as she was not medicined into a stupor, my aunt might take the air with me upon the upper terrace, but such shared mornings were the exception. In the latter days of June and first weeks of July, Lydia suffered megrims of exceptional severity. Since I had come to learn the meaning of this kind of wretchedness, in Spoleto, I was not so quick to begrudge my aunt what limited relief she might find in her laudanum. Indeed, I continued to resort to it myself on evenings when my customary insomnia (for such it had become) was compounded with headaches of any intensity. By taking a very small dose I found that I could cheat my pain without incurring the penalty of dreaming. I slept as if I were dead, that sleep of utter un-being that is the envy of Hamlet and all intending suicides.

Once that sleep was over, my inner landscape brightened as quickly as that which I could see shining in through the shutters, the thin pale horizontals of the dawning day. By the time I had dressed and gone down to the terrace, the outer and the inner worlds were in full accord, as though a single sun lighted them both. I would always wait till I was there in the garden before I said my morning prayers. I am told it is a mark of a theist to prefer to pray out of doors. If so, it is the only heresy that I have ever begun to understand.

The Villa's gardens had once been very grand, in the approved Italian style of box hedges and clipped avenues, but years of neglect had transformed their spheres and cones and mazes to trees and thickets of no geometrical pretension. There were elaborate water-works, as well—fountains and cascades, fed naturally from the springs of Santa Restituta, which issued from a cavern in the hillside southwest of the Villa. These had been less pervious to the ravages of time. The waters flowed and spouted more or less as the architect of this little Tivoli had intended: pouring from the mouths of lions and trickling from the mossy eyes of tragic masks, arching from the lifted conch of a mutilated Triton or swirling idly in the lotus pool. To complete the mournful impression of this melancholy wonderland, there was a tomb at the center of the garden, where the cascade parted to form an oval islet. There, under the perpetual frown of a marble Athena, rested the mortal remains of Vittoria Agnese Visconti, who had killed herself, no one ever learned why, on the fourteenth of August, 1739, the morning of her twentieth birthday.

Alone, I have said; yet not quite alone, for the garden was haunted by its own peculiar nymph. My step-daughter, another early riser, was left at liberty to romp through the garden unattended, the terror of the carp in the pool, of lizards warming themselves to life on sunny ledges, and of myself, when she would adventure beyond the Triton fountain at the end of the cascade, where the waters spilled over a final precipice into the sea. Clara Maria was not yet two years old, and though she displayed a precocious agility, her judgment was still in many ways that of an infant.

When I expressed my anxiety to Niles, he insisted that the child's nurse "always had an eye on her." No matter that I had never seen this protecting eye open before noon! Like all lazy parents, Niles excused his neglect with the high-sounding principle that experience is the best teacher. On this theory, children are to learn to climb stairs by falling down them and to avoid fires by being incinerated.

As there was no way to reason with Niles on this point, I tried to take the place with Clara Maria of her absent nurse. This proved equally impossible. She would not come when I called and vanished into the shrubberies at my approach. Only at such times as I ignored her, when I had opened a book or was gazing at the daily pageantry of cloud-wrack round the head of Epomeo, only then, like some shy squirrel, would she come near me. As for talking with her, except for a few simple imperatives, such as "Look!" or "Come here!" we might as well have been mutes, for all that those early efforts at communication achieved. One might suppose that children, with their smaller vocabulary and more naïve syntax, would be excellent companions for a foreigner learning their language, but it is quite the contrary. Only someone in perfect command of his language and with a sympathetic ear can hope to sort out an intended meaning from its phonetic realization in the prattle of the very young. Foreigners require another kind of patience, which children do not possess. Add to these difficulties that Clara Maria lisped in a dialect that many native Italians find incomprehensible. No wonder she thought me a curiosity: an adult who could not speak, who could imagine no entertainment livelier than peek-bo, who never ventured off the gravel paths, who could not run or shout or splash her feet in the fountains, and who, despite these manifold disabilities, persisted in coming to the garden every day! So I imagine I appeared to her.

And she to me? Was I to make good my intention of loving her? Never as a daughter, no, if only because the time allotted was too short; but as the garden's tutelary goddess, perhaps. What was strange in her and alien I respected from as near a distance as she allowed me to approach.

It was nearer than Niles could ever come. Against him she was never to relent, and Niles, for his part, demonstrated little of affection or interest in Clara Maria. He had been deprived of his daughter, and she of him, during those crucial months of first growth and dawning intelligence, when, if ever, the bond is forged between parent and child.

If Niles would show no affection and I could not, this did not mean that Clara Maria was unloved. In her more expansive moods Zaide seemed quite to dote upon her grand-daughter. This doting might sometimes wear the aspect of an amused fondness more properly bestowed upon a pet than a child, as when, in letting her take a peppermint from her pocket, she would address the girl as *scimmietta* (literally, "poor little monkey"). But in that she was not very different from most grandmothers. We are all of us notorious for indulging our darlings heedless of the damage we wreak upon their characters.

Clara Maria had another and (I believe) still dearer friend in the gardener who tended these groves. Jack Drinkwater, Zaide called him, anglicizing his more resonant name of Gioacchino Bevilacqua. A stranger nor an apter companion for the little nymph could not have been discovered on all Ischia than this aged satyr with his sun-darkened face, rough and wrinkled as the bark of a tree; his gap-toothed smile, which no one but the nymph knew how to invoke; his mismatched legs and crook-backed, crouching walk. An ugly fellow, Jack, but he wore his ugliness with such a pride one was almost persuaded it was a kind of beauty; perhaps it was. Clara Maria was certainly of that opinion, for she would sit upon his lap for whole minutes, tugging at the bits of string that served as buttons on a blouse of coarse blue canvas and listening to his mumbled monologues with an expression of quite idolatrous respect.

Because I tried to keep Clara Maria under my survey and because she liked to follow Jack Drinkwater about at his chores, we three tended to be much together, moving from one terrace of the garden to the next as though joined by bands of subtle magnetism; nor were these conjunctive wanderings determined solely by the gardener's rounds, since Jack, for his part, was inclined to drift towards any quarter of the garden where I might have established myself for any length of time, so that our movements formed, over a morning, a kind of slow ring-dance, intricate as a cotillion.

Then, on a Sunday in the middle of that July, I awoke fully dressed and seated upon a low stone bollard that marked the garden's lowest and farthest extent, where its waters, tired of their duties, spilled from the cascade and across some boulders to drop the last hundred feet into the sea. I had no recollection of having dressed nor of coming to the place, but I noted my surroundings without alarm and without the vertigo I had felt here at other times, when I had been concerned for Clara Maria's safety.

A fishing boat moved slantwise across the wide expanse of opal towards the just-risen sun. I felt a peculiar peace, as though I were as far removed from my own fleshly body as from that silent fishing boat; as though I had become another liquid, like the sea, utterly yielding in all my being, a mere film for the light to play upon.

From this waking I was again awakened by a poke from the handle of a rake. There at my side, gape-mouthed and wide-eyed, was the grizzled Gioacchino. Satisfied that I recognized him, he laid down his rake and, touching the warped brim of his ancient hat, addressed himself very earnestly to me. When I failed to take in his meaning, he repeated his words, and I realized that he was entreating me in my own language to return with him to the upper terrace. This seemed so extraordinary, in a pleasant way, that I did not think to take offense. In truth, I must have been no more than half-conscious, for, even understanding him, I remained unresponsive. At last by taking the flounce on my sleeve gingerly between thumb and forefinger, he was able to lead me back towards the house, which still lay sleeping in the long morning shadows. A lamp burned dimly in a window of the third floor, which I knew to be unlived in. This little incongruity more unnerved me than all that had happened heretofore. My sluggish imagination stirred, and I drew back from the gardener with a start. Whether he thought I recoiled from mere fastidiousness or from some deeper motive, he made no protest but only looked on sadly as I took my leave of him.

I went directly to Niles' rooms, not to my own. They were empty, his bed not slept in. The clothes he had worn to dinner the previous evening were draped on the backs of chairs or lay crumpled on the carpet, seeming in their casual disarray an allegory of our marriage.

Like low plains swept by a great tide, my earlier peace of mind was submersed in a flood of self-pity. I did not reason my way to that misery then, and I shall not attempt now to make it seem reasonable. I felt myself to be alone, unloved, despised, not by Niles only, but in the absolute.

That tide was ebbing, though the tears still flowed, when my aunt discovered me, bent double on the carpet, hiding my face in my skirts.

"I shall be fine now," I assured her quaveringly, as she helped me into a chair.

"Of course you shall be, my dear," she soothed. "But first you must have your cry, and then you will feel better. No, you needn't try to talk. Only let me smooth your skirts. So! And now, another chair."

Niles' trousers occupied the armchair nearest mine, but Lydia, surmounting her scruples with scarce a wrinkle of her nose, removed them and pulled the chair still closer. With my hands in hers, I let myself be calmed and comforted. Once she had coaxed the first self-deprecating smile from me I thought she would leave, satisfied she had done her duty and restored me to a state of rational decorum. Instead, she took a firmer grasp upon my hands and asked me if I felt equal to some minutes of serious discussion.

I said I hoped I was.

"Because, you know, I don't want to upset you more."

"I'm done crying now. And it would be a comfort, truly, to talk. I have so wanted someone to—" I stopped short, conscious of the unkind implication of that beginning.

"And I have not been there, I know. But I mean to alter that. Today shall mark a new beginning. You must hold me to that promise, dear, and if ever I seem to you to be withholding my full confidence, for whatever reason, you must take me to task for it at once. Is that a promise?"

"Yes."

"And you, in turn, must be open with me. No!"—pressing a finger to my lips, before I could agree to this—"I have no right to coerce *your* confidences; or if ever I did, I forfeited it long ago by my too-much reserve. Yet I *will* ask you, if I may—I really *must* ask you about this morning. Only about this morning."

"I went down into the garden quite early. As I usually do, you know. . . ." But my purposed half-truth wilted before Lydia's level scrutiny, and I could not go on.

"Let me tell you first," said Lydia, "what I heard that caused my alarm and set me searching for you. This morning, your mother-in-law came to my room before I'd finished dressing, which is a considerable departure from that lady's custom, because of the little quarrel we have been having over my hangings. But you have heard enough of *that*! She was seeking you. It seems that that decrepit gardener had insisted on having her awakened and then alarmed her with a story, though I knew it to be perfect fiddle-faddle, and told her so, for the poor man is certainly not quite accountable."

"Certainly. But what did he say that was so alarming?"

"That he'd seen you come out of the house while it was not yet light and walk to the lower end of the garden. He says he followed you, first at a little distance, but when you seemed not to notice, more closely, and at last he crossed your path. He says you walked on as though he were not there, which, to be sure, is just how one ought to deal with such an inquisitive old scoundrel."

"And then?"

"Little else that wasn't his, or the Countess's conjecture."

"Which was?" I insisted.

"He had heard—indeed, how is one to prevent servants hearing and discussing such matters?—he'd heard of the young Contessa's death in England. He said he thought you might be in a similar state—I mean, of sleepwalking—and that he feared, if you had approached too near the edge from which the water spills. . . ."

"And how closely did I approach to it? Did he say?"

"Do not *you* know, Clara?"

"I know where I was sitting when I woke. All the rest you've told me I have no more recollection of than if it had happened to another person." Then I described what I have already set forth here.

Lydia could ill disguise her apprehension. "So he was not mistaken," she said, when I had finished. "You *were* sleepwalking?"

"Apparently."

"Was this the first time?"

"To my knowledge. But how is one to know? If I had returned to my bed and if I'd not been witnessed, I might not have known of this. Perhaps I am an inveterate somnambulist!"

"But your husband. . . ?"

"Lately Niles and I have slept apart. My insomnia need not prevent his rest as well as my own."

"Your headaches have returned?"

"Some times, in the evenings, yes."

"You never mentioned it."

"Is it mannerly to speak of such things if it can be avoided?"

"Indeed. Indeed. And have you been able to alleviate the pain? I mean, to put it bluntly, Clara, have you been taking the Sulphurous Compound?"

"Yes."

"Last night was one such time?"

"The worst that it has been. I took rather more than usual, and the headache vanished at once."

"Then it's all I feared." Lydia shook her head. " 'God shall bring every work into judgment, with every secret thing, whether it be good, or whether it be evil.' "

"Aunt, you shouldn't upset yourself needlessly over what is done and can't be helped. I am sorry for what I have done, and in future I shall certainly know better and shall refrain from—"

"You, Clara! *You?* Oh no, my dear, you don't understand me. I should be much blinder even than I have been, if you think I could blame *you* for my vices!"

"Really, Aunt, to call your medicine a vice!"

"If we are to be candid, Clara, we must begin somewhere. I've always known how you regarded it, but I *can* be blind when it suits me. Moreover, I knew you were right. Long ago, I *knew.* The dreams that it brought, together with the easing of the pain— they were wicked. I knew that. But so delicious, too, and except for you, my dearest Clara, they were my only pleasure. Josiah railed against it, said we must accept what pain God cares to send us, but when my megrims came on me he soon relented. And now to think that he was right! Yet it never seemed to be a *harm* to anyone, unless to myself, and for that I didn't care. Truly, it had ceased to matter whether anything I did was for good or ill.

Except for you, my dear, except for you. And that is how I have been punished. 'God shall bring every work into judgment, with every secret thing.' I'm sure I never would have believed it."

"Aunt, you are exaggerating the harm that has been done."

"Let us hope so, indeed. And let us say no more on the matter. For my part in it, I'm ashamed and deeply sorry. There was one other matter I should like to discuss with you, a matter of some urgency, but it can wait until this afternoon, if you'd prefer."

"I think that it had better, Mrs. Jerningham," said Niles from the doorway.

Lydia shot from her chair and stood facing Niles with such an air of defiance and dislike as I had not seen since the time of her last confrontation with her husband. "I am sorry to be an intruder in your room—"

"Not at all," said Niles, with a bow that his nightgown would have made ironic if his smile had not. "You're always welcome, wherever you are found."

"But," she went on, pretending to be deaf to this interruption, "my niece was in some distress when I found her here, and so I stayed to comfort her."

"My mother has told me something of the matter, and that was my only meaning when I asked to be left with Clara."

Lydia returned him bow for bow, and quitted us with a promise to be in her own rooms throughout the afternoon, should I have need of her.

"Are you quite well, Clara?" Niles asked in a tone that somehow defied me to answer in the negative, so little did it promise by way of sympathy.

"I am well. I slept poorly and was up before my usual time."

"The gardener saw you walking, as he believed, in a kind of trance."

"He was mistaken."

"He said he followed you, and you paid no heed to him."

"Should I have?"

"Unless you were meaning to give the man a fright, Clara, which you certainly did, and to stand the house on its head, which you have also done, I cannot otherwise account for what he said were your actions."

"*My* actions, Niles! He frightens me half out of my wits, so that I'm put into a perfect panic and come running to your room, which I find empty—and you question *my* actions?"

There was enough of truth compounded in my lie to give it a ring of authentic grievance. Even then I knew that in speaking so I made a scapegoat of poor Jack Drinkwater, who had intended no harm to me; nor can I offer any excuse except to say that I had acted without reflecting.

Niles, being put on the defensive, explained that he had spent the night in another bedroom to escape from an hungry horde of mosquitoes that had entered at a window left open in the evening, attracted by the lamplight. It had not been my intention to make Niles account for his absence, but it served my purpose as well as if I had, for Niles did not pursue his inquiry.

Manfredo announced himself at the open doorway with a brisk rap and entered with the materials for Niles' morning toilette—the only time I can recall ever being grateful to see him. I excused myself and went to my own room, where Rose was waiting with a cup of cold coffee and my first delivery of mail since we had left Venice. Four issues of *Blackwood's Magazine* had come all at once, and there were seventeen letters from charitable institutions and missionary societies. I read through the lot of them as carefully as if they were so many closely reasoned arguments persuading me that I was, indeed, the same Contessa Visconti to whom they were addressed, a wealthy young married woman from England, though living now in Italy, who could be relied on for ten or twenty guineas in a good cause.

CHAPTER FOUR
Sources of Distress

THAT SAME MORNING, after we had talked, Lydia emptied her entire supply of Macpherson's Sulphurous Compound, twenty-two quart bottles, into the sea. Then she rinsed each bottle in a solution of soapy water, so there would not be even a teaspoonful left.

"For it is all very well to have good intentions," she concluded, "but then one must act on them."

"You needn't have done it on my account, Aunt," I assured her. "I should not have tempted fate by taking any more of it."

"Now fate can't tempt you—or me, for that matter. It is something I have had in mind to do for almost as long as I can remember. Perhaps your spell of forgetfulness this morning was an act of Special Providence. Let us hope so."

"Was there not another matter you wanted to discuss?" I asked, when she lingered in the doorway.

"Yes, but I'm afraid it may prove a new source of distress. If you would rather wait. . . ."

I shook my head.

After closing the door carefully, she joined me on the sofa, one of the pieces Niles had had copied by the Jerningham manufactory. Though she never said no, I think Lydia had come to share my distaste for these simulated reminders of our London lives. It was as though by showing us that the home my aunt had created could be duplicated by the mere expenditure of a sufficient amount of cash Niles were questioning the unique worth of that home. His impulse towards irony was so over-mastering that it led him to mockeries even where he meant only to be kind. But the sting of it could be felt—by my aunt as much as me—like prickles lodged just beneath the damask of the upholstery.

Lydia composed her hands carefully on her lap and drew a deep breath in a manner suggestive of challenge accepted and perils braved. "You'll recollect, Clara, that some time ago, in Venice, you asked me a very direct question on the subject of marriage and . . . children. I was not quite candid in my answer to you. It is not, of course, a subject a third party can easily speak of, and usually some experience of married life renders such spellings-out unnecessary. Yet I have often looked back on my response and wondered if it were not too brusque. Indeed, I'm sure that it was, and I'm sorry for it. If you should wish, today or any other day, to resume that conversation, I shall do my best to answer whatever question you may care to put to me."

I thanked my aunt sincerely, for I knew what a sacrifice of her own scruples this offer must have cost her. I told her of my approach to Mr. Mainwaring and of his referring me to Mrs. Lacey, though I said nothing of the price exacted of me, afterwards, for my curiosity.

Lydia was grateful to be spared the explanations she had so much dreaded, but her hands did not loosen their resolute clasp. "There was another matter, too, concerning your maid." She paused, as though hoping I might once again be able to relieve her of the need of speaking out.

"Has she been rude to you?"

"No, and in fact I am not *quite* certain that it was Rose that I saw. The woman was veiled, and much too finely dressed. My first thought was that it must be you. You had mentioned to me just that morning—the Tuesday of last week—that there were still gowns packed in your closets that you had never worn. I thought this might have been one of them and that you'd tried it on in an idle hour. It was a broad sort of redingote, looped up at the side, gray over red."

"If it's mine, I have no recollection. Unless it might be my poplin Isabeau?"

"No, I'd have known that at once, as I helped you pick it out. This was a much bolder red, and there was an inordinate amount of trim. I would not have supposed it was you at all except I couldn't think who else it *could* have been."

"Zaide, perhaps?"

"I'd never confuse the two of you. She's much too tall. And then, when . . . this figure . . . became aware of me, she took fright and ran up the stairs to the floor above this."

"How odd. No one ever goes there." Though even as I said this, I remembered the lamp I had seen burning that morning.

"I was of half a mind to follow after, thinking it Rose. Then I considered that it might be a visitor. And yet, that isn't likely either. Whom would she be visiting in those empty rooms? And then, you know, she was dressed so improbably, as though for a ball. It must have been Rose, for of all the servants only she is vain enough for such a folly."

"I shall ask her."

"To what purpose, Clara? If she ran from me, would she not deny it to you? I'd simply keep a closer watch upon my things. I would not have mentioned it at all, except that—" She stopped short, trembling with the effort of maintaining her composure. "Except that—" Her eyes closed. Her forehead knotted with pain.

I thought: "Her megrims have come back already."

"Lydia." I tried to take her hand, but she pulled away from me,

"I did not want to tell you, Clara! This morning, when I promised myself that I'd keep back nothing any longer, I did not think that my promise would require me to bring such . . . an uncleanness to your attention. Oh, Clara, it was so awful! And so . . . deliberate. Though he will *say* it was an accident, I know."

"My dear Lydia, whatever can it be? Has Niles—"

She shook her head vigorously. "Not Niles, no. His manservant. Oh, I cannot tell you what looks I have endured from him. The sneers he makes when I am not supposed to hear."

"He is the same to me, Aunt. Indeed, I do not know what is to be done. But if you will tell me what has happened, I will speak to Niles about it."

"I'll tell you, but on condition that you *don't* speak to your husband. He will excuse the fellow, or claim that he was painting him at the time."

I let this tacit accusation pass unchallenged. For reasons already evident, and for others I must momently lay forth, my faith in Niles was not so firm as it had been. He had as much as told me in an odd moment of candor some weeks before that he would not scruple to lie to me, if pressed to it. "Marriage is the root of all falsehood. One learns more than it is good to say, and so one suppresses unbearable truths or invents comfortable fictions. It might as well be written into the vows—love, honor, obey, and beguile." "Except," he had added, "ourselves." But in such a tone that it seemed an illustration of his thesis more than an amendment. "*We* can look at matters squarely."

"It happened this morning," Lydia went on with her story, "when I was disposing of my medicine. I was returning from the lower terrace with the last four empty bottles. He was standing on the little island, by the gravestone of that poor girl. He heard me approaching and turned right around. He stood there only six or seven yards away. What was I to do, Clara? I dropped the bottles and turned and ran the way I'd come. And he laughed!"

"I don't think I understand."

She tried to speak, but tears came instead of words.

"Lydia! What is it?"

She brushed the tears away angrily. "He *showed* himself to me! Like . . . like the statues that we saw in Florence."

"Naked?"

"He had dropped his . . . trousers. It is not unusual here, I think. I've noticed before, even in the cities, that the poorer class of men have no shame. If you mention this to Niles, that's what he'll say, that it's a commonplace. He'll make a joke of it, and I would prefer to be spared that."

"But you say he turned round and stood in your path."

"Oh, I've no doubt he meant to provoke me. But it's all a matter of emphasis, as your husband would say. For form's sake he might deliver some mild rebuke to his man, but what would that mean, for me, but a further humiliation? They'd both be laughing up their sleeves."

Even this I let go by, though I had more faith in Niles' compassion than in his strict veracity.

"But if we do nothing . . ." I protested feebly.

"As for that, I don't mean to allow the fellow another opportunity. I shall avoid the garden in future, and keep to my own rooms as much as possible, which will suit me better in any case."

"You will make yourself a prisoner!"

"Nonsense, Clara. I shall make myself comfortable. See if I do not!"

CHAPTER FIVE
Lydia Strikes a Wager

SHE WAS AS GOOD AS HER WORD. If those first weeks in Venice had been my heyday, these midsummer days on Ischia were Lydia's. By force of will, without any show of discontent or suffering (though feeling both), she created an England whose green and pleasant bowers were co-extensive with her own two rooms. These

were, at her own request, of modest dimensions and faced inwards
to a courtyard, so that, with the curtains partly drawn, one would
never have supposed, either from the view or the brilliancy of the
sunlight, that one were painfully far from Charing Cross. The
patchy frescoes had been covered up with paper-hangings in a contemporary design that interwove Scottish thistle, Irish shamrock,
and English rose. The stark stone floors had been carpeted, and
whatever furnishings insisted too much on their Italian origins had
been civilized with shawls and antimacassars. The overall effect
was pleasantly impromptu, as of a company hastily costumed
for charades. Though the illusion was imperfect, with fancy
assisting it managed to solace if not to deceive.

I would gladly have lent some of my furnishings to fill out
this masquerade, but such a charity would have been all too clearly
an instance when giving is more blessed than getting. In any
case, they were my wedding gift from Niles, and so entailed, as it
were, to my own rooms. I limited my generosity to letting my aunt
take the Dimoline pianoforte, which belonged to her, in any case,
by usufruct, or right of use.

In the particular of music, if not in many others, my marriage
had taken a conventional course. From the moment I had spoken
my vows, I had ceased to play. Some times I sang, to oblige my
husband or my aunt, but only such songs as I already knew or did
not require preparation. In proportion as my accomplishments
had atrophied, Lydia's bloomed. In Venice, we had had the
privilege to hear the supreme musician of the age, Franz Liszt, play
two private concerts for Count Wrbna. I was too little fluent in
the language that is music (as in all languages I have studied) to
catch more than hints and flashes of his mighty meaning, but for
my aunt those two evenings had been, in the most literal sense, a
revelation, and she became a convert to Bach and Schubert. She
had been acquainted with their works before, of course, but in the
way that lukewarm Christians are acquainted with the tenets of an
unfelt faith; lukewarmly. Now they were her all-in-all.

Liszt had shown my aunt the heights, but he could not help her
scale them. For this she must rely on her own strength, and her
first view of the task ahead was daunting. She was fifty-five, and
who at fifty-five does not hesitate before undertakings of too

much magnitude? Like Moses stopping upon Pisgah in view of the Promised Land yet not entering, Lydia sought out the music she had heard and studied it, but she would not perform it. Then, on the afternoon of the day she threw out her medicine, she began to play. The poor Dimoline, untuned by its travels, was scarcely equal to the demands she placed on it, but her enthusiasm rode roughshod over the piano's limitations and her own. Nor was this a triumph of the spirit only; she did not play perfectly but she played well, some times superbly.

"I can't believe it is your aunt," Niles told me one evening, when I found him listening outside her door. "Not Lydia Jerningham of Worcester Terrace in Bayswater. Some wandering spirit has taken possession of her and plays on her as on a living keyboard."

Even as he said this, her left hand faltered and the music broke off. Niles and I stared at the closed door with a single accord, willing Lydia on, and in a moment she resumed, only to be defeated again by the figure in the left hand.

"It's rough, of course," Niles went on, "but only at the edges. The great central mass is alive and singing. Listen: now it changes."

And we listened.

"What is she playing?" he asked.

"The andante movement of the B-flat sonata. It is one of his last works."

"I seem to hear her trumpeting all my darkest secrets, loosing them to every wind that blows, and all the while they remain fast in my heart. Would she let us, do you think, sit in some corner of her room and listen?"

"I will ask her."

"If you do, she'll say yes. Do you think she'll play less well, though, if we're there?"

"She says that she plays better for an audience. From my own experience I think that after a minute or two she forgets altogether that anyone else is with her, and she is alone inside the music."

So began our custom of assembling at five in the little *Inghilterra* of Lydia's drawing room. After a light tea together, Lydia would sit down at the Dimoline, I would take up my embroidery, and Niles, in the darkest corner of the room, would stroke the rich, plum-colored plush of the sofa with a flowing movement sympathetic not to the overt, fleeting rhythms of the music but to the deeper pulse impelling it onwards. The music seemed to be a kind of spirit-mirror, before which he would place himself in sundry lights and costumes: now angry, now anguished; in sweet sadnesses and bitter; scorning himself, adulating himself, but always (such is the genius of music) self-absorbed, unable to take his eyes from the phantom eyes he beheld in that mirror. That this is unfair to Niles and to the genius of music, I must confess. It was my attention, not his, that was improperly bestowed. I kept waiting for him to betray, by a word or a smile, that his real interest in these musical evenings was the occasion they provided to be with me. I wanted to believe that the secrets that the music spoke to him were the secrets of a love that had died and was struggling to be reborn. I thought that *I* could hear such meanings, but only indistinctly and for a little while. In fact, when Niles was present I neglected to mark the music very closely, except when some phrase of peculiar expressiveness would cause him to wrinkle his forehead or bite at his lip. Then, if it had been in my power, I would have stopped my aunt from playing more and taken Niles aside to demand that he translate his feelings from the language of music to a language I could more fully understand.

Yet when the music did cease and words began, the gap that widened our two selves was increased rather than diminished. I felt I stood on the deck of a ship whose embarkment Niles watched coolly from the dock; that my departure was already an accomplished fact in his thoughts, which turned, accordingly, to more urgent matters. There was no acrimony. Niles was pleasant; I was pleasant; my aunt, I'm sure, was pleased to think that these little levees were helping to strengthen the conjugal bond. We read aloud the first chapters of Mrs. Oliphant's latest continuation of the saga of Carlingford, *Miss Marjoribanks*, which was appearing serially in *Blackwood's*, and were united in admiration of the author's cleverness. I dare say we were often clever ourselves.

When we could not manage on our own to be amusing, when the sirocco had blighted our tempers or when other events of this time made it impossible to behave like genial strangers whom chance had thrown together for a long week-end, there was still one recourse left in the society of Monsignore Egidio Tabbi. Just as, in England, Lord Rhodes had had the livings of Rodmell and Glynde in his gift, so in Italy it is thought to be a normal expense in any aristocratic household to endow a chaplaincy. But to say that Monsignore Tabbi was our chaplain gives altogether a wrong picture of his role, which was more nearly that of a poor cousin whose charge it is always to be affable, to fill the silences with pleasant chatter, and to know when to become invisible. Though he appeared at the Villa almost daily, he lived in the nearby village of Casamicciola, but in neither place had he any discernible ecclesiastic duties, unless, as my aunt suspected, his duty were to ingratiate himself into our household and effect the conversion of its two heretics, as the Roman Church regards all Protestants. If this were his duty, he performed it, in the first article at least, to perfection. So winning and withal so youthsome a septuagenarian I have never known, yet for all the grace of his manners and live-liness of his talk there was nothing in either to compromise his dignity as an elder statesman of his church. A saint, Niles called him. My admiration was more moderate. I thought him the ideal neutralizing presence to introduce into a situation of latent con-flicts; in short, the perfect bachelor. Without appearing to, he counselled us, and the drift of all his diffident advice was simply that one ought to wait, to place oneself trustingly into the hands of God and let Him act, Whose actions are always wiser than our own.

Sage as Monsignore Tabbi was, and welcome as his presence was in drawing room and dining room, I would not have jeopard-ized his chances at eventual canonization by introducing him into these pages, except that he was to forge, all unwitting, some few links of the inexorable chain. Like many other visitors to Ischia, then and now, the Abate (which he was by virtue of his chaplaincy) believed in the efficacy of its waters in the cure of all human ills whatsoever. It was a second creed to him, and nothing gratified him so much as to recite the properties of the waters issuing from Ischia's innumerable springs and the peculiar ef-ficacy of each. The Acqua de Nitroli was a specific against renal diseases and hypochondriasis, and the source of longevity besides, to which latter benefit Monsignore Tabbi could personally testify. The Acqua del Fornello was a cure for stone, and was of value against ulcers and scrofulous swellings. The Acqua de Castiglione, taken as a tonic aperient, was a remedy for stomach complaints, as were the waters of at least a dozen other springs. Somewhere on the island there was a cure for any disease or disability, so that a skeptic might well wonder how the natives of Ischia ever died, being thus proofed against Death's armory. That I was such a skeptic, I think I have sufficiently conveyed; not so my aunt Jerningham. Even before she had forsworn her old medicine, the Abate had converted her, in theory at least, to this new one. Why else, as he reasoned, should the Creator have introduced volcanoes and all their related ills into the plan of His creation unless by this seeming evil He hoped to accomplish some greater good? More persuasive than these arguments, he could bear personal witness to a dozen remarkable cures accomplished by the waters of Ischia: cures of dropsy and of gout, of lesions, of *grand mal*, of rheumatisms and sciaticas.

So long as my aunt had relied on her own panacea, the potency of Ischia's springs was of interest only as a curiosity, but once she had jettisoned her supply of Macpherson's Compound and when, in due course, her megrims returned with all their wonted strength, she was then prepared, with no more prompting, to see if the waters would fulfill the Abate's promise. What harm in trying? Accordingly, she set out upon that pilgrimage from spring to spring that occupies the time of most foreign visitors to the island and that is the mainstay of its economy. She was immersed in water both hot and cold; she drank it by the gallon; she even breathed it as it issued from the fumaroles in vaporous plumes. The result of all these experiments was uncertain. Her megrims would vanish some times, but they would invariably return, and the same spring would seldom be so efficacious upon a second visit, or else the regimen proposed to her would be so strenuous, or so time-consuming, that she would have had to devote all her waking hours to being cured, which she was not prepared to do.

This search for the one true fountain involved a great deal of junketing, and it is my own heretical notion that this daily necessity to be up and doing, rather than the specific properties of the different waters, is the source of whatever heightened well-being visitors to Ischia may enjoy. I often accompanied my aunt on these outings, though I never took the waters, and yet on the days of our excursions I felt a distinct "bloom" and on those evenings I was able to sleep without my usual difficulties. However, I had the good sense to keep my theories to myself and let my aunt achieve good health by her own principles.

On the most adventurous of these outings, towards the end of that July, Monsignore Tabbi accompanied us on an exploration of the Aragonese castle at the far eastern end of the island. Once, in the age of piracy, the whole population of Ischia had been sheltered within the natural ramparts of the Castello, which name scarcely does justice to it, for it is an island and a city quite to itself. Even before the Aragonese were driven out, earthquake and plague had reduced the population. The Bourbon kings used it as a prison for their political enemies, and thus a great many heroes of the present day, including the worthy Professor Minghetti, have been its recentest inhabitants. Now it is deserted and falling into ruin.

One expects the temples of vanished religions to exist in a fragmentary form, and poets have accustomed us to consider the chapels and abbeys of the Middle Ages as worthier of attention when in a state of solemn desuetude. But to see a church of the Rococo already being decomposed, its windows gaping and moldings fallen to the floor, its frescoes faded and flaking—that is very strange. To such a church, inside the walls of the Castello, did Monsignore Tabbi conduct us.

"It is melancholy, is it not?" he asked, after an interval sufficient to allow us to draw the same, inevitable conclusion. "One cannot look at it without reflecting on the vanity of all our undertakings here below."

My aunt, as always before assenting to one of the Abate's more philosophic remarks, paused to consider whether it savored of Papist doctrine or were more generally receivable. At last she agreed. "And yet," she argued, "I dare say we'd never let this happen in England."

"No?"

"With just a little effort it could be fixed up very nicely.

Why, look how they allow the plaster to lie about on this lovely floor. And this carving here—see how the rain has warped the wood. A terrible waste!"

Lydia had a susceptibility for well-turned wood more than for all the plastic arts together, the last vestige of loyalty to the Jerninghams, whose trade it was. Her finger traced the curving lituus of a scroll with unaffectd admiration, skipped across a Latin inscription, and felt the ruffled outline of an acanthus leaf.

"Indeed, Mrs. Jerningham, there is justice in what you say. The parish church in Lacco Ameno is presently in need of a confessional, and this—"

Lydia's hand recoiled from the wood as though it were on fire. "A confessional! Is that what it is?"

"Why, yes. I supposed you knew. There is scarcely a church in all of Italy that doesn't have one."

"I've seen them, but I never thought to ask myself what they were."

"Would you like to try it?"

"I beg your pardon, Monsignore!"

"I mean, would you like to sit in it? It is only wood, as this church is now only bricks and rubble."

"Yes, but after all, it *is* one of your sacraments!"

"Ah, Mrs. Jerningham, do you really think we are such terrible idolaters as that? The sacrament is not here"—he rapped lightly upon the side of the confessional—"in a piece of wood. It is in the human soul."

"I am glad to be mistaken, but I should still not want to go into a confessional. My poor dear husband, who has been dead it will soon be three years, would turn in his grave if he knew I were now inside a Roman church, even a ruined one such as this."

"And talking with a Papist priest," the Abate suggested, "even a ruined one such as myself."

"Indeed, Monsignore." My aunt, despite herself, returned his smile.

"But here you are, Madam, and no great harm seems to have come of it. I am sure your husband is watching you from Heaven at this moment, and the question of whether you step into that confessional or not is of absolutely no consequence to him. What sort of Heaven would it be if our spirits did not become a little larger there?"

"That is as it may be, but all the same I shan't go in. One must draw a line."

"Do you scruple at gambling, too, Mrs. Jerningham?"

"Pardon?"

"Would you be willing to accept a small wager, to amuse an old man, and possibly to win a shilling, if that is not too steep?"

"What is your wager?"

"That inside of a week you shall have set foot within this same confessional."

"Done!" said Lydia, offering her hand to the priest.

Monsignore Tabbi turned to me. "Contessa, you are our witness."

CHAPTER SIX
Lengthening Shadows

THOSE WERE THE FAIR TIMES: the mornings in the garden, the afternoons with Lydia, the occasional excursion from the Villa; all the rest was shadow, or darkness absolute. Niles avoided me and added to the hurt of this by claiming not to. He must go into Naples, he would say, to settle a dispute with an official of the new government. Once there, bad weather or a good friend might prevent his return for two or three days. Even when at home, his presence was elusive, his rooms empty or the door locked. If I sent Rose to him, she would return with a message from Manfredo that the Conte was at work, or indisposed, or walking with his mother in the gardens. Since I could survey the whole of the gardens from my bedroom's balcony, it was an easy matter to determine if this were so; and it was not. Soon I knew better than to seek him out. Soon, indeed, I had reasons of my own for avoiding him.

Niles' neglect was painful chiefly by contrast to the warmer relation a wife may legitimately hope for. With my mother-in-law, it was a case less of neglect than of active hostility and open dislike. Initially, it was my aunt, more than myself, whom she abused with her sarcasms; slyly at first, and only by inference; then, as with any vice that is exercised in small ways, enlarging to insult and argument. Lydia, for my sake, tried to adopt a placating tone, and so for a short time their contention was in search of a bone for which to contend.

The issue that at last engaged them was the scheme of decoration that Lydia proposed for her rooms; in especial, the item of paper-hangings. To paper over a fresco, even such an one as this, ill-painted and in bad repair, was, in the Dowager Contessa's eyes, a crime against civilization, while Lydia would happily have papered over half the frescoes in Italy, as being either indecent or idolatrous. My aunt was accused of being a barbarian. She replied by charging Zaide with intemperance and slatternliness. If the Contessa disapproved of her taste, very well! But decent people could not be expected to live in the daily presence of squalor and disorder without bestirring themselves. Zaide inquired scornfully whether my aunt were interested in working as her housekeeper, and Lydia replied she would accept the post happily, were it offered by the *real* mistress of the Villa. Meaning myself? Zaide wanted to know. Whom else? Lydia demanded. Niles finally had to intercede, with the result that she and Zaide abandoned all pretense of civility between themselves. Zaide had her luncheons privately and Lydia her dinners.

How I dreaded those meals of heavy food and heavier silences! Zaide ate frugally and drank copiously, which, given the quality of the food that came to the table and the excellence of Ischia's wine, was a reasonable preference. Most travellers agree that the Italian cuisine becomes noticeably coarser below Rome; some would say south of Bologna. Yet the recognized inferiority of the Neapolitan cookery could not excuse cold soups and raw joints, salads that had not been washed and sauces that had not been seasoned. No, these faults sprang from a kitchen so mismanaged as to be in a state of permanent insurrection, and for this state of affairs, as for the general disorder of house and grounds, Zaide had to bear the blame.

At one of these dismal dinners, from which both Niles and Monsignore Tabbi were absent, Zaide informed me that she had dismissed the gardener who had frightened me the previous day. I protested that I had not been frightened, that on the contrary the old man ought to have been rewarded, or at least praised, for his zeal on my behalf.

"I cannot, of course, pretend to know whether your fright was real or only assumed. Niles said you were beside yourself afterwards, and I acted on that basis. Now the fellow's gone and I'm glad to be rid of him. Ugly clubfoot that he was! Though *that* is often an advantage, for then they know that they must work. I would fire the lot of them, except it is summer and I can find no one to replace them. For now they must be scratching in the dust of their own gardens during the one hour of the day in which they work."

"In general, that may be, but I have never seen this gardener idle. For his years he is very industrious."

"You mean he is so old he should have a sinecure?"

"I meant he keeps very busy."

"As to that, I shan't gainsay you, Clara, but have you observed just *how* he improves the shining hours? By extirpating flowers and planting weeds. I don't know whether spite or senility impels him, or whether it represents his notion of an English garden, but I have seen him cultivating neat rows of thistles and borders of spiny spurge. Quite, quite mad! Drink, I should suppose." She raised her wineglass, as if to toast me, and wet her wide lips at the brim.

I would not take this bait, and so she offered another. "I see your aunt has not come down to dinner. I hope she is well?"

My aunt had not come down to dinner for two weeks, so there was no way to interpret this question except as a taunt. I pretended that it required no answer and worried a wilted leaf of lettuce with my fork.

There are families (I know, for I have been their guest) at whose table such contumely is regular sport, a kind of piquant sauce for the better enjoyment of their food. I have heard daughters rail against a mother's ignorance, that mother to ridicule her offspring's taste in suitors and in clothes to and criticize—cruelest cut of all!—the shape of her darling's nose; and all before the first removes had left the table. Perhaps Zaide was of such warrior stock herself, and only offered combat out of a dawning sense of family feeling. If so, I was unable to meet her challenge in the same spirit of playful animosity. Not even when, afterwards, I would accompany my mother-in-law to her rooms, there to be initiated into the mysteries of bezique, did I provide any larger amusement or livelier sport.

I cannot play cards. I tried then, I have tried since—I cannot. The rules fly from my head. The cards drop from my hands. So invincible is my incompetence that even three-year-old children, playing snap, have given me up in despair. It is not that I try to spoil the game in order to be let off from playing it (as has been suggested more than once); it is only that I cannot quite believe in what is happening. A Christian asked to take part in the ceremonies of Hindoos could not feel much more ill-at-ease; and then, think—if those ceremonies were to go on for hours and hours, night after night!

With Zaide, my native inability was compounded by a profound inexperience. A series of rainy, purgatorial afternoons in Venice, when she and Niles had tried to teach me to play whist, represented all the gaming I had ever done. That little learning proved, as we are warned it may, a dangerous thing, for I managed to confuse the half-learnt rules and strategies of that game with those of bezique, to which, alas, they bear no relation. Moreover, I was so fearful of offending that, even when Fortune was most preposterously favoring, I contrived to lose. At last (it was upon the same evening that she had announced the gardener's dismission), annoyed as much with my consistent bad play as with my consistent good luck, Zaide laid down her cards and said with a sigh: "So, Clara, once more—against all odds—you've let me win."

"Ought I not to have played the queen when I did?"

"Brava! Yes, that was your worst mistake. If you'd played any other card you'd have been able to declare a double bezique the next time round."

"And to think I didn't see that. I'm truly sorry. I should like to offer you better sport. I think I do understand the rules at last, but not what I'm to *do* with them. If you see what I mean."

"What you want, my dear, is motive. You must play to triumph over me, not to placate me. Perhaps if we played for modest stakes . . . ? What would you say to a shilling a point?"

"A shilling! But goodness, I have been losing each game by hundreds of points—I should never be able to pay you."

"Tut, my dear. You have millions."

"That may be, but—" I shook my head emphatically. "I never, never could play for such sums. Never."

"Do I hear the accents of the admirable Jerninghams? Have a care, Clara, not to be too loyal to your upbringing. It is all very well for tradesmen to have a pious horror of gambling. It is quite something else for *you* to shiver every time you come within sight of a green baize table. Altogether apart from the amusement that gaming may afford—and cards will help one through a dull evening better than most novels—there *are* appearances, and you must keep them up."

"Oh, I assure you, there are many ways I should relish being extravagant. If I let myself go and followed all my fancies in matters of housekeeping, I'm sure that I could bankrupt us within a decade."

"But that's not extravagance—it's work! Such matters are the concern of the Mrs. Laceys of this world—not ours."

Though I realized that I was treading dangerously close upon the grounds of contention between herself and my aunt, Zaide had so far succeeded in overcoming my reluctance to oppose my opinions to hers that I plunged on regardless. "Then I am irreclaimable, I fear, for I like nothing so much as taking up my little basket of keys and jingling them all over the house, putting things in order and setting them to rights."

"As against myself, who would rather let those same things slide to perdition? Well, I confess it. At least with regard to our present domicile. I hate this place, and always did, and have no relish for investing my labor, nor your money, into it."

"Then why—excuse me, but I don't see how the question's to be avoided, having said this much—why are we here?"

Zaide pursed her lips and narrowed her eyes. The silver point lattice of her wrinkles became a skein of dark, deep-graven lines. "Ask your husband that, my dear."

"I have, and he says it's at your behest."

"Then I should say that *one* of us is lying to you. And since *I* am not about to admit to it, that brings us to something of an impasse, doesn't it?" Saying which, she swept up the cards spread upon the table and began to shuffle them. "But I'm so sorry— *c'est à vous à donner!*" And she handed me the deck to deal.

Thus it was, against both judgment and inclination, that I became a gambler. For an hour or more on any evening that Niles was absent from the Villa I would be impressed for a game of bezique with my tormentress. Rarely did the experience cost me less than ten pounds. All too often the price exceeded fifty. If I did not acquire the knack of winning, at least I learned what Zaide had declared was so essential to my station—the art of losing with aristocratic nonchalance.

She, by contrast, did not win with notable noblesse. With each increment to her score, were it only ten points for turning up the seven of trump, her smile grew broader, her eyes brighter, her manner gayer. This transformation was not only, or even principally, a psychological one. The advance of her ivory marker across the rosewood board seemed to effect her quite like an *elixir vitae*, smoothing Time's rough imprint from her face line by line until, with the climactic settling of my debt, a phoenix would rise from the ashes of the old Zaide, a matron of vivid impulses and lively appetites, a woman wholly and heartily of the world. Then the I.O.U.'s I had paid her would be folded and tucked inside her purse, and the flames would fall and fade, and all that would be left of her brief youthfulness would be the ember-like glow upon her hollow cheeks.

Amid these tribulations, I found that I possessed an unexpected ally in Rose, who was in rebellion against the heat of the Ischian day and the uneventful quiet of its night. It was not for such a pastoral life that she had entered the service of a Contessa, who was, to boot, an heiress of some *réclame*. All this she complained of to me with discreet bitterness, as to one presumed to share her resentment against such a cheat. That Manfredo no longer paid her those courtesies that I had been an unintending witness to in Venice may have contributed to her discontent, but this must be my own inference, for on that score she had the sense to be silent.

So well was I persuaded of Rose's essential good will that when my aunt had told me of the figure she had surprised, whom she suspected to be Rose, I did not hesitate to question her directly on the matter. Rose denied all knowledge of the event. Perhaps she would have, guilty or no, but she displayed so avid a curiosity for the details of what my aunt had seen that I was persuaded of her real innocence.

She was especially puzzled on the point of the dress. "For," she explained, "as my Lady knows, there is nothing precisely of that cut and color in my Lady's wardrobe. Unless it were her poplin Isabeau."

"No, my aunt was definite as to that."

"And *I* surely have nothing of the sort. But perhaps the little Italian who waits on the old Contessa. She is old, but as vain as any coquette. If my Lady wishes me to inquire . . . ?"

"Indeed, Rose, I do not. I only mentioned it at all because my aunt wondered, quite naturally, whether it *might* have been you whom she saw. Now that I know that it was not, the matter need not concern either of us."

Rose accepted this with a nod of grudging assent, but she nonetheless took it upon herself that afternoon to make a minute analysis of the contents of all my closets; without, however, discovering anything more untowards than that there was a smutch, small but irremovable, low on the hem of my favorite blue travelling dress.

Some days later, Rose returned confidence for confidence. In the midst of helping me to dress for dinner she laid an envelope upon my dressing table. Though sealed with wax, it bore no stamps or other marks of having come through the posts.

"It is from the gentleman you met in Florence," Rose announced simply. "He sent a note to me, through the butcher's boy, asking me most respectfully to meet with him. I went out this afternoon and he was very civil."

"He asked to *meet* with you?"

"Indeed, I had my suspicions, too, my Lady. But I thought it could do no harm to discover what he wished, and it was only that I might convey this note to you. If my Lady is satisfied with her hair . . . ?"

"Yes. Quite. Thank you."

Rose curtseyed and left me alone with Mr. Mainwaring's mysterious letter.

Madam, it read,

Having received no acknowledgment of my previous letters, I remain in doubt whether you have received them, and therefore I am taking the liberty, which I know to be censurable, of addressing myself to you in this clandestine fashion. Forgive me if this renewed expression of my good will comes unwelcomely.

First, I beg you to accept my most profound apologies for my ill-judged efforts to mediate between you and Count Visconti. I regret the loss of his friendship and trust; even more, I must rue any unpleasantness or pain my well-intending folly may have cost you.

Further, I should like to renew my earlier pledge of friendship and to insist that at any time you may feel need of my counsel or of my more material assistance I am at your service. The bearer of this note will be able to convey in strictest confidence any reply you may choose to make. However, if you disdain to engage in a correspondence by such questionable means, I shall accept your silence as a merited rebuke.

> *Believe me,*
> *Madam,*
> *Yours very truly,*
> *Godfrey Mainwaring*

CHAPTER SEVEN
The Plan of Clarapolis

"How did she die?" I asked Niles, one time that we were sitting by the gravestone of the unfortunate Vittoria Agnese.

Niles lifted his pencil. He had been sketching the garden's mutilated Athena and mistook my meaning. "Goddesses can't die, my dear. Leastways, not Greek goddesses. At worst, they are forgotten. In the Norse theogony I believe it's different, but even so I can think of no specific deaths. They all went down together."

"No, I meant your long-ago cousin."

"Oh, Vittoria: she was a suicide. It seemed quite unmotivated. There was not even a predisposition to melancholia. And such a lovely creature, too, it really was a pity. You must have seen her in my mother's sitting room, the girl in the low-necked dress with the white spaniel in her lap. She opened her wrists here in the garden, over by the carp-pool. When they found her, poor little Fiordeligi—the spaniel in the picture—was lapping at the bloodied water. They killed the dog but not the fish."

"How dreadful."

"And how unfair. The poor creature could not have known it was doing wrong."

"It is *all* so dreadful. How could anyone ever be so desperate? Especially one who believes in God."

"Why assume that she believed in God?"

"In the portrait, there is a crucifix on the chain round her neck."

"Oh, in Italy that signifies no more than if she wore shoes. In any case, I would dispute your original premise. I suppose that I believe in God, in a lazy sort of way, and yet that hasn't ever interfered with my considering suicide at one time or another."

I blushed, and wondered why I should be blushing, and blushed all the deeper for its seeming so inappropriate.

"It's nothing I'm ashamed of," Niles went on, interpreting my reaction more quickly than I had. "I suppose every serious person, by the time they've reached thirty, and usually well before, has given thought to the matter. I have a distinct recollection of the first time *I* did. I was twelve. The whole world seemed ordered to make me unhappy, and as far as I could see into the future I foresaw nothing but toil and bondage and falseness. I remember being allowed to climb up alone to the porch of St. Mark's while my tutor had an ice at Florian's. I had a coin in my pocket, a six-kreutzer piece with Franz Josef's profile on one side and the Austrian arms on the reverse. I flipped the coin, swearing that if it came up heads I would *hurl* myself upon the paving stones. It came up heads, to my no little alarm. I decided then to go for two out of three. Twice again it came up heads. It was some time before I finally managed to bring Fortune around to my way of thinking. You're smiling, and yet I swear that the difference between my imaginary suicide and the actual one of this poor girl may have been no more than a hair's-breadth apart. A slightly worse run of luck than mine, that's all."

"It is wrong of you, Niles, to make fun of another person's unhappiness. Even your own."

"Even *your* own, do not you mean, Clara?"

"Perhaps that was my meaning." I met his look steadily, not challenging him and yet not seeking to disguise the sadness controlling me.

Niles' eyes answered mine with a calmer, more rational sadness. He, after all, did not have to waste his strength on self-deceptions. The pain that he felt he could follow to its source and his dread had an object, while I was still laboring mightily to be blind, in the belief (which I would have denied) that only my blindness kept us from being sundered.

"This is not what we promised ourselves, is it?" he said, speaking straight to the point even as he avoided it. "We are not leading that fine, brave, free life we spoke of when we stood in prospect of Helvellyn. Instead, it is the same cramped, inglorious travail that is the reward of all such romantic expectations. Gall and wormwood in the mixture as before."

"It is not our hopes that have been at fault, Niles. It is ourselves. We have made no strenuous effort to realize those hopes."

"Then, let us. Let us leave Ischia, all secretly, just we two, and go to Australia."

"Australia?" I laughed. The leap from my mild reproof to Australia was so broad that I did not believe he was serious.

"Why not, Clara? I could buy a farm. In Australia I could probably buy whole counties. We shall create a new society from scratch, ignoring all the old worn-out rules and making up our own to suit ourselves."

"But Niles—"

"Think of it: Viscontia! And its capital city of Clarapolis. We'll do it along the lines of Fourier. Living together in great dormitories, sharing the meals and the work equally, dressing like Quakers. Women wouldn't have to wear bonnets, if they didn't want to. In Australia they probably don't in any case."

"My aunt would never stand for that."

"Your aunt shan't come with us, nor my mother, nor anyone but us."

"Then who," I demanded, still not seriously believing in Niles' proposal, "is to live in these great dormitories with us?"

"All the convicts! England has been transporting felons to Australia for a century. They've stopped at last, only because it's been filled up. But you mustn't set your heart against them for that, my dear. They're *honest* criminals, unlike the bunch of us here in Europe. That's where the future is, you know. Australia! Australia and Texas."

"But do you think it is the future for us?"

"Oh, we'd have to be transformed from top to bottom, no doubt at all. But isn't that just what you were saying we had to do anyhow?"

"Must it be so drastic? Couldn't we reform ourselves little by little?"

"That's so English! You might be the Member for Ipswich arguing against universal suffrage."

"Well, possibly he has good reasons to argue against it. I'm sure I don't know."

"There are good reasons against anything, if one *looks* for them."

"I begin to think you are serious, Niles."

"I'm perfectly serious. I'd pack my bags and set off tomorrow, if you'd agree to it. The morning packet to Naples. Naples to London, that's three days; less, with luck. Then a clipper round the Cape, and we would be in Brisbane, ready to start life anew."

"What of your mother?"

"I would write friendly letters from time to time. Seriously, my mother is quite able to look after herself, here or wherever she chooses. There is money enough to let her live as she will. Your aunt, ditto. She might have the run of Blackthorne, if she wishes. It's standing empty. *Someone* should have the benefit of living there."

"Lydia would be as wretched without me as your mother would be without you."

"As wretched as we all are, here together?"

"There is no *need* for us to be wretched!"

"No need to be here, either. Will you come to Australia? Answer me that."

I smiled uncertainly, not wanting to oppose him even in his folly, so long as that folly proceeded from a genuine impulse towards a better life.

"*Will* you?" he insisted.

"*Must* I?" I countered, with perhaps some hope, dim and absurd, that he would answer yes. I was so unhappy and so unable and unwilling to understand my unhappiness that any action that promised to remove me from my everyday dilemma, however misguided, seemed preferable to the moral stagnation of the present.

When I made no more answer than thus to return him question for question, he grew silent and returned to his sketch of the stony Athena. I, having no other task to occupy me, sat looking on. The pencil strengthened the steep curve of the drapery falling down her thigh. It shaded in the shadows cast by shield and helmet until the goddess was lost within a cloud of angry pencillings. When the drawing was quite spoiled, Niles tore it from the tablet and crumpled it.

"I wish you wouldn't *look* at me in that way, Clara!"

"I'm sorry. It must be provoking to have me looking over your shoulder. I shall go inside."

"That isn't what I meant at all."

I had risen, but I paused, waiting to see if he would say what he did mean.

"When you look at me, Clara, there is something unspoken in your eyes. Don't deny it, for I see it now. Some judgment you've made against me, which I can't appeal because you never *speak* of it, but only *show* it, like some mute ghost pointing to its wound."

"And you, Niles—when you look at me? Is there nothing unspoken then? And have I ever demanded to know, or offered to interpret? Have I shown impatience or disloyalty? Have I, Niles?"

"I am sorry. I spoke without considering."

"What would you have me say? That I have felt your coldness sealing up my heart like the approach of winter? Indeed, I haven't spoken of the pain that coldness costs me daily. I was so foolish as to suppose it a virtue in myself that I did say nothing. I must be patient, I told myself. I must be submissive, and this way I shall more deserve his love. *Those* are the thoughts I have kept hidden from you, Niles. But now let *me* ask *you*—"

But my passion of anger was spent and it was followed by as great and as sudden a passion of tears. I ran from Niles, hardly able to keep to the path. When I knew, certainly, that he did not mean to follow after, then my grief seemed to strike roots of pain into the core of my being; into, quite literally, my heart and bowels. All other sorrows I had known were mere vagrant vapors compared to this, which I could feel coiling and uncoiling within me, a palpable presence, restless and unappeasable. So I came to taste the sorrow of all sorrows the most bitter, the certain knowledge that I was not loved, a doubt no longer, but incontrovertible conviction.

CHAPTER EIGHT
A Broken Vow

I HAD READ RENATA'S DIARY. That key she had long ago entrusted to me I could not at last resist turning in the lock. Perhaps I had always known I would. Often and often I had sworn to burn it and so remove the temptation for ever. Still, I left it in its hiding place in a parcel of old school-books, complete from my first battledore to the ledger in which I had learned to cast up household accounts. This latter volume was nearly identical, in fact, to the ledger-book Renata had given me, and for the good reason that this had been an account-book, too, which Renata had purloined from the housekeeper's room at Blackthorne. When we were leaving for Venice, I had insisted that that box of books should not be left behind, and when we departed that city, the box (its wrappings still intact) had been sent on ahead with the furniture and other bulkier effects to the Villa Visconti.

Once, in Venice, on the evening of Manfredo's notable insolence, I had come near to giving the ledger-book to Niles. I was then of the belief that what Renata had written was a confession of her illicit relations with Niles' valet, and I thought to use her words as a weapon of last resort against my enemy. What Niles told me that night had shaken this belief, but still I supposed that the contents of the ledger would be a painful surprise to Niles, not an accusation *against* him. It was for that ignoble motive—to cause Niles pain—that I at last opened the door to the Bluebeard-chamber of that book. From the moment we left Florence, all through the long train-ride south, it was my set purpose to read those pages I had vowed never to read, and, having read them, to tell Niles. Wounded and humiliated by him, I wanted meanly to wound and humiliate in return.

The day I arrived on Ischia, I had unpacked my box of school-books and taken out the ledger. The first pages were filled with reckonings, in Mrs. Lacey's hand, of Blackthorne's laundry expenses over a period of four years. Then these reckonings left off and Renata's tale began. I had meant to read conscientiously, checking each word I was unsure of in the dictionary that I had bought for this purpose before leaving Rome. Instead, I raced headlong through the obscure scribblings, understanding only a sentence here, a phrase there, and misconstruing much. One other time, some years after this, I was in Holland during the awful days of the Paris Commune, when it seemed the whole of civilization was in its death-throes, and I read through a dozen Dutch newspapers with the same avid incomprehension. This time, it was not civilization that stood in mortal peril; it was my marriage and my life.

I made myself return the ledger to its hiding place, and the next day I began a line-by-line translation. What Renata had dashed off in a few stolen hours at Blackthorne took me twenty-three days to decipher, and even then I could not be sure, always, of *what* I had read, much less whether it was to be entirely credited. Renata had been incapable of a clear sequential laying-forth of her wrongs and misgivings. I write this account at many years' remove, and it is hard enough, but who is there so cool, so merely rational, as to be able to convey in a few judicious words the extremity of a present fear? Of a fear which all the ordinary rules of polite behavior would prohibit any woman even to mention? Again and again, a womanly reticence prevented Renata from committing to paper what I supposed she meant. Indeed, how is such a meaning to be expressed? Her conventual training had given her an ornamental style and hand better suited to the issuing and accepting of invitations than to the terrible, humiliating purpose to which she had been driven. Desperate to express herself, yet terrified of discovery; never certain when she left off writing one day whether she would be able to resume the next; rebuffed by Mr. Mainwaring when she tried to present the ledger to him, who alone of all the guests at Blackthorne could have been expected to comprehend its anguished outpourings; seeking then to tell over the same tale in simpler terms that *I* might comprehend; ransacking memory for its slender, useless stock of English words; begging and beseeching me to make the effort to understand, yet all the while, I am sure, persuaded that I, too, would refuse even to accept the book: it is no wonder if, under these pressures, her letters writhed out of recognition, if her so formal sentences collapsed beneath the weight of their own awful meaning.

Yet there were passages so unambiguous as not to allow of the least doubt in their interpretation, passages all the clearer in that the tale they unfolded was essentially my own. *"Non fui la sposa del mio marito,"* she had written in the pages meant particularly for me. *"Non sono la sua moglie. Sono la sua prigioniera, la sua vittema, la sua facezia, nient' altro."* ("I was never the bride of my husband. I am not his wife. I am his prisoner, his victim, his joke—and nothing more.")

She had tried to escape from him, soon after their wedding, in the spring of 1862, and was prevented. She had written to her parents, asking them to rescue her from the mockery of an invalid marriage; Niles had torn up these letters before her eyes and forced her to write milder messages of his own dictation. Her maid was taken from her, and the other servants were forbidden to speak to her—except for one, who was her torment. Need I name him? Renata *could* not, her loathing was so great.

Between them, they subdued her. The shy, fair girl that I had met at Blackthorne, four months a bride, bore no visible resem-

blance to the dauntless fury who, by her own account, had smashed
through windows in her resolve to escape, and drawn the blood
of those who would restrain her. Niles had pleaded for her to be
patient. I could hear the echo, in Renata's distraught outpourings,
of sentiments he had addressed many times to me, of the same
bargains offered, the same excuses ever renewed. Zaide, too, seeking to mollify her, had tendered bribes of clothing and jewelry, of
opera tickets and, some time or other, of balls. Then, when
Renata showed herself deaf to their reasons and uncorruptible by
their gifts, she was handed over to Manfredo, as a recusant heretic
might have been returned to the torture by officers of the
Inquisition.

Renata's journal does not record by what means Manfredo at
last compelled her acceptable deportment and made her submissive
to her husband's and mother-in-law's requirements. I suspect that
at the time she wrote, it was no physical coercion that Manfredo
exercised over her, but the compulsion, rather, of threat. Not until
later, at Corme Hall, was that threat carried out. This, though,
was my suspicion, unsupported by anything Renata had written.
For the confirmation of it, I had only to step from the secretaire
where I carried on my secret work of translation to my little
balcony overlooking the garden. There of an afternoon I would
often see Renata's daughter being bounced on the knee of her
true father, or running from him in a pantomime of fear, shrieking
and laughing, as once her mother must have run from him with
fear unfeigned. Seeing them together, I wondered at my blindness,
and the blindness of the world, that could witness these evidences
so openly displayed and not see to what conclusion they led. Niles'
unfeeling coldness to the child; Manfredo's warmth; the manner-
less way Clara Maria was allowed to act, as though no one intended
she should become a lady; how she had been shipped away to
Italy—and in Manfredo's keeping!—before her poor mother had
been put within her grave. Her very complexion, seen in the
raking light of these revelations, seemed to betray the shame of her
parentage.

But these suspicions, terrible as they were, were not the worst.
Renata declared, not once but repeatedly, that she stood in peril
of her life. *"Egli desidera uccidermi! M'uccidera!"* ("He wants to

murder me—and he shall!'") Nor could I be in any doubt as to whom she meant; it was Niles.

As well as I could gather from the tangled text, the reasons she imputed to him for his intended crime were greed to possess her dowry, and mistrust. For, as often as she had sworn to him she would be compliant, as many times had she gone back on her word as soon as occasion seemed to allow of secrecy. If she should leave him and obtain an annulment, the dowry must be restored, and so (Renata believed), in order to forestall such a disagreeable contingence, he meant to murder her.

Could *I* believe this of the Niles *I* knew? Given the facts that I possessed, was it still possible for me *entirely* to doubt and deny? That Niles had entered on his first marriage largely for mercenary motives he had confessed to me long since, and that he would not scruple at causing pain I could believe. Even that he had consented to Renata's enforced stupration I had reluctantly to admit as probable, though the degree of his consent, and whether obtained before or after the fact, I could not estimate. But Niles, to murder?

How is one to reason on such matters? Though I could say, with Renata, that Niles was not a husband to me, yet there *was* a tie; a tie too close for me to judge objectively whether and in what circumstances he would be capable of the most heinous of crimes, the taking of another human life.

I could not believe it of him, finally. Not for any reason I could then articulate, but because I could not *see* it. Yes, to be sure, I had glimpsed in his eyes, behind their glint of irony, shadows that hinted of a kind of guilt—but not *that* guilt. Niles lacked the quality of absolute, unswervable conviction in his own imperious hungers that I believe is the mark of a true murderer. Instead of this brand of Cain, Niles' brow was stamped with the more common ones of weakness, irresolution, and self-doubt.

To have acquitted Niles of the blackest guilt was a meager consolation while doubts remained as to what wrongs he *had* performed, or what consented to, and what he might still intend. For these deliberations were not conducted at the comfortable height of a judicial bench, but in the hourly presence of those whom Renata had accused. Wherever I went, whatever I might try to do, these doubts were my companions; but especially, of course, when I was with Niles. Then I would study his face, his gestures, his words, as though among them I might find the clue that would bring an end to these Gorgon doubts. There was no end to them. Every fair appearance—a warm smile, a gentle speech—suggested the possibility of a deceit, of a deliberate effort to throw off my suspicion.

Why had he married me? This question, more than all the rest, obsessed me. For my inheritance, as he had married Renata? I could not suppose so, for he had proposed when I was poor, and when I had become rich he had withdrawn his offer. These were scarcely the actions of an adventurer. But (tormenting myself more) might he not have known in advance that Lord Rhodes' fortune would fall to me, and shaped his actions to suit that knowledge? Perhaps; but then what was one to make of Zaide's so evidently sincere chagrin at the reading of the will? No theory of Niles' character allowed me to think of him acting except in concert with his mother. No, I could not think he *proposed* for the sake of my money, though of course when the money was there, it was welcome.

Why, then? I had to know, for if he had asked for my hand in good faith, and accepted it so, then I was truly his wife, though yet our marriage might want the seal of our entire conjugality. And if I were truly his wife, then my vows required that I love, honor, and obey. Yes, and more—they required that I overlook what had gone before.

Finally, even in this broader sense, I realized that I did believe in Niles—believed, that is to say, in the honesty of his love. It was a faith that required some exertion of the will, but may be it was all the firmer for that.

So, because I believed my duty required it, I burned Renata's diary and the translations I had made of it. One day, in the dead hush of midafternoon, I made a hearth upon my balcony—the one that looked towards the sea—with shards of old clay tiles I had brought up from the garden, and on it I burned, page by page, the entire document, including even the reckonings in Mrs. Lacey's hand at the beginning of the ledger-book. Then I crushed the ashes to a powder and let them drift down like a fine black snow to the waters beneath.

It was not so easy a matter to wipe out my memories and my misgivings. They were not laid to rest by burning the book that had brought them into being, nor exorcised by declarations of faith, which I would repeat like anxious prayers. They had a life and will of their own. They might be gone in the morning, but at evening they would return, like mice emerging from their hiding holes or birds coming back to nestle in the eaves. I refused to heed them, but to no avail; their rustle and scurry kept me awake through the long, sleepless hours of the night, and at no time were they ever so far away that I might not hear them scrabbling in the walls or glimpse the shadow of one skimming across a gravel path. This, I think, is what it means to be haunted: to deny, yet always to be in the living presence of that which one denies; to turn one's eyes away and still to see; to say, "She is dead, I have forgotten her," and to hear not one's own strenuous denial but the hoarse whisper of the unquiet spirit.

At the time of my talk with Niles that was so greatly upsetting to me, I had been in possession of Mr. Mainwaring's letter for nearly a week. It had been my intention to make no reply to him, knowing that Niles would have seen such a correspondence, carried on without his knowledge and with a person of whom (however unjustly) he disapproved, as a challenge to his authority as my husband. I cannot accuse Niles of any unusual coldness or cruelty to me that day. Nothing in his scheme of emigrating to Australia, though I thought it ridiculous, had caused me real distress. His very accusation that I had made some judgment against him that I would not speak of—was it not true? Why, then, as soon as I had reached the privacy of my room, did I feel morally at liberty to reverse my earlier resolve and write to Godfrey Mainwaring? For a simple and sufficient reason: because Niles had not followed after me when I had fled from him; because he had witnessed my anguish and made no effort to soothe it; because I had ceased to believe in his love. Without that belief, of what validity were the vows I had made to him? Even as I wrote my brief note, saying only that I had received the letter he had sent me through my maid, that I was grateful for the friendship he proffered and would appreciate some time the benefit of his further counsel—even as I penned these treacheries I hoped that Niles would come to comfort me, to tell me that indeed he did love me, to urge me once again only to be patient and time would do its work of healing and growth.

But he did not, though I took the time to copy out the letter in a fairer hand. I folded the note-paper, sealed it in an envelope, and rang for Rose.

She seemed to understand all at a glance. She took the envelope with a curtsey and promised that it would be delivered into the gentleman's hand by the morrow.

When she turned to leave, I sought to put a gold sovereign in her hand. It was as inept a piece of intrigue as ever made woman blush.

Rose seemed to consider of the matter coolly, then gave the sovereign back. "That is not necessary, my Lady. The gentleman has already rewarded me for my labors. If we were in town it would be another matter. There money vanishes like water, and it seems quite natural. But here, how would you account for it if you exhausted the little supply you have? Eh?" She smiled and folded my fingers round the coin with a shrewdness so warm almost to merit the name of affection.

Never in my life have I known a deeper shame or a profounder humiliation than when I stood there clutching that hateful piece of gold.

CHAPTER NINE

Where Is Clara Maria?

THE HEAT! THE EVER MORE AWESOME heat of that midsummer! I marvelled at it quite as though it were a spectacle to be ranked with Epomeo or the wide amazement of the surrounding sea, something so wonderful that I could accept its attendant hardships almost uncomplainingly, as one accepts the toil of an ascent for the sake of the summit's view. Everything gentle in nature withered. All flowers died, except the bougainvillaea, whose glaring purple and crimson blooms are not flowers, properly speaking, but masquerading leaves. Grapes swelled, and ripening figs burst their outer skins, attracting congresses of enormous hornets, who became, along with much else that creeps and stings and swarms, the true possessors of the island.

From within one's shuttered room, one listens to the buzzing midday and waits, torpid and incredulous, for the rescue of evening.

Even Clara Maria showed herself reluctant, with the coming of August, to adventure out of doors as blithely as before. Partly, no doubt, this was because she had recently learned from Niles' favorite instructor, Experience, why it is that scorpions are to be avoided; but chiefly because it was so unbearably hot. This is not to say that she became sedate; rather, she treated the interior of the Villa as though it were a second out of doors. There were, of course, certain rooms sacrosanct to grown-ups where, though she might be welcome, she would be obliged to observe grown-up conventions with regard to chairs and tables and the contents of drawers; but there were other, more noble regions where liberty was uncurtailed: a dark romantic cellar, breath-taking staircases, a laundry room of steaming tubs, the kitchen and pantry with their odorous mysteries, leagues of empty corridors, and acres of ghostly guest rooms, their furnishings swathed in dust-covers and cobwebs.

Despite such possibilities for explorations, the mornings could be very lonely, and I was not surprised when, one Friday morning, she came on a visit to my rooms, hoping with the gift of a peach she had purloined from the kitchen to bribe me to put aside my sewing and play with her. I admired the peach and gave it a place of honor on a dish of old majolica. Then I had to close my eyes while Clara Maria hid from me. She had advanced considerably in sophistication since our earlier games of peek-bo, but even so our game of hide-and-seek was elemental. She had a single hiding-hole, which was behind an ornamental fire-screen made from a fragment of old tapestry that depicted a faded goddess pointing portentously to the Visconti coat-of-arms. Each time she hid she would go back of this screen to scuff her feet and giggle frantically as I wondered aloud whether she might be behind the window-curtain? No, not behind the window-curtain. Or under the table? No, not there either. Or possibly inside the lowest drawer of the bureau? *No!* she would declare, unable to contain herself longer. *She was here!* And I would find her, and we would start again.

On the fifth or sixth enactment of this little rite, Clara Maria seemed to sense that I was becoming bored. She went back of the fire-screen (I must confess that I was cheating shockingly by peeking through my fingers) but then came out again. One could see the idea dawning that she could hide *somewhere else*! I thought her first alternate hiding place would be the curtains, the table, or even the bureau drawer, but, as she understood the rules of our game, these were just the places where one did *not* hide. Instead, she left my room and raced down the corridor towards the stairs.

She nearly escaped me altogether; for, coming to the staircase, I assumed she had gone down to the ground floor and thence out to the garden, to some hiding place dear to memory. Accordingly, I descended to the first landing of the stairs, when I heard from above the closing of a doorway and the pattering of her feet.

Only once, on the day after our arrival, had I been through the rooms of the third floor. They were lumber rooms, or simply empty. When the Villa had had a full complement of servants some may have lived there, but for the most part I think the third floor had never had any purpose beyond allowing its architect the satisfaction of building in the grand manner and its possessors the satisfaction of possessing similarly. So, if the upper regions of the Villa were unknown to me, it was because, like America before Columbus sailed westwards, they had remained unimagined, a blank.

Into the *terra incognita* I followed after Clara Maria, opening the door at the top of the stairs just in time to see another closing at the far end of the corridor. I hastened to this door and, finding it not quite shut, called through the cracks, as fair warning: "*Dove è Clara Maria? Dove è la mia fanciulla?*" ("Where is Clara Maria? Where is my little girl?")

The room was empty. Bands of glaring light slipped in through the louvers of the closed shutters, striping the bare floor, the bare walls. Dust motes, stirred by Clara Maria's passing, whirled and sank and soared in a great sunlit commotion.

There was a door to my left and another to my right; both were closed. That to the left opened to a deep closet that might have been passed off, with some charity, as a small dressing room. A shabby cotton camisole hung from a nail driven into the plaster. In one corner a straw hamper overflowed with rags of some indefinable fragrance.

I returned to the empty room and tried the other door. When I heard a tell-tale scuffing of shoes inside, I knew my quarry had not eluded me. A glance explained why she had sought out this remote corner in which to hide, for here, in a heterogeneous clutter of retired furnishings, was the twin of the fire-screen in my room. This portion of the dismembered tapestry showed a threadbare Mars dressed for battle accepting a shield blazoned with the Visconti arms.

"Where is Clara Maria?" I asked loudly, in Italian.

A giggle replied.

"Is she behind the curtains?" I asked, and drew to the side a tatterdemalion curtain strung from a wire across the middle of the room, such as children might put up to turn their nursery into a theater.

Behind this curtain, the purpose of which was to control the level of illumination in the room, Niles had made a second studio for himself, an humbler but much busier workshop than that which he maintained on the ground floor of the Villa. There, in a space ample enough to stable horses, the walls were bare, except for a large bright landscape lifeless as the insides of a watch; here there was not room upon the walls for all the canvases. My first impulse was simply to admire such profusion of energy. Then, when I had taken in some of the particulars forming that profusion, I pulled the curtain to. "The child," I told myself, "must not see these." Yet if it were her feelings I wished to spare and not my own, would I not have taken her from that room at once? Instead, I lingered indecisively by the curtain. Slowly the revulsion for what I had seen subsided and the fascination of it took hold. I looked again.

It was clear from the unfinished painting of her that glistened wetly on the easel that Clara Maria was no stranger to this studio and the pictures on its walls. She was shown nestled, unclothed and asleep, in Manfredo's lap. It was not nearly so improper, in Niles' painting of it, as it must seem in the telling.

So with the other paintings: even when their subjects were not candidly indecent there was something morally disquieting about them, as though their very excellences were derived from some unseemly accommodation with the basest elements of human nature. To say, exactly, how this came about would involve me in unwarrantable digressions, yet I must ask my readers' indulgence to describe one from among the many. A woman of my own age, in exaggerated embonpoint, was depicted, nearly life-size, seated at a small round table. Though alone, a gentleman's silk hat and gloves

rested on the table-top. An image of almost insipid banality, such
as one might glimpse in any city hurrying past some retired café,
and executed (like the other paintings here) in a sprawling, spattery
style that yet conveyed more of truth than all Niles' paintings heretofore. Even so, I could not help but cringe from what was shown,
for it was an awful truth, a truth unworthy bearing witness to. The
smile on those carelessly rouged lips, what did it bespeak but a
despair grown so familiar it had lost all power to oppress? There
it was in her ruined eyes, too, undisguised—a sadness past curing,
a dullness past caring. I wanted to protest against this painting,
against them all, against the occluded light of their smoky rooms,
against the glaring absence of whatever in human nature merits
admiration and love. That, most of all—that they were loveless. The
woman cried out for kindness, and Niles had painted her.

Clara Maria was signalling her impatience by a discreet rattling
of the fire-screen. I left off looking at the painting and set about
once more on my pretended search.

"She isn't behind the curtains," I declared. "Perhaps she is
under this table."

There was a scrap of cloth that smelled of turpentine and a
wizened apple core, but no Clara Maria. "Where could she be, if
not under the table? Could she be . . . ?"I approached the fire-screen,
which drew back some inches to avoid my attention, and put forth
the traditional hypothesis that she *must* be in the lowest bureau
drawer.

Standing before the bureau, a homely affair of white deal close
by the fire-screen, I began to have misgivings. In all likelihood its
drawers were empty. My concern was only to bring our game to a
conclusion and to take Clara Maria back downstairs. If there were
something within, I need not look at it. Would it be prying in
that case?

"*Cerchi nel cassetto!*" Clara Maria called out. In her excitement
she had come halfway out from her hiding place. If I had not looked
in the drawer, as she insisted, I am sure she would have looked
for me.

If there were any other alibis by which I might have excused
myself, I did not think of them. These sufficed, and I opened the
drawer.

Though it was folded so that I saw only the bodice, I knew the dress at a glance. The whole of it, allowing for what the table concealed, had been represented quite faithfully in the painting that hung not ten feet off, though the colors were all so much darkened that I had not recognized it there: a broad sort of redingote, looped up at the side, gray over red; just as Lydia had described it.

My first consciousness that I was not alone with Clara Maria came when she burst out from behind the fire-screen with a shriek of pure pleasure and rushed towards the doorway. The figure that had been standing there was gone in the time it took me to rise from my stooped position and turn round to glimpse the departing, dove-gray flicker of a skirt. I called after Clara Maria to come back, but she had passed beyond obedience into the very ecstasy of hide-and-seek.

Her pursuit ended almost before it was begun. There was the emphatic slamming of a door, and Clara Maria, balked (for she was still too small to reach the knob), battered at the closed door with fists and feet. She screamed, she demanded, but all uselessly. I was as grateful for these signs of her frustration as if they had been music. Whoever our onlooker had been, and for the moment I would not speculate, I was glad to have been spared a confrontation. My relief was short-lived, for when I went after Clara Maria into the adjoining room, it was to find her hammering not at the door to the hallway, as I had imagined, but on the door of the deep closet in which I first had looked for her. Instead of escaping, the intruder had been trapped.

"Clara Maria!" I insisted. "*Smettila!*"

But she would *not* stop! As well chide a pack of hounds who have brought their victim to bay. Nothing would do at last but I must pick her up, still raging in all her limbs and carry her down to my room, to end the game where it had been begun.

When she was calmer I asked her whom she had seen in the doorway.

"*La donna,*" she answered sullenly.

"What lady? Do I know her?"

Clara Maria shook her head, and then nodded, uncertain which answer I wanted her to give.

"What is the *name* of the lady?" I asked.

She smiled. "Nana."

"Nana?" Somehow I did not believe that Clara Maria's nurse

would have ventured so far in search of her, or that, once having found her, she would have been put to rout so unaccountably. "Was it *Nana* you saw?"

"No."

"Who, then?"

"Clara!"

"No, not me, my dear. The lady you saw in the doorway—what was *her* name?"

"Polly."

"Polly?"

"Polly," she declared, with a slight twist to the foreign vowels that left no doubt of the matter.

When my further questions annoyed her, she decided not to understand them. Taking the peach she had bribed me with, she left me to ask them of myself.

CHAPTER TEN
The Wager Is Lost

THAT SAME FRIDAY was the last day of the week in which, under the terms of Monsignore Tabbi's wager, my aunt must either enter the confessional or keep without. In all that time, though the Abate was a daily visitor, he had never reverted to the subject, even by indirection, nor ever suggested a return visit to the Aragonese Castello, nor acted in any way that might have advanced his cause.

"Yet he had seemed so confident, you know," Lydia said, as we watched for his approach from the tribune of the principal *sala*, which overlooked the Villa's long white drive and iron gate.

"You sound disappointed, Aunt."

"I suppose I am. Where is the credit in resisting a temptation that is never offered? I shall feel quite guilty taking the poor man's money. I would almost go into his old wooden box for pity's sake, if it were not for Josiah."

"Perhaps that was Monsignore Tabbi's calculation."

"Clara, what can you be thinking! I'm astonished at you. For all that he's a Papist, Monsignore Tabbi is a very simple, straightforward man. I dare say if you knew him a little better—"

"Aunt! Are you well?" I reached for her hand, supposing from her sudden silence and the stricken look that had succeeded to the good cheer of only a moment before that one of her megrims had come upon her.

"No. Please." She spoke in the barest of whispers. "Do not alarm yourself—and do not, I beg you, make such a commotion. It's nothing. Only, I would rather not be noticed . . . by them."

She nodded to where, on the lawn below us, Contessa Visconti, supported on the arm of Manfredo, was taking the air of late afternoon. They walked in the shade of a row of plane trees, whose broad leaves intermittently obscured both their figures and their speech. Even witnessing them from this far remove, I could not escape the impression (which I knew Lydia must share) that there existed between these two an intimacy, an easiness, a lack of reserve much in excess of that which ought to exist between mistress and manservant. She was dressed in a light peignoir more suited to the morning hours and the privacy of her own rooms than to the semipublicity of a path that skirted the Villa's main approach, while he was attired with even less regard for decorum—lacking hat or jacket, his shirt-sleeves rolled to his elbows, his cravat hanging loose, his waistcoat unbuttoned. What could be heard of their conversation, which was in Italian, seemed of a piece with their appearance, the free and animated dialogue of equals, unmarked by deference on his side or condescension on hers.

I have already spoken of my suspicions with regard to Manfredo's position in the Visconti household. I was not greatly startled, therefore, by this glimpse of a moment shared by the confederates (as I knew them to be, from my reading of Renata's ledger-book) of a crime so prolonged and so indelicate that nothing beyond a mere *conventional* reserve could obtain between them. What did distress me more than their intimacy was their carelessness in letting *us* observe them at such a time. Had it altogether ceased to concern them how I, or my aunt, or passers-by upon the public road might regard their conduct? Even as I framed this question to myself, I realized with a start of guilt how much my own behavior had been compromised by the necessity of pretending to be ignorant of theirs, how much my actions were governed by the mere, unseemly need to keep up appearances before the world, and especially before my aunt Jerningham.

When I suggested to Lydia that we might go in off the balcony, she declined to do so; whether from a stubborn reluctance to yield ground to an enemy, or from a fear of drawing attention to our presence, still unobserved by the couple below, or from simple curiosity, I do not know. Surely, my own motive in not opposing her more forcefully was some compound of these, and so we stayed, and from having been inadvertent eavesdroppers become conscious spies.

I had long since discovered that Zaide's explication (on that second morning in Venice) of the continued use of my name among Ischiotes in its antique significance of *chiara* was a fiction. Consequently, I knew it had been no idle fancy when I had supposed Manfredo to be making sport of me before Niles. Now again I heard my name upon his lips and again the context was one that incited his listener to laughter. This time I was in no doubt as to the cause of their mirth. I knew he must be telling Zaide how I had discovered Niles' studio that morning, and been discovered there myself. I had not supposed that the young woman of the paintings —"Polly," as she was known to Clara Maria—would have kept our near-meeting a secret from her confederates. But that having told of it, it should become no more than a joke! I felt a kind of chill pass through me, quick as a surgeon's knife, that left me, afterwards, quite numb, as if my body had become a lifeless shell wrapped round an emptiness, void of heart and blood and breath and feeling. Even today, remembering that sensation, I feel ashamed. It seems so spiritless of me, so weak, so wanting. Yet it is very hard to defy an enemy for whom one does not exist, an enemy to whom one's terrors and sorrows are so utterly inconsequential that they can regard them as a fit object for their jokes. In both a literal and a figurative sense, I did not exist for Zaide and Manfredo, and so, for a little while, I did not exist for myself. I became what they must have often wished I were, a nothingness.

When they had passed round the east side of the Villa and out of sight, Lydia limited her reprobation to one dry comment on the Contessa's mode of dress, nor did I, short of agreeing that there was no excuse for it, seek to impart any more of what I knew, or suspected, or feared. An unspoken compact was formed between us not to expand the effort nor to expose ourselves to the pain that a larger honesty would require. For our mistaken reticence we would both soon pay dearly.

After another ten or fifteen minutes, the long-awaited Monsignore Tabbi appeared, striding down the road that led to the gate. The sight of him, all black but for the crimson glint of his monsignorial stockings, seemed at once to dispose my aunt to a happier frame of mind. She waved to him and called aloud (in reply he touched the broad brim of his hat), and wanted to go down directly to meet him in the drive. It was for me to act the part of duenna and insist that she receive her suitor in the drawing room.

We did not long remain indoors, however, for Monsignore Tabbi announced he had a surprise prepared for us, which we must come with him to see. He would neither confirm nor deny that it concerned the wager.

West of the Villa, behind a screen of cypresses, was a kitchen garden, which now lay fallow for a season of aestival ease. Thither, past festoons of withered bean-plants and one last precious row of living salad greens, the Abate conducted us, to the wall that marked the western boundary of the Villa. Just as I had not explored the rooms of the third floor, so I had ignored this unprepossessing corner of the grounds. Altogether it was to be a day of venturings. Monsignore Tabbi led us out through a gate in the Villa's wall and along a path barely distinguishable from the rugged terrain it traversed. Dense, low shrubs of cistus, or rockrose, formed a dark, green mantle on either side of our path. The Abate explained that the gum of this plant is the source of the myrrh which the Magi bring as offerings in the Gospel of Matthew, and he showed us the little beads of aromatic gum on the undersides of the leaves. This gum is gathered by shepherds, who comb it out from the beards of their goats after they have been grazing; for which purpose (we discovered) a wide skirt works quite as well. But as for where we were going or what we would find there, not a word! We climbed until we had a splendid view down over the roof of the Villa and along the north coast of the island; then the path descended and our destination came into view.

"You are taking us to the convent," my aunt declared in a

hushed tone, though whether it were the hush of reverence or of scandal would be hard to say.

If we had been quite honest with ourselves, we would have realized as soon as we had passed out the Villa's side-gate that there was nowhere the Abate could have been taking us except to the Convent of Santa Restituta, which was squeezed into the one portion of the peninsula not belonging to the Viscontis. Its buildings lay out of sight and out of mind behind the hill we had just circled, and connected to the public highway by a different road from what we used.

The chief reason, however, for our taking so little note of our neighbors was that we had none. The convent had been unoccupied these twenty years, a victim of two mighty and incalculable forces, fashion and diastrophism. At the beginning of the century, thanks to its ownership of the Acqua di Santa Restituta, one of Ischia's best-reputed *terme*'s, or spas, the convent had been prosperous and populous, but there are fashions in springs as in other things. The convent's *terme* attracted an older and older clientele, which meant, over the course of time, a smaller and smaller one. Before the wheel of fortune could come round and bring Santa Restituta back in vogue, the definitive disaster occurred to blast the convent's hopes forever. An earthquake brought down the roof of the main cloister and considerably damaged the fittings of the *terme*. God's Judgment was plain to be read, and the nuns, all having miraculously escaped injury in the roof's collapse, were ordered dispersed among other houses of their order on Ischia and the mainland.

This brief history was related by Monsignore Tabbi as we followed him down the steep, twisting path to the convent's gate. What one could see of its buildings over the top of the high encircling wall illustrated most poignantly the Abate's theme of abandonment and ruin. There were the spars and timbers of the fallen roof, stark as a crucifixion. The other buildings ranged about this were scarcely in any happier condition, having become a kind of hanging garden of weeds and wild shrubberies. The windows all were gone; some had been boarded with planks, but most were gaping holes, so that all those deserted cells had been colonized over the years and made into dovecotes and other aviaries.

Reaching the gate of this ruin, Monsignore Tabbi announced our arrival by the jangling of a bell mounted on its own little campanile.

To whom? I wondered, though out of respect for the spirit of the occasion I did not ask. At last eyes appeared at the metal grating; a bolt was drawn, and then a second bolt, and the gate opened with a groan.

The aged nun who had performed this labor came without and Monsignore Tabbi introduced her as Suor Incarnazione, who had been, in her youth, a postulant within these walls. For once, Lydia's sense of Propriety failed her, and she stared at Suor Incarnazione with abject ignorance of *what to do.* But more astonishing than the gray-habited nun (who, after all, had a certain ghostly *à-propos*) was the other, more familiar figure that still kept within the gate.

"Antonia!" my aunt exclaimed. "Whatever brought you to this place?"

Her maid curtseyed and lifted up a basket brimming with linens. "I was told you would require these, Madam." And when Lydia still showed no sign of comprehension: "For your bath, below."

"I am to take the waters *here?*" she asked incredulously of the Abate.

"You may consider of it, and if the waters meet your approval the key to this outer gate shall be yours, a gift from your neighbors, who, alas, are your neighbors no more."

"But, why?"

"As a favor, through you, to the Conte; and to please me, too, a little. This good woman with other former residents of the convent have been employed all this week to put some part of the *terme* into acceptable order. While I may not judge of their work, since it is forbidden any of my sex to go within this gate, you may ask your maid whether it might meet your approval."

Antonia assured my aunt that both the changing room and the bathing cabinet were quite decent, and Monsignore Tabbi went on to cite the specific virtues of the waters, which contained a larger proportion of the muriates of soda and potash than any of the island's other springs, not excepting even the Gurgitello, which had done Lydia so much good on the two occasions she had gone there. Finally, it could not be denied that this was incomparably more convenient than the far-off Gurgitello, should it prove beneficial.

Suor Incarnazione had listened to the Abate's discourse with the closest incomprehension and a growing urgency to uphold the oriflamme of Santa Restituta. At last she testified in a voice reedy with age but still resonant with a fanatic faith. As her outburst had been too passionate for me to follow, Monsignore Tabbi had to translate. "She says that by comparison with these waters—she calls them 'holy,' but that is only her way of speaking—the Gurgitello is a mere pickle barrel."

Suor Incarnazione spoke again, and more emphatically.

"A laundry tub!"

And finally, knotting her poor old hands into fists: "A cesspool!"

At last, if only to appease this aged pythoness, Lydia had no choice but to accompany her to the spring and put her word to the test. Necessarily I must go along as interpreter and *fidus Achates*.

"To think, my dear," said Lydia, as we followed Suor Incarnazione across the little jungle of the courtyard, "that we should have entered a convent of nuns! Though, to be sure, they have long since ceased to live here. Even so, I should never have consented to come here, if I had not dreaded hurting good Monsignore Tabbi's feelings."

"Aunt, you protest too much."

"Well, perhaps I have *my* reasons, too, though"—and she smiled enigmatically—"I can't think *what* they might be!"

We were conducted into the *terme*, a kind of hotel lobby forsaken by its guests and pillaged of its fittings, and thence down a staircase of remarkable depth and gloom. Warm clouds of steam climbed the steps as we descended, forming aureoles round the wicks of rude clay lamps fixed to the sweating rocks of the walls. After we had passed the last such lamp, the narrow obscurity of the stairs broadened to a vista of obscurity incalculably larger, which Suor Incarnazione declared to be the grotto of Santa Restituta. While Antonia showed my aunt to her changing room, the gray-habited Virgil of this nether-world pointed out its distinctive features quite as though they were visible to us from the vantage of the broken balustrade by which we stood. *There*, just before us, was the pool of Santa Restituta, measuring fully two *moglii* in length by one *moglio* in width, which, as I could see nothing at all and had no notion of a *moglio*, might have made it as small as a bath-tub or as large as a lake. *There*, in the blackness to the right of us, were the cabinets, thirty-four in all, in which the bathers took the waters, the pool itself being much too hot to enter directly, as the water came from the mouth of the spring at a temperature very near to boiling. *There*, to the left, was the fissure by which the waters left the grotto to take their winding course through the middle-earth, mingling with other springs to become at last the tamer, cooler streams that played through the gardens of the Villa Visconti, rising in its fountains, filling its pools, rushing down its cascade.

Lydia rejoined us, clothed in a white bathing-gown. Suor Incarnazione approved this transformation, remarking that she looked like a novice going to take her vows, a compliment that, though harmless, I thought wiser not to translate for my aunt.

Following the nun, and followed by Antonia—both of whom held lamps aloft to show us our way among the boulders, which were the *terme*'s legacy from the great earthquake—we ventured forth into the blackness. The steam became ever thicker and hotter till we reached the water's edge. The pool stretched out, darkly indefinite, as far as the lamps would shed their light. A *moglio*, evidently, was a fair distance. Back of us, following the crescent of the shore, were the thirty-four bathing cabinets, which, standing in every degree of relation to the vertical, resembled nothing so much as a row of funeral monuments in an ancient, untended graveyard. To the most upright and farthest of these sepulchers Suor Incarnazione conducted us. When we stood before it, she held up her lamp in a gesture of regal munificence and announced that it was a gift to Lydia from the worthy and venerable Abate.

Not much work had been required to make over the confessional into a bathing machine. It was raised up on stilts so as to stand level on the rough, unpaved floor, and a basin was set into the center of it, in which the beneficent waters of the pool were allowed to cool. One entered this basin by means of a little stile affixed to the side, where once a penitent would have knelt.

After I had translated for my aunt our guide's full praises of the Monsignore's generosity, I asked, in my own character, whether there had ever been a gift more elaborately wrapped.

"But, Clara, how can I accept it without going in?"

"Having come so far, Aunt, how can you do anything else? Even leaving Monsignore Tabbi's feelings out of account, one must consider the nuns who have worked all this week to put the place in order. Besides, it may do you good. This may be the spring to end all your questing."

"But think, my dear—if Josiah knew!"

"As Monsignore Tabbi pointed out last week, when you made your wager with him, it is only wood, and now it is so much altered from what it was that the strictest Protestant should have no qualms."

"And so you think I should?"

"If your conscience at all permits it, yes."

"Well, then I will! But, mind you, it doesn't signify." With this assurance and a sigh, she entered the basin of steaming water within the confessional.

CHAPTER ELEVEN
Mr. Mainwaring's Views on Art

A WEEK AND A DAY from the events of that Friday, at the candescent center of the afternoon, Rose entered at the oven-door of my sitting room to announce that a gentleman was waiting below to see me. Sensing from the way she smiled that my visitor must be Mr. Mainwaring, I protested that I was not in a state fit to receive, having unlaced against the heat. Rose tut-tutted and assured me I looked quite pretty. With only the least bedabbling of toilet water—So!—and one or two strands of hair reordered—Thus!—I might receive whom I liked. Surely, after he had come all this way, and in such weather, too, it would be the worst cruelty to refuse him my presence only because I was *en déshabillé*. The more she argued, the greater grew my flutteration. I was persuaded and then, at a glance into the pier-glass, I was un-persuaded. Rose must ask the gentleman to wait below for a moment and then come back and help me dress. When she returned from this errand I was still undecided what to wear.

"Your Garibaldi shirt," she suggested unhesitatingly. "With the Zouave jacket and a black silk shirt. That would be very smart, and he will not have seen it, as you never wore it all the time you were in Florence."

"The colors are so bold. That is why I never wore it."

But Rose brushed my objections aside and dressed me to suit her own fancy; nor when she was finished, ten minutes later, could I sincerely fault her choice.

"Now for your hair, my Lady," she said, leading me to the dressing table in my bedroom. "No, no, he can be patient a little longer. Your hair was well enough before, but now you are *en grande toilette* it looks too negligent. I shall be done in a moment. And there is a little matter you may wish to know, before you speak with your caller. I have taken the liberty, which I believed my Lady would approve, of putting some few necessary articles together into a portmanteau, one of my own, which is deposited at a house in the village of Casamicciola."

"Indeed, Rose, you have taken a great liberty! And quite unnecessarily."

"I hope so, my Lady. I can't think what was in my mind to make me do such a thing. It's at the house of Mr. Mainwaring's acquaintance, through whom he some times contacts me. Signore Stopponi. His house faces the little church of San Rocco."

"But, Rose—"

"Please, my Lady, I cannot work if you move about so. There is no money in the case, nor any jewels, except some beads and such of no value at all, for it seemed wiser not to tempt good Signore Stopponi's honesty too far."

"Rose, have you considered what would happen if by any chance it became known what you have done?"

"Yes, my Lady, I have. It would be thought that I have grown tired of serving here and mean to run off with your blue travelling dress and some of your nicer stockings. For that is what I should say. If my Lady wishes me to retrieve the portmanteau. . . ?"

"Of course I do! But you have fussed me quite enough for now. No, none of your powders! Fetch Mr. Mainwaring and don't talk any more nonsense about portmanteaus."

No sooner had she curtseyed in acquiescence and gone out the door than I realized that in my harum-scarum haste I had neglected to change my straw slippers for a pair of shoes. Lacking time to repair my mistake, I told myself that with a little care it need not be known.

Mr. Mainwaring, when he appeared, seemed even more ill-at-ease than myself, though not from any consideration so slight as his clothing, which was of the rough-and-ready order, more suitable for a day of boating than a social call. His misgivings proceeded rather from his having been turned away, earlier that day, with a message that I was "not at home" and his uncertainty whether that message were my own and a true indication that I did not wish to see him.

"Dear Mr. Mainwaring," I protested, offering my hand, "please do me the honor to believe I am *always* at home to you. After my aunt Jerningham, I do not think I have a friend in this world whom I more implicitly rely on."

This was so much in excess of what courtesy required that it put Mr. Mainwaring somewhat at a loss for a reply. At length, mutely, he raised the hand that I had placed in his and kissed it.

Far from adding to the fluster of my feelings, his kiss seemed to quieten and calm them, as some times the sudden revelation of a shining sky when first the blinds are raised will erase a whole night's history of uneasy dreams.

"I wish, Contessa—"

"No, please. After such a declaration of friendship you must call me Clara. At least when we are by ourselves. I have never felt quite at home in my title, I'm afraid."

"Some times, Contessa—" He broke off, smiled, shrugged, and resumed. "Some times these formalities can be helpful. The purpose that brings me here is a grave one, one that you may regard as improper or compromising. Certainly, others would regard it in that light."

"Well, then, the forms don't matter. As to purposes, I have too high a regard for you, Mr. Mainwaring, to suppose that yours could ever be other than correct."

"Even if it be to urge you to leave your husband and seek an annulment of your marriage?"

However often he may have rehearsed these words to himself, now that they were out he seemed to stand aghast at his own intrepidity in speaking them.

"Even then, of course."

"You speak with no hesitation."

"I feel none, with regard to your probity. It is a serious course. I'm sure you must have serious reasons for urging it. But, please, before we are more deeply involved, let us be comfortable."

I sat down, careful that my slippers should not peek out from my skirt. Mr. Mainwaring sat facing me on the high-backed replica of my uncle Jerningham's favorite chair. I doubt either of us were notably more comfortable, but there was a low table between us, and it seems to be a part of human nature that discussions of serious matters may be conducted more easily in the presence of a table.

"My reasons, then," began Mr. Mainwaring, "though before I speak of them, I should caution you that if your relationship with Count Visconti, as it exists today, is not such as to allow you to consider such a course, then all I have come here to say might be better left unsaid."

Two impulses warred within me: to tell him everything—how Niles had treated me that last night in Florence, what I had learned from Renata's journal, what else I had surmised—and then, recoiling from this, to take the way he now was offering and allow him to suppose me Niles' true wife. Neither contrary could overcome the other, and the result was a silence that Mr. Mainwaring at last interpreted as a tacit admission that my marriage had remained imperfect.

"Let me say, too," he went on, "that my grounds for urging an annulment are not narrow or legalistic—that because annulment *might* be possible, it *ought* to be. That has never been my thought— not when, so imprudently, I approached your husband in Florence, and not now. What is more important is the spirit of the marriage, whether the vows were sworn in good faith, and whether, while the marriage remains unconsummated, that good faith persists."

"In that particular, Mr. Mainwaring, I can assure you that it does."

"I have never doubted it, Contessa—of you. And until yesterday I have believed it of the Count as well. But I have seen that which utterly contradicts any charitable interpretation."

"My husband is in Naples. You saw him there?"

His eyes would no longer meet mine but stared down, fixedly, at the table-top. Partly in anger and partly in embarrassment, his cheeks, already darkened by the sun, grew darker with a sudden rush of blood. "It is always a sorry business to bear tales, especially if they reflect against those who have trusted us. I would not sully you with an exact account of what I have seen, yet to observe an ordinary reticence might be the means of doing you a worse injustice. Forgive me, then, for what I am about to tell you."

"Perhaps I have a better idea of what you saw in Naples than you would suppose."

"No, Contessa—you could not."

"It is easier for me to show you what I mean than to explain. If you will come with me upstairs, you may judge for yourself."

I was halfway to the door before I recollected that I was shod only in my straw slippers. There was no help for it. I shuffled along as best I might, but finding myself unable to shuffle up a staircase, I let them slip off and proceeded barefoot the rest of the way, conscious of every imperfection in the cool dusty tiles of the corridor.

The outer room was as before, empty of all but the bands of sunlight that came in through the louvers of the shutter. The door to Niles' studio was closed but not locked. Had he trusted to my timidness or to my reticence that I would not return here? Or was it of no import to him? Surely he knew of my intrusion of the week before. The woman who had seen me and whom Clara Maria had chased into the closet must have told him.

The tattered curtain partitioning the space into sitting room and studio was drawn. I parted it. The picture of Clara Maria sleeping in Manfredo's lap was finished and hung upon the wall. The easel held a new painting, the thinnest sketch as yet, though the woman's gown was already recognizable as that which I had discovered in the bureau drawer, and the furniture was the furniture of this room. Otherwise, there had been no change.

"Your husband has *shown* these pictures to you?" Mr. Mainwaring asked, frowning.

I explained how I had discovered the studio, and been discovered myself. "So," I concluded, "if we may suppose that the lady who saw me here—I presume that is she in the painting just begun—told Niles of what she saw, to the degree that he makes no effort to conceal them from me, he shows them."

"He never spoke to you about your having been here, or what you saw?"

"No; nor I to him. What is there to discuss? The pictures are more expressive than anything we might say. The woman lying on the couch—how he has understood her!"

"But what a terrible thing to choose to understand—the degradation of a woman's soul."

"Is that what you see? I see pain, and a great loneliness, and an intolerable bitterness. Even humility, of a kind. I have never met such women, but I believe they must be very much as Niles has pictured them."

"Forgive me, Contessa, but I cannot speak of these matters so coolly. My work in London for the Magdalen Mission has made me acquainted with many such women. I don't dispute that there is a kind of truth to these paintings. But the fact that they exist at all is inexpressibly shocking. Surely you see that? To paint evil itself as though it were a . . . a bouquet!"

"It's for you to forgive me, Mr. Mainwaring. I should have prepared you for what you would see. I was shocked—how could I not be?—when I first saw these. What they suggest of the life that Niles may lead away from me is, as you say, very shocking. But admitting this, what of all the wives who have made such a discovery after the bond of matrimony is indissoluble? Are *they* not obliged to forgive? And is my case so very different?"

"If it were not, Clara—and I address you so advisedly—if it were not, I would not have caused you needless distress by coming here and speaking of these matters."

"Have you considered this—that Niles may not be sunk quite so deep in this iniquity as we have been assuming?"

"I don't know how any more charitable assumption is to be made. Only look about you. The evidence hangs on every wall."

"But what does the evidence prove? That Niles has a penchant for painting improper subjects, no more. But perhaps you know what I do not."

"Do you suggest that your husband may frequent brothels for aesthetic purposes? And that the woman your aunt saw in this house came here only to *pose* for him?"

"Is it not possible? Painting can be a passion. As you say, the evidence hangs on every wall. Look at them. Tell me what you see."

"Coldness. Indifference. A perfect willingness to let the world stew in its old corruption."

"Have you ever seen the paintings of Piero della Francesca, Mr. Mainwaring?"

"But, my dear lady—there can be no comparison!"

"There is a painting of his that has haunted me these many weeks. It shows Christ coming from the tomb. I thought it appalling, and for just the same reasons. There was nothing of radiance or triumph in the scene. No warmth, no tenderness. But in a strange way these become excellences in Piero's work. I do not say that Niles has achieved the same thing in these, but I have learned enough to know that that is what he has been after."

"Well, suppose they were as good as you think—though I don't see it—what then? Because a man paints well are we to think him estimable? There have been many fine painters who, I fear, were scoundrels, thieves, even murderers."

"But it isn't so much that his paintings are better than before. They're more *human*. He has seen these women as he did not see me, when he attempted my portrait. There is a struggle going on inside of him between the person he has been and the person he wishes to become. If I left him now, I know that he would return to his old way of life. People fall into evil little by little; may they not be led the same way back into the light?"

"Yes, that is so. There must always be some preparation, even if it is no more than a hand held out at the right moment."

"Then can you still look doubtful, Mr. Mainwaring? Isn't it clear that I must stay by him so long as he allows me?"

"But that may be years!"

"Did I not vow to be his till death should part us?"

Mr. Mainwaring was silent for some time, considering. "I don't know what to say, Contessa. I admire your choice. I must even approve it, with reservations. But I fear for you as well. You'll have no allies in what you undertake, and I foresee one certain enemy."

"Manfredo, do you mean?" Then, realizing that the name would mean nothing to Mr. Mainwaring, I indicated the picture of him. "His valet."

He would only nod in reply, though the look he gave the picture was eloquent of high feelings. There must have been a considerable provocation.

"What you foresee, Mr. Mainwaring, has long since come to pass. We're enemies of long standing. But as for fearing him, that isn't necessary. There are bounds to his insolence, which he is careful not to overstep."

I then suggested that we return to my sitting room, to which Mr. Mainwaring assented with alacrity. It was well that we chose this moment to bring our trespass to an end, for as we were returning along the corridor, the door that gave onto the staircase opened and my mother-in-law greeted us with an altogether in-genuine affectation of surprise. In one hand she held the slippers I had lost upon the stairs.

"My dear Mr. Mainwaring, how wonderful! You were lost and now you are found! When I thought it *might* be you, I tried to summon you back, but I was too late. The servant thought you wished to speak only to my son, who is in Naples. But you re-turned. I'm *so* glad."

He accepted her offered hand and murmured, "Contessa."

"You have been showing him over the Villa, Clara?"

"Yes," I said, grateful to be spared having to lie for myself.

"I must say you are being thorough about it. The good Lord knows, Mr. Mainwaring, that visitors are rare enough here. When they do come, we must all exert ourselves to keep them with us. You *will* stay to dinner?"

"I should like nothing better, believe me, Contessa, but I was just saying good-bye to your daughter-in-law when you dis-covered me."

"Nonsense, my good man. You will explore the attic and not even glance at the gardens? The gardens are famous. 'The Tivoli of the South,' Ramage calls them in the charming book of his travels, and he even claims to prefer our copy above the original, though that, I think, is rather overdoing. Clara, you must add your voice to mine, if only out of charity to me."

"I do, and most sincerely. Please stay to dinner, Mr. Main-waring. We all stand in need of some novelty. My aunt Jerning-ham should be most upset to think you had been here and she had not seen you."

"You see, Mr. Mainwaring! You must yield to us now."

Mr. Mainwaring bowed his head as a token of submission.

"Good! I shall tell your aunt, Clara, and if the Abate is still with her, as I think he was only an hour ago, I shall compel him to dine, too. You, meantime, must show Mr. Mainwaring round the garden. Oh, but first—I neglected to ask: these are not yours, are they?" She held up the slippers.

I shook my head, and I suppose that I blushed.

"No, of course not. What can I be thinking of? Oh, but one last thing: Mr. Mainwaring, I trust that you like game?"

"Yes, very much."

She took her leave of us, and then, barefooted, I showed Mr. Mainwaring through the length and breadth of the garden. The day was still fiery hot, and the gravel like so many heated coals against my tender soles, but I scarcely minded. I was happy.

What we spoke of in the hours Zaide had given us does not properly concern this narrative. For minutes at a time we did not speak at all. The sea glittered, and the fountain foamed. Gulls rose up from the rocks of the shore and rode the southern breeze and dropped from sight. The clouds about the summit of Epomeo slowly became suffused with pink. Too soon the day ended, too swift the night came on.

CHAPTER TWELVE

Doubts and How They May Be Overcome

THERE WERE FIVE OF US at table: Mr. Mainwaring sat at my right hand with Zaide beside him, Monsignore Tabbi on my left, next to Lydia. There was not one of us, as I see in retrospect, who was not acutely conscious of being in a false position; not one whose conscience could or (at the least) should have been entirely at ease. Mr. Mainwaring regarded the dinner as having been got up specially as a punishment for himself, which, in a most literal sense, it was. As for my aunt, though she was visibly in distress all that evening, I supposed this due to her having been dragooned into sitting down to dine with Zaide, the battle of the wall-hangings being still a present reality for them both. That it was rather my own and Mr. Mainwaring's presence which was disturbing to her I would not then have believed. Monsignore Tabbi alone seemed in his element, but that must be because the kind of intrigue he was then involved in was precisely his element. The same, of course, could be said for Zaide, who had arranged all these discomforts on purpose to amuse herself. And yet, to listen to our table-talk, you would have thought there was not a single cross-purpose among the lot of us.

Though I sat at the head of the table, it was Zaide who played the part of hostess and wrought this illusion of cordiality. She plied Mr. Mainwaring with questions about the latest discoveries at Pompeii and Herculaneum and extracted from Monsignore Tabbi a very interesting account of the cultivation of figs. She described her ascent of Vesuvius some thirty years before and wrung from Mr. Mainwaring a reluctant promise to organize a party to make the ascent together, when the weather moderated. Then she began making plans for all of us to go on a tour of Sicily! Even Lydia, who scorned to be a hypocrite, entered into these hollow discussions for the mere sake of filling the silence agreeably.

All the while we talked, courses of inedible food were brought to the table and removed untasted, except by Mr. Mainwaring, who stoically got down a portion of everything that appeared, and by Monsignore Tabbi, whose appetite I had never seen to fail him. Truly, the Villa's cook outdid herself that evening. King Phineus, whose dinners were beset by Harpies, never ate so wretchedly. The worst dish of all was appropriately the main course, a kind of rabbit stew the receipt for which Zaide claimed to have discovered herself in the ancient cook-book of Apicius.

"It uses a spice that is almost unknown to us now," she explained, as it was brought round the table in its tureen. "Asafoetida —the Romans made it into a kind of Universal Sauce, called *liquimen*, which they poured over almost everything to bring out a 'high' flavor. As you English are known to be partial to game when it is at its gamiest, I was certain it would please you."

For all her praises, I noticed that she took not a bite herself, nor did my aunt and I. Monsignore Tabbi, after a suspicious

morsel, put aside his fork and concentrated his attention on the
wine. Even I drank more than is my custom, only to have the
fumes of the wine at hand to counteract the odor rising from
the stew. But Mr. Mainwaring not only ate the better part of what
had been served him; he then outwent Zaide by insisting she give
him a copy of the receipt.

Shortly afterwards, I pretended faintness and said I must take a
turn in the garden to clear my head. Mr. Mainwaring promptly
offered me his arm. As soon as we were out of doors, we parted
by mutual consent.

"Thank you, Contessa," he said, rejoining me on the lower
terrace. "I do not think I would have lasted much longer."

"You needn't have been so accommodating to her for my sake.
The dinner was a deliberate affront. You'll note *she* didn't eat it."

"But, you see, it was a challenge. If I hadn't eaten, she would
have had the better of me, and my stiff-necked pride wouldn't
allow that. I trust I won't be any the worse for it by tomorrow. Indeed, Contessa, I would eat my way from one end of Apicius' vile
cook-book to the other, if I could always be guaranteed such
delightful company."

"You're very kind to me, Mr. Mainwaring."

"I wish I could be kinder. For all my good intentions, my
visit cannot have added to your peace of mind."

"Oh, but it has, and very much! You have approved me in the
course I've chosen for myself. It has not been an easy choice—"

"As it will be no easy course, I fear."

"And for that very reason your sanction is reassuring. I feel
more able to do what must be done."

"Ah, Contessa, do not give me too fine a notion of the power
of my advice. I approved only reluctantly, when I saw that I
could not persuade. If I thought that I might make you change
your mind. . . . But you already are tilting your head at its obstinate angle, and I see it is useless to go on. There, you have my
approval, but I wish, instead, you had my doubts!"

"I do have doubts, of course. Who is ever quite without them?
But I learned, some time ago, how to get the best of them. When
I was fourteen I was much disturbed by doubts as to the central
doctrines of religion. How, I asked myself, could an all-loving God
condemn souls He had Himself created to the everlasting fires of

Hell? How could there be such a weight of unmerited suffering everywhere in the world? I knew better than to ask such questions of my uncle Jerningham, but at last I could not bear to keep them all to myself. I went to my grandfather, Augustus Reeve, who was the curate of St. John's Church in Clerkenwell, and laid forth all my scruples and misgivings. He listened very patiently, but when I'd finished he did not attempt to answer any of the problems I'd posed. Instead, he instructed me to crush the very shadow of a rising doubt with a short quick prayer. That was all; no arguments and precious little sympathy for my distress."

"It was very good advice, if one has the strength to accept it."

"I found the strength."

"And now you use it to dispel doubts you may have about your husband?"

"Once I have thought my way through to an understanding of my duty, I do try not to agitate myself with pointless specu-lations."

"Your self-command is daunting, Contessa; and I say that, whom you have seen eat this evening's dinner."

"I say I try to. I don't always succeed."

"I shall not urge you any more against your conscience, and yet I cannot say that you leave me altogether at my ease. What I witnessed yesterday—"

"Please, Mr. Mainwaring, say no more of that!"

"This much, at least: that if you ever feel your own strength begin to fail you, send for me, or come to me direct; that if new events should dispose you to reconsider the possibility of an annul-ment, that you discuss the matter with me *before* you broach it to your husband."

"I'm not sure that what you ask is quite proper."

"In all candor, I am not sure myself. I ask it selfishly, for my own peace of mind."

"If it will really assist you to that, you have my word, Mr. Mainwaring. And now we had better go within. Let us hope we have missed the dessert."

As soon as we returned to the dining room, Monsignore Tabbi began praising Lydia's musicianship. At his urging, and mostly, I think, to rescue us from the dining room, she agreed to perform.

She played a Schubert fantasia and then accompanied me in

one of Beethoven's Irish songs. In the second stanza, quite unaccountably, I began to cry. Lydia came to sit beside me on the
sofa and held me till I was once more in control of myself.

"But what is it, my dear? What has upset you?"

"It's nothing, Aunt," I whispered. "The music suddenly affected me. I'm quite over it now. Let us start over from the
beginning. I shan't spoil it this time."

But she could not be persuaded, though we all urged her. I was
never to hear her play again, for on the next morning she was
dead.

CHAPTER THIRTEEN

Darkness

A BROAD HEDGE OF OLEANDERS formed the boundary between the
kitchen garden, which was the servants' demesne, and the formal
gardens, which were ours. To the shade of these bushes I had
come on that fatal Sunday morning, thinking to avoid Niles, who
had returned from Naples late the night before. I dreaded the
questions he would ask, foreseeing I must either lie or quarrel with
him, not a pretty range of choices. For all my high motives and
professions of fidelity, I could not escape that moral law (as in-
fallible as Newton's) which states that any single lie that is
persisted in engenders seventeen more, until even one's candor is
infected by the all-pervading duplicity. With Niles I could never
be simply who I was, but must always be calculating how to make
my words and actions consistent with my recentest untruths. But
I shall spare my readers a full accounting of such unworthy
thoughts, for the events of that day and the days following threw
out all my calculations and showed them up as the vanities they
were. May God preserve me from ever again seeing the crooked
made straight at such a cost!

Because my chosen retreat was near to the gate in the Villa's west wall, I was the first to hear Antonia when she entered at that gate, her shrill alarms rendered mostly incoherent by fear and a frantic haste. When she saw me come from behind the oleanders she began to wail, as though the mere sight of me were accusation and judgment against her. When I demanded to know the cause of her distress, she would only tell me, with eloquent wringing of her hands, that it was not her fault, that she had done her duty, that more could not be asked. Without conveying any information, she managed in this way to communicate all her anxiety, and soon my questions shared in the distraught illogic of these replies. I gathered that in some manner too awful for Antonia's words my aunt had suffered a mischance, and immediately my imagination began to frame hypothetical accidents which might have befallen her, the very direst of which fell short of the reality I was to find.

I did not question Antonia more closely, but, bidding her to rouse other servants in the house and send them after me, I set off along the path to the convent, fearful at every turning to see Lydia prostrate among the cistus plants. But the hillside was deserted, except for a little flock of goats, which I scattered in my flight. When I reached the prominence, from which I could survey the path ahead to the very gateway of the convent, I knew my fears had been a kind of hope, a stratagem by which I had averted darker thoughts of what might be.

From the crest of the hill I saw a familiar figure in a black cassock and wide-brimmed hat hurrying towards the convent's gate from the direction of the public road. At any other time, the sight of the old priest would have been reassuring, but distance and distress made him a figure of ill omen. While I paused to catch my breath, Monsignore Tabbi entered the convent; he, who before had been so scrupulous not to venture within the abandoned cloister! This time there was no ringing of the bell, no nun on sentry duty at the grating, no drawing of heavy bolts. The gate gaped wide, and through it, some minutes later, breathless with running, I followed after him. I made straight towards the *terme*, where I found the Abate rattling the handle of the door to the stairway that led to the pool. He continued some while, unawares, in a spirit rather of pique than of alarm, and this pique was not lessened when, leaving off in frustration, he turned round and found himself observed.

"Contessa!"

Any reply, even the speaking of his name, was beyond me.

Momently Monsignore Tabbi seemed to take a more hopeful view of my appearance, or at least recognized that it must be dealt with. "Ah, you arrive most opportunely, my dear lady! Has your aunt then spoken to you of her intentions? Believe me, Contessa, I have urged her repeatedly to be open with you. 'Tell her,' I would say, 'now, *before* you commit yourself.' But she feared that you would try to prevent her, and she was not confident of her own strength, should you choose to oppose her."

"Oppose her? I don't at all understand. Is she below? Antonia came running and in such a state, but I would not stay to listen, for she wasn't making sense."

Nor, to judge by the look of Monsignore Tabbi, was I. "Contessa! Your hand!"

"Bother that! We must find my aunt. Something has happened!"

"Allow me, please."

"No, really, it's nothing, a stumble on the path."

We engaged then in a bizarrely inappropriate combat whether or not I would let him wrap my cut with the handkerchief he had dug out from the pocket of his cassock. His persistence in this trivial courtesy at such a moment exasperated me beyond bounds. I clenched my hand into a fist rather than permit him to bandage it.

"If you will not let me help you, you ought to return to the Villa and have it looked after there. It is a very nasty cut."

"I have no intention of going anywhere without my aunt. Do you *know* where she is?"

"I have assumed she is down by the pool. I was to meet her there. We arranged the matter last night. She was to leave the gate open for me, and so she has. But now *this* door is barred."

I went to the door and tried it. As he had said, it was fastened —presumably by a bar or bolt within, for there was no keyhole. She must, therefore, still be below; or *someone* must. I called aloud to her and pounded on the door, but it was thick, and I knew the stairwell to be deep. If she were by the pool, it was possible she might not have heard me. When at last the futility of my clamoring had to be admitted, I left off.

"Contessa, I believe you had best go back to the Villa. No, hear me out! The case is more serious than I thought. I fear there is someone with her. Her maid's alarm, the bolting of this door, the lack of any reply—everything points that way."

"She may have fallen on the steps," I protested.

"And then barred this door?"

"Or may be she has changed her mind with regard to meeting you."

"Yes, that must be our hope—that she has locked the door herself."

"But who else could have?"

"We cannot know, until we go down. That is why I urge you again to return to the Villa. We lack the tools to force this door, and in any case, without knowing whom we may find behind it, it would not be wise for *us* to do so. I would go, but that would leave you here alone. Or not alone, as it may be."

I still protested, but his arguments were too forceful to be long resisted, and so, with many a backward glance at the convent's sorry roofs and gaping windows, I returned hastily along the way I had come, holding my skirts high, so they would not snag upon the cistus plants. At each twist of the path, I expected to meet Antonia returning with other servants, as I had bidden her to do, but I encountered only the grazing goats, who this time went on browsing imperturbably among their aromatic leaves. The sun mirrored its burning whiteness in the wider blue expanse of sea, and the ground around me, quickened by the August heat, writhed and wriggled with superfetation of life, while deep within that earth was Lydia, and whether she suffered or had passed beyond all suffering I did not know, and would not think, and still the path stretched on before me, and still I ran.

The Villa, when I reached it, was in a usual state of Sunday somnolence. The scullery maid was alone in the kitchen, teasing a cat, and to all questions I addressed her she would but goggle and agree with meaningless nods and smiles. Rose, when I found her, was somewhat more helpful. She explained that the other servants had gone in to Casamicciola to attend Mass.

"And my aunt's maid, have you seen her about?"

"Antonia? Only a while ago. Something had made her late, and she was hurrying to join the others."

"She said nothing to you?"

"Except to complain of the heat, which she does every day."

Only later, when the police apprehended her at the quay of the port, where she was waiting for the packet-boat, was this least of mysteries solved. Antonia, after encountering me in the garden, had bethought herself of the likely consequences of that morning's misadventure. Whatever its issue, she judged it certain that she would lose her position, and so instead of alerting the household, as I had bidden her, she went to my aunt's rooms, emptied her jewelry case into her pockets, filled a small valise with other coveted items, whose value she greatly misconceived, and decamped. (For which ill-considered felony the foolish girl was to receive a sentence of twelve years of servitude in a Neapolitan prison.)

Such an explanation, however, was very far from my supposal as I talked with Rose. The only way I could then think to account for Antonia's contradictory behavior was to assume that Lydia's plight was, after all, not such a desperate one. Such pretexts one may find for hope! such straws to clutch at!

I continued my search through room after empty room. Niles' own were empty. In his dressing room a basin of soapy water had been spilt upon the tiles, and a lizard had come in at the open window to refresh himself at the puddle; who, when I appeared in the doorway, darted up the wall and over the sill with the lightning caution of his kind.

At last I admitted to myself the necessity that I had been avoiding and went to my mother-in-law's rooms to secure her help and advice. There I found Niles as well, entertaining Zaide with her favorite game of bezique. I told them of the fright Antonia had given me, of my going to the convent, and of Monsignore Tabbi's dark suspicions, all which, from a mistaken sense of duty (thinking to spare my aunt later embarrassments if this proved a false alarm), I rather minimized. Zaide, indeed, did not seem to think she could be in any danger, and showed more curiosity to know why she should be trysting at the grotto with Monsignore Tabbi than to take alarm over hypothetical dangers. Niles, on the contrary, reacted as I had when Antonia first startled me. He rang for a servant and, when none appeared, went himself to order up the carriage. He was that urgent he even took a hand himself with the harnessing of the horses.

His alarm fed my own, demolishing the frail structure of false hopes I had been constructing, and as the carriage jolted along the Villa's drive and turned onto the public road, it came over me with a certainty as certain as the sunlight that Lydia, wheresoever she might be, was dead. Each winding of the road round tongues of rough limestone declared it; the horses' hooves repeated it; and I knew, though still I could not bear the weight of it, I knew.

Niles must have known as well, for when we had reached the convent's gate he bade me wait within the carriage, which I refused to do, and when the coachman broke the door from its hinges with an iron bar, I ignored his more insistent urgings and followed after the three men down the stairway to the pool. The clay lamps along the wall had not been lighted, and our only illumination was from the two carriage lamps, one of which the coachman carried, while the other was entrusted to Monsignore Tabbi. At intervals, as we descended, we would pause and I would call out her name, but there was no reply from the nether darkness, only the rising billows of the steam, the distant mutterings of the spring, as it rose, boiling, from the rock.

At the bottom of the steps, within the changing room, we found Lydia's walking-dress hung upon a hook. I was constrained to remain upon the landing with Monsignore Tabbi, while Niles and the coachman ventured ahead to the pool itself, and even then it was nothing he said that persuaded me, but the sight of the pistol he entrusted to the priest.

Yet when, a moment later, the coachman's oath echoed through the cavern, I could not restrain myself, but ran to where I saw the other lamp gleaming feebly through the steamy air.

Where the confessional had stood, only a broken scaffolding remained. It was as though a known constellation had been ripped from the sky to leave a blank, blind absence. Niles looked at me fearfully, knowing what I did not.

Then I saw the confessional behind him, afloat upon the black water of the pool. Darkness and steam rendered the smaller object floating beside it indefinite in all respects but its humanity. Crying her name aloud, not thinking what harm I might do myself, I plunged my foot into the burning stream and reached out to grasp the collar of the drowned figure.

Niles and the coachman were instantly at my side to pull me back upon the shore. I had grasped the cloth firmly, and as they drew me back the corpse rolled over in the water.

It was not Lydia. For that small mercy I must be thankful. She had died, trapped within the confessional when it fell, and I was spared the sight of what that hellish water had done to her. The body I had burned my hand and feet to recover was that of the dismissed gardener, Gioacchino Bevilacqua. Though his features were bloated out of recognition, he could be known by the bits of string that served as buttons on his canvas blouse.

Somehow, between them, Monsignore Tabbi and my husband were able to persuade me to leave the pool. For a while the pain of my burns served as an anaesthetic against the worse horror of Lydia's murder. But, when the coachman was carrying me up the steps, a kind of paroxysm overcame me, a strong involuntary trembling in every part of me that was, nevertheless, a deliberate struggle to free myself from the man's arms. I very nearly toppled both of us down the steps before the fit had passed.

I was put into the coach and taken to the Villa. Niles and Monsignore Tabbi remained behind. At the Villa, Rose treated my burns, and Zaide brought a cup of tea, which she said would soothe my pain, and which I adamantly refused to taste.

CHAPTER FOURTEEN

Sorrow

I COULD NOT KEEP in my own room. The constant play of waters in the garden, the splash of fountains, the cascade's gentle purl were always audible, always reminding me of where I had been and what I had seen and how my aunt had died.

I went to her sitting room. Nothing had been changed. Her treasures and her souvenirs, except the few Antonia had absconded with, were disposed on shelves and table-tops where she had placed them. The music she had played last night still stood open on the music-stand. Mrs. Oliphant's new novel, parcelled out in the several issues of *Blackwood's*, lay ready to hand next to her favorite chair. I sat in it. The room was still. Footsteps traversed the corridor without, sometimes to pause before the door, then passing by. No one intruded until, in the evening, Rose brought my meal to me. Though I had no appetite, I ate enough so that my abstinence would not serve as a pretext to violate my sanctuary. Niles came by twice, and Zaide once, but both were respectful of my need for privacy. I spent that night in Lydia's bed, sleepless but strangely content.

The next day, though, Niles would not leave me to myself. There were questions he must put to me on behalf of the police. When I had answered these, he began to explain the facts surrounding the murder, so far as they had been determined from questioning Antonia and Monsignore Tabbi. I begged to be spared knowledge that could only be a source of horror.

"But, Clara, you can't just refuse to know. She was your aunt. You can't *want* to remain ignorant of how she died."

If I had any desires left, ignorance and oblivion were surely what I chiefly longed for. Yet I had not the strength to say so. Niles held up the basilisk, and I gazed upon it.

It seems (by his account) that almost from the moment of meeting Monsignore Tabbi my aunt had begun to be tempted to apostasy. What had principally kept her from going over to the Church of Rome had been her fear of my disapproval. The entire scene enacted at the Castello, ending with Monsignore Tabbi's wager, had been in the nature of a conversation between lovers, which seems quite bland to those who overhear them and yet is pregnant with more passionate meanings. In the drama of any conversion there is usually some element of romance, if not, indeed, of seduction. The love that leads us to God is not really so separable from love in its profaner aspect. In any case, after resisting Monsignore Tabbi's urgings for some weeks, my aunt at last consented to be baptized by him and received into the Roman faith, for which purpose they had arranged, like lovers planning an elopement, to meet secretly at the pool of Santa Restituta. There she had gone early that Sunday morning, accompanied by her maid. Arriving betimes, she had opened the convent gate with the key entrusted to her and gone down to the pool with Antonia, stopping to change into her bathing costume, which was to have been, this time, the gown of her baptism. After she had helped my aunt to change, Antonia was sent above, to wait in the cloister of the convent.

What then followed was unclear. Apparently the Villa's former gardener had entered at the gate left open for Monsignore Tabbi and followed my aunt down the staircase to the pool. Somehow he avoided the attention of Antonia (probably while she helped Lydia to change), who first was apprised of an intruding presence when my aunt's screams were heard issuing from the *terme*. Horror of scandal (for which she feared she must bear the blame), together with uncertainty of the actual dimension of the danger, reduced Antonia to that condition of hysteric helplessness in which I had encountered her some minutes later.

That the old gardener who had dealt so kindly with me on that morning he had found me sleepwalking, and then been so unkindly dealt with himself, that *he* should have assaulted my aunt, and in circumstances so peculiar—how was it to be thought? Yet what deed of violence, what sudden death is not, essentially, unthinkable? Had Lydia been engaged on some more ordinary business, had her assailant been some unknown vagrant and his crime committed in daylight by the public road, would it then have seemed more plausible? Perhaps; yet I could not bear what Niles was telling me and *would* not believe it. It was not that I rejected his explanation, for indeed, I scarcely heeded it; it was rather the mere brutal fact of my aunt's death that I refused to countenance.

And yet, when he departed, the images he had evoked lingered on, like some vile odor that sinks into curtains and upholsteries and obdurately clings. I tried to direct my mind to other matters. Uselessly; as well might I have tried to keep from breathing. All my thoughts led me to that locked door and down those damp stone steps and through the darkness to the pool. Again and again my imagination strained against the enveloping obscurity to see my aunt within the confessional, waiting, or praying may be, for a broken rosary was found in fingers. Then I would hear her, as through the thickness of that door—first the unbelieving exclamation, then the piercing screams when, instead of the priest, another figure approached her through the roiling vapors. Surely there had been a struggle, she within and he without, in the course of which the scaffolding supporting the structure had buckled. Had the confessional, as it went over, toppled the old man with it? Or, finding himself a murderer and cut off from escape, had he perhaps *chosen* this death as the easier and more honorable end?

Though such speculations only deepened the wound and kept it open, I could not leave them be. In truth, I did not want to. The pain they afforded was a kind of homage I paid to Lydia; as well, perhaps, it was my tribute to that all-powerful ravisher, Death. For though I would not admit it myself, I was afraid, passionately afraid, that what had happened to Lydia would happen also to me. I knew, or thought I knew, that her murderer had died with her, and yet it seemed I could hear him still, pacing the hallways of the Villa, stopping at my door, and passing by; waiting for me; abiding with me, as patient as Atropos and as unpersuadable. Every deeply felt grief, I think, is accompanied by such fears, though they are dumb, like the mutes who accompany the body of the beloved to the grave. The difference, for me, was in the persistence of those fears, day after day, as though after the funeral service the hired mutes should not depart but always follow at one's side, accepting no payment, indifferent to one's pleading.

Without acknowledging these fears, I fed them with the self-replenishing horror of phantasy. By staying in Lydia's rooms I kept her alive in my heart, where, hourly, I must bear witness again to her death; which then, a moment later, going to the piano and playing some few bars of the music she had played, I would deny. She lived on, too, in the books from which she had read to me, and I would read through them again—not for their meaning, for they had no meaning any longer, but for the dear echo they had the power, briefly, to awaken. Trinkets I had seen her purchasing in Brighton and in Venice became as relics, made precious by her touch. How could she be dead, while yet the water in the glass upon her bedside table was not evaporated? While letters still arrived for her? While she still inhabited my dreams, the same as when she lived?

If I had seen her in death, that might have helped, but Niles advised against it, advice that I accepted with a secret gratitude, though outwardly I protested against it. When the time came to set off for Rome (outside which, in the Protestant Cemetery, Lydia was to be buried), I could not bear to leave those rooms in which she still seemed so present and alive. Niles set off alone and was the solitary mourner by her grave.

But Death will not be cheated. By too much fingering, my relics lost their magic, and the prose that seemed to echo Lydia's voice became mere lifeless spatterings of ink upon a page. Only the music seemed to possess the power to revive her, but always it was a harder struggle to evoke her from the recalcitrant keys of the pianoforte. My fingers, still smarting from the scalding they had had, faltered, and my judgment failed, but I labored on, and some times there would come the reward that I labored for. Lydia would speak to me and I would hear.

More and more, however, it was the *music* that engaged me, though I did not see that then. Lydia's spirit was lost in the brighter glow of those other vanished souls, from whom the music first had sprung and whom always we honor and mourn when we play the music they have bequeathed us. In this respect, all music may be a form of sorrow, but one in which sweet and bitter are inextricably commingled. In the greatest works of the supreme composers, I always hear, distinct as the trumpets of Judgment, an echo of St. Paul's mighty challenges: *O death, where is thy sting? O grave, where is thy victory?* And though music, at last, is unable to reply with an affirmation as grand and soul-comforting as the Gospel's, it nevertheless may take us much closer than as many hours vainly employed poring over the words of promise, while their meaning is sealed from us in a winter numbness of despair.

CHAPTER FIFTEEN
Terror and Flight

A MONTH PASSED SO, though in the changeless warmth and brightness of Ischia's summer it seemed not to. My whole effort was to make each day identical to the day just passed, a ritual of mourning endlessly re-enacted, and this seemed Nature's effort, too. Yet all the while her secret processes accomplished a slow ripening, until, by mid-September, from every sun-drenched hillside arose the spontaneous fragrance of wine, as some of the clustered grapes would burst their skins before they could be harvested and put within the press. In my heart, as well, a change took place, unwitnessed by me, until one morning, as I took the air within the Villa's garden, it was complete. I did not see it, even then, as *my* metamorphosis. Rather, it seemed that a curtain had been parted from the ordinary lying aspect of the world, which I saw revealed for what it truly was—the hunting-ground and battle-field of all living creatures; an endless, pitiless, blood-soaked *abattoir*.

Every object that met my sight confirmed this sudden, terror-stricken intuition: the cat the kitchen girl was used to teasing, the lizard that he stalked, the hornets buzzing round the pool, the carp within, the water itself, which was fed from the spring in which my aunt had drowned. Even the trees seemed to be struggling against each other to be the first to reach the light and have it to themselves. The very blue of the heavens appeared inimical to me, for it no longer was the seat of the God I had believed in. What Lord of Love and Mercy could have formed a world so cruel?

If Nature, in her most casual aspect, looked malign, the face that the Villa turned towards its gardens seemed to bear the very brand of Cain. It was as though in some unguarded moment I were to witness a look of immitigable enmity in the eyes of an old acquaintance. The terror of it was all the more terrible because it seemed a kind of madness. Nothing had changed from what it had been. All was harmonious and orderly in the approved Palladian manner. Except where the rusted hinge of a shutter on the topmost floor had stained the wall's whiteness with a mineral red, nothing broke the regular rhythm of double pilasters and greenshuttered windows. An archetype of architectural reticence, yet so profound was this sense of something inexpressibly sinister lying behind the Villa's courtly, genial façade that I could not persuade myself that it was a mere subjective impression. In aftertimes, passing by certain residences in London, I have felt the same dismaying conviction of an evil immanent in brick and stone. No longer do I try to account for it, but go by as quickly as I may and remember in future to order my walks and my drives so as to avoid those buildings.

As is the case with any fear, the longer I looked, the more that Gorgon-face rendered me incapable of any action but still to feed my fear with looking. A bell rang, announcing luncheon, but I did not stir. Rose came outside to ask if I meant to eat. I said I had no appetite. She asked me if I felt quite well, and I nodded, for I did not trust my voice. How much longer I may have sat, transfixed, I do not know; nor what my thoughts may have been all that while. Fear at that pitch does not allow for thought in any ordinary sense: the body rebels, the blood runs riot, and feeling reigns supreme, like some resistless hurricane that breaks into the body's little room and whirls about, battering and shattering. One cannot question such a vastation. It is too large; it has no object. One can only hope to last it out.

When the worst was over (I remember), I stood up; which simple act was accompanied by an amazed conviction of my own self-mastery, as though I had arisen from a months-long confinement to a sick-bed. As I stood, I thought: I *shall not* go inside! I did not consider how it was to be avoided or where I would go instead. The essential thing was that I had decided, that after the hour I had spent I was still capable of decisions.

Notwithstanding this brief elation, my fear did not abate. Now, though, it was opposed by the determination I had come to— never again to enter the Villa. I had only to look at that building, swollen with its own malefice, to see that to do so would be inconceivable. Indeed, I could not any longer remain this near.

I went away by the gate in the western wall, without any regard for its associations. To have left by the drive would have exposed me to the view of anyone who glanced out a window, and so the path through the cistuses was to be preferred. Here was where the goats had grazed, and here a lone century plant lifted its spiky leaves above the lower-lying shrubs. Here I had stopped to catch my breath, and here, where the path turned sharply, I had stumbled and cut my hand. I noted these points along the way rather as milestones marking the distance I had put behind me than for their power to awaken memories. Even the gate of the convent I passed without a qualm. Had it been required of me, I am sure I could have gone by the very spot where my aunt had been murdered without breaking stride. Fear made me strong, as well as foolish.

Only when I came to the public road and had to choose between left and right did I stop to ask myself whither I was bound. Leftwards was the island's port, a four-mile walk beside the shore; to the right, the road led to the fishing village of Forio, then climbed the lower southern slopes of Epomeo, making at last a full circuit of the island. That that was where I was—upon an island—I had not till this moment considered. My two legs might take me from the Villa Visconti; but to leave Ischia. . . ?

Suddenly I understood the full dimension of the choice I had made. In leaving Ischia, I was leaving Niles. The last frayed fiber of the bond between us had parted, unperceived, and I was free— perfectly, appallingly free! For what use had I for freedom in a world such as I had come to understand, in which all creatures were ranged against each other in phalanxes of unappeasable appetite? Better a prisoner in some cell of blind, blithe domesticity! Yes, and what of all my brave talk to Mr. Mainwaring of faith and fortitude and how many wifely virtues else? Gone, vanished; it mattered naught! The choice had been made at some level of my being too deep for me to unmake it. If it were an immoral choice (as I believed it was) I did not care. It seemed regrettable that Niles, when he should learn that I was gone, would misconstrue my motives; it could not be helped. Passion was my excuse, and in this I resembled a myriad other faithless wives, with the difference that mine was rather a passion of fear than of love.

As I stood perplexed which way to turn, a mule-cart appeared far down the east branch of the road. I let this be my omen and turned in that direction. All the while that the cart, laden with grapes bound to the wine-press, drew near I could feel the gaze of the young countryman who guided it appraising me. No doubt from my dress of heavy mourning and our nearness to the Villa Visconti, he must have known I was the young Contessa, niece of the murdered Englishwoman, and so an object of legitimate curiosity. Yet when we passed each other he raised his cap and wished me a good-evening with a diffident courtesy that would have done credit to any nobleman.

So it was the entire distance that I walked. No one stared, though I must have made an odd little figure, in my bulky black dress and bonnet hung with heavy crepe, trudging resolutely along the dusty road towards no conceivable destination. No one spoke to me, or smiled, or showed me by any sign what I was so certain of at every step—that I was trespassing upon *their* world, that in all the complex bonds and knots of this island's society there was not one by which my own existence among them might be recognized and ratified. No doubt in my general unease I had exaggerated the real degree of my estrangement; yet I wonder if that may not have been a truer perception of our situation when we are travelling abroad than our usual assumption that the English are everywhere welcome and everywhere safe.

As the road went through the village of Casamicciola it took me past the dwelling of Monsignore Tabbi. Twice since my aunt's death he had called at the Villa; both times I had sent back his card to him without a message. When he had written, I destroyed his letter, unread. Having no one else I might blame for what had befallen Lydia, I had made the Abate my scapegoat, though by his own lights, I suppose, his actions had been above reproach, and even meritable, believing as he must that all Protestants were heretics and therefore damned through all eternity. So Niles had pleaded on his behalf, but I was intransigent against him, and he had ceased to call.

Now all my resentment and my rudeness were vanished, and I went up to his door as decisively as if it had been my whole purpose that day to pay a visit to him. No one answered to my knocking, and when I tried the door I found it locked. No matter; I would wait. When he came I would barter my forgiveness for a night's lodging and fare on the packet-boat. Fear makes us humble, too.

This improvisation might even have succeeded, had I been permitted to put it to the test, but after I had waited an hour outside Monsignore Tabbi's door, an elderly woman, who had been studying me from an upper window of the neighboring house, informed me that the Abate had departed Ischia a week ago and was not expected back before December.

Dusk was thickening to dark, for even on Ischia the days grow shorter as the summer wanes. Surely at this point I might have allowed myself to abandon my scruples for one evening and gone back to the Villa, if only to make a more rational preparation for my journey. But no, on that I was absolute. I would sooner have passed the night in an open field. Indeed, I was deliberating just this possibility when I bethought myself of the portmanteau that Rose had deposited at a house in the village. Even if she had obeyed me and retrieved the portmanteau, I might be able to send word to her through these people and she could bring my purse to me. But who were they? She had told me the name, but I could remember only that they lived opposite to one of Casamicciola's churches. There were three. The largest was Santo Spirito, which I had passed on the way, and which looked out over a small fleet of beached fishing craft to the open sea. There remained the little Baroque chapel of Santa Agnese and the still littler church of San Rocco. Opposite each of these were dwellings of almost identical character and size.

It was fully evening before I made up my mind. Choosing the house that faced San Rocco, as seeming friendlier, I introduced myself to the man who came to the door, as valiantly as any commercial traveller. He regarded me with the suspicion that an unannounced visit from an unknown Englishwoman at such an hour surely merited. I said that I believed he was acquainted with my maid. His eyes grew narrower; he said he could not remember. I suggested that she might have left a parcel with him a month or more before; which he would neither affirm nor deny, but only repeated the word I had used interrogatively: "*Uno pacco?*" Yet

I knew, from his intonation and the way his eyes avoided mine, that he understood me quite well. After enough practice one develops a good sense of when one is being lied to.

I decided to risk all on one cast of the die and ask, point-blank, what I had meant to come round to by degrees. Would he be able to have conveyed a message to my maid, in secret, while I waited within for her reply?

"Signora," he said, in honest perplexity, rubbing the stubble of his beard, "you must forgive me. What you ask is not possible. I am a little man, you understand? And your husband is very great." Then, with a valedictory smile of apology, he shut the door in my face.

I returned to the village street with nothing like that sinking of the spirit one might expect after one's last hope has been extinguished. True gamblers have assured me that a swift and spectacular loss can be, for a moment, as good a tonic as a mighty win, and perhaps this principle may be extended beyond the gaming table.

An urchin was sprawled on the single step of San Rocco, smoking a cigarette and contemplating me through the haze of it. No doubt I represented that evening's and may be (unless I flatter myself) that month's prime curiosity. I remember envying him the coolness and comfort of his rags and the probable fitness of his bare, blackened feet relative to my own, cramped in their stylish, buttoned boots, and taking these as the text for a short sermon to myself on the uses and benefits of adversity. Then, as I turned on my way, his face joined the populous limbo of strangers noticed and forgotten. He, however, was not ready to be dealt with so summarily, and some hundred yards later he was at my side to tell me that I had taken the wrong direction.

"Is this not the way to Ischia Porto?"

"Yes, Contessa, but you live at the Villa, which is—that way."

"And how are you—" I had replied with the formal *voi*, being unpracticed in the familiar *tu*, which my grammar book prescribed when an adult addresses children. But had my grammar had such a child as this in mind, with a cigarette pendulous from his upper lip and his little baritone voice so sedulously gruff and gravelly? I thought not. "How are you (*voi*) so certain where I live?"

"You're the new Contessa. Everyone knows that."

"Say that I am: may I not walk where I please?"

"Yes," he said, but so doubtfully and with such a look! If I had been the devil himself come to bargain for his young soul, he could not have been more guarded or more delighted.

He walked along at my side with the grave courtesy of children too soon required to be grown-ups. Some hundred or so yards down the road from where he had joined me, we passed the high wall of the *terme* of the Acqua del Fornello, and my escort informed me that we had come to the end of the village.

"Yes, I see that. But I must keep going."

"To Ischia Porto?"

"Have *you* never walked that far?"

"Oh yes, but. . . ." He shrugged and smiled with virile self-deprecation. "For a man it is not the same."

"How long will it take me to walk there?"

"At this pace, most of the night, I think. And the road is very lonely."

Lonely it might well have been, had I been alone, but my young friend seemed minded to put me under his protection. He did not say how far he meant to accompany me, nor did I ask. We spoke as little as two strangers sharing a compartment on a railway carriage, but this was the silence, on both our parts, of shyness rather than of suspense. Never for a moment did it occur to me to suppose that he acted from any motives but kindness and a natural curiosity.

After a while the moon came up, gibbous, its silvery features distinct as the profile on a new-minted coin. The sea stroked the narrow beach, and sighed and foamed, and deep below, the soothed Typhoeus slumbered in his chains. Some times late travellers would pass us, going towards Casamicciola, and raise their hats, and wish us a good-evening. For each such greeting I felt as grateful as if it were a solemn benediction specifically invoked to stead me on my way, and I would stride on a little more briskly.

When, to judge by the height the moon had climbed to in the sky, it was nearly nine o'clock, Giuseppe (which was my escort's name) made me stop and sit upon a whitewashed boulder. I obeyed gratefully, for my legs and every part of me were protesting against these unaccustomed exertions.

"You will wait here," Giuseppe said, in a tone of natural authority, "and I will return—soon."

He scrambled down some rocks forming a natural staircase on
the seaward side of the road, and a moment later I heard his tiny
baritone issuing new commands, which met a various medley of
objections, but all spoken so rapidly in the dialect of Ischia that I
could not tell their import. Giuseppe, however, carried the day
and returned momently with what he had been demanding: a
flask of wine, a glass, and a plate of bread and pungent goat's-milk
cheese. I balanced the plate upon my knees and held the glass while
Giuseppe poured from the flask.

Thirst and gratitude made of that first taste of the warm wine
something transcendent. Even the second taste was wonderfully
delicious, and with the third I emptied the glass.

"The bread is dry," Giuseppe said apologetically, speaking
slowly and with a conscious effort to tune his accent to mine. "But
it was all they had. I looked."

"Won't you join me?"

"Thank you, I've eaten."

"Some wine, at least."

"So you are not alone, a drop. They would not trust me with a
second glass. Enough!"

"It was kind of them to give us this. I'm most grateful."

"They would not believe me at first. Then they sent up the
little girl, Amalia. You didn't see her?"

"No. This cheese is excellent. Are you sure you won't. . . ."

"Perhaps a crumb. The wine is harsh, I think?"

"I thought it delicious."

"Time will improve it, even so." He poured a second glass for
me, and I sipped it with a mellow appreciation of the coolness of
the evening, the kindness of strangers, and the way the moonlight
filtered through the long needles of an umbrella pine.

After Giuseppe had conveyed the emptied dishes and my full
thanks to our unseen hosts, we set off once again towards Ischia
Porto. Giuseppe gathered courage as we went along and put questions to me, each chosen after prolonged and solemn deliberation, as
if they were wishes and, in consequence, not lightly to be asked.
How many jewels did I have and how did I wear them? Did I like
to walk on the river when it froze? And did I like the Queen of

England? He seemed skeptical when I told him in neither case had I the experience by which to know my preferences. I supposed, though, that I should be quite fearful walking across the ice, and he thought he should be as well. As for the Queen, I said she was to the last degree admirable but so far above our stations that liking and disliking could not enter in; a notion that, with my little Italian, took me from one hilltop to the next properly to convey, from which new vantage, to my astonishment, the dark cirque of Ischia's crater-harbor could be seen in the distance, ringing a silvery disc of sea. I was delighted but a little disconcerted, too, since I had got used to the idea of passing the night tramping down the road, while now I must begin to consider loitering about the quay instead.

The nearer we approached the town, the more earnest became my escort's questioning. Did I like Ischia and would I ever come back? (I had not told him I was leaving!) Did I like Garibaldi? Did I believe in God? For his own part, he informed me, he was a free-thinker, but this must be a secret strictly between the two of us, for if it became too generally known, his mother would learn of it and it would surely break her heart.

On the outskirts of the town Giuseppe once again left me to confer at the doorway of one of the houses facing the road. He returned to say that the lady of the house had agreed to put me up for the evening. I protested that I had no means to repay her for her hospitality.

"That does not matter, Contessa. You will remember her possibly another time, and in any case it is a privilege to be of service to so beautiful and distinguished a lady." This pretty compliment was accompanied by a bow as nicely executed as one might find in any grand hotel or royal court of Europe. "Now I must take my leave of you, though, for I will be expected at home."

"Oh dear, must you return at once the long way we have come? Of course, if you must. You've been so kind to me, Giuseppe. I shall not forget." I felt in my pocket for something I might offer as a memento. There was only a crumpled handkerchief that my aunt had hemmed and embroidered. Giuseppe accepted it as though it were the Order of the Garter.

He pointed inquiringly to the letter *C*.

"That is for 'Clara.' My name."

"Would you. . . ?" He removed the string that went round his neck and vanished under his rag of a shirt. A square scrap of cloth was stitched to the string. I accepted this with due deference and held it close up to see if there were any word or emblem on it to hint of its significance. "It was blessed by the archbishop," he explained, "and it's very lucky."

"Then it is just the thing for me." I undid my bonnet strings, removed my bonnet, and put on the scapular (for such it was). "Thank you a thousand times."

I held out my hand, meaning him to shake it, but this was too mild a farewell for the gallant boy, who pressed a respectful, tender kiss on the hand I had offered him. Then, with an impulse of shyness as sudden as his kiss, he bolted off without a word and vanished into the night.

CHAPTER SIXTEEN

Apprehension

THE PACKET-BOAT DEPARTED the mainland at dawn, docked for an hour at Ischia, and then crossed the bay southeastwards to the island of Capri, before it returned to its nightly berth in the harbor of Santa Lucia, an itinerary that describes a triangle of roughly equal sides. Had tourism been so extensive in the year 1865 as it has since become, so that there had been separate boats plying to each island, my tale might well have taken, like the boat as it sailed from Ischia Porto, a very different turning, but whether for better or worse I would not hazard a guess.

Having learned from Giuseppe simply to take what I needed, I boarded *La Sirena d'Ischia* with neither ticket nor means to purchase one. Such was the power (thought I) of blatant self-assertion that the ticket collector never even approached me. I stayed within the first-class cabin on the upper deck all the time we waited at the dock and while we sailed out of the harbor and around the Castello at the island's eastern end, but once Ischia was fairly behind us and the sharp facets of Epomeo were blurred by distance to a uniform lavender-blue, I went out on the deck to taste my freedom in the spray the wind lifted from the waves and to feel it in the rolling and plunging of the boards underfoot.

A hand in a glove of soft gray kid appeared by mine upon the railing. Except that no other person might have presumed upon me so, Niles did nothing else outwardly to declare his dominion over me; yet had he placed shackles on my wrists I would not have felt the meaning of that hand next to mine more acutely. My new-fledged freedom withered fast as a flower that falls upon a bed of glowing embers.

"I am so glad," he began (when that flower was quite reduced to ash), "that we are at last going to Capri. I cannot think how many times I must have urged it. Nothing equals the Blue Grotto in loveliness. Addison goes on about it, Fenimore Cooper goes on about it, Lamartine goes on about it, and we all do go on about it, because. . . . Well, you shall see, Clara. Words are inadequate."

I was too dismayed to deal with Niles as I was dealt with by him, but I felt just as unable to speak from my heart while he regarded me from behind this cold, comedic mask.

When he had tired of observing me in the pillory of this silence, he asked: "Did you leave a note for me at the Villa? No? I would have thought I merited at least that much farewell. At first, seeing you on the dock, I supposed that you'd come down to welcome me, but then, as the boat drew closer, it was harder to take that cheery view, for you looked very unwelcoming. And not a little bedraggled, I might add, though that is by the by. What *are* your intentions, if I may be so bold?"

"I haven't thought beyond this minute, Niles."

"Mainwaring's out of town, you know. Since he had called at the Villa, I thought I might return the compliment. But when I at last discovered his very modest lodgings in Resina, a serving-girl informed me that he'd gone off with his aunt and some visitors to look at the ruins at Paestum, and thence to Amalfi."

"It was not to him I was going, though perhaps I might have come to that."

"If not to him, where did you purpose to go?"

"To the British Consul. Anywhere. I really can't say."

"You came away without luggage? Without even a purse? How would you have dealt with the ticket collector if I hadn't been on board?"

To none of these questions could I make any answer more coherent than a distracted sigh.

"You've been at loggerheads with my mother—is that it? It was inevitable, given your two characters. But you must come in out of the sun, for my skin's sake if not your own. Come within the cabin. We have it to ourselves, and the steward will be bringing up a lunch for us, which I ordered when I saw that we'd be crossing to Capri. I see it's no brief tale."

I let myself be led within the cabin, where Niles continued to soothe away my initial constriction of fright with such smooth, pleasant patter, like rain falling on a pane of glass, which one listens to intently, not for its sense but for the feeling of calm and regularity its rhythms can impart. After a while, I was able to describe, if not explain, the events of the previous day.

"And is it just the Villa then?" Niles asked, when I had concluded.

I shook my head helplessly. How was I to answer? It was the Villa, yes, but it was, as well, Lydia's death; it was an hundred particular slights and as many nebulous fears; it was Niles' falseness, his coldness, his all but entire absence. And it was much more than all these summed together.

"Forgive me, Clara. Of course it is not so simple a matter as being 'just the Villa,' nor am I so simple as to think so. The habit is so engrained of twisting words to my convenience that even when I mean to be candid I keep at my old ways. But please credit that I *would* be."

"Candid to what end, Niles? I don't blame you. I don't blame myself. Only, I can't go on."

"God knows, Clara, you might blame me many times over, and yet it's not so I may beat my breast and cover my head with ashes that I beg to be heard out. It's because"—he smiled and hunched up his shoulders, bending his well-padded morning coat into an awkward shape—"I love you. Make of that what you will."

"Niles, I can't go back to the Villa. I can't."

"Nor shall I ask you to. After what has happened in these

months just passed, it is a wholly understandable aversion, and indeed, I share it. But the world is full of habitable dwellings, and there are few we can't make our own, if we should fancy them. But there I am, galloping off into another daydream! Let me explain, Clara. I ask no more than that. An afternoon, while we take a carriage about Capri. If it is to be a parting, then let us try to make it an affectionate one. I ask not for my sake—although, of course, I do—but for yours. You should know very well that if you act too impulsively now, even allowing your impulse to be right, that next week or next year your conscience will eat you alive. And then, as I said before, you have never seen the Blue Grotto."

This seemed so extraneous a consideration that despite myself I had to laugh. "Nor yet the Pyramids, Niles, nor the Great Wall of China!"

"Well, you may laugh, but it *is* sublime. You'll see—or you won't, if that's your choice."

I consented to see the Blue Grotto and hear Niles' explanations, and he, having gained his point, was content to pass the hour remaining of our voyage in rapt contemplation of the island we were approaching.

Like Helen and Cleopatra, Capri is notorious for its beauty, but even so I wondered that Niles could be so insistent to have me for a listener and then break off talking the moment I said I would hear him out. Yet as we came nearer I had to admit the justice of his silence. Viewed against the majesty of those cliffs that soar up from the waves at a single sheer bound, all human words and most human feelings seem vanities unworthy of notice or expression. Ischia is a mountain set in the sea; Capri is the blunt, broad massif, abrupt and unbelievable and utterly unhuman, such as a climber might come to as the reward of a day's exertions, but which we moved towards with no more effort than the eagle that rides the currents of the air home to his high eyrie.

As the boat glides into the tiny harbor, roofs and trees and varied signs of commerce establish a scale in which mere mortals in hats and bonnets can again exist, and by the time one has stepped from the quaking gangplank to the grimy deck, one is thumbing one's Baedeker in search of the glowing paragraph that originally propelled one to this remote, uncomfortable place, where one is cautioned against the food and lodgings, where a dozen giant flies have already lighted on one's veil and a dozen giant boatmen are clamoring for the privilege of rowing one to the *Grotta Azzura.*

For the enchantments of that faerie place, however, I must refer my readers either to the Baedeker or the boatmen aforesaid, for I was never to see it. Niles had hired a little donkey-drawn cart to take us round to a beach close by the entrance to the Grotto. This route, though more time-consuming, promised to be less arduous than the director, seaward way. However, after a strenuous zig-zag climb, when we had reached the upper road traversing the island east and west, Niles ordered the carter (who trudged ahead of us, carrying the traces of his beasts) to take us to the Villa Jovis. Even with my little knowledge of Capri's geography, I knew this destination to be at odds with that first stated, and I wondered aloud why, after all Niles had said, we were not to go to the Blue Grotto.

"I must confess, Clara, that I set out deliberately to deceive you. Let us hope for the last time. My lie was intended for Manfredo, who was on the boat with us and who, I strongly suspect (and, indeed, I know), was on the deck below ours, and later outside the cabin, listening to all we said. There was no way I could mislead him as to our destination without, for the time being, misleading you as well."

"And you allow that? To a servant?"

"There is very little I *can* refuse Manfredo, if he means to have it. It would be nearer the truth to say that I'm his servant rather than that he's mine. There have been times, indeed, when I could have wished to be treated with *that* much dignity."

"But *how* did you let him gain such an unnatural ascendancy over you?" I insisted.

"Unnatural, Clara? Not at all: Manfredo is my older brother. My half-brother, strictly speaking."

"You mean . . . your father . . . ?"

"Not my father, darling. He's Zaide's, sired by the great poet. You heard the story from our mother's lips, all but the tag-end, for she had shame enough to keep from proclaiming her complete disgrace."

"I could never understand why she should have told as much as she did. If, as you say, she is capable of shame."

"Because she is proud, too. Not that Manfredo is much to be proud of. Once, indeed, he was handsome, but now even his looks have left him. But were he a clubfoot like his father, and an imbecile besides, it would not have altered the case that she had had him by the best-acclaimed stallion in the whole stud of Europe. It was a time unlike ours that formed my mother's character, when maiden modesty was not the *sine qua non* that it is for us."

"I've understood that, Niles, and made allowance."

"As have I these many years, which, among other errors, has helped to shape me into the false, misformed creature that I am."

I reached for his hand, which fled from my touch as though by its own volition; but mine pursued and grasped it and offered a wordless contradiction of his self-reproaches.

"Clara, please!" he protested, pulling free. "You don't know. You can't imagine. The rottenness within! The way it grows and spreads!"

"But to have seen that, and to repent it, and amend—"

"Ah, if it *were* that simple! But the corruption stains the flesh as well as the spirit, and worst of all, corrodes the will. When I speak with you I think myself a saint; but when I am with *him*, I become another person, and I *want* what he tempts me to, and nothing else seems worth the having."

"Then put temptation from you. Send him away."

"I have tried to, Clara. Oh, the sums I've offered him, the pledges of money that has come from your inheritance. He is glad enough to spend it, but he won't be satisfied, I fear now, with less than all. He has always been jealous of me—jealous, rather, of the accident of my legitimacy (for I will grant him that it's only that). For me, for my person, he has only contempt."

"Why need you bargain with him? Command him to go!"

"I have—so many times it has become a kind of joke between us. First, I recall, was when I was fourteen. He had accompanied me to Oxford. We quarrelled, I ordered him away, and he left me for three weeks—until the purse I'd sent him off with was empty."

"Even then he had such a hold on you?"

"He knows me, Clara. He has known me for over twenty years. There is not a weakness in my character, not a blemish on my skin, that is not familiar to him, and which he has not some time exploited."

"Your mother understands and tolerates this?"

"And encourages it. It is why she set him over me originally. To mold my character."

"To corrupt you!" I burst out, with no regard for the implication.

But Niles did not take offense. "She would not like to hear it said, but doesn't it amount to that? Oh, it seemed quite innocent when I was a lad of ten. We made a cozy family, the three of us, and that my dashing so-much-older brother should play the part before the world of my valet seemed no wickedness, only a kind of game of pretending, in which I had the flattering role of being master to a servant whom else *I* must obey! Where was the harm of it?"

This was not a question requiring an answer from my lips, and so for a considerable while we pursued our several thoughts to the steadying cadence of the donkeys' slow ascent.

"There is so much to tell you, Clara," Niles resumed. "And I do mean to, though it will be painful both in the telling and the hearing. But first we must ask ourselves—what are we to do?"

I looked at him in perplexity; a look Niles answered with a complaisant smile that perplexed me all the more.

"Well, well—you think I run ahead of you. In fact, my dear, it's you who are too fast for me. You've *decided* what to do, and as usual your instinct has been right. To escape! So the question is not *what* to do, but whether you will let me do it with you."

"I should say the question of what to do very much remains with us."

"The immediate problem is to take our leave of Manfredo without his witting of it. Which, if we take this cart to the little harbor on the southern shore, can be accomplished with relative ease by the hiring of a small craft to convey us across the strait to Sorrento. Then, as directly as we may, to Australia! Well, Clara?"

I shook my head, less in refusal than regret.

Niles understood me. "Yes, I know. If only we'd come to this a month ago."

"When you asked me if I would go away with you. . . ."

"And you asked me if you *must*. I should have insisted yes."

"I would have obeyed you, Niles."

"But I lacked the strength. Even now, the strength and will to act have been yours. But is that wrong? How may the weak become strong except they share the strength of those who have it in excess?"

"My strength, Niles? It is very small."

"Only if you say it is. Call it great and you shall feel it grow."

"Oh, it might suffice to carry us to the antipodes, but what is great in that except the fear? Now that I know a little better your situation and your motives, it seems all the more suspect a solution. If we went to Australia to create a new, better life for ourselves, then . . . perhaps. But if it is only to *escape!*"

"If I told you *all*, Clara, you would not be so harsh."

"Which is to say that you mean still to keep me in darkness and tell me only what it's convenient I should know? No, Niles, I can't live so. What is there so terrible that my imaginings aren't worse?"

"Yes, yes—you're right, of course," he said, as sullenly as if it were an accusation. Then, more cautiously, "What *have* you imagined?"

"I have been to your studio and seen your paintings there. You must know that."

"Yes, I was told so."

"By Polly?"

He smiled. "So you know of Polly?"

"Only her name, and what you tell of her in your paintings."

"You shall leave me nothing to confess for myself. 'Thou turn'st mine eyes into my very soul; and there I see such black and grainèd spots as will not leave their tinct,' as the Queen remarks to Hamlet."

"I believe she says that after she has asked him to speak no more about her sins."

"Well, but that wasn't *my* implication. Proceed, proceed! Lay me out flat!"

His lightness provoked me—his smile that seemed to mock at

his own guilt, as though it were no more than a suit of clothes that fit him absurdly rather than a disfigurement of his essential self—and his nonchalance, even at such a moment as this, as though all moral actions were to be viewed as landscapes, something one passed through briefly and regarded with more or less approbation, and then forgot, except as it might provide matter for some future conversation. I resolved to tell him what he could not smile away.

"I know that you were never Renata's husband, any more than you've been mine. And this is no mere surmise of mine—I've read it in her own words, which she entrusted to me at Blackthorne. For years I resisted reading those pages. Now that I have, my regret must be that I did not read them soon enough to have helped her."

"Or, at the least, soon enough to have helped yourself?"

"I would be false if I denied it. Have *you* no regrets?"

"A lifetime's. But what became of this damning document?"

"As to that, you're quite safe. I've burned it."

"But why?"

"Because I believed it my duty."

"To protect me? Would it have been so damaging?"

"Yes, though I'm no lawyer, I think it would."

"Did you ever discuss what you read? With your aunt, or with Mainwaring?"

"I came near to doing so, but always held back."

"Never even threw out a hint? Never a 'Well, well, we know,' or a 'We could, an if we would'?"

"No, never a hint. Though I did bring Mainwaring to your studio. But only when he had come on purpose to tell me what those paintings already had revealed."

"And what *did* he tell you?"

"That he had seen you in Naples."

"Surely he was more particular than that."

"He found you in compromising circumstances, I was led to suppose."

"And when he saw the paintings—what did he say then?"

"You mean, did he admire them? No, I'm afraid he was a rather severe critic. He said you painted evil as though it were a bouquet."

"That's sound Ruskinism, but not exactly what I meant."

"I said I wished to know nothing more particular, and he respected my wish. Was that your meaning?"

He replied with a look from which all trace of smiling was expunged, but said no more. Having achieved my aim of shaming him into seriousness, I was content to share his silence.

At the foot of a steeper gradient, the track we had been following changed its nature from rough but continuous roadway to broad, cobbled steps, and the carter gave us the choice of walking on the rest of way ourselves or riding the unharnessed donkeys up these *gradino*. I said I would prefer the exercise, and, after Niles had addressed some words aside to the carter, we set off on foot for the Villa Jovis.

Centuries of exposure to the elements and plunderers have robbed Tiberius' famed palace of its grandeur, but even the residue of bare-bone masonry has power to impress, if only by its extent. It rises above its encompassing vineyards in tier upon tier of tumbled walls and shattered arches, obscured by the conquering grass and broom, shadowed and humbled by tall Aleppo pines.

"Shall we see the cliff from which he threw his prisoners?" I asked.

"Il Salto? Yes, it is only a little farther. We are on the path."

CHAPTER SEVENTEEN

Il Salto

As one approaches the precipice, a wind gently and steadily rises from that abyss, curling over the sudden edge to stir the grass and caress the long, drooping needles of the pines. It seems a suspiration of the vast Tyrrhenian itself, the last, sublime reminder of the waves that break against the rocks seven hundred feet below. A thousand and a thousand and again a thousand years of human turmoil and consequence dissolve into a single panorama of shining bay and shadowed land and high-drifting cloud, as though one could take in all of history in a glance. There, to the south, at the very limits of vision, are the Doric temples of Paestum; and there, almost as far to the north, the ancientest of Italy's cities, Phoenician Cumae, where Aeneas landed, and Hannibal fought, and Petronius Arbiter feasted and died. Between these, towering, Vesuvius presides and prevails, the admiration and the terror of all who live under his wide and timeless empire.

Here we came and stood, and here I told my husband the last secrets I had withheld from him. I told him that Renata had accused him of desiring her death. I told him what she had written of Manfredo's persecutions, and of what more than these I had surmised concerning the true parentage of Clara Maria. This last he admitted by a tacit lowering of his eyes, not guiltily, but as we turn away from a pain too large for our pity to comprehend.

Elsewise, he never flinched nor looked aside. When I had finished, he was silent a long time, as though searching in my eyes for accusations still unspoken. When he seemed satisfied that I had disburdened myself of all, he said, "My dear, you are being either foolish or cruel. I don't know which fault in you could more surprise me."

"I have said nothing, Niles, that has been untrue or unconsidered."

"No, of course not. But you have brought me to such a place as *this* to say it. To Il Salto! What! Did you think I would push you off the edge? Or that I'd play the part of another Tiberius, and after entertaining myself by torturing you I would command you to leap?"

"It was *I* who brought *you* here?"

"Yes, and planted us on this dizzy brink and then tempted me to do my murderous worst. Don't shake your head. It was the meaning in your eyes, Clara, all while you spoke. I saw it there— the challenge!"

"You saw pain, I know, and doubt. But the only challenge I intended was to return me your candor for my own."

"What would you have me *say*, Clara? Do you want the whole long wavering history of *my* suspicions? Whether my brother is a murderer? Whether the mother that I love has known this and has helped him to conceal his guilt from me? Whether he means to kill you? Whether he means to kill me? All this I have speculated on, yes, but I kept my doubts hidden from you, because. . . ." His voice quavered, its timbre altering and pitch rising under the pressure of high feeling. "Because I love them, Clara. And because I love you as well. I have tried to reconcile those twain, and at last I see that I have failed. But there was one doubt I never had until today. I never doubted your love."

"My love, Niles? I don't know what love is any more, or where to search for it. Fear? Yes, I could show you that. And bitterness, and several kinds of pain. And a great confusion of words that I wander in when I'm alone. May be love is one of those, but I know it isn't here, where others claim it is."

I took his hand and placed it on my heart. When I could feel that warmth resting there, tears started to my eyes, contradicting all that I had just said. With his other hand Niles wiped them away, and I watched him at this task through all the tears that flowed, as though it were some solemn task assigned him to do and me to supervise, an endless counting and sorting of glass beads.

When the last was blotted away, Niles kissed me. I felt the kindness of those lips against my own almost as a kind of burning, as a thing to fear. Indeed, there was some cause to fear, for those minutes of crying had put all the muscles of my body into a state of tremulous weakness, which, though a wonderful relief from the knotted tension I had felt before, was a condition altogether inappropriate to where I found myself.

Without my asking, Niles led me from the edge of the precipice to a glade near at hand, where the pines and the uppermost slope of the Villa Jovis formed a kind of natural atrium, enclosed all round but open to the sky. Here he sat beside me on a low mound of grass-grown masonry, and held me, and was silent.

Even this far removed from the cliff, one could hear the susurrus of the wind, steady and unvarying as the spring of a timepiece. The sky began to darken, and through the boles of the pines I watched Vesuvius vanish into a mass of golden clouds.

At the first evidence of night's approach, Niles said he must go off to make certain that our carter was still waiting below and would continue to. I knew he wanted to compose his thoughts, and so, though I dreaded to be left alone, when he asked if I wished to go with him, I refused.

"Not yet," I said, as though that choice were mine.

CHAPTER EIGHTEEN
A Prayer and Its Answer

FROM THE MOMENT THAT HE, on the deck of *La Sirena d'Ischia*, espied me waiting on the quay, it seems probable that Manfredo was resolved to put aside his hesitations and murder me with no more ado. What later, as the boat crossed the bay to Capri, he may have overheard me say to Niles would only have confirmed what my solitary presence had clearly enough foretokened—that my despair had waxed to the full and I was abandoning the role of Contessa and resuming the honester character of a Miss. Manfredo, though caring nothing for these nice distinctions, knew that in resuming my old name I must resume my fortune as well, and this he would go to any length to prevent.

Even so, Niles' precaution of misstating our destination almost had its desired effect, for when he had seen us set off in our cart, Manfredo left the packet-boat and immediately commenced bargaining with one of the assembled boatmen to be taken to the Blue Grotto. He had even stepped into the fellow's boat, when some last-minute misgiving caused him to change his mind. Perhaps it was no more than a consideration of the likely publicity of any encounter in the spot to which all Capri's visitors first resort.

So one may speculate. This much is known with certainty— that he followed us by land instead, asking along the way whether an English milord and lady had lately passed by. When, taking the westward branch of the road that leads to the *Grotta Azzura*, these inquiries produced only puzzlement and denials, Manfredo realized he had been deceived. With that realization his purpose must have become more settled than it had been before.

Reaching the base of the *gradino*, which we had climbed on

foot, he discovered the carter stretched out in his own cart, awaiting our return. Manfredo roused him and ordered him away, saying that his passengers had decided to return to the lower town without his aid, and when Manfredo had added a certain weight of silver to his request, the carter did as he was bidden.

What, if any, Manfredo may have heard of my conversation with Niles as we stood on the edge of Il Salto cannot be known. Perhaps he did not discover us until we had withdrawn into the glade of pines. Certainly he was at hand when Niles took leave of me, for it was only a moment later that he emerged from the dense shrub of myrtle back of which he had concealed himself.

Seeing him, I rose. He stopped where he was. There was, as there had always been between us, an exquisite and instant understanding each of the other. The ordinary obscurity of human motives was illuminated as by a lighting flash. I knew his nature, and hated it. I foresaw his purpose, and dreaded it. What he saw in that moment I cannot with the same authority declare, but what it was provoked a smile—not, like Niles', ironical, but such as an epicure might smile in view of a well-laid table, the conscious relishing of a hunger soon to be appeased.

He bowed to me. "My Lady must forgive me if I have startled her."

"Not at all."

He approached some paces nearer and halted. "The Count your husband bids me to say that he is waiting for you to join him. I am to show you the way." To deliver this arrant lie, he struck a stance of calculated insolence, feet spread wide apart, hands grasping either end of a heavy walking-stick, his tall silk hat tilted to the side. In the arrogation of such items of dress, as well as by the cut and costliness of all else he wore, he evidenced the final stage of a months-long metamorphosis. Nothing could be detected now of the former valet except the noticeable absence of a gentleman behind these assembled tokens of gentility; that, and the pretense which he still maintained—doubtless, for his private delectation—of treating "My Lady" with something like respect.

How far, I wondered, would Niles have gone along the path? Too far, I was certain, for him to have heard me if I yielded to my fear and cried out for help. Was that not why Manfredo lingered now, cat-like, teasing me—so as to make me declare my fear? Then I would not.

"Very well," I replied. "But first please to fetch my parasol for me. I have left it by the look-out."

"My Lady is mistaked. She had no parasol with her today."

"The word is 'mistaken,' and it's you who mistakes. I came with a parasol and left it . . . just there." Despite that it represented a diminution of my Lady's full dignity, I pointed to the imagined parasol.

After a moment's hesitation, he strode off towards the precipice. I had judged him rightly: he was too proud to be the first to abandon his own game of cat-and-mouse.

When he had nearly passed outside the circle of pines, I set forth in the contrary direction. He stopped, as, after some few more precious steps, did I. Every inch that I could put between us now, while we yet maintained the forms of civility, was of vital importance. So nations use the remaining interval of peace to exchange diplomatic messages all the while they deploy their armies at each other's borders.

"Well?" I asked, facing round. Not more than twenty yards separated us. It would not be enough.

"If my Lady will wait—"

"To what purpose? I know the way, and Niles, you say, requires me." With all I could muster of a regal indifference, I turned my back on him and continued towards the path, nor did I, even as I left the glade and broke into a run, once look back.

Running, I could not hear if I were pursued, but I knew it as surely as every hare that has been coursed or woodcock flushed from covert. If only I had shared, as well, such powers of flight! But all I wore seemed made on purpose to impede me—my wide and weighty skirts, my buttoned boots with their small unsteady heels, my bonnet's flaring brim that let me see only what lay immediately ahead. Worse than these was the body within them, so un-sinewed by a lack of exercise that scarce had I reached the first turning of the path before I was gasping—and all uselessly, for I was laced too tightly in my dress properly to draw the air into my lungs.

Yet I had got this far and still was running! And farther, to where the path diverged. Downwards it led by many windings through the lower levels of the Villa Jovis to the broad cobbled steps of the *gradino*, the upward path went only a little way and stopped before the massive base of an ancient lighthouse. Certain that, if I trusted only to my feet, Manfredo must soon overtake me, I chose the latter way, though first I pulled my bonnet off and flung it down the path I did not take. A crude deceit, perhaps, but it succeeded. While I lay beside the path, only half hidden by the prickling branches of a juniper, I saw Manfredo snatch up the false spoor. He let out a cry of mingled delight and threat, as a huntsman halloos when his quarry comes in view.

The shattered lighthouse occupied the whole summit of this spur of land and offered little more concealment than the fire-screen that Clara Maria was used to hide behind. Yet where was I to go? To return to Il Salto and its glade would be an inconceivable folly; to follow after Manfredo a larger one.

The answer lay before me, across a brief wilderness of broom and myrtle, in the deep-shadowed mazes of the Villa Jovis. What the architect of that labyrinth had neglected to provide for my concealment the gathering twilight would supply, and to it I hastened down the trackless hillside, which to my right merged by imperceptible degrees of steepness into the sheer face of the cliff. Leftwards, too, the land fell away, less precipitately, but filled with a danger no less grave, for somewhere in that terrain, unseen, Manfredo must have paused in his pursuit and taken thought and known that I had eluded him. Now he would be seeking out a prominence from which he might scan the hill behind him for some sight of me while yet a little light remained.

Reaching the Villa Jovis, I took refuge behind the first shard of masonry that rose up high enough to conceal me. My relief was short-lived, for though I could not be seen by one coming the way I had fled, from other angles, and especially from the higher levels of the Villa, I was all too visible. So, reluctantly, and quailing at each footstep lest I disturb the debris I walked through, I retreated to those upper levels along a ramp that some times became a narrow canyon, some times lost itself in an acre of maquis, according as the circumjacent walls had survived or lay strewn upon my path.

For a while I hid behind an extant doorway in a room still vaulted over, but the very darkness covering me became a source of dread. The terror of waiting in uncertainty grew to surpass the terror of active flight, and so again I fled. Often, encountering a cul-de-sac, I would be obliged to retrace my steps until I found a staircase by which I might mount to the next level, until by these random means I reached the heart of the maze and summit of the hill. Far off, across the blackness of the bay, the streets of Naples glowed with a dim, gas-lit refulgence. In the other direction, as few and distinct as the stars that could be discerned at this last violet pause before absolute night (and seeming as far away and alien), shone the lights of Capri. Kneeling and clasping the trunk of a pine so as to become a single shadow with it, I scanned the labyrinth through which I had just come, but the darkness I invoked to protect me concealed my pursuer, if he were there, as well, nor could I hear any sound except the familiar bleating chorus of the cicadas.

As before, the suspense of waiting overcame my better wisdom, and I left my vantage point at the foot of the tree and crossed the level summit to the seaward edge, where a rude unwindowed hut offered an illusion of greater security. Crouching low, I made my way to its door, which stood ajar, inviting and then insisting. I went within.

The feeblest of rush-lights revealed a crucifix upon the rough-hewn block of the altar, as well as a statue of the Virgin Mary, who (though of this fact I then was ignorant), under the name of Santa Maria del Soccorso—Our Lady of Perpetual Help—was the name-saint of this shrine. But these signs that my chosen sanctuary was literally such I failed at first to recognize amid a contradictory clutter of homelier artifacts, baskets and shovels and faggots of wood, which gave it the appearance, much more, of a common gardening shed.

When I saw where my flight had brought me, all my fears transformed themselves into a sudden blaze of superstitious hope. I prayed then—not to the God I had worshipped heretofore, the One Supreme Being, but to the fly-specked idol of this shrine, who held out her little arms as though to receive me in them. I knelt to her and implored her, with tears and whispers, to keep me hidden, to save me, to let me live. I remembered the scapular I had been given on the night before and drew it from my dress, as though it were a pledge she must honor. I kissed her plaster hands and feet and promised her a lifetime's devotion if she would preserve me from my enemy.

How much time was occupied in this self-abasement I do not know. Perhaps the blaze was brief as bundled thorns, perhaps it lasted as long as a stout log, but when it had died down to a smoldering anguish indeterminate between hope and dread, I heard footsteps approaching the chapel. I sought to hide myself behind the altar-stone, but in doing so my skirt brushed against one of the ranked implements and sent it clattering on the floor. The footsteps paused—and recommenced more slowly. I could not move nor breathe. The door opened, and at the sight of him, holding high his stick, I screamed. The sound of it seemed to issue not from my throat and lungs only, but from every part of me at once, as though I might transform myself into one great reverberating roar of denial that I was here and this was happening. For a moment, he stood frozen on the threshold. Then, as I drew breath to scream again, he turned and fled in terror.

Too late I realized it was not Manfredo. I picked up the stick he had dropped in his panic flight, a pine branch all gluey with pitch where I had touched it. The man I scared off was the tender of the lighthouse fire, a hermit who had lived the last thirty years on this hillside and who was supported in this life of eccentric piety by the islanders in gratitude for his service in keeping the lighthouse beacon burning through the night. It was to kindle his rude flambeau at the altar's rush-light that he had come to the chapel, just as he came every night at the first hour of darkness. Santa Maria del Soccorso had indeed heard my prayer, and even answered it, and all her help I had wasted in a breath.

I had not long to wait before the entire consequence of my error was manifest. The same outcry by which I had frightened off a potential rescuer had, as surely as if it were meant to signal him, advertised my whereabouts to Manfredo; who now appeared by the tree where I had stood, a gasping shadow, winded by his long and, till now, fruitless search through the length and breadth and height of the Villa Jovis.

Not knowing where, I ran from him. The plateau of the summit left off and became a slope steep as a mansard roof. At every step, the earth crumbled away from my foot, and I half-clambered, half-tumbled down the dark hillside in a self-avalanche of indefinite extent. Even as I scrambled thus, my face was pelted by the dirt and stones Manfredo loosed in his no less abrupt descent. At last my body lodged against a stump of wall, back of which there was a sharp drop to the next terrace fifteen or twenty feet below. I picked myself up and ran beside this wall at a lamed, stumbling gait, for the heel had been torn off my right boot in my long slide down the hill. The wall I followed varied in its height, some times towering over me, some times not there at all. Once I tripped, and when I was on my feet again, his hand was on my shoulder. I tore loose, screaming. He struck me with his fist, and I collapsed against the wall, but it was not there, only a void through which I fell still screaming, as though I would defy even the elements that had betrayed me.

The ground's impact took my breath away, but in another moment, as much in wonder I was still alive as in terror of Manfredo, I had begun to scream again. He, with a curse that was as well a groan of exertion, grappled a great block of mortared rubble from the ground beside the wall. I saw him strain to raise it over his head, but this proved beyond his strength. Though I perceived his intention, horror paralyzed me and I could only watch, supine, the great mass of it swing backwards in his cradled arms and then, released, drop through the blackness.

When it hit the ground, I felt my body lifted up and smashed down again, like a doll tossed into a toy-box, but still I lived to feel that pain and to know I had been spared. The block of tufa had buried itself in the ground beside me, crushing my skirts and crinolines beneath it. I pushed at its resisting mass without the least effect.

Manfredo regarded my futile efforts from his natural balcony directly overhead and laughed at the spectacle of my ideal helplessness. "My Lady," he called out, quite gaily. "My Lady, O listen! I want to tell you . . . what I will do now."

Has there ever been a prisoner brought before the bar of justice, however defiant otherwise, who will not be silent for the reading of his sentence? I ceased struggling against the block that pinned me to the earth, and in the stillness following that cessation I felt. . . .

What can never be named, for it is an absence of sensation, a nullity. Just as joy that is too intense may lead to tears, so there is a fear that passes beyond the spirit's reach into a strange, nightmare calm, where terror ceases to be terrible. One sees as from an immense height, with a marvellous and joyless clarity, the worthlessness and folly of all our feeble strivings. Men will risk their lives for such a moment, climbing to the frozen pinnacles of mountains or voyaging to arctic wastes, and all to feel . . . nothing. The cold penetrates to their bones, and the immensities of stone and ice deride their littleness, and each breath tells them they are perishing, and it matters not at all, for they have passed through the gates of fear into the bright, quiet realm of their deaths; and they believe—O last and rarest vanity!—that the icy dust on their lips is the taste of eternity!

Manfredo, as I lay thus in the ecstasy of terror transfixed, had unclasped his belt and loosened his trousers to reveal himself in that indecent manner in which he had one time exposed himself before my aunt Jerningham. Reverting to his native tongue, he said much that I could not understand—though the drift of it was clear enough—that I should not be allowed the benefit of death until I had learned from him what I had never learned from Niles—what it meant to be a woman. Indeed, I doubt if his words were meant for any ears but his own, as a kind of caressing incitement to the deed.

All the while he did this, I looked on with that same icy calmness. I understood my own helplessness, and I believed Manfredo capable of any evil he might intend, and yet, against all reason, I felt secure against him. It may seem presumptuous of me, but I have often wondered if this sensation were not akin to that which sustained the early Christians at the hour of their tribulation, and which is the boon that the Psalmist and the writers of the Gospels pray for under the name of *righteousness*. If so, I may claim no credit for it: it was not "mine own righteousness, which is of the law, but the righteousness of God."

Sustained by this last cold flame of hope, released by it from the paralysis of horror, I called again for help—and this time my call received answer. I cried out more loudly, and when Niles replied again I knew him to be near at hand, though my angle of vision was such as to prevent my seeing him.

Manfredo warned Niles to keep back, with curses as incomprehensible as his obscene endearments of a moment before, curses Niles returned on him with shrill vehemence.

All through their struggle, which I witnessed only intermittingly, as a spasmodic combat of shadows lurching into view, then disappearing on the ledge above, I tried to free myself from the encumbering block of tufa. Abandoning a direct assault on its too great mass, I tried instead to rip open the heavy silk of my dress, which had already been torn in sliding down the slope. By thus surrendering some few yards of silk, I thought to escape this present trap as I had escaped the fanatical women of Cascia. Without scissors, however, this was a slow task, and before it could be well begun, with a double cry, the interlocked combatants fell.

Manfredo's head struck against the rock that his own strength and malice had heaved below, and instantly he fell silent. A sudden liquid warmth seeped through the rent I had started in my dress. The blood continued to flow from his shattered skull till I was quite drenched with it, nor was there aught I could do to evade this terrible declaration of his death and my release.

Niles had sustained no greater injury in his fall than the straining of a muscle in his back, but this was sufficiently alarming that he gave all his attention in the first moments after the initial shock to exploring the dimensions of this pain. Then, seeing that Manfredo neither stirred nor groaned, he forgot his own hurts and went to him. One touch told all.

I could not then understand, nor shall I now try to interpret what Niles felt at that moment, except that it was all for Manfredo. He would call down curses on the corpse and on himself indifferently, and then a moment later, would kiss its lifeless lips and staring eyes until his own features were dark with blood. For as long as we were alone, he gave himself over to this empassioned and voluptuous grief, and only when he saw the approaching torches did he hasten to repair the shameful disarray of the dead man's clothing.

The hermit who tended the lighthouse, when I had scared him from his chapel-shed, had sought out the people dwelling nearest to the Villa Jovis, and returned with a small contingent of them to the summit of the hill. There they had heard my screams and the sound of Niles' struggle with Manfredo. When they found us, their first business was to lift Manfredo and roll aside the stone that trapped me and to raise me up.

That strange calm that had sustained me at the worst moment of trial had departed long since. Gradually, out of the tumult and tumble of my contradictory feelings—the sheer, dazzling relief to be alive and out of danger, an almost hysterical disgust at the blood that drenched my skirts and my person—one emotion emerged supreme. It was fear.

It seemed to have no object. What need now for fear! There were only friendly and solicitous faces in the torch-lit circle round me. Then I realized that Niles' was not among those faces. It was for him my fear had arisen. Somehow I had sensed his purpose—but too late to prevent it! He was gone—and I knew where.

At first my would-be rescuers tried to prevent my following after him. How could I explain my misgivings, my certainty that my husband meant to kill himself?

It was Santa Maria del Soccorso, or rather the hermit who tended her shrine, who helped me at this hour, when all help else had been in vain. When Niles had left the group of islanders, while they were concerned with me, something in his manner had alerted the Virgin's votary, and he had followed after him along the dark path that led to Il Salto. By the time I had persuaded the others to return there with me, Niles had already been subdued, and the old man was no longer troubling to restrain him. Niles' own unchecked weeping had rendered him quite helpless.

CHAPTER NINETEEN
Hôtel des Étrangers

LIKE THE SURVIVORS OF A STORM who sit upon the saving shore and
watch benumbed the wreckage that had been their ship washed up
about them on the beach, so we, once established in a Naples hotel,
found ourselves incapable of sharing our thoughts and, almost, of
forming them. Whatever present need there might be for explanations was met, many times over, by the interrogatories of the
Neapolitan police. These, though relatively superficial (glossing
over all considerations of Manfredo's motives, as though it were not
at all out of the commonplace for valets to assault their masters'
wives), established the chronology of Manfredo's actions from his
arrival on Capri to the moment of his death.

Such times, on that following day and the next, as the police
would leave us at peace, Niles occupied himself with writing to
his mother, or he would sit at the window and meditate upon our
view across the bay, wreathed in the smoke of his cigar, or he
would sleep, fully clothed or in his nightgown, upon any cushioned
surface that offered itself—chair, sofa, or bed. Not once did he
display his grief, though only hours before, in the extremity of
sorrow and guilt, he had tried to take his own life. Besides assuring
me that he had quite got over that foolishness, as he called it, he
showed no sign of what he felt.

For my part, I was as grateful for this silence, as if it were
truly the gift of his love rather than (as I suspected) the prelude
to renewed equivocations. Altogether apart from the craving for
quiet companionship that is the natural successor to any violent
event, I had my own well-deliberated reasons for reticency. I
knew that I must leave Niles. In all the complexity of my feelings
for him, and his for me, there was nothing of the conjugal, nor

could I now believe there ever would be. I had seen his features
when they were touched by love, and in that moment he had
seemed a stranger.

I knew this, but I feared to say it. There was in his silence
a quality of desperate inner debate that intensified with each
passing hour, and I believed that the course on which he meditated
was suicide; which if he were to attempt in this more settled
frame of mind would be more likely of success. How could I, in
such a case, add to his present distress? If this were not cause
enough, there was, as well, the promise I had made to Mr. Mainwaring, not to broach the subject of annulment with Niles till I
had first spoken with him. My stated purpose—that I visited Mr.
Mainwaring chiefly as one seeking the counsel and the consolation
of the Church—seems somewhat disingenuous to me now, as it
must have then to Niles, but he did not begrudge me the comfort
of a visit, and it was with his full knowledge and permission that
I set off on our second day in Naples, a Sunday, to Mr. Mainwaring's residence.

Resina, where he lived, lies on the lower, vine-clad slopes of
Vesuvius. The modest, modern village rests like a funeral monument over the buried city of Herculaneum, whose excavations had
even at that time become so extensive as to threaten the existence of
the living *municipium* above. Mr. Mainwaring's house stood at
the very border-line of these two worlds, where Resina ended
and, forty feet below, Herculaneum began.

Mr. Mainwaring was not yet returned from his expedition to
Paestum and Amalfi, but was expected by noon of the next day.
I found the necessary inconvenience of this delay upsetting out
of all proportion to its consequence. I asked the servant if I might
be allowed into the sitting room to compose a note to my absent
host, and though I was allowed pen and paper and Mr. Mainwaring's own desk I was unable to compose either a message or
my own feelings, but could only sit and gaze, enjoying the fugi-
tive warmth of him to whom I could approach no nearer.

The room I had been shown into was a happy blend of the
high-minded and the homely, being furnished, to the delight of any
antiquary and the dismay of an over-nice housekeeper, with shards
and fragments sifted from the nearby ruins and brought here to

be examined and catalogued; and with, as well, as cozy an assemblage of furnishings as one might find jostling each other at
the jumble sale of some suburban church. I would gladly have remained at that desk until its possessor reclaimed it from me, but,
after a bare fifteen minutes, the serving-girl was showing signs of
impatience. I told her that I had decided to return the next day,
and so there was no need, after all, to leave any note except my
name, which I scrawled on a slate, which Mrs. Lacey had thoughtfully provided for those callers who might not have cards. I deliberately neglected to put down my present address at the Hôtel
des Étrangers, lest Mr. Mainwaring think himself obliged to call
upon me. Much as I longed to see him, I did not want the meeting
to be there.

Though I fear my readers may be impatient with me, I must
pause in my narration of these last consummative events to introduce some bare description of that hotel and our rooms in it.
The hotel was located in a quarter into which most casual visitors
to Naples will never penetrate, a neighborhood in which antique
splendor and modern squalor co-existed in a shouting, rank hurly-
burly of the most vivid paradoxes, much as if Ratcliffe Highway,
the Haymarket, and Belgrave Square, with all the inhabitants
thereof, were to be compressed into a dozen winding alleys. The
Hôtel des Étrangers shared the mixed character of its environs,
for though its lobby and public rooms were questionable, if not
actually sordid, the chambers Niles occupied there were sumptuous
to the point of gaudiness. Nothing that could take an application
of gilt had been spared, and what else remained was covered by
plush and damask. It was profusely evident that Niles had not
come to this establishment nor taken his apartment here at hazard,
but that he and Manfredo had long been established as residents.
The closets and bureaus were bursting with their personal effects,
and there was, as well, a considerable supply of feminine garments
of decent quality, though much too flaunting for a genteel taste.
Despite this want of taste, the sorry condition of my own clothes
obliged me to avail myself of these until a local dressmaker could
assemble a gown better adapted to a condition of mourning. I
might, of course, have sent word for Rose to bring some part
of my already excessive supply of clothes from the Villa Visconti,

but this Niles dissuaded me from doing, since a request to Rose would certainly have brought Zaide down upon us, a confrontation for which we neither felt ourselves equal.

"I brought you here precisely so she would not find us—till, that is, we cared to be found. Let her digest the letter I have sent her. Once she's spent her first anger, and her first grief, then . . . we shall see." Such was Niles' counsel.

Among the items I had recognized as belonging to Niles there was a box covered in green baize, which I observed first upon the mantel of the drawing room, then upon Niles' bureau among his toilet articles, and at last on the carpet beneath his bed. I could not but regard such a progression as ominous, knowing the box to contain a brace of duelling pistols, which he had bought at a Florentine silversmith's—for the sake, he had then assured me, of their exquisite workmanship, only for that.

The impulse to be my brother's keeper proved irresistible. That same Sunday that I had made my useless trip to Resina, and while Niles was talking with the police in the adjoining room, I abstracted the pistol (there was only one) from its case and placed it in a large handbag of red Russia leather, which I had already availed myself of, along with the other feminine fineries that were so conveniently at hand.

Thinking that Niles may have foreseen my well-intentioned theft and so removed the other pistol from its case in anticipation, I went through the apartment's bureaus and wardrobes systematically in search of it. Though I found much to embarrass and offend (for Niles had been allowed very little time to whisk away the evidences of these rooms' libertine character), there was no trace of the second pistol. Thwarted so, and feeling quite as mean and prurient as if I had acted on purpose to spy out the secrets of the place, I gave over my perquisition and resigned Niles' well-being to God's and his own care.

CHAPTER TWENTY
Polly

ON THE MORROW, Monday, I rose early, aided by such an insistence
of human voices and bustle in the street below as would have prevented anyone but Niles from sleeping. Dressing in the discreetest
of the costumes the closets could supply, a very full walking-dress
of green muslin delaine and a spoon-shaped straw bonnet with a
caul of golden silk, I went downstairs. My first intended business
was to go to the shop of the modiste who had promised to have
ready my mourning, and, while setting about this, I meant to dispose
of the pistol, which I brought with me in the Russia handbag.

However, as I was departing the hotel, a young woman who had
been sitting in the lobby, fanning herself with a painted fan, roused
herself with a gladdened shriek and came bounding to me for all
the world as though we were friends of long and intimate acquaintance. She had very nearly embraced me before she knew her
error, but in that same moment I recognized *her* as the woman Niles
had so often painted.

"Excuse me, love," she said, taking my hand and squeezing it
as familiarly as if she were still under her first false impression. "It
must be the hour. I thought I knew you, and then I thought I didn't,
and now I can't tell which, for you seem to know me. Or is it just
seeing another English face? You can't tell me you ain't English!"

"Is it so obvious, then?" I asked, in what I thought was her own
bantering vein, for I had resolved, almost from her first words, not
to take flight nor stand over-much on my dignity, but to learn what
might be learned.

"Oh, I can always tell, though you mustn't ask me how. There's
a certain I-don't-know-what, as dear old Poll would say. You do
know Polly, don't you?"

I smiled, and inclined my head equivocally.

"To be sure, you must know her if you're wearing her dress.

What I thought, when I called out and gave you such a start, was *you* was Poll."

"That's just who I thought you might be, at first," I said, not untruthfully. "Just fancy!"

"In this draggle-tail thing?" She caught up a handful of her limp skirts and scowled at it. "Not likely! But it's been such a night, I can't tell you! What are we doing here I should like to know! I'll tell you what *I'm* doing, precious heart—I'm saving my ducats and carlinos and buying a ticket back to London, and if you ever see me more than five miles from the Burlington Arcade, my name isn't Emily Annie Shiftney."

She accompanied this oblique introduction with a low, burlesque curtsey, to which I replied that my name was Clara Reeve. And that was true, too.

"Well, Clara Reeve, it is almost eight o'clock in the morning and I have been waiting in this dusty hole for three hours and I begin to think the gent ain't coming back. So what do you say— shall we sit in the corner and share a bit of satin and pretend we're at home? I haven't heard a word of honest English for the entire week, except for one poor sod of a dodger who wanted me to take tea with him, which I did, and we discussed my soul, and how black it was with sin, and how very lovely white it might be if I washed it in the blood of the Lamb. Peculiar blood that, I told him, and he blushed like a girl. But such a handsome lad, and not a day over twenty-two, I'd wager, and the manners of a duke, so that I could have fairly let him have his way with me just for the sport of it. Only it wasn't his way! Well, I stayed prating his nonsense and sipping his cold tea all the afternoon. But as for helping me to my fare back to London, do you think he'd talk of that? Oh no! *That* got him going on about Mary Magdalen and her alabaster box of ointment. Well, I told him off properly then! Alabaster box! As if it wasn't all I could do to pay for my room in this wretched city. I called him a whitened sepulcher and poured my tea on his boots and told him if he wanted me to wipe it off with *my* hair he'd have to pay me a pretty price for the favor and left him flat. And good riddance!"

Making this her toast, she unstopped a bottle of spirits, which she had taken, along with two doubtfully clean tumblers, from behind the unattended desk of the hotel. For all her complainings, she seemed very much at ease and at home at the Hôtel des Étrangers, for she had settled us unerringly in the lobby's two most comfortable chairs and was quite liberal with the appropriated gin. "What a life it is, Clara," she said with a sigh. "I declare—what a life! How do we get through it, I should like to know?" Then, with a philosophic smile, and as though in answer to the question just posed: "Cheers!"

A shared conviviality seemed the price I must pay to satisfy my curiosity, and I raised my glass in salutation, and wet my lips at the brim.

"So you are a friend of our Polly. How is she, poor thing?"

"I . . . don't know. I haven't seen her lately."

"Oh, but she's here, you know. I saw her only the day before yesterday, or no, it was Friday, about this time of day. Looking so woebegone and dressed in those togs of hers, which *I* could never fancy doing myself, though, to be sure, she brings it off more natural than *most* can. A born actress. I wanted to go up to her and say, 'Polly my love, *leave* him!' Don't you agree?"

"Oh yes, absolutely!"

"What a life she could lead if it wasn't for him! You'd think, to look at her, or to listen, that she'd been born a proper gentlewoman. Like you, my dear—the genuine article. *I'm* something else. Ah no, it's true, sad but true, though *here* I may pass myself off to such as don't know the difference. But that's just why the likes of her and you—excuse me, dear, taking such liberties—are wasting your time here. But then, say I, what else is time for?"

"That is a very melancholy saying," I said, unable altogether, even for the sake of curiosity, to suppress a reforming impulse.

Miss Shiftney, however, took my reproof in good sort, and even, after another meditative taste of her "satin," tended to agree. "Indeed, indeed! It's the hour again, for I can't think what else should make me so low. I certainly haven't *her* excuse. The brute! Which I can say from sad experience. A brute and a bully and a braggart—may God strike me dead if he's not!"

"Niles?" I asked, surprised into candor. Though I could imagine many pejoratives used against him, none of these would have been among them.

"Is that his name then? With me, he's always Manfred, or Fred, when he's in his cups. I had a feeling that was sham, though, like his flummery tale that he's the son of an English lord. Him! Does he think we're deaf and blind? Lord Newgate, maybe, of Newgate Gaol. The long and short of it, my sweet, is that all men are beasts— and here, as our dear Poll would say, if she were here with us, is to their extermination!"

Knowing, as she could not, that what she proposed was already accomplished, in the particular case of Manfredo, I burned my tongue once more with the fiery gin. "And if he's truly as bad as that, why does she stay with him?" I asked, hoping to steer the conversation towards Niles. "Doesn't she know anyone a bit more gentleman-like?"

"Why?" Miss Shiftney winked. "Why else? Though, to be sure, she *ought* to leave him, and I've told her so, and she agrees. Perhaps, who knows, she may be driven to it yet. This last month has been even worse. I think he deliberately searches out the lowest types just to torment her. As though she were some 'leggers' mott from Wapping High Street."

"And where *is* she from—do you know?" For the terrible suspicion was at last dawning in my mind.

"No, she says very little of who she is, but I have my own idea. I think she was a governess with some very good family, and that *he* was in service with them, too—for he has that kind of hand-me-down manner of a flunky dressed to the gills for his afternoon off. And I suppose they ran off together after she was ruined. Lord knows, it's happened to others."

"And why a governess in particular?"

"Ah!" She lifted up her finger shrewdly. "It's what she does, you see. She draws, and does a capital job of it, too, with every little detail set down just so. Hasn't she ever asked you to sit for her? Oh, she will, when the occasion offers. Little Jenny Colbert even *bought* hers, the likeness was so striking. Say now, you're not leaving! We've just begun to chat."

"I'm sorry, but I really must. There's something in my room."

"Just as you please, love. But what do you say—shall we all have a nice supper tonight, the three of us? And Jenny, too, if you're up to her French. It would do us all the world of good."

"Yes. I don't know. Perhaps."

"Don't forget your purse, my dear," Miss Shiftney called out after me. "My, whatever can be in it?"

"Thank you," I said, accepting that article from her. "But now you really must excuse me."

"Tonight?" she insisted, catching at one of the ribbons dangling from my bonnet playfully.

"Very well, then," I agreed. "Tonight."

"Good. I'll tell Polly, and we'll all meet in my room at six. Maybe you can let us all have a nip of it"—nodding at the handbag—"if it isn't gone by then!"

"At six," I repeated, only in order to win release.

At the foot of the stairs I glanced back, and Miss Shiftney, lifting her tumbler in a final toast, called out, "*À toute à l'heure!*" which, as she rendered it, became a cheery "toodle-oo."

I found Niles, as I had left him, asleep in bed, his mouth agape, his hair fanned out in damp ringlets upon the wrinkled linen of the sheet. Nothing I could detect in his sleeping form either confirmed or contradicted the suspicion I had formed. Surely there were many men whose cheeks were as soft, whose limbs as small, whose hands and feet as delicate. Yet there was one proof that must be incontestable, and I determined, if I could, to rid myself of all uncertainty.

Quietly I approached the side of the bed. Carefully I drew back the sheet that covered him. He stirred, and sighed, and tried to win back that vanishing warmth. Instead of the sheet, he grasped the fabric of his nightgown, unconsciously assisting at my task of discovery.

I waited until his breathing was again quite regular. Then, stealthily, I touched the hem of his nightgown, and raised it up— and knew, beyond all possibility of doubting, that Niles could never be my husband.

CHAPTER TWENTY-ONE

An Outing in Admirable Weather

To HAVE BEEN SO LONG, so utterly, the dupe of this deceit! Never once, among all my suspicions, to have suspected this! And that the perpetrators of the fraud could have practiced on—and taken in— not only myself, whose ignorance must have made me an ideal prey, but all the world besides! I repeated these amazements to myself, as though they were the bizarre doctrines of some strange creed, the truth of which had been demonstrated to me by a miracle. Then, by a single look at Niles' sleeping face, these incontrovertibles would be lost in the glare of my habitual faith. It was *his* face I saw, *his* hand that rested limply on *his* nightgown. It was *him* I feared to wake and confront with the fact of what *he* had done. Only by a strenuous effort of thought, as when we speak an unfamiliar tongue, could I bring the proper gender to bear and think of Niles as a woman. Even as I write this, long after the events that it records, I find myself unable to refer to him except in his adopted masculine character. So great is the weight of custom when placed in the balance against the feather of truth.

Though fearful of a solitary confrontation, I nevertheless could not take my leave of Niles without some gesture of repudiation. With a rueful smile for my own folly in ever having let them be put on, I removed from my finger the ring of his false-sworn vow and the ring of his unmeaning promise, and placed these on his bedside table. They had belonged to Zaide, I had been told. Let them belong to her again!

As there could be no thought of going to a dressmaker, in my present state of mind, nor yet of lingering in the hotel, I summoned the barouche that had taken me to Resina on the day before and once again set off for Mr. Mainwaring's. The four miles of that journey were by no means long enough for me to review the entire history of my relation to Niles in the light of this new knowledge. What I had learned represented a revolution of my preconceptions no less momentous (though far more singular) than my dark meditations during the train-ride, three months before, from Florence to Naples. However, I shall not inflict even a part of these reconsiderations on my readers. Where would we begin or end? My whole past, everything I have written in these pages, would need to be re-envisioned and revised, and even then I would not be done, for there were to be further revelations ahead of me on this same eventful morning, and the process of re-interpretation would have to be begun afresh.

Let us suppose, then, that my racketing barouche had the wonderful properties of certain conveyances in the *Arabian Nights*, and that I arrived at my destination at the very instant I set out from the Hôtel des Étrangers. By several signs—the parted shutters, an empty carriage waiting at the gate—I was persuaded that Mr. Mainwaring was returned from his trip, and I could scarcely keep from running down the little path to his doorway from very gladness.

Before I had reached the door, it was opened, and Zaide, resplendent in a gown of purple and gold, came down upon me, like the Assyrian in Lord Byron's poem, vulpine and voluble with welcome.

"Clara, my dear, I'm so *relieved* and so *delighted*! You can't imagine how you've worried us, but here you are, and looking prettier than I've ever seen you. We *hoped* you might come by before the appointed hour of twelve."

I looked at her disbelievingly, and she returned me a look of defiance, as much as to say, "You can't make me behave otherwise!"

"Have you not received Niles' letter?" I asked her.

"Yes, my dear." Matching my lower tone, but quite undaunted even so. "And we shall discuss it more at length. But first you must come in and meet Mr. Mainwaring's guests, for,"—dropping to a whisper—"they're quite the drollest creatures I've ever seen."

To have found the Contessa Visconti in apparent possession of the rock of my refuge was so confounding that I could not gainsay her, but tamely let her take my hand and lead me within. Three strangers in the strictest, most upright English style were standing to attention in Mr. Mainwaring's drawing room, which had come to seem, by contrast, much less respectable than on the day before; and (with three of us in crinolines) distinctly smaller as well.

"Clara, let me present Mr. Langdon Humphreys."

A substantial, solemn old man looked out at me from behind a pair of very thick spectacles and bowed.

"Mr. Humphreys," she added, in a tone that the gentleman referred to seemed to take as duly deferential, though I could detect the inflection of her sarcasm, "is the treasurer of the Magdalen Mission Society."

She turned from Mr. Humphreys to a young lady of no more than fourteen years, who was dressed with as much care and cost as if she had been a matron of forty.

"His daughter, Miss Humphreys."

Miss Humphreys made a low obeisance but with an air rather of rendering to Caesar than of respect for anyone present before her. From the verdict of Miss Humphreys's first glance there could be no reprieve: anyone wearing such a gown and such a bonnet as mine could not conceivably be a lady. No doubt, too, if Zaide had long been at hand, Miss Humphreys may have incurred a considerable debt of condescension, which she intended to pay back upon my less formidable head.

"And Mr. Jonathan Saintsbury, also of the Magdalen Mission."

Mr. Saintsbury, a fair young man who, like Miss Humphreys, had gone to a great deal of sartorial effort to seem ancient, grave, and reverend, bowed to me, rather lower than need be, blushed (at which my intuition told me that here was the original of Emily Shiftney's tale of her attempted conversion), smiled very warmly, and seemed about to speak, when he recollected that I had not yet been presented to the company.

"And this," said Zaide in a tone of affectionate proprietorship, "is my dear niece and dearer daughter, Contessa Visconti."

"No," I said, "excuse me, but that I am not."

Astonishingly, having cleared that hurdle, the first and most formidable, I found it had not been at all hard—except for the rest of the company. Miss Humphreys gave an audible gasp. Mr. Saintsbury bloomed roseately above his stiff collars and did not know where to look, while his co-missioner smiled a smile of deathly charity, much as if I had just qualified myself for the assistance of the Magdalen Mission.

Zaide, accepting my defiance with composure, quickly and in-geniously smoothed over its roughness by remarking: "Ah, do you still think I am so jealous of my lost plumes? No, my dear, I'm really much *happier* with the title of Dowager. *But*"—preventing me from again contradicting her—"that wasn't your whole mean-ing, was it? Perhaps, gentlemen and Miss Humphreys, if we might have a moment by ourselves. . . ?"

"Excuse me, but it was my sole intention, coming here, to speak with Mr. Mainwaring. Is he not at home?"

"Our host," said Mr. Humphreys, "has gone to hire another conveyance to make the ascent. When we first understood that you were to be expected at noon, we thought we should have to forego that pleasure, but"—he regarded Zaide through his thick glasses uncertainly—"your good friend has assured us that you would be kind enough to join our party. She says that you had even formed plans to do so, some time since."

"I'm afraid I do not understand."

"To go up Vesuvius, you know," explained Miss Humphreys. "It will be *so* thrilling. The crown of our whole experience of Italy."

"And you wouldn't, would you, take that crown away?" Zaide insisted. "This is to be the last day the Humphreys and Mr. Saints-bury shall have here, and so I took the liberty of pledging your company, and my own. It is *such* admirable weather, and nothing is wanting but your consent and another coach, for the scoundrel who brought me here refused categorically to accommodate us. But perhaps your driver shall not be so unyielding. Let us put him to the test."

I let myself be swept from the room as meekly as I had been taken in, but when we were again out of doors I pulled loose from her grasp brusquely.

"Are you quite mad? Can you possibly suppose I am so spiritless as to go on acting the part of your dutiful daughter-in-law? Know-ing all I know! And being wronged as I have been!"

"Tush, my dear, we're alone now, and there's nothing to be gained by such displays. I should not have risked my own safety seeking you out if I had not that to propose which I believed you would pause to listen to. Whatever you know, even if it is all that Niles can tell you, is less than you *ought* to know before you act.

I ask nothing but that before you speak to anyone else, even the benevolent and wise Mainwaring, you should read this."

From a handbag as capacious as my own, she removed a large, sealed envelope swollen with its contents to a condition of almost perfect cylindricality. "I believe it will explain itself. Read it. Consider what it proposes. I ask no more."

"What right have you to ask anything of me—except my pardon?"

"Good heavens, do not be so obtuse! Don't you realize what I have put in your hands? It is my confession. I have been scribbling day and night since Niles' letter was delivered to me, and that is not the first impulse of a bereaved mother, believe me. Oh, you needn't arch your brow. I don't expect you to credit me with feelings. But an intelligent regard for your own interest should suggest that you at least listen to the terms of my surrender."

"You mean to bargain. I thought as much."

"I throw myself at your feet, my dear, and ask you to trample on me. You may call that bargaining. To me it is an humiliation of some dimension."

"And yet you speak of making terms?"

"Clara, what do you gain by this contention? I have written what I could never bear to speak, nor you to listen to. Read it while we make the ascent, and then—"

"Do you know, Contessa—you share a most unaccountable disposition with your daughter."

She hesitated only a moment before replying, unruffled: "And what is that, my dear?"

"You both go off sightseeing at moments of extremity."

"Vesuvius? That was improvisation, though I should hesitate to stand in the way of the redoubtable Miss Humphreys once she has declared her pleasure. I have no doubt that Mr. Mainwaring would sacrifice her wishes to yours, if you require it of him. But why should you? There will be time, while we ascend, for you to read my letter, and an opportunity, at the summit, to speak rationally—and so I shall have gained *my* point. And *you* shall have me under your eye the whole while, virtually a prisoner. The Humphreys and Mr. Saintsbury shall have had their "view," and Mr. Mainwaring shall have been spared the scandal which you and I shall otherwise certainly create."

"Oh, you make it seem quite plausible!"

"What do you think, Clara—that I mean to entice you there to hurl you off the edge? Manfredo having already fared so ill against you in similar circumstances, I'm afraid I would lack zest for such an undertaking."

I had thought myself proof against her heartless jesting, but this last audacity fairly took my breath away. Zaide, as though my dumbfounded silence were a compliment to her wit, smiled her broadest smile, nodded pleasantly, and left to rejoin the company indoors.

I was not left alone for long. Soon an open victoria stopped at the gate and Mr. Mainwaring and his aunt stepped down. Their expressions when they saw me were a rare mixture of delight and consternation. Mrs. Lacey, especially, seemed perplexed to see me in my borrowings. In her anxiety not to seem over-curious, she had no sooner offered me her cheek to be kissed than she was excusing herself.

When she was gone, Mr. Mainwaring grasped my hands in his own and assured himself, by wordless inquiry of my features, that I was well; or else that I was not, for I cannot imagine what of all I had experienced in the hours just passed may have been registered in my face. I do know that my gratitude at seeing Mr. Mainwaring and feeling his strength at hand brought me close to tears, but when I tried to express my simple thankfulness it became lost in the tumult of all my other feelings, and I was mute.

"Your mother-in-law is here. Did you know that?"

I nodded.

"She came first yesterevening, looking for Niles and you. She saw your name upon the slate, and was quite abusive to the girl, trying to learn where you might be found. Have you quarrelled with her?"

"Has she said nothing, then, of all that's happened since Thursday?"

"Only that you and Niles had gone to Naples and were, I gathered, hiding from her. I assumed there was some provocation, but—my dear Clara, whatever *has* happened?"

"So much! But I can't begin to tell you now. Your guests—"

"Don't speak of them. When I knew that you would call I made it clear to them that I could not possibly accompany them today.

If they refuse to go up without me, they have only their own timidity to blame. The *vetturino* speaks English sufficiently well, but they act as if every Italian were a bandit. They had resigned themselves (though with no very good grace) to returning to the Bourbon Museum, when your mother-in-law arrived to stir up their hopes. I'm much to blame myself for having so far submitted to her bullying as to have gone off in search of another carriage."

"Sorry? Why, how else should I make the ascent?"

"Clara, there is no necessity."

"It's not only for the sake of your guests' pleasure, and our own. There is also this." I held up Zaide's bulky letter. "My mother-in-law, as you term her—though I have told her to the scandal of your guests that she is not—has written what she says is her confession. As you can see, it is no trifling document. She asks me, before I speak to you of what else I know, to read her own account. That seems a fair request, though I'm under no obligation to be fair to her. Still, it is true that what I read may affect how I decide to deal with her."

"What does she stand to gain by this?"

"Time."

"And is there time to spare?"

"Not as much as she may hope for, but the afternoon at least. That is, if *you* are willing to go with us up Vesuvius. For I shall make the same stipulation as the Humphreys and Mr. Saintsbury. I won't stir from this house without you."

CHAPTER TWENTY-TWO
A Very Long Letter

WE MADE THE ASCENT in three carriages. Mr. Mainwaring and Zaide rode in the first, the Humphreys in the second, Mr. Saintsbury and myself in the last. Mrs. Lacey remained at home, having from the first declared that just by living in Resina she had a better view of the volcano than any rational being could want.

My state of mind, even before opening the envelope and beginning to read its contents, was not calculated to make me a careful observer, and indeed my whole impression was that there was nothing to observe. After a mile traversing the vineyards of the lower slopes, we climbed up an interminable track through an endless desolation of black stones, where the only living existence besides ourselves and our toiling beasts were lonely bushes of broom, the stark flower of this desert.

While we climbed, I read Zaide's letter. It was a worthy companion to the landscape we inhabited, of infertile ash and brittle lava. But, ah, what use? No curse of mine, no commination could do justice to her own articulate evil. She condemned herself as no accuser could. I reproduce her letter, therefore, without comment or apology, and without a comma changed.

Dear Miss Reeve, it began.

Having acknowledged all that that salutation implies, little more need be said: —You have never been my daughter-in-law, Niles is not my son, and life is a dream. We are all equally deceived; —You, by the fraud we practiced on you; we, by our own delusive hopes. I confess that I have always seen you as something of a joke, my dear, and now you may return the compliment. There is much pleasure to be had by inflicting pain on those who have regarded us as *their* victim. I know from experience. And so (because my shame increases your luster) I present here not the little that need be said, but the entire Newgate Calendar of my life; not from the vanity of wanting to appear a blacker cut-throat than I have been, but rather as a fillip to your delight. You have triumphed, Miss Reeve, & are entitled to see me dragged through the dust.

Pour recommencer: —As I'm sure you've surmised, my relations with Lord Byron did not cease once he'd had his laugh at me. That humiliation had been but the *avant-propos* to my fuller debauchment, a process that was not completed until the following evening. Whether from incapacity (which I prefer to believe) or as a refinement of cruelty, he did not accomplish the actual defloration himself, but delegated this duty to his manservant, a fellow he'd chosen from among all the helots of the Mediterranean for a single qualification: like himself, the man was a clubfoot. Gioacchino Bevilacqua—or, as his master styled him, Jack Drinkwater—had no other graces to recommend him; the face of a monkey, the stature of an ape, the intelligence of a baboon; his only faintly human quality was an insatiable appetite. So long as we remained in Genoa, he would appear at my window and renew my dishonor as regularly as the sun set.

I had come bearing my treasure in hope to lay it at the foot of the altar of my god, only to have it filched from me by a beggar on the steps of the church. Think of the ignominy! Imagine my chagrin!

In May, to my no little relief, the Blessington party left Genoa; in July, to my distress, I found myself to be pregnant. As there is some cachet in having been the mistress of a world-renowned poet, I encouraged Lady Blessington to believe that I owed my disgrace to Lord Byron. Alas for my vanity! If I'd told her the truth, she would not so readily have let me become the object of scandal. Anyone may be forgiven for having failed in her duty as duenna with respect to the author of *Don Juan*. But to be outmaneuvered by a Neapolitan *valet de chambre*? It isn't done; and if it is, it's well concealed. Undoubtedly, if Lady Blessington had known all, she would have helped me to be rid of my embarrassment betimes, but a bastard of the bard could not be sacrificed to such scruples! As to seeking help from my seducers, or even, with my reputation lost, abandoning all pretense and fleeing back to my seducers—alas, it was too late! Man and master had departed for Greece.

Rumor of my disgrace had reached my father, who crossed the Channel post-haste to confirm it. In my eighth month I was not in a condition to contradict a truth so blatant. Accordingly, I was established in a convent of Augustinian nuns who catered to such cases as mine, where the babe was born and christened Manfredo, after an earlier production of his presumed author, who, very soon, would be dead and unable to deny his authorship.

The next years, at the Convent of Santa Bibiana, were the hardest. Every morning the nuns would rouse us (there were four other repentant Magdalens besides myself) to attend a mass in their dismal chapel, where we could study in the flaking murals the example of the virtuous Bibiana, who had defended *her* honor, some fifteen hundred years before, at excruciating cost. I always felt that the abbess of the convent—Mother Nemesis, as we styled her—meant to revenge their saint's tortures on us, for having pre-ferred the course which *she* had so steadfastly resisted; —Indeed, it came to seem a preferable fate to be whipped to death, like Bibiana, all at once, rather than to eke out one's pain over a number of years.

As you may imagine, I addressed a voluminous correspondence to my father, proclaiming my repentance and promising amend-ment, if he would only remit my sentence, or at least consign me to a more congenial gaol. His infrequent replies counselled patience and a deeper contrition. I became desperate, foreseeing myself grown gray among the beastly Augustinians, & began to interleave my sighs with threats: I would flee the convent and live a life of sin! I would prostitute myself upon the Strand in plain view of all his friends! My father was unmoved. I attempted one escape and was apprehended within seven hours, in an olive grove.

I'd learned my lesson. For the next three years I concentrated on perfecting the two skills that promised to be most useful in my then situation, Italian & hypocrisy. In my letters home I grovelled, but more discreetly; I developed a vein of false good humor, re-counting anecdotes of conventual life, redolent of an unconscious pathos. In short, I learned to display those qualities of unctuousness and self-misrepresentation which are worth so much more in the marriage market than the usual little accomplishments of young ladies.

At last, as if in recognition and approval of my transformation, my father agreed to put me up for sale, after making it clear that despite my so much strengthened character, I could no longer ex-pect to command a very high price. I was also to understand that my release was to be conditional upon my agreeing to a perpetual banishment to Italy (unless a husband could be found in Russia) and the surrender of Manfredo. He could not have made any stipu-lations more painful than these. After four years of absence, Eng-land looked like Arcadia. As for my son, my love for him was, expectably, immoderate and obsessive. Whom else had I had to love this while? Yet if I had been asked to sacrifice him on the altar of the convent's chapel I would have, if that were set as the price of my freedom. I vowed to myself that I would one day have Man-fredo back, and, too many years later, I fulfilled my vow, and revenged myself on my old warden, the abbess, in the bargain by reporting to her superiors in the Augustinian order the *real* amount of the bribe I had paid in order to find out my son's whereabouts. As I'd suspected, Mother Nemesis had gravely misreported her gains, and I had the satisfaction of learning that she spent the last years of her life working in the kitchen of the convent she had formerly governed.

I shall not burden this account with a catalogue of the longueurs and indignities of the next three years. That it should, despite my name and dowry, take so long as that, expresses it all. At last a taker was found, a bargain was struck, and my honor, lost so long, was restored to me; —I married.

Nor shall I recount my four years of wedded life. The Conte Visconti was a miser, a bore, a fool, and a sot, but he was no worse than most men. He had such virtues as sorted with his vices: he was cunning, companionable, and too lazy to be actively cruel. Yet can I honestly say I regretted the necessity of killing him? I think not.

He owed his death, in good part, to the shrewdness of my father's solicitor, the same Hautboy *père* who connived at defaming and disinheriting my brother (your grandpapa) Howard. In the marriage settlement that Mr. Hautboy had negotiated, it was stipulated that I should act as sole executrix of my husband's estate until his heir (if any) should reach his majority. To this hint, I added some knowledge gleaned from an excellent Renaissance herbal that had been in the library of the convent. While I was in my final month with child, Conte Visconti died quietly in his sleep, after two weeks of mild indigestion.

Immediately upon my husband's inhumation, I quitted Ischia; and with not much time to spare. Within hours of my finding a den to whelp in (assuming the name, once more, of Zorina Stanley) my time had come.

It is an old wives' tale that a child carried low in the womb will be a boy. This had been true in my first pregnancy. During the second, the same token persuaded me that I would bear another son, but I had labored, so to speak, under a false impression. My son—the Conte's heir—was of the wrong sex! I was of half a mind to let the midwife who'd assisted me assist me still more by losing my darling on some convenient doorstep, as she proposed.

The other half of my mind was cannier. I kept the child, dismissed the beldam, and took thought.

To this point, the story of my life has been representative. All through history young ladies have lost their virtue, been tucked away in convents, plighted their troth to troglodytes, and been disappointed in the sex of their progeny. A good many, I have always suspected, have even murdered inconvenient spouses. But who among them has thought to accomplish by Art what they have been cheated of by Nature? There I may lay claim to originality.

My motive was great. If my husband died without male issue, I was to receive the meagerest of pensions; his daughters, if he'd happened to have any, would have done even less well. Even the scabrous old Villa (which, believe me, Miss Reeve, I loathed as heartily in my day as you in yours) would be forfeit to some twice-removed stranger who happened to bear the same coat-of-arms. If any proof be needed for the contention that our sex are not regarded as human beings, only reflect that these are commonplace provisions in the drawing-up of wills. One must be grateful, I suppose, that Europeans do not follow the simpler practice of the Hindoos and roast their widows on their own funeral pyres.

To revert somewhat, but not to digress. . . . What was true in Italy would be true, equally, in England. Having secured a husband for me, my father felt he'd done his whole duty, and struck my name, along with Howard's, from his will. Niles came along too late to effect a change of heart, for the heart in question had ceased to beat some months previous. Douglas had inherited title and all, in the year the Parliament House burned down—'Thirty-four. You saw me once at a moment of high disappointment, in the office of Hautboy *fils*;—My behavior on that later occasion was temperate by comparison to what I felt in being thrown over by my father. Fortunately, that rage went unobserved. I had learned, in the convent, never to send a letter that had not aged one week; —The practice stood me in good stead, for when I did send the new Lord Rhodes my condolences, and congratulations, my note was a marvel of all the sisterly virtues (among which the chief is humility). Douglas accepted my deference, as he did his title, as his due.

I knew better, of course, than to expect anything from Douglas in his lifetime. But who is such a pessimist as to think he won't outlive an elder brother? Howard was already dead, and his daughter (your mother) so much stained by the dishonor of his supposed illegitimacy that I could not conceive of her as a rival. And then—who else? No one! I was confident, moreover, that Douglas would not fill that happy vacuum with progeny of his own. I forebear to give my reasons, except to say that in my girlhood I had a passion for peeping through keyholes. In this case, events confirmed my expectations, and Douglas remained a bachelor through all his dreadfully long life. And so, if *I* should have a son, Douglas would have little choice but to make him his heir. If he did not, the will could be overturned.

And I was to be cheated of all this—my husband's tidy fortune and my brother's inconceivable wealth—because of the accident of a child's gender? Not while I had breath to lie!

The greater part, after all, of what is thought of as sexual differences is nothing but ornament. Men wear their hair this way, women that; men affect trousers, women skirts; a man's calling card is three inches by one and one-half, a woman's generally larger. All these usages, being dictated by custom rather than necessity, may be turned topsy-turvy in a moment. Beyond that: among civilized nations, the differences that cannot be dissimulated are not on public display. Only one's mother, nanny, wife, and tailor need to be acquainted with these most intimate details. I was Niles' mother; he had no nurse; you and Renata were his wives. As for tailors, they did indeed pose a delicate and trying problem, but even in this case the tendency of the times towards bulkier garments more loosely cut has been to our advantage.

He, I have written; and *his*; the habit is so engrained that I would think it equally absurd to see Niles constricted by corsets and swollen up with crinolines as to refer to him in any gender but the masculine. If I, who initiated this deception, am so far deceived, who may not be? You, my dear Miss Reeve, will appreciate the length to which such an imposture may be carried!

The secret, finally, of all good deceptions is that they be practiced so consistently as to take in even the deceiver. Tartuffe, I am sure, believed himself to be an exemplar of piety, and malingerers—like your aunt Jerningham, God rest her soul!—dupe their bodies into producing the symptoms of their imagined ailments.

Niles, all through his boyhood, thought himself to be a boy. By the time the truth could no longer be concealed from him, he was rational enough to appreciate the advantages of continuing the pretense.

Men, as every woman knows, lead larger, freer, finer lives. All that is worth doing in life, all that is enlivening, ennobling, or enriching, every career and all professions excepting one, they have arrogated to themselves. What is left is either drudgery or sin. Given a choice, what woman of spirit would not prefer to be a man? Ah well, *baste pour cela!* You would think I were Mrs. Godwin or Mr. Mill, and this some vindicating pamphlet!

To resume: —Once my claim to administer my son's estate had been acknowledged, I removed to Venice, stopping along the way to leave my bribe at the convent of Saint Bibiana and to buy back my first-born from the orphan-home, where he'd been employed from the age of six in the manufacture of pins. The darling, for all he'd been abused, was still not wholly crushed. A gleam of intelligent and, when you consider, not unreasonable malice gleamed in his eye; his figure, thin but not stunted; his face, a fallen angel's. Altogether he was worthier of his pretended father than of the actual one, whom he favored only in the item of appetite. He was too young, and too dear, to employ as a servant, nor did I wish, as yet, to enlighten him as to our real relationship; —Though, to be sure, he had the wit to detect the truth well before it was told him. I established him in a Jesuit school in the town of Sirmione on Lake Garda, where the early defects of his education were remedied by a regimen no less severe than the pin-factory's, if more improving.

Venice represented my first taste of that intoxicating beverage, Independence! I commend it to you, Miss Reeve, though you must beware at first, as it goes to the head. I had come to Venice with the noblest intentions of bettering my lot by a prudent marriage; instead, I made the mistake, once again, of falling in love. You have met the gentleman, Rudolph, Count Wrbna and Freudenthal. I was a widow of thirty; he, an officer of twenty-five; a score of French novels will tell you all the rest. Indeed, my only regret has been that Rudolph should have been so entirely satisfactory and loyal a lover, for I never had an opportunity, for more than a week at a time, of being out of love with him. Though he urged me always, unselfish as he was, to add, as he said, a husband to my accomplishments, I could never exert myself with sufficient persistence or energy; —My heart was bespoken. It continued in that state as long as Rudolph remained alive, with what modifications such a span of years implies. My changed feelings for you upon our reunion at Villa Visconti, my sometimes hostility and unvarying resentment were due largely to the part that you and your foolish aunt had played in Rudolph's assassination, Unfairly, no doubt; —I might have laid the blame at my son's door (that is to say, Manfredo's) as justly, for it was his sporting with Mrs. Jerningham that set in motion the tragic and absurd chain of mischances that led, at last, to La Ricci's stiletto in my dear Rudolph's breast. *Sic semper tyrannis*, as Mr. Booth lately proclaimed; but I shall miss my darling all the same.

Niles, during these balmy years, was growing up to be a model young gentleman, sweet-tempered, high-spirited, and precocious in all his studies. By the age of six he could entertain adult acquaintances in any of four languages; by eight he could enrage them by his superior address & logic; by ten he was grown so wise that he foreswore argument and resumed his earlier manner of droll amiability. He was small, but what of that? The one half of mankind that is not tall is short. My only real concern in those days was for the morality of his tutors, for it would not do to have the *abbé* who instructed him in Latin or the distressed gentlewoman who gave him drawing lessons seek to impart knowledge to their little charge beyond that which they were commissioned to impart. But our luck held, and Niles was educated.

In that same decade, I had taken young Manfredo more and more into my confidence. He had his own manner of pleasing, very different from Niles', but just as effective against a mother's heart. Rudolph obliged me by employing the boy on some missions for the Austrians, and Manfredo proved as able as discreet. His character withstood every temptation we set in his way, including a bribe of one hundred silver zwanzigers that Rudolph, affecting to be jealous of the boy's dark charm, had offered him if he would quit my household. He remained, and I discovered to him the secret not only of his own birth (or rather the one half of it, for I let him assume, from hints and blushes, what he evidently wanted to assume concerning his paternity), but of Niles' as well.

The truth is that I needed a confederate. Niles was growing apace; his little body was proving as precocious as his mind. He required daily attentions of a personal nature that I had neither the leisure nor the inclination to give him. His brother agreed to become his manservant and oversee not only the countless details of the child's toilet but as well to tutor him in the finer elements of his impersonation and to offer him, in his own person, a model to be imitated. All those graces which young boys customarily learn from their peers—the arts of swearing, drinking, and smoking; how to be insolent to inferiors and to hold one's ground against bullies and swaggerers; how, above all, to boast of, or imply, exploits that reflect credit on one's manhood—all these matters Niles studied at his brother's knee.

A thriving time, but clouds were already gathering. Your birth, my dear, was one of those clouds. Another, in the unappealing shape of a club-footed vagabond, appeared on the doorstep of the Palazzo Albrizzi. It was Jack Drinkwater, grizzled into a state of consummate ugliness. He had been a whole year hobbling about Italy seeking me out, and except for my own folly he would never have succeeded. Gioacchino had gone to the Convent of Santa Bibiana, from which in the first imprudent months of my confinement I had smuggled a letter to Byron ingenuously beseeching him to come to my rescue. It arrived at Missolonghi too late to lighten the poet's last fevered minutes and served only to inform Gioacchino that he had fathered a son and where that son and I might be found. Many years and much misfortune had whittled down his spirit before he acted on the clue and applied to the door of the convent, nor would that visit have profited him in the least, had it not been for the wakeful malice of my old enemy. When I'd settled my score with Mother Nemesis by betraying her to her superiors, I had given that woman, quite unnecessarily, a motive for revenge. She it was who provided the scent he had needed to run me to ground. There is no tale so sordid but that an improving moral may be found in it, and the moral of this tale is *Never needlessly inflict a wound*.

A lesson, alas, I had still to learn, for now that my old co-ravisher had placed himself in my hands, I could not refrain from seeing what harm might be done him. To be practical, I ought to have had Manfredo dispatch him, but shrewd as he was, the lad would have discerned my motives and realized that I was urging him to parricide. Why else should a lady have a taliped beggar murdered unless he is blackmailing her? And what, in nine cases out of ten, is the reason ladies are blackmailed? Manfredo believed himself to be the bastard of an English milord (his supposed father's *poetic* reputation was of no account to him); —What a comedown to discover the truth! But, in all honesty, I must confess that my motive was less to spare the son than to make the father as wretched as lay within my power. The man was already so abject that his effort to blackmail me had provoked me more to pity than to scorn. An hundred zwanzigers was all he asked! I gave him double that amount, and hired him, in addition, to help in the garden at the Villa Visconti. He thanked me! You have witnessed yourself the extent of his final abasement, but even he, ground as he was into the dust, reduced almost to idiocy, retained the power and the will to avenge himself. But of that, in its place.

During the stormy days of 'Forty-eight, Niles, accompanied by Manfredo, went to England and was matriculated in Balliol College at the remarkable but not unprecedented age of thirteen. At Oxford he comported himself as a prodigy and a gentleman, charming and astonishing all his elders; which is to say, everyone. It was during this period, during a recess of the college, that you first encountered him, at your mother's funeral.

As to the offer I made to the Jerninghams shortly thereafter, to bring you to Venice to live with me, that was largely Niles' inspiration. Even then he was smitten with your spaniel eyes and wilting manner! Admittedly, it was a politic idea. Where better to place the rival claimant to an inheritance than under one's own thumb? I even speculated that you might, in time, make a match for my Manfredo. (How differently it has proved in the event!) But while a judicious aim, it was not an essential one, and when your uncle Jerningham denied our request we were not greatly cast down.

Even before Niles came to England, and increasingly upon his presenting himself at Blackthorne, my brother Douglas had professed a partiality for his nephew that augured well for the future.

Without his original intercession, Niles would not have been admitted, so precociously, to the university, and without his later interventions, Niles could not have continued there, for while his own habits were unexceptionable, his brother had begun to develop a taste for the costlier vices. At first, Niles sought to curtail Manfredo's debaucheries by refusing to honor his debts, but Manfredo would retaliate by pawning his young charge's books and clothing down to the last ragged grammar and next-to-last piece of linen. Protests were futile, and Niles was obliged ever and again to appeal to his uncle, who, I suspect, rather approved his nephew's prodigality than not. After all, it was the only respect in which the boy seemed to take after him.

Niles continued to excel in his studies, and there was every reason to believe that he would distinguish himself in whatever field he chose. Then the all-too-foreseeable disaster occurred to nip these hopes in the bud: He fell in love.

The object of his affections was a freshman, the son of a Birmingham steel merchant. Niles, though in his third year at Balliol, was still the fellow's junior by a considerable margin. When Shakespeare's Rosalind, *en forme de garçon*, kindles a liking in Phoebe's unwary breast, it is an absurd spectacle; but Phoebe's inclinations are at least superficially excusable, and Rosalind did not set out to encourage her folly. But what can we think of *this* romance? Ridiculous as the situation was, it was also one of peril. If Niles, with the candor of the empassioned, were to reveal himself to his beloved shopkeeper, who could calculate what that boy, in his amazed disappointment, might not be capable of? There was no help for it; —I telegraphed to Niles that I was dying and that he must return to Venice at once. He departed Oxford dutifully, and did not return.

Speedily as I had acted, it had not been fast enough. A scandal had been avoided but a suspicion lingered, like one of those clouds that cluster round the brow of Epomeo, muzzy yet of not altogether unspecific shape. Douglas was curious why his nephew should throw up a career so well begun. Some kind of answer was patched up: that the climate of Oxford was insalubrious; that Niles, being at last of age to matriculate at Tübingen, preferred to finish his course of studies there, under the illustrious Ferdinand Baur. To Tübingen he did go, but he worked with a much diminished brilliance, and it was only by a signal act of charity that he received a degree.

Up till this moment Niles' life had been a steady mounting upwards from success to success, a history of precocities fit to be set alongside those of Macaulay and Hume. With each new success, I felt my program of education confirmed. Imagine such a genius wasting itself upon embroidery frames and novels! Then, at the age of eighteen, Niles went into a decline. He professed himself indifferent to his masculine prerogatives and interested himself in just those pursuits with which any woman of intelligence and leisure might have busied herself. He became, in short, the futile dilettante you married. I always thought that by affecting to despise those advantages my guile had won for him he meant to spite me for having lured him from Oxford and romance. But I may be wrong. Had Niles been, in very fact, the figure he masqueraded as, he might have enlisted just the same in that legion of idle young men who fill the drawing rooms of Europe with their self-important prattle.

Not that I cared, especially. I had lost a son in whom I could take pride, and gained a friend in whom I could take comfort. In the ranks of dilettantism, Niles commanded, at least, a colonelcy. He had every superfluous merit—wit, grace, taste, and a happy disposition. How the time flew!

It was never my intention that Niles should marry. Indeed, I assumed that marriage represented precisely the outer limits of his imposture, to which it might tend but never touch. That he did marry, and not once but twice, requires some explanation. Because of her father's friendship with my departed husband, there was an understanding between their two families that Niles and Renata should some day be married. I had encouraged this understanding in perfect bad faith, assuming that by the time Renata was of age to be wed, Niles would have come into his inheritance. Meanwhile, other efforts at matchmaking might be discouraged by insisting on this spurious commitment. My brother, however, proved to be more tenacious of life than I had hoped. Renata bloomed into womanhood like a bill that falls due. It is natural that my simile should savor of money, for Renata was well-dowered, and the

Visconti coffers were nearly depleted. I had not been improvident, nor was Niles; the fault, if fault it must be considered, lay with Manfredo.

I shall not seek to extenuate my son's failings, as I foresee that it would be wasted ink. His vices, like his virtues, were of that military, self-asserting cast which it has become fashionable to denigrate; —Though I should like to know how the business of this world could be accomplished without men of Manfredo's temper. Howbeit, he did spend money faster than it could possibly be supplied to him. Impatient with playing the part of valet, resentful of his social subordination to Niles, whom he regarded (like all women) as his inferior, Manfredo insisted on having his own way with respect to money. In fact, he rather held us to ransom at times. It was at his insistence, and for the sake of the dowry, that first I and then Niles was persuaded to undertake this more perilous impersonation. The wedding took place in Naples at the church of San Bernardino, in February of 1862.

We had trusted to the girl's convent education to render her innocent of the realities of conjugal love. Our trust was misplaced. Renata knew what was due her as a bride, and despite her professed antipathy for her bridegroom, she insisted on receiving that due; nor would she accept less than full measure.

Niles has informed me that Renata honored you with her written account of the first months of her marriage, so I shall not seek to anatomize her sufferings here. As with other heroines who make it their merit that they patiently endure worse and worse indignities, I had no patience with the girl. Her insipid presence, especially at Corme Hall during the eternity of her pregnancy, was an intolerable weight on my spirit, and I for one was happy to see the last of her. You, my dear Miss Reeve, were, by contrast, a welcome addition to our household, and I shall always regret that a more settled existence could not have been arranged for our little family.

But I am running ahead of myself. Renata's pregnancy, no less than her death, must be accounted for. It was Manfredo who accomplished what, in both cases, the circumstances demanded. Renata had made it clear that she would go to any length to reclaim her freedom and her dowry. What could be a more effective proof of the reality of her union with Niles than that it should seem to bear fruit? Hence, Clara Maria; —In whom, poor dear monkey, her grandfather's features were once again asserted.

Had Manfredo been content to serve as Niles' proxy only so long as strict necessity required, Renata might eventually have resigned herself to her lot; which would not have been, after all, such a very extraordinary one. Manfredo, however, had inherited his father's appetite, and Renata was to be made to appease it. Her desperation became unbounded, and her efforts to escape Corme Hall reached such a pitch of panic that she might fairly have been said to be mad at the end.

A great embarrassment, you must admit; but, even so, Niles forbade any overt attempt on her life. Reluctantly, I concurred in his prohibition. In the event, she was not so much killed as hunted to death. She escaped Corme Hall, as she had many times before, by her own ingenuity. Manfredo followed her; —But dressed, as she was not, to brave the elements. She saw him behind her and pressed on as though the blizzard were naught but a spring shower; —Manfredo following, but refusing to overtake. He was persuaded that if she were made to admit defeat by turning back to Corme Hall of her own volition, her resistance would for ever be crushed; —A theory to which no less an authority than Shakespeare lends his authority in *The Taming of the Shrew.* Renata's spirit outwent her strength. Even when she had collapsed for the last time, in the ditch at the foot of the thorn tree, with the last glimmer of life and intelligence she continued to defy her enemy. For that, all we lesser spirits may envy her.

And now it is the diminutive presence of Miss Reeve herself that must occupy the foreground of my tale—the Princess of Bayswater, as I have heard her denominated! Why, you may ask, immediately upon being quit of one so great encumbrance in the person of Renata, should Niles seek to saddle himself with another? The answer is—Prudence. We knew of your uncle Jerningham's effort to force you into matrimony. We feared there would be other askers after your hand, whom you might not so determinedly resist; —One other, particularly. Godfrey Mainwaring had already mentioned to Niles, at Blackthorne, that he thought you a fetching creature. If he were to unite his mild prospects of inheritance with your claims (which we supposed, at that time, the lesser of the two!), who could tell what bounty Douglas might heap on such a pair? We had learned from your aunt that Mainwaring had become a caller at your house. Judging his motives by ours, we supposed that he delayed openly courting you from a doubt as to the soundness of the speculation. What I've since come to suspect was that his motives were exactly opposite to this; —He had learned, through Mrs. Lacey, of the fourth Lord Rhodes' confession, the effect of which, if Douglas published it, would be to make you the mistress of Blackthorne. It was Honor that stood in the way of a proposal! Honor that forbade him to court a lady who, unbeknownst to herself, was his superior in fortune and rank! Such, at least, would be my wager.

The surest method of averting such a match, the kindest, too, was to present you with a better opportunity. Eventually, at my urging, Niles agreed to pay court to you, with the understanding that it would be only a feint. He swore he would never subject another creature to such an ordeal as Renata had been through, least of all yourself.

In those first weeks after Renata's death, Niles was in such a state of Conscience as I have never witnessed in any human being. It was not as though he had had a hand in her death, though to hear him repine and repent you would have thought he was the guiltiest wretch since Bluebeard. It was all I could do to keep him from going to the constabulary and confessing himself to the magistrate. As for Manfredo, his presence so exacerbated these unwholesome impulses that he had to be sent off at once to Italy, ostensibly to deliver the infant Clara Maria to her maternal grandparents.

It was your company, more than my reasons, that at last persuaded Niles that life might go on as it had gone on theretofore, pleasantly and day by day. There was, I think, an element of wistful sincerity in his courtship. He told me once—it was outside St. John's Clerkenwell on the morning of your wedding—that he had intended to arrange matters so, that when he came into his fortune and threw you over, you would be compensated for your loss with a handsome sum when you sued him for breach of promise! He really was, and ever remained, fonder of you than your merits seemed, to me, to warrant. But isn't this every mother-in-law's complaint?

He asked for your hand, and you stood at shilly-shally for weeks and months. Since it was time that we sought, nothing could have suited us so well as this blessed irresolution. Douglas was sixty-six; he *could not* live for ever! As my not-quite-beloved Lord B. reflected, apropos a similar trial to his patience:

> *"Yet doth he live," exclaims the impatient heir,*
> *And sighs for sables that he may not wear.*

When at last he was blown to bits, I gave thanks to the Spirit of the Age that had made possible the camphine lamp; —But not for long. Douglas had prepared an humiliation for me bitterer than any I had ever tasted. All my life's effort was in vain! You witnessed what effect that disappointment had on me. I think I would have killed myself the same afternoon if Niles had not returned to our hotel with the news that you had at last yielded your consent. I couldn't believe that anyone could be so wanting in all calculation as to accept Niles' offer precisely at the moment it had become worthless. I still do not understand your motives, but I trust you've learned your lesson. Next time, my dear, you *must* think twice.

Niles, in withdrawing his offer, had acted in good faith; —If with a sense, like mine, that you must have decided to reject him then in any case. When, instead, you accepted, what was he to do? The fortune that he'd lost at a single *coup de malheur* was his again for the mere effort of pocketing it. He had meant well, but the temptation was too great and he succumbed.

Your own story is known to you; —Nor shall I exercise my lagging pen to demonstrate how in each of an hundred instances it may be linked to what I have already revealed. During most of the term of our residence at the Palazzo Alari-Uboldo it seemed possible that your *soi-disant* marriage would settle into a mold of complaisant nullity; —For your innocence, unlike Renata's, was whole and entire. Though events were to take another course, Niles was not to blame; nor I; nor even (for all your stumbling efforts to enlighten yourself) you, except insofar as you made an implacable enemy of my son.

Manfredo had always been inclined to regard you as a joke. Your total ignorance of what was to him the central fact of existence was a source to him of constant mirth, and he was forever inveigling Niles to tell him stories of *la donna inglese* and *la piccola Madonna,* as children beg to hear fresh accounts of their favorite piglets and bunnies. Then, thanks to his rencontre with your aunt and her *impossible* cook and the awkward aftermath of his harmless jest, thanks still more to your discovery of him and Rose in the garden and *its* aftermath, you ceased to amuse him and became instead a thorn in his side; —Which he determined to pluck out.

But independently of his good or ill regard for you, he would eventually have sought your death, for the full accomplishment of his aims could be achieved in no other way. What Manfredo wanted, above all else, was to become *himself* the Conte Visconti. He must have deliberated this transformation for many years, for when he first presented the idea to us, shortly after Rudolph's death but before we had departed Venice, he had worked out its details to the last contingency. In brief, Manfredo's plan was this. You were to be killed and your corpse disposed of secretly. We were then to set off—he, Niles, and I—to Alexandria (or Saratoga; he was un-decided), where he would take over Niles' identity, while Niles would assume yours. In emergencies—that is, should there be visitors who had known the *old* Niles—he might reassume his former self so long as the danger of discovery lasted. There was even less to fear in having Niles' impersonate you, since your past life has been, socially speaking, an exemplary blank. The plan was more elaborately conceived than this bare account would hint at, but since it never actually was put into execution, I shall let it go at that.

I was at first of two minds: I bore no animus against you, but Manfredo was, after all, my darling and my only boy. He'd labored long and patiently, & deserved some reward. Niles, though, was adamant against this scheme. No doubt he did not relish losing his ascendancy over Manfredo, or the appearance of it. He was used to being a man and having a man's freedoms. Also, I think Niles rather feared such a metamorphosis. Manfredo was too much in the habit of murdering, or meaning to murder, young ladies who went by the name of Contessa Visconti, which name he was now asking Niles to assume. I confess to having had some misgivings myself along these lines.

These were not reasons one could urge in discussing the matter with Manfredo, who, as a good Italian, extremely resented any expression of distrust or even reserve among members of the family. What Niles did urge, and not without truth, was his affection for you. Manfredo had all the money he could desire, and if he wished to go off to some other quarter of the globe and call himself Conte Visconti, Niles had no objection. But he would never countenance a scheme that required any indignity to you; still less, your death. He loved you, he declared, quite as if you were his wife; and indeed, in a larger sense, a sense that Manfredo, brutish as he was, could never appreciate, you were!

Before I can explain, in more detail, how this issue was joined, I must discover to you one last guilty secret. Manfredo and Niles were more than brother and sister; they were, and had been for some time, man and wife.

Of all sins, incest most naturally shrinks from the glare of publicity, but I must be excused from expressing too profound an horror of my darlings' transgression. I did speak out against it now and then, but I was not in the best position to preach virtue to my children, having so often permitted, and encouraged, their wickedness. Eventually, one found, as with other varieties of sexual relations, that the specific act did not so much alter the existing bond as express it more completely. But enough of this mellow Wisdom & more of Facts!

Despite the daily intimacies that Niles' careful toilette had involved them in (the binding of breasts, the imposture of a morning "shave," etc.), neither Niles nor Manfredo had ever felt for each other anything but a kind of merry complicity; nothing very tender or very warm. Moreover, there were resentments on both sides, mostly unstated, but liable to burst out on a little provocation into threats, taunts, & tirades; and, in Niles' case, into tears. Manfredo satisfied his needs below-stairs and about town; Niles, except for his brief, issueless infatuation at Oxford, had never seemed to have needs, except for amusing books and pretty pictures. The advent of Renata destroyed this comfortable stasis. While avoiding her caresses, Niles could not always repress his own. He would play with those blond tresses or stroke the silk of her gown or her stockings interminably. His fascination was undiminished even when the dress was hanging in a closet, the stockings folded in a drawer.

Then one fateful afternoon, Manfredo discovered the young master seated at Renata's toilet table and attired in one of her gowns. Some words were exchanged, & some blows; —In a trice, twenty-seven years of unmolested virtue were set at naught. Thereafter, the same deed was re-enacted on several occasions, always to the same pattern—Niles discovered in Renata's clothes, a defiance, and finally a debauchment. When accidents are thus repeated, one begins to suspect they are not accidental. Though he would never say so, either to Manfredo or myself, I believe that Niles was in love with Manfredo; —Or half in love, at least.

But suppose he was not in love at all; suppose he felt nothing for Manfredo but what he claimed, a disgust tempered to courtesy by the force of fear. He remained, for all that, a woman, with a woman's needs. He—foolish pronoun! What was the significance of Niles' dressing himself in Renata's dresses, of his rouging his cheeks and twining masses of false hair in with his own, except to escape, for a moment, from the tyranny of he and him and his? And if Manfredo showed himself willing to extend still further the bounds that Niles might go, why then so much the better!

As for Manfredo, he saw that Niles, by these indulgences, was placing himself more securely in his power than he had previously done. This, for Manfredo—the exercise of an ever more autocratic force—took the place of the tender emotion. A similar instinct for conquest had made him hound Renata to her death. In this case, the contest was more even, less a persecution than a duel; and really, aren't most other marriages just the same? For the woman as much as for the man? Our weapons may differ, but they are no less powerful. Consider your own aunt Jerningham, and how she triumphed over her tormentor. Consider, my dear, yourself!

(While on that subject, there is a droll side-light to this romance which you must have often puzzled over. At Blackthorne, after your clandestine visit to my rooms, you were accosted by Manfredo in a darkened stairwell and benefited from attentions he had meant for another. Did you ever ask yourself for whom? And was your answer—as we always supposed—Renata? No, you may be sure she, who so much loathed and dreaded Manfredo, did not make midnight trysts with him. It was Niles, at that time in the full shame and glory of self-discovery, & so giddy with desire that the danger of being found out and exposed acted as a tonic to his pleasure. A small confusion, doubtless, but an amusing one.)

During our sojourn at Corme Hall, Niles' passion gradually subsided into a mere itch. He spent as much time as he might in the society of our neighbors, or in London taking you to plays, whither Manfredo could not pursue him; —Where, too, Renata was not on hand to remind him of her wretchedness. After Renata's death, Manfredo, as I've noted, was required to depart for Italy as a condition of Niles' not sacrificing all of us to the police. They did not see each other again till Venice, where they established themselves on their old footing of genial partnership. Our joint goal had been achieved, and we were rich as three Croesuses. Nothing was wanting but leisure to sit back and enjoy our success. I had Rudolph; Manfredo had Rose, and whatever rarer blooms he chose to pluck from the multiflorous streets of Venice; Niles had Tintoretto, and you besides.

Manfredo, however, was not satisfied being only a member of a triumvirate. He demanded ascendancy, and in due course proposed that scheme for achieving his desire, of which I gave some sketch above. Niles refused to consider the plan, called it mad, wicked, impracticable. Rather than debate with Niles, Manfredo sought to re-establish their old bond, judging that once the substance of his proposal had been achieved, Niles would be more willing to agree to its full, formal realization. Niles still resisted, in consequence of which he got that black eye he displayed to you in Spoleto. All through the term of your nervous debility, Niles and Manfredo had been venturing off to other towns; not for the sake of their art treasures but so that Niles might publicly display himself there *en grande toilette*, in frocks and bonnets filched from your own travelling closets. For while Niles still strove to resist Manfredo's intimate attentions, he could not so resolutely refuse the attentions of a crowd.

At length, Niles let Manfredo have his way with his own person, though not with yours. Even when so foolishly you forfeited the inestimable pearl of your ignorance, Niles would not allow Manfredo to deal with that awkwardness as he had dealt, years before, when Renata had threatened to seek an annulment. You may have thought his behavior cruel at the time, but he was prompted by a sincere concern for your well-being. So do physicians let blood, by a lesser pain hoping to avert a greater.

Under seal of strictest secrecy, Niles told me what had taken place in Florence, & so you owe it to my good will, as well, that Manfredo was never given that additional cause for alarm which might have precipitated his more violent precautions. I must admit, despite my fondness for my son, to having wondered myself how far he might proceed in the interest of *complete* independence. So, though I left it to Niles actively to oppose Manfredo's intentions, I made it my principle to promote an atmosphere of *far niente,* of doing nothing comfortably. That is my last language lesson for you, Miss Reeve, as well as the whole of my philosophy. I hope it may serve you a little better!

Manfredo was determined to have his way. As relentlessly as he had pursued Renata, and still more patiently, he sought to bend Niles' will to his own. To this end, he would take Niles on those excursions into Naples which threw us two together for so many evenings of mutual aggravation and gloom. There Niles was painted and exhibited along the quays like the canvas of some squalid Bohemian; —& sold. I cannot tell you of these weekly displays in any greater detail, for I forbade Niles to bring his complaints to me. If he went into Naples with Manfredo, he must look out for himself. Despite his complainings, he *did* go, and I averted my gaze. A mother's interest in her children must end *somewhere.*

I would say no more on this painful subject, except that these weekly sorties were not without a more substantial consequence than the piasters added to Manfredo's purse, or the sketches to Niles' portfolio. One of the gentlemen that Manfredo solicited for the enjoyment of his "Polly"—such was the name that Niles had adopted for his new career—was none other than your old friend, Reverend Mainwaring, up to his usual missionary tricks, no doubt! In any case, whatever motive had originally drawn him to that obscure quarter of the town, once Manfredo approached him, it seems likely that Mainwaring recognized him. Mainwaring, however, had so altered since last they'd taken notice of each other three years before, at Blackthorne, that Manfredo, all guilelessly, led him to the brothel in which he and Niles had taken an apartment. There was no grand confrontation. Mainwaring was obliged to wait outside Niles' chamber while a prior engagement was concluded. He stood upon the threshold of the room only long enough to recognize the figuré stretched upon the bed before him, and then departed in the utmost haste. That same afternoon, he hired a boat and presented himself for supper at the Villa. I gather from the fact that you did not decamp with him *tout à coup* that he didn't tell you all he had discovered. Nor, if one reflects, had he discovered *all*. Niles' misconduct was plain to him, but not the vital detail of his sex. Perhaps he had heard—from Douglas or from a fellow-Oxonian—rumors concerning Niles' abrupt departure from Oxford.

Had Mainwaring been less reticent, or you less forgiving, we might all be happier at this hour, and my son might be alive. Manfredo returned to Ischia in a state of high alarm, vowing to kill you at the first opportunity and set out for Ultima Thule; —Which he might well have done (Niles' fright having made him temporarily more tractable), had not chance interposed and led him to commit two other murders instead—your aunt's and his father's.

Jack Drinkwater had for some time been a source of annoyance to Manfredo. Though the old man wisely did not acknowledge his near relationship, he could not avoid throwing out hints and, once he had understood her to be his grand-daughter, showing a proprietary interest in little Clara Maria. Finally, at Manfredo's insistence (using your little episode of somnambulism as pretext), I gave Jack a liberal honorarium and told him to go.

Thus it stood on the morning after Mr. Mainwaring's untoward visit. Manfredo, after a sleepless night, was pacing the hillside west of the Villa and meditating various means by which you might most inconspicuously be murdered, but to every scheme he could invent there was always one great impediment, your aunt Jerningham; —Who, as though summoned by his dark thoughts, appeared below him on the path to the convent, followed by her maid, Antonia. Irresistibly, he followed her, keeping always to the higher ground. While he lingered without the gate, which had been left ajar as though by invitation, he witnessed the entry of the dismissed gardener. Before he could make up his mind to join this little throng, Antonia came flying out the gate. It was a miracle she did

not see him, for (by his account) they nearly collided. Manfredo
hastened to the *terme* and down the steps to the pool, guided by
your aunt's screams and Jack's exhortations to be quiet.

Cloaked by the steaming darkness, Manfredo overheard the
gardener's garbled warnings and inchoate account of the conspiracy (so much as he had fathomed) that we had formed against
Renata and now against yourself. Was there ever so patient a
revenge or a malice so meek? For years he had spied on us and
picked up gossip from the other servants, had schemed and speculated, and at last had struck; —Only to be defeated by an old
woman's obstinate prudery! For your aunt refused to listen. Even
if she had stopped screaming, it is doubtful whether she would
have gathered much meaning from Jack's ill-remembered English
commingled with the idioms of Naples. Manfredo himself was hard
put to decipher what the fellow was saying, though one fact
emerged clearly: he was not, as he'd believed all these years, the
love-child of an English milord, but instead the bastard of this
scrofulous old beggar. This, more than all the rest of Jack's gib-
berish, decided him. He sprang upon his father and threw him into
Restituta's pool, where in an instant he was boiled and drowned.
Your aunt stared at her deliverer, undecided whether gratitude
was more in order, or horror. Manfredo did what was needful.

His immediate escape was baffled, as you know, by the arrival at
the *terme* of Monsignore Tabbi and yourself. With a prudence and
coolness which even you must commend, he forebore a confrontation with the priest, but concealed himself instead in one of the
bathing cabinets in the nether darkness. Then, at the engrossing
moment when the corpses were discovered, he left, undetected, returning to the Villa as he had come.

Thereafter, he spent the weeks that you mourned for your aunt
mourning his lost pretensions and abusing me for my lack of virtue
and judgment in having given him such a father as he had just murdered. I was in no very good temper myself, nor was Niles; nor, I
think, were you. Altogether, it was a very weary time.

The rest you know better than I; —Except for one telling detail, which Niles makes much of in his letter to me, as illustrating
the remarkable scale of his brother's evil (always his strongest
point). That struggle between Niles and Manfredo, which you

witnessed only in glimpses from the terrace below, had an object you could not have suspected. Manfredo was endeavoring, as he contended with Niles' so much smaller strength, to divest him of his masculine garments and then—before you, and as a kind of exemplar and pre-vision of your own rape—to have his sport first with his sister's flesh. A work of supererogation, surely, but he must have judged it the most effective means not only to subdue Niles' will to his own but, as well, to elevate your last earthly moments into the Empyrean of terror. Though he failed, one must respect the magnitude of the endeavor. Had Manfredo been born into a higher sphere of life, I have no doubt he would have become one of the supreme statesmen of the age.

Having laid that wreath upon my darling's grave, let us advance to matters more pressing. It has been one of my purposes in addressing these many pages to you that you may implore Niles to return to me. And if he should, what then? I have steadily opposed the idea of Alexandria and Saratoga, but perhaps I shall be reduced to venturing off to some such exotic spot at last. All hangs on your kind indulgence, my dear. You may, if it suits you better, have the police upon me in a moment. You may choose to entertain yourself, over the next decade, with the letters I shall be forced to write to you from prison; —For even there I shall have no bread but what you can provide for me. Or you may let me escape and know that, if only from a regard for my own safety, you shall never hear from me again.

I should prefer to be with Niles, as I think, upon deliberation, he would prefer to be with me; —It must be as you determine. But spare *him*, at least, I beg of you. What is his guilt beside mine? Consider that the fraud he practiced was also, for all the years of infancy and youth, practiced as well upon him. Consider, too, that you owe him your life; —Ought you not therefore to make him the gift of his?

I would not plead that you perpetuate an injustice, for I know you'd not do that. But what is required, beyond this full confession, to return to you that which is yours? With this letter in your hands, your marriage may be annuled ten times over; —& with the prudent assistance of Mr. Hautboy, the unpleasantness of wide publicity may be avoided, too. Your marriage was unconsummated,

and your would-be spouse has disappeared; —That is all the world
need know. If corroboration of this letter be required, discreet inquiries may be addressed to the management of the brothel in
which Manfredo and Niles passed so many week-ends. They may
find out, in turn, some of the gentlemen who were acquainted with
Niles in a professional way. Their testimony would surely satisfy
the most skeptical judge.

But if you cannot find it in your heart to pity the guilty, then
pity the innocent. Think what will become of little Clara Maria
if you go to the police. Were Renata's family to learn the whole
truth of their daughter's misfortune, they would deal with the
child exactly as if Renata's dishonor had been of her own seeking.
Will you not so far honor Renata's memory as to allow the fruit of
her suffering to inherit the decayed remnant of her fortune? Give
the Villa to her by deed of gift. Then return to England and pursue
your annulment there.

For my own part, you have my solemn promise never to intrude
upon my grand-daughter if you honor this request. If my promise
means nothing to you, you have my written confession. The truth
is a powerful weapon, but like any other, it may be employed for
good or ill. I pray you, Miss Reeve, take thought; & have mercy
upon—

Your undeserving Aunt,
Zaide Visconti

As best I might, I tried, while I read these pages, to control my
feelings, and when this was not possible, to conceal them. Only in
the discovery of the true circumstances of Lydia's murder was the
attempt beyond my strength, and even then my tears were quiet
rather than convulsive. What else I felt—the pity, the abhorrence,
the sheer astonishment—I was able to moderate by virtue of a con-
tending indignation, that grew stronger with each fleering sarcasm
that I read.

My companion had been advised by Mr. Mainwaring that I
should need to employ my time with him in this way, and so all
this while he had sat beside me, respectful of my privacy and unobtrusively sympathetic to my distress, always forebearing to
speak. But when I had finished with the letter, and folded it and

placed it in my purse, the pressure of his own need could no longer be withstood, and he burst out, with wonderful earnestness and a disconcerting lack of preface, imploring me to use my influence with Mr. Mainwaring and to urge him to return to London and accept the direction of the Magdalen Mission.

When I protested that my influence with Mr. Mainwaring was very slight, Mr. Saintsbury replied, "On the contrary, Contessa—" He blushed fiercely, becoming mute as suddenly as he'd found his tongue a moment before.

"Miss Reeve," I said quietly. "I am sorry we were not properly introduced."

He nodded, and resumed. "I meant to say, Miss Reeve, that, on the contrary, he has the greatest admiration of your character, and in especial, your judgment. All the while we have been with him he has been full of your praise. So I am sure a word from you would have considerable weight. You may believe, of course, that his time is better spent here in Italy. I know nothing of archaeology. Mr. Humphreys maintains that it is a great waste of Mr. Mainwaring's talents for him to be digging up broken pots and bits of statues to add to the shelves of museums that are already full to bursting with such vanities, and I should agree, if it were anyone but Mr. Mainwaring, for whom I have the very highest admiration. Indeed, I could say without exaggeration that his example has been the beacon of my life."

"We are agreed in two things, Mr. Saintsbury—our innocence of archaeology and our respect for Godfrey Mainwaring. But is his importance to the Magdalen Mission so very singular?"

"Since he has left, Miss Reeve, I could almost say—if it were not disrespectful to many gentlemen much older and wiser than myself —that the Mission has ceased to exist. Mr. Humphreys is very good in approaching our subscribers and appealing to their generosity, but in the missionary aspect of our work, which is, after all, the more important one, we have not been at all successful. In fact, without Godfrey we are *all* at sixes and sevens. You will think it impious of me, perhaps (Miss Humphreys did)—but *I* think the reason we have fallen off so . . . or, rather, the reason *he* so much succeeds, is—that he is a true Christian. Not, to be sure, that Mr. Humphreys isn't, or that I'm not. I'm sure we try. But Godfrey acts as Christ would have acted, if He where alive now and in London. That isn't easy, you know, given the specific task of the Mission. Somehow one is always condescending, or bullying, without meaning to. But that isn't Godfrey's way. I'm sorry if I've offended you. It wasn't my intention."

"Not at all, Mr. Saintsbury. Not at all."

The warmth and, even more, the openness of this testimony came at the psychological moment. I could have embraced Jonathan Saintsbury for the sheer gratitude he made me feel—the gratitude and the relief! His praise of Godfrey Mainwaring was grateful not only in itself but as a powerful specific against the soul-deadening *tone* of what I had just read. Even those elements of his person that could be judged droll—his blushes and awkwardnesses, or the fact, which I now noted, that it was not his elders in general that he modelled himself after, but his hero in particular, whom he emulated with a fidelity and literalness of detail that would have done credit to a waxwork at Madame Tussaud's; coat, collar, cravat, the very parting of his hair and tilt of his hat were copied from him—even for these absurdities I was grateful, for they showed me that my relish for this side of human nature need not be the mark of a cankered soul (which the example of Zaide's poisonous wit had made me believe), but that it might be a form, just as well, of fondness and a source of joy.

I promised Mr. Saintsbury that I would give thought to his request to use my influence with Mr. Mainwaring. He thanked me and instantly, losing his gift of tongues, fell to blushing and thence into a silence.

Assuring myself with a glance at the black heights still to be scaled that there remained time, and to spare, I took out Zaide's letter from my handbag. With a colder eye and a steadier purpose, I read it through again from the beginning. When I was done, I knew my own mind, and we had reached the summit of Vesuvius.

CHAPTER TWENTY-THREE
The Volcano

"AND WILL YOU COME right to the door of Hell and not look in?"
Zaide asked me, for I had refused both Mr. Saintsbury's arm and
Mr. Mainwaring's, saying that for the moment I preferred to rest
within the coach.

"I have looked quite deep enough, thank you."

"And your verdict, my dear?"

"Of what I see there? I can add little to the general opinion—
that it is cold and ugly and full of hate, that its denizens affect to
be proudest when they ought most to be ashamed—"

"Don't omit that we are desperate creatures, too."

"No doubt."

"But yet the most remarkable thing about us, I believe—do
step down from the coach, Clara, for you are putting the poor *vet-
turini* into a frenzy of speculation—the remarkable thing, I say, is
that we are so ordinary. Daily life in Hell is the same as elsewhere,
the same trifling worries and pleasures. We look at the clouds that
go by—and how lovely they have been this afternoon, all gold and
silver, like a miser's dream—and we take just the same impermanent
delight in their fleeting loveliness."

"So much the worse your wickedness then." I was resolved not
to let her charm me to the least concession, not even to a reciprocal
pretense of civility.

"What a stern judge you are. But then it is not your good
opinion I am asking; only that in your triumph you should exercise
mercy to those you've defeated."

"Is it a triumph, then, to have escaped your toils?"

"All things are relative, Clara."

"And my poor aunt—where is her triumph?"

"I had no hand in Lydia's death."

"You knew her murderer and concealed him. And you continue, in your malice and in the face of what you call my triumph, to praise his crimes. But I will not argue with you. It is too demeaning."

"Then on that we're agreed. But look, there is Capri, that violet smudge beyond Sorrento. You almost can't see it for the haze. In a year's time, or less, it will be just the same with the events that happened there. A little distance puts all things into perspective. As with yesterday, so with today. What looms so vast that we can't comprehend it will become, once we have returned to the plain below, the striking and familiar profile of Vesuvius. And next week—who knows?—it may be below the horizon, both the place and the moment."

"By which, I gather, you mean to suggest that I should let you off scot-free."

"Are you not content with the spoils? What do I ask except to be spared but the horrors of imprisonment, assuming I might escape the mercy of the gallows?"

"Plead with your judge, Zaide, not with me. In what you wrote to me you forgot your own wise precepts—not to incur a needless enmity, and not to dispatch a letter that hasn't aged one week. I am not the dewy, guileless innocent you jeer at so merrily. Perhaps I was, but knowing you has changed me. I may say that your imprisonment is rather a pleasant notion than otherwise, and my only regret must be that I shall not be long enough in Italy to pay regular visits to your gaol."

"And my gray hairs?" she flung at me. "Won't you pity them?"

"Age never seemed to curtail your rapacity. Why should it alter your deserts? Next you'll be urging my duty as a Christian!"

"And why not—since you profess to be one?"

"The God in Whom I believe created a Hell for such as you, and till you go there, prison is good enough."

"Damn *me* to your Christian Hell then, but what of Niles?"

"What I feel for Niles is no concern of yours."

"You cannot throw me to the wolves without sacrificing the sharer of my fetters. Our guilt unites us, Niles and I."

"Contessa, if I *pitied* you, I should still give you over to the law."

"You're resolved then?"

"I am resolved to show what you have written to Mr. Main-waring and to follow his advice implicitly. And I am confident what his advice will be."

"No less am I."

"That is as much as to say that you *know* that every reason you have offered me is specious."

"As I have known you to accept *worse* offers, it seemed worth a try. But since I find you are unyielding, I shall trouble you for the return of my letter."

"You gave it to me with no conditions except to read it. I've done so, and now if you'll excuse me, I mean to give it to Mr. Mainwaring."

"Wait at least until we have returned to Resina."

"Indeed I won't! If you mean to escape, you shall have to make the attempt from here."

The three coaches, beside which we had conducted this em-broilment, were clustered on a narrow plateau, where the rough road ended and a rougher flight of steps was graved into the hard-ened lava of the volcano's upper cone. Up these steps, through a fog of sulphurous steam issuing not only from the crater but from the black, brittle ground itself, had Mr. Mainwaring mounted with his friends towards the ever-beckoning, ever-elusive summit, and up these steps I followed after him. Zaide did not set off after me at once, but lingered a while below to confer with the two coachmen who had remained beside the coaches. We later were to learn that she had taken my gibing advice in good earnest and tried to bribe the coachmen to set off back to Resina with herself as sole passen-ger, leaving the rest of us to return on foot. This they had refused to do, either from a charitable regard for our well-being, or because the bribe offered was too small.

After the equivalent of not less than nine or ten long flights of stairs, I came to the crater's brim, and stood there, stupefied and half-asphyxiated. What I had not imagined, and what no one can explain, is the extent of it. The Thames from shore to shore is not so wide as the distance across the crater; and the Thames is not burn-ing.

The *vetturino* had shepherded his flock to another part of the rim from which they might survey to better advantage the whole inner dimensions of this Malebolge, but as I could not know whether they had gone to right or left I was obliged to wait where I was. Though I was not made reckless, anger and high resolve rendered me strangely impervious to my terrible surroundings. I viewed the roiling white smoke and the lambent mineral mass from which it issued rather as obstacles in the way of my purpose than as phenomena objectively (and indeed, awesomely) existing outside myself. In short, I felt the insensibility and blindness of true courage.

As I was pinioned thus, indecisive between left and right, Zaide appeared behind me on the steps, short of breath, her eyes tearing from the smoke. Below us, at an incalculable depth, earth was transfigured to liquid flame that flickered like the lightnings of a far-off storm, but Zaide was as unaffected by this tellurian spectacle as I. One thing only mattered, and that she stated curtly: "The letter, Clara—I must have it."

I shook my head and backed away from her, fearing what reckless evil she might be capable of in her despair. In this I erred not by a want of caution, but by lack of imagination.

At first sight of the pistol she took from her handbag, I believed she had stolen it from me by some incredible sleight of hand. Then, by the unchanged heft of my own bag, I knew this was not so. The pistol in her hand was rather the mate of mine, which had been missing from its case, and for which I had searched so fruitlessly in the rooms of the Hôtel des Étrangers. Why that search had failed was now clear, though the manner by which Zaide's pistol had come to be parted from its twin, whether innocently or in premeditation of some other, unaccomplished crime, must remain a riddle without answer. Here is a hint, if not proof positive, that the pages of her confession might not have been so unsparingly truthful as they suggested by their tone of shameless cynicism. What secret conflicts among herself and her children may thus have gone unrecorded? What snarlings of wolves? What snares and toils and springes?

"Clara, this is no idle threat. One way or other I will have it." Her thumb strained at the pistol's great silvery scroll of hammer. She was obliged at last to use the full strength of her other hand to draw it back.

"It will do you no good to kill me. I have already given the letter to Mr. Mainwaring."

"Who has gone off to sit on the edge of *Vesuvio* to read it? Nonsense! It is in your purse, or you would not clutch it so to your chest."

She stood not ten feet from me, holding the pistol at her arms' extended length, and though I fully believed she might fire it, I felt no more fear of her than of Vesuvius' fiery pit, but only a degree of indignation, mounting almost to rapture, that she could stand there, steeped in all her sins, and still assert her foolish, fruit-less, desperate demands. By her own admission she was a thief, a liar, an adulteress, a murderess, and the unrelenting corrupter of her own children. If there were any crimes she had neglected to commit, it was only from indolence and that lack of ready op-portunity which she decried as woman's lot. Now that her schemes had come to nothing, why would she not admit defeat? It was that which gave me strength still to oppose her—a desire, passionate as any *she* had known, to see that proud, ancient face admit, if not her guilt (for may be she had passed altogether outside the realm of conscience), then at least some *consciousness* that she had failed!

"Well then, the guilt is not on *my* head," I said calmly, reach-ing into my own handbag. "But you must understand that I do this reluctantly."

"With what quodlibets you will, so that you give it to me."

It was a measure of my coolness at that moment that I had observed her cocking the hammer of her pistol and was able, with my hand still concealed within the purse, to duplicate this action, though I only dimly understood it to be essential to the weapon's effectiveness.

When she saw her weapon mirrored in my hand, there was a tightening of the seines of wrinkles about her eyes and mouth that suggested, however, no more than her next words: "Clara, you surprise me, and not only because you should rise to the occasion, but that you should have come so well-prepared for it. You have begun to use your pretty head. *Brava!*"

"I am prepared to use this pistol, too, and I shall, if you don't return yours to your purse."

"Ah, Clara, that's not how duels are fought. We must follow the logic of our weapons now." As she spoke, the pistol seemed to waver in her hand, with the dream-like, erratic movements of a planchette across the letters of a ouija board, and I stared at it with

the same hypnotized attention that object commands from those
who believe in its prophetic power.

"But though you have grown so much larger under the instruction of adversity, you still want life's sublimest lesson—disappointment! To love and then to lose, for ever, the object of that love—
nothing else builds character quite so solidly. Myself, for instance,
am a monument to disappointed love. And now, my dear, *that* shall
be my parting gift to you."

She pressed the trigger, and the pistol discharged. Only then
did I realize that it was not I who had been her purposed target,
that the movements of her pistol had not been erratic but had been
trained upon the form advancing towards us through the rolling
smoke. Because I had been facing Zaide, I did not see *him* until,
after the second shot she fired, I turned round in horror to see the
body collapsed upon the stone.

She threw the spent pistol at my feet, and dusted her gloved
fingers together.

I closed my eyes and fired, and in the very instant that she fell
I knew that she had had her victory over me, by awakening my
malice, and enflaming it, till I became no better than herself, a
murderess; and then, like a judgment of mercy, I felt his arms
around me, arms I had believed would never again be instinct with
life.

When she looked up from where she had fallen, it was to witness her error. Mainwaring lived; the figure she had espied through
the sulphurous haze had been young Saintsbury, the victim of his
own admiring imitation. Then, and only then, did I see her admit
defeat, but even this was the merest lightning-flash against the
black night of her soul.

She turned her gaze to me, and spoke, in a tone in which were
gathered up the last frayed remnants of her pride and resentment,
and yet with a kind of melancholy fondness, too: "Well, my dear,
do finish what you've begun."

At first I did not comprehend that she wished me to act as her
executioner.

"The pistol, Clara," she explained patiently. "There is a second
ball in it."

As when children, playing in the garden, wound a viper with

a stone and then find themselves afraid either to kill it or to leave it in its pain, so we regarded her, with helpless horror. Slowly she raised herself to her knees; and, with a groan, to her feet. The blood of her wound seeped from her shoulder to spoil the gold and violet of her dress, spreading in a delta pattern down to its hem.

"Contessa," said Mainwaring, "it is not wise, in your condition, to be on your feet. Your wound should first be bound, and then—" He broke off, seeing that she did not heed his words, except to smile at them, and shake her head, as if in mute commentary on a visitor's solecism.

Then, lifting her ruined skirt, with a little wince of pain, she walked to the edge of the crater. Too late I called to her to stop, too late Mainwaring reached out his hand. With a calm disdain, as though she were lighting from a coach, she stepped from the edge and fell, without a cry, into the Hell of Vesuvius.

CHAPTER TWENTY-FOUR
The Pyramid

ZAIDE'S MARKSMANSHIP HAD BEEN no better than my own, and Mr. Saintsbury survived to become, only a month ago, the suffragan bishop of Colchester, and with no other enduring ill-effect (as I have heard) than a proclivity on evenings of high festivity to remove his shirt and show the gentlemen of his company the two small scars commemorating his so memorable ascent of Vesuvius.

There was, necessarily, a great deal of unpleasantness to be gone through in the hours that immediately followed the events of the last chapter, but, like Mr. Saintsbury's wounds, none of it was of lasting consequence. Mr. Humphreys was outraged, and his daughter hysterical, and both were incensed that Mr. Mainwaring's attentions, during the whole descent, were divided between the unconscious Mr. Saintsbury and myself, to their almost entire exclusion.

After we had reached Resina and deposited the Humphreyses with Mrs. Lacey, I insisted on accompanying Mr. Mainwaring on into Naples. Though we would have preferred to make our first approach to Niles without such an escort, it was needful that two policemen go with us to the Hôtel des Étrangers; and needless, too, for we came many hours too late. Niles had fled the hotel, and the city, shortly before noon, leaving all his masculine apparel behind —and leaving, with it, his identity as Niles. Some part of her habiliments and all the more valuable gauds that had belonged to "Polly" were gone, as well as the rings I had left on the bedside table.

The rings must have aroused suspicions, which a visit from Emily Shiftney, announcing that evening's supper for "the three of us," then confirmed. Yet my discovery had but advanced the hour that could not, in any case, have been much longer post-poned. Niles knew me well enough, certainly, to know I would not have become a conscious party to a continued fraud. The very recklessness of our coming to the Hôtel des Étrangers, where "Polly" was so well known, is explicable only if one supposed that it had been Niles' intention from the first to abandon a role he no longer had the strength nor the wish to support. This it was, and not his suicide, which he had contemplated in those brown studies by the window of the hotel room. Are the two acts, after all, so very distinct? Wasn't it, in the strictest sense, a kind of self-slaughter to surrender the name and mask of "Niles Visconti"? And is it any wonder he should hesitate before the deed, and require, at the last, the impetus of immediate peril? Perhaps, too, he had lingered in order to allow his mother an equivalent op-portunity to evade the hand of justice, but that must remain con-jecture, since his letter to Zaide was never discovered. Presumably it had been incinerated, with herself, in the furnace of Vesuvius.

My own departure from Naples was not to be effected with such enviable dispatch. The attempted murder of Mr. Saintsbury, my wounding of Zaide and her own self-immolation, taken in conjunction with the remarkable revelations in her letter, and all these following hard on the events that had already excited the attention of the police, made a longer stay in Naples inevitable; nor was it only the police who must be satisfied. Renata's family had to be informed, and some determination made for the future of the orphaned Clara Maria. This was not accomplished without considerable acrimony and debate. The Vannis had persuaded themselves that their grand-daughter stood to inherit not only the Villa Visconti but a considerable portion of my own inheritance as well, under the theory that it had passed irrevocably to Niles upon my marriage. That there had never *been* a Niles, and that therefore this devolution of the Visconti fortune was wholly without basis—this was, understandably, a notion that they resisted with some vigor. However, once the certainty of it was established, they became, as Zaide had predicted, as obdurate against the unfortunate child as they had previously been energetic in her interest. Two considerations, at last, persuaded them to adopt a more charitable view: a desire not to involve themselves in their daughter's posthumous disgrace, and the discovery that the Villa Visconti, with all its pertinents, had passed, effectually, into my possession. It had been so deeply mortgaged at the time of my marriage to Niles that only deep infusions of the money obtained from my inheritance had preserved it from foreclosure. Its disposition, therefore, rested with me (since the authorities were prepared, at the Vannis' powerful insistence, to forget whatever they were asked to).

I took the advice of Zaide's letter and made over the Villa to Clara Maria by deed of gift. A more strict regard for the law would have led me to restore the estate to the heir of the murdered Conte whom Zaide had originally defrauded, but this gentleman was long since deceased, and his estate had passed to a collateral branch of the Visconti family in Milan, whose wealth was even more considerable than mine. Further, I felt a debt of guilt towards Renata: having accepted the ledger in which she had summed the wrongs done against her, I should have read it, or caused it to be read by an impartial judge. It was a small amends, therefore, to give Clara Maria an estate purchased at the cost of her mother's dowry, honor, and life.

While matters were thus arranged with the Vannis and the Neapolitan police, I lived at the Albergo della Villa di Roma, alone and without attendance. Rose, despite the failure of my aunt's Antonia in a like undertaking, took advantage of the confusions of this time to make off with all my jewelry and a choice part of my wardrobe. Lacking the heart to expose her to the stern punishment Antonia had suffered, I did not report her misdeed to the police. She had stood by me at a parlous time, and I was content to let these spoils be her reward. To tell the truth, I was grateful for her departure, as it solved the question of how to be rid of her. I desired nothing at this time but to consign Italy, and all its associations, to oblivion.

The night-terrors and headaches that had kept me wakeful so many evenings since Spoleto resumed at the Albergo della Villa di Roma with some of their old strength, and so it often happened that I would hear, through the long hours of the middle night, the wauling and yowling of innumerable cats, sounding now like the endless lament of some brute purgatory, now like skirmishes, ever renewed and never concluded, in that great warfare of all against all, which I had first become aware of at the time of my flight from the Villa Visconti. A dreadful sound, and not to be escaped by removing to another hotel, for Naples, I had observed in my various passages through it, was as much a city of cats as of people. Because I could not sleep, I listened, night after night, with a kind of meditative horror, to the unredeemed anguish of these poor animals, until the sound of it came to seem the ground bass of all existence. Oh, how I longed to leave Naples—or even to be deaf!

At last the energetic efforts of Mr. Mainwaring and the British Consul availed, and my passport was visaed for departure. As soon as my freedom had been won for me, I was on the train, with Mr. Mainwaring beside me (Mrs. Lacey had already gone ahead to Blackthorne to prepare for my arrival), and each premonitory hissing of steam or blast of the whistle was as thrilling to me as the first noodling of the violins in the pit of the orchestra before the rising of the curtain on the sublimest and best-acclaimed opera of the world's supreme genius. I was free! I was leaving! I never need return!

Though it had been my purpose to make for England without stopping anywhere along the way, when our train pulled into the Rome railway station, I bethought myself of Lydia, and of her grave, which I had never visited. Since, in any case, the schedule of the trains obliged us to pass some hours in Rome, Mr. Mainwaring engaged a coach and we drove to the Protestant Cemetery, which lies just inside the city's ancient wall, by the Porta San Paolo.

The earth had not yet settled over her grave, and the marker, by contrast to those around it, had a crisp, unweathered whiteness that would have been unbearably bitter, were it not for the message carved upon the simple marble tablet: *The dead shall be raised incorruptible, and we shall be changed.* Whether by design or inadvertence, Niles had chosen the same epitaph for Lydia as that which he had helped me to read, so many years before, on my mother's gravestone.

There was a small bouquet at the foot of Lydia's grave, of red roses mixed with white. The blooms were still fresh, despite that they had not been put into a vase. A square of stiff paper had been pushed in among the thorny stems. I stooped and took up the bouquet, and worked the paper loose. It was one of Niles' cards. In one corner he had scrawled the traditional formula of leave-taking, *P.P.C.*; in the other, *Good-bye.* I replaced the card among the flowers and put it back upon Lydia's grave.

All the while one is within the Protestant Cemetery, one feels the presence, beyond its low brick wall, of the Pyramid of Caius Cestius, which stands beside Rome's eastern gate as a kind of summary of all the more modest vanities and pomps assembled here in honor of death's empire. When I returned to the gate of the cemetery, where Mr. Mainwaring had been waiting for me, he suggested, with an earnestness I could neither fathom nor deny, that we direct our steps towards this strange monument.

The pyramid's western and southern slopes glowed in the golden light of the Roman afternoon. So simple a thing; so merely massive, you might think; and yet there was more of dignity in it, and even the power of inspiration, than in many structures more lavishly endowed, more articulately beautiful, and more nobly dedicated. Or is it memory that lends to the neutral bulk of it a moral significance that derives from associations personal and accidental?

At the sunken base of the pyramid, unapproachable by steps, there was a narrow moat of grass, and this little meadow was inhabited by a commonwealth of cats. There were cats of every age and color and condition: toms and tabbies and tortoise-shells; weary veterans and gravid dames; an hundred of them at least, and very likely more. Some few of the youngest pursued an energetic social life, but the majority were content to enjoy the steady warmth of the October sun. It was hard to think that in a few hours these same benign and philosophic-seeming cats might be carrying on the brawls and miseries of their cousins in Naples who had given such an unpleasant shape to my thoughts for so many sleepless nights—and yet it was certainly so. That is all. I draw no larger moral from the matter of that moment. I saw a number of stray cats at the base of an ancient funeral monument, and I felt strengthened for the sight. It did not, by any means, heal every wound of my spirit, but I am sure it marks the moment when that healing truly began. God bless you, Caius Cestius, and all you genial cats, and all of your descendants to the seventh generation! May you enjoy many more October afternoons as bright and calm in the warm hollow of that pyramid!

Crediting my friend with an arcane pre-vision of the effect this sight would have on my spirit, I thanked him profusely for having brought me here, as though he had had no other purpose than to act as my soul's cicerone. "I'm *so* glad," I insisted. "There is such peace. I had forgotten there could be such peace."

"It is just to disturb that peace, though, that I want to speak with you."

"If it's you who say it, Godfrey, I cannot think it can be un-settling."

"I should have spoken before this, but almost every day, it seemed, we were involved in another explanation, more labyrinthine than the last. And now, here is yet another. I have put it off and put it off, telling myself it's in consideration of your feelings, though it was no more, may be, than cowardice. In any case, Clara, I cannot put it off longer."

"Please, Godfrey, if you are referring to Contessa Visconti's reckless imputations against you—"

"Reckless or not, Clara, all her conjecturings, so far as they concerned me, are substantially true. I love you. I have loved you almost from the moment that we met, yet there has never been a moment, in all that span of time, when I could honorably tell you so. Now it would be dishonorable if I did not tell you, despite the pain it may immediately give."

"The pain, Godfrey? Can you say so? Isn't my own case just as clear? It was to Zaide. She saw what I had tried so hard to conceal even from myself, and she knew how she might have destroyed all hope of happiness for me, and she would have, only her strength was not equal to her malice. I have only waited for you to speak—and I knew you would, when the right moment declared itself, as it has now. Now you have spoken, so may I. I love you, Godfrey, and if you'll ask me—"

It was only his kiss that kept me from proposing first.

EPILOGUE

Graceful, but grave, her brow he kiss'd,
And bade her terrors be dismiss'd.

—SIR WALTER SCOTT,
The Lady of the Lake

WE WERE MARRIED the following summer in the parish church of Glynde. The years were kind to us, and though Godfrey and I were to know our portion of disappointments and sorrows, the shadow cast by these has never been so deep as to make us unaware of, or ungrateful for, the wider realm of sunlight we so long inhabited. Good marriages, however, need no chroniclers. Indeed (speaking *ex cathedra* from the throne of my more than sixty years), it is their special quality that their goodness can never adequately be expressed, except to the sharer of our happiness. It is no wonder, then, so many books leave off, like this, just when their principals have commenced upon their larger life.

While this must represent the termination of *my* story, there have been other destinies so closely linked to mine that my readers, if they have read so far, will be concerned to follow these other threads to their natural conclusion. It is the purpose of these last few lines to gratify that curiosity, so far as a present retrospect allows.

The saddest of these brief life-stories is surely that of Clara Maria, who was buried in the collapse of the Villa Visconti, during the terrible convulsions of 1883 that took so many other innocent lives. She was not yet twenty. Her death has always seemed to be, somehow, the last of Zaide's murders—as though her spirit had remained within the fiery core of Vesuvius, gathering a slow strength, like the pearl that forms about a speck of dust, to spend itself at last in one final cataclysmic outpouring. But I have been told that such a notion is heretical. The power that shook

Ischia was the same that raised it from the sea, and it is a power that no human mind can hope to fathom, for it is God's.

There have been happy endings, too. Mrs. Lacey returned to Blackthorne to resume, for a short time, her position as house-keeper, but on the day of my marriage to her nephew she retired (to our regret, though doubtless wisely) to her own property of Coppleswith, in Rodmell, taking with her the invaluable Mrs. Minchin. There, every Thursday, we would come to celebrate the conjoint genius of these two good women in dinners that added to every other excellence the precious ingredient of a long-enduring affection.

Another figure in my story came to a better end than perhaps, by a strict accounting, she deserved—at least, if one may judge from a recent report in the newspapers concerning the remarkable sensation produced at the casino of Baden-Baden by one Lady Elizabeth Towton of High Wycombe. Lady Elizabeth (concerning whom nothing is discoverable in Debrett's) excited the popular press to such a deal of admiring attention by her *sang-froid* in losing and then regaining a small fortune that there can be no doubt that she and my maid Rose are one.

But this has been another's story equally with mine. What then of Niles? This was the question I have asked myself all the while I have been writing these pages, and the answer was given me only as I have reached this terminal point, in the form of a letter arriving in last Wednesday's post, though the postmark on the envelope shows that it left Melbourne many months ago, at the very time, indeed, when this account was begun.

Let the last words, then, of this long book be Niles', for he says all that remains to be known.

Dearest Clara, the letter begins.

Yesterday in a London newspaper I read of your loss, and so I am breaking the resolution of many years to write to you, thus belatedly, in vain commiseration. Indeed, by the time you receive this letter, time may have so well done his healing work that my sympathy will only serve to re-awaken the pain. I would much rather make you smile, as I smile now, remembering our life to-gether—so foolish, so false, so brave. Dear, dear Clara, I still love you—and all the more because you are so far from me, and because it is so certain we shall never meet again.

Do you remember, when we stood before Helvellyn, and I borrowed some lines from Wordsworth to propose to you? Have you returned to that poem lately, and have you noticed how it resumes, from where we left off? And is it not prophetic?

Dear Clara, it is enough, almost, to trace the letters of your name (albeit in a hand something stiffer than what you may recall), and to know that you shall see it in some few months, and hear my voice, like a bubbling in the well of memory, addressing you across the whole circumference of the earth.

Did you know that I realized my daydream of coming to Australia? I made Godfrey promise he would keep it secret from you, but I've always wondered if, in the course of time, he might not have judged that the promise had expired. I'm sure I would not blame him if he had. He found me in the Portsmouth Hospital only a little while after my flight from Naples; but that little while had wrought a large difference, in flesh and spirit both. I cannot think now what I could have felt then to make me so eager to waste myself. Perhaps I believed that a career of sinful self-despite would be a penance for my former sins. Certainly, I conceived it as an alternative to suicide; it was nearly the equivalent. But I survived my long sickness, and Godfrey, in the course of his work for the Magdalen Mission, found me, and lifted me up, and taught me, with Christ's help, to forgive myself, and gave me my passage-money to this new land and new life. I became a wife, a mother, and in the course of time, a widow, too, and lately, to my wonderment, the grandmother of a little girl who is surely the loveliest and best in Australia!

It has been a good life, and I have been grateful to the higher Mercy of God and to the humanity of your dear husband. May that same Mercy now be his! And yet—

There is a part of me that still is wed to you. Forgive me, Clara, but I feel it so. It was in your clear eyes that I first saw the glimmering light of whom I might become. In loving you, I learned to love myself. If that is not marriage, it is something deeper and more precious, and so. . . .

But I can only say again what I have said so many times before, without ever understanding the words myself—that I love you, and that your happiness has been, will always be, dearer to me than my own. But let him say it, who says it so much better—

> *Therefore let the moon*
> *Shine on thee in thy solitary walk;*
> *And let the misty mountain winds be free*
> *To blow against thee: and, in after years,*
> *When these wild ecstasies shall be matured*
> *Into a sober pleasure; when thy mind*
> *Shall be a mansion for all lovely forms,*
> *Thy memory be as a dwelling place*
> *For all sweet sounds and harmonies; oh! then,*
> *If solitude, or fear, or pain, or grief,*
> *Shall be thy portion, with what healing thoughts*
> *Of tender joy wilt thou remember me,*
> *And these my exhortations! Nor, perchance—*
> *If I should be where I no more can hear*
> *Thy voice, nor catch from thy wild eyes these gleams*
> *Of past existence—wilt thou then forget*
> *That on the banks of this delightful stream*
> *We stood together. . . .*

Dear Clara, whom I love—again: Good-bye!

Your cousin,
Niles

The End

A Note on the Type

THE TEXT OF this book was set on the Linotype in Janson, a recutting made direct from type cast from matrices long thought to have been made by the Dutchman Anton Janson, who was a practicing type founder in Leipzig during the years 1668–87. However, it has been conclusively demonstrated that these types are actually the work of Nicholas Kis (1650–1702), a Hungarian, who most probably learned his trade from the master Dutch type founder Dirk Voskens. The type is an excellent example of the influential and sturdy Dutch types that prevailed in England up to the time William Caslon developed his own incomparable designs from them.

Composed, printed, and bound by
The Haddon Craftsmen, Inc., Scranton, Pennsylvania.
Typography and binding design by Gwen Townsend.